PRAISE FOR THE
BESTSELLING BOOK RETREAT MYSTERIES

"[A] suspenseful and compelling read."

—Kings River Life Magazine

"[A] delight . . . An idyllic mansion in a quaint village complete with secret passages and books, books, and more books—what could make for a more ideal setting for a cozy murder? . . . Ellery Adams spins a fine tale full of jealously, love, greed, aspirations, and poison . . . Highly recommended."

—Open Book Society

"Adams . . . combines clever clues, a smart and courageous heroine and an interesting setting in a whodunit that will inspire readers to make further visits to Storyton Hall."

—Richmond Times-Dispatch

"Adams makes Storyton Hall come to life . . . Readers will relish the way Ellery Adams weaves together books, mystery, and fantasy."

—Fresh Fiction

"A mystery that takes place at a book-themed resort—it doesn't get any better. The author has woven in a bunch of suspects that will keep cozy mystery lovers guessing. The story is well paced and keeps you reading until you find out whodunit."

—MyShelf.com

"Adams has skillfully crafted a fantastical world for bibliophiles, as well as a puzzling cozy mystery . . . [A] fabulous start to a new series."

—Book of Secrets

NEW YORK TIMES

Berkley Prime Crime titles by Ellery Adams

MURDER *in the* SECRET GARDEN

Ellery Adams

BERKLEY PRIME CRIME, NEW YORK

An imprint of Penguin Random House LLC
375 Hudson Street, New York, New York 10014

MURDER IN THE SECRET GARDEN

A Berkley Prime Crime Book / published by arrangement with the author

Copyright © 2016 by Ellery Adams.
Excerpt from *Killer Characters* by Ellery Adams copyright © 2016 by Ellery Adams.
Penguin supports copyright. Copyright fuels creativity, encourages diverse voices,
promotes free speech, and creates a vibrant culture. Thank you for buying an authorized
edition of this book and for complying with copyright laws by not reproducing, scanning, or
distributing any part of it in any form without permission. You are supporting writers and
allowing Penguin to continue to publish books for every reader.

BERKLEY® PRIME CRIME and the PRIME CRIME design are trademarks
of Penguin Random House LLC.
For more information, visit penguin.com.

ISBN: 9780425265611

PUBLISHING HISTORY
Berkley Prime Crime mass-market edition / August 2016

PRINTED IN THE UNITED STATES OF AMERICA

10 9 8 7 6 5 4 3 2 1

Interior map: © 2016 CW Designs by Carol Wilmot
Sullivan. All rights reserved.
Interior text design by Tiffany Estreicher.

This is a work of fiction. Names, characters, places, and incidents either are the product of
the author's imagination or are used fictitiously, and any resemblance to actual persons,
living or dead, business establishments, events, or locales is entirely coincidental.

If you purchased this book without a cover, you should be aware that this book is stolen
property. It was reported as "unsold and destroyed" to the publisher, and neither the author
nor the publisher has received any payment for this "stripped book."

Penguin
Random
House

To "Captain" Phil and Sandi Hughes.

Thanks to Frank Romero for his expertise and assistance and thanks to all first responders for all that you do each and every day.

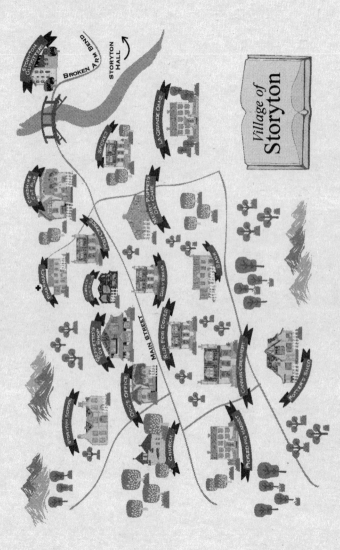

WELCOME TO STORYTON HALL

Our Staff Is Here To Serve You

Resort Manager—Jane Steward
Butler—Mr. Butterworth
Head Librarian—Mr. Sinclair
Head Chauffeur—Mr. Sterling
Head of Recreation—Mr. Lachlan
Head of Housekeeping—Mrs. Pimpernel
Head Cook—Mrs. Hubbard

Select Merchants of Storyton Village

Run for Cover Bookshop—Eloise Alcott
Daily Bread Café—Edwin Alcott
Cheshire Cat Pub—Bob and Betty Carmichael
The Canvas Creamery—Phoebe Doyle
La Grande Dame Clothing Boutique—Mabel Wimberly
Tresses Hair Salon—Violet Osborne
The Pickled Pig Market—the Hogg brothers
Geppetto's Toy Shop—Barnaby Nicholas
The Potter's Shed—Tom Green
Storyton Outfitters— Phil and Sandi Hughes

The Medieval Herbalists

Vivian Ash
Hannah Billingsley
Kira Grace
Tammy Kota
Claude Mason
Sandi Hughes
Constance Meredith
Nico and Michelle Scannavini

ONE

"I don't like killing things," Hemingway "Hem" Steward told his mother as she handed him a garden trowel.

Jane Steward—single mother to twin boys and manager of Storyton Hall—gave her firstborn a skeptical look.

"I don't," Hem insisted. "Except for mosquitoes and flies. And everybody hates them. I should get paid to kill them."

"What about spiders?" Hem's lookalike, Fitzgerald Steward, otherwise known as Fitz, poked his brother with the tines of the hand rake Jane had given him. "You squish them because you're scared of them."

Hem glared at Fitz. "I am *not*."

"Are *too*."

Jane stepped between her sons before their argument turned physical. "You shouldn't hurt spiders, Hem," she said. "Many species eat the mosquitoes and flies we dislike so much. And since Fitz is so comfortable with spiders, ask *him* to relocate them outside from now on."

Fitz paled slightly over this suggestion, but with both his mother and brother watching him, he decided to put on a display of bravado. Puffing out his chest, he said, "Fine. I'm not afraid."

"Good." Jane grabbed one of the plastic buckets stacked in the maintenance shed and beckoned for her sons to follow suit. "Let's get going. I'd like to finish this chore while we still have some cloud cover. It's supposed to be really hot today."

As they walked, the twins grumbled over having to work on a Saturday, especially since school had only let out for the summer yesterday. However, their complaints weren't very impassioned and Jane suspected that both boys were looking forward to digging in the dirt. They enjoyed being outdoors, and though they occasionally complained about their chores, they usually settled into a given task by turning their work into a game. Jane noticed that even the most mundane job could become the equivalent of swabbing the deck of a pirate ship or sweeping out a dungeon prison cell. She put her sons' vivid imaginations down to their constant exposure to books and book lovers. Even at the tender age of seven, they were reading, and understanding, books meant for a much older audience.

The three Stewards lapsed into silence as they walked to their cottage, which was formerly the estate's hunting lodge. Like the behemoth manor house it faced, the lodge had been dismantled in the 1830s and transported from its original seat in the English countryside to a remote valley in western Virginia. These days, the cottage served a dual purpose. The front half was occupied by Sterling, the head chauffeur, and the back, by Jane's little family.

One of the things Jane loved about her home was its walled garden. Because she and her sons lived on the grounds of a resort where the majority of the guests enjoyed long strolls, it was difficult to obtain much privacy. Luckily, both an evergreen hedge and a low-wrought iron fence protected their small yard from prying eyes or nosy parkers.

The only way to gain entry was to pass through their gate, and as Jane now unlatched it and pushed against it with her right hip, it squeaked in protest.

"Ugh." She winced. "I need to oil those hinges."

Fitz patted the gate as though it were an obedient dog. "Isn't it kind of like a burglar alarm? When it squeaks, we know that someone's coming in."

"Yeah, and then we can show them our moves!" Hem dropped his bucket in order to demonstrate several air punches. All three of them had been taking Tae Kwon Do lessons from Sinclair, the head librarian, and the boys were always looking for an excuse to show off their latest punch, kick, or defensive maneuver.

"Save your energy for the weeds," Jane advised. "I've let them go for too long, and with all the rain we've had, they're threatening to overtake the entire vegetable patch." She pointed at a dandelion growing next to a potato plant. "Just look at the size of this one! Its roots probably go all the way to China!"

Hem and Fitz exchanged glances of amazement, but then, Hem frowned. "No, Mom, it couldn't do that. Fitz and I read a book about dinosaurs and there was a picture showing what's in the middle of the earth."

"A giant fireball," Fitz informed her sagely. "It would burn a plant like that!" He snapped his fingers.

Jane smiled. Over the past winter, the twins had devoured every book they could find on the subject of dinosaurs, but by the end of the school year, their interest in the resplendent reptiles had waned. By May, anything to do with magic spells and wizardry utterly captivated them. Their night-stands were stacked with the books they'd purchased with their allowance, and they were also listening to the Harry Potter series on CD. These were a birthday gift from Aunt Octavia. Jane liked to play them while she was cleaning up after supper. This way, the boys could take their dessert to the living room sofa and spend an hour with Harry with the lights on and their mother close by in the kitchen. After all, there were some frightening scenes in those stories, and though the twins adored being scared by fantastical tales, Jane deemed it best that they listen to them in her presence.

"You're right, the roots don't go to China, but they do go surprisingly deep. You can't just yank the plant out by its top or the whole weed will just regrow."

"Like a lizard's tail," Hem said, studying the dandelion with admiration.

After casting a brief glare at the offending plant, Fitz lunged at it. "I bet I could get it out."

Before Jane could protest, he gathered the weed in his fist and pulled. The dandelion snapped at the base, leaving a white eye of a root staring up at them.

Seeing the dismayed look on her son's face, Jane squeezed his shoulder. "Don't worry, it happens to the very best of gardeners. What you need is the proper tool."

Fitz took the item she proffered. "It looks like a stick for s'mores."

"It does," Jane agreed and showed her sons how to push the divided head of the weeder into the ground. Grasping the remains of the root with one hand, she worked the tool under the root until it finally released its hold of the soil and slid free. She placed it in the bucket with a triumphant flourish and then, with the boys on their knees beside her, pointed out which plants were weeds and should be removed.

"All this grass has to go, but it's tricky stuff so leave it to me," she said. "You two focus on the dandelions and chickweed. See which ones I mean?" She pointed at multiple examples. "Bad, bad, bad. Got it?"

"It's not very nice to call them bad," said an unfamiliar voice.

Jane glanced up to see a woman standing at the edge of

the garden bed. She wore a black dress, black boots, and a black sun hat with a large brim. With the sun behind her, her face was completely cast in shadow. The hair that framed her face was dark and wiry. The stranger had come upon them soundlessly. She now stood, looming over them, as though she had every right to be there.

"Take the dandelion, for example. You can eat the young leaves, make wine out of the flower, and roast the root to produce coffee," she said in a deep, authoritative voice. She pivoted her head slightly, addressing the boys. "The root can also be turned into very useful medicine. You need a really big one, though. It has to be about this thick around." She curled her fingers until they formed a circle of approximately an inch in diameter. "It can help people with kidney or liver problems. Those are organs, which are located here and here." She indicated the areas on her torso. "Pretty handy for a *bad* plant, wouldn't you say?"

Jane, who'd been momentarily entranced by the dandelion trivia, looked over at her sons and saw that they were staring at the woman with a mixture of fascination and alarm. Their expressions forced Jane's maternal protective instincts into high alert, and she swiftly got to her feet, weeder in hand, and took a step toward the intruder.

"May I help you?" Jane asked.

There was something innately sinister about the woman's black garb and the manner in which she'd noiselessly appeared.

"This is a private residence." Jane struggled to maintain a cordial tone. After all, she was the manager of Storyton Hall. She couldn't allow a stranger—and possible guest—to note her discomfort. "Maybe you didn't notice the sign on the gate."

"Oh, I saw it," the woman replied breezily and smiled.

The twins exchanged anxious glances.

Hem pulled on Fitz's sleeve and muttered, "The gate didn't squeak. How did she get in without it squeaking?"

And before Jane could ask another question, Fitz squinted up at the lady in black and whispered, "Are you a witch?"

Jane's eyes widened in horror. Despite the fact that the same word had also crossed her mind, she glowered fiercely at her son and intoned, "Hemingway Steward! Apologize this instant!"

However, the woman startled them all by tossing back her head and laughing heartily. The movement caused her sun hat to slip, revealing molasses brown hair threaded with filaments of gray and a nose sprinkled with freckles. "Young sir, you wouldn't be the first person to call a lady with a keen knowledge of plants a witch. Personally, I prefer the term 'cunning woman.' These women used herbs to heal people during the Middle Ages. As for me, I'm better at healing gardens." She smiled at Jane. "That's why I'm here. To help you with your garden."

"I'm sorry?" Jane was totally confused.

The women held out her hand. "I'm Tammy Kota, a member of The Medieval Herbalists. I came a day early for our gathering because I wanted to read, explore the area, and spend a little time with Mrs. Hubbard before the scheduled activities begin."

Jane relaxed a little. "You're a friend of Mrs. Hubbard's?"

"A new friend, yes," Tammy replied. "After our president, Claude, booked this event, he asked me to take charge of our celebratory feast. I gladly agreed, and Mrs. Hubbard and I have been pen pals ever since."

Tammy shifted position. Sunshine fell on her dress, and Jane realized that it wasn't solid black at all. The cotton fabric was actually dotted with tiny white flowers. The light also washed over Tammy's face, revealing a woman in her late fifties with sun-speckled skin and a generous number of laugh lines.

Something clicked in Jane's memory, and she suddenly

recalled Mrs. Hubbard mentioning how much she'd grown to admire the woman now standing before Jane.

"Forgive me for not recognizing your name right off." To hide her embarrassment, Jane hastily introduced herself and the boys. "Mrs. Hubbard told me about the line of products you've created using herbs and plants from your garden. I can't wait to see them at this weekend's fair. Mrs. Hubbard also said that you were brought in as a consultant in the restoration project of the gardens at The Mount, Edith Wharton's home. That is so impressive."

"It was more of a courtesy invitation," Tammy said. "That project was led by Vivian Ash. She restores historic gardens for a living and is not only a fellow Medieval Herbalist, but also a lovely and generous woman to boot. She knew I was dying to watch The Mount's garden come to life again, so she got me on staff for a few weeks."

Jane caught the glimmer of excitement in Tammy's eyes. "Was it wonderful?"

"It was." Tammy sighed nostalgically. "I particularly loved the walled garden. There's nothing like being inside a walled garden at night. Even the most ordinary plants are transformed by moonlight. Their scents, shapes, and the very shadows they cast render them suddenly alien. In the dead of the night, plants can either turn into total mysteries or they can reveal their secret selves."

Jane didn't know how to respond to this unusual remark. Judging from the way her sons were gaping at Tammy, they still believed she was a witch.

With a rather forced laugh, Jane gestured at her modest vegetable patch and said, "This is hardly comparable to a garden bed at The Mount. I'm sure you have better things to do than—"

"Examine your spinach?" Tammy smiled. "I love diagnosing sick plants. It's a hobby of mine. May I?" She pointed at the row of spinach.

Jane nodded in assent.

Tammy knelt in the dirt and cradled a spinach leaf in her hand. She peered at it intently before gingerly folding it inward and peering at it some more.

"Infected," she murmured gravely and then waved for the boys to come closer. She tapped the leaf. "Do you see how the veins have turned yellow?"

"Yeah," said Fitz. Jane nudged his rump with the toe of her shoe and he quickly amended his answer to, "Yes, ma'am."

"This is caused by a disease spread by leafhoppers," Tammy explained.

Hem cocked his head quizzically. "Is that like a grasshopper?"

"More like a cicada." Tammy touched the leaf's paler underside with the tip of her index finger. "When the leafhoppers feed, they inject toxic saliva—their drool—into the plant. They also carry teeny tiny virus bugs around with them that they spread from plant to plant."

"Gross," Fitz grimaced, but leaned closer, his eyes gleaming with interest.

Jane, on the other hand, was genuinely repulsed by the idea of insects spreading disease among her vegetables. "What can I do?"

"We'll start by removing the infected plants. It's time to harvest the healthy ones before they bolt. You can plant another lettuce variety in its place." Tammy looked at the boys. "The leafhoppers can't jump all around the garden like it's a big hopscotch board if we make life tougher for them. To do that, we need to get rid of all the weeds. Are you up for the challenge?"

The twins responded with a unified cry of, "Yes, ma'am!"

She smiled widely at them before fixing her attention on Jane again. "Once we're done with the harvesting and weeding, you can plant marigolds around the perimeter and right down the center of the vegetable patch. Marigolds deter a host of garden pests. How does that sound?"

"Wonderful. Thank you so much." And before Jane could offer Tammy a cold glass of water or escort her to the gate, the expert gardener had helped herself to one of the hand trowels and had begun to dig up one of the diseased spinach plants. "Please," Jane said, feeling uncomfortable. "You're a guest of Storyton Hall. You shouldn't be working in my garden."

"But this is where I'm most content," Tammy said. "Please let me stay. I'll sit on the other end and be very quiet. You won't even know I'm here."

Having no choice but to acquiesce, Jane offered to get Tammy a set of tools and a pair of gloves. When she returned from the maintenance shed, Tammy and the twins were chattering away like old pals. Clearly, if the boys still considered her a witch, they'd come to the conclusion that she performed white magic.

"What about mosquitoes and flies?" Hem was asking her. "There were a billion last summer!"

"You could plant basil," Tammy said. "Those bugs hate basil. Your mom could also use the leaves to make a salad with fresh tomatoes and mozzarella cheese."

Jane handed Tammy her tools. "Sounds delicious."

Fitz pointed at the small pile of dandelions in his bucket. "Can we do something with these, Ms. Tammy? Didn't you say they weren't bad?"

"They're not bad, Fitz. No plants are, but we have to make choices about which plants we want in our gardens. We've chosen not to include dandelions in this garden." Tammy pursed her lips in thought. "You could feed them to a goat. Or a pig."

Fitz and Hem grinned at each other. "Pig Newton!"

By the time they'd finished telling Tammy about the most famous pet in Storyton Village, the spinach plants had been pulled, and the twins were making excellent progress with the chickweeds. Jane, who'd given herself the job of rooting out the dandelions and invasive grasses, made a silent vow to weed the garden on a more regular basis in the future.

Much later, four hot, sweaty, and dirt-encrusted workers crossed the back lawn leading to the manor house and paused by the kitchen door. "Are you sure you won't come in for a drink?" Jane asked Tammy. "Mrs. Hubbard always keeps a supply of sun tea and lemonade on hand."

"What I want most is a shower," Tammy said. "Between my morning hike and the lovely hours spent in your garden, I probably smell worse than Pig Newton. I'll take a rain check on the sun tea." With a wave, she headed for the guest entrance.

"Pig Newton doesn't smell," Hem said, instantly coming to the pig's defense.

Fitz looked at Jane. "It's true. Mr. Hogg put a baby pool under the tree behind The Pickled Pig Market. Mr. Hogg tosses some Cheerios in the water, and while Pig Newton's busy eating, Mr. Hogg gives him a good scrubbing."

"We could all use a good scrubbing," Jane said. "Wash up to your elbows, both of you, or Mrs. Hubbard will have a fit."

As though the mention of her name had conjured her from thin air, Mrs. Hubbard appeared from inside the closest pantry. "Hello, my darlings! You're just in time for lunch." Her apple-cheeked face was more flushed than usual. She exhaled loudly and put a hand over her ample chest. "I've been running around like a madwoman making sure we have everything we need for the Billingsley-Earle wedding, but I've gone over my list three times now and I'm satisfied." Sliding a notepad into her apron pocket, she smiled at Jane and the boys. "As for you three, you can be my official taste testers. I want to add new sandwiches to the Rudyard Kipling

Café's summer menu. Take a seat at the counter and I'll be right back with the first candidate."

She paused to issue orders to the kitchen staff and then returned carrying three plates. "Turkey club with herb mayonnaise. I mixed fresh parsley, thyme, and basil in with the mayo. There's locally grown lettuce and tomatoes and crunchy bacon too. I know how much you boys like your bacon."

"Is this spinach?" Fitz lifted off his top slice of bread and pointed at a few pieces of mayo-smeared lettuce. Jane caught the apprehension in her son's voice and knew that he was picturing the diseased leaves from their vegetable garden.

"No, honey. That's romaine." Mrs. Hubbard put her hands on her hips. "Now put your sandwich back together, have a taste, and tell me what you think."

Hem hurriedly yanked the tomato slice out of his sandwich before taking an enormous bite. His right cheek inflated like a balloon and he grinned at Mrs. Hubbard and gave her a thumbs-up.

Though Jane took a more conservative sample of her sandwich, she was immediately impressed by how many flavors and textures Mrs. Hubbard had managed to squeeze between two slices of bread. The fresh tomato and lettuce slices lightened the heaviness of the crispy bacon and salt-and-pepper seasoned turkey, and the aromatic creaminess of the herb mayo provided the perfect finish.

"This is a keeper," she told Mrs. Hubbard.

With a nod of satisfaction, Storyton's head cook walked to the prep station and returned with three small bowls. "Watermelon salad with fresh mint to round off your meal."

"Ms. Tammy says that mint helps you digest," Hem informed her.

Mrs. Hubbard looked pleased. "She found you, then? Good!"

"She knows *everything* about plants," Fitz said. "She's

like Professor Sprout in the Harry Potter books. Ms. Tammy could teach herbology at Hogwarts."

"I believe she would take that as a high compliment." Mrs. Hubbard gestured at their empty plates. "Tammy encouraged me to experiment with different herb combinations based on recipes from the Middle Ages. You should see my kitchen garden, Jane. Tammy kindly mailed me dozens of seed packets shortly after we first started corresponding. With her help, I'm now growing a real medieval herb garden right out there." She pointed toward the back door, which led to both the loading dock and a raised garden bed enclosed by a low stone wall. "I have the more exotic plants at home because they require more care. I even have licorice!"

"Can you make candy?" the boys asked in unison.

Too caught up in her narrative to be misdirected, Mrs. Hubbard winked at them and prattled on. "I'm growing ginger too. Can you believe it? I hope to harvest my first crop of baby ginger in October. To me, these herbs are as precious and wonderful as one of those illuminated manuscripts would be to you, Jane, my dear."

At the mention of illuminated manuscripts, Mrs. Hubbard's voice faded as Jane's mind turned to thoughts of Edwin Alcott. The last communication she'd had from the man she'd fallen hard and fast for had arrived in the form of a mysterious package. Inside the package, Jane had discovered a missing page belonging to the Gutenberg Bible hidden in Storyton's secret library. Edwin had recovered the page from an untold location in the Middle East and had sent it to Jane in an attempt to prove that he was not a book thief—not in the pure sense of the word anyway. He promised to explain himself when he returned to Storyton, but that had been months ago, and Jane's doubts about his character had grown more and more with each passing day.

I should just forget about him, Jane chided herself for the hundredth time. *He must be a thief and a rogue. Why else would he stay away? Why else would he make his sister worry? Or make me promises that he never meant to keep?*

"Mom?" Fitz waved his hand in front of Jane's face and she blinked.

"Sorry," she said. "I drifted off for a second there."

Mrs. Hubbard studied her closely. "You should stick your nose in my rosemary plant and take a deep breath. That'll clear your head. If you're not growing any in your own garden, take some of mine. You could whip up a lovely rosemary-lemon chicken for supper—it'll help focus all of your minds."

"We don't need to focus," Hem countered. "It's summer!"

Smiling indulgently at him, Mrs. Hubbard said, "So it is. But there's a saying about idle hands and the devil." She shot a conspiratorial glance at Jane. "If it's all right with your mother, I'd like to hire you boys to weed and water my kitchen garden. The groundskeeping staff is too busy to deal with it. And in all honesty, I think you two would take better care of my plants. Not because the groundskeepers aren't hard workers," she hurriedly added, "but I believe you boys will come to love the garden as I do. You'd have to tend the plants for an hour every day except for Sundays. I'll pay you on Friday. In cash. Are you interested in the job?"

The twins laced their fingers together and made begging motions. "Can we, Mom? *Please?*"

"Only if Mrs. Hubbard and I can come to an agreement about your wages," Jane said. "Thank her for the delicious lunch and then go play while we talk."

Hem and Fitz hugged Mrs. Hubbard before racing out of the kitchen. As soon as they were gone, the two women settled in for a good-natured haggling session.

"They should be doing the job for free," Jane began. "Stewards have been maintaining Storyton Hall for centuries. Even my great-aunt and -uncle have assignments, though their tasks are far less physical."

"But Master Hem and Master Fitz are just children," Mrs. Hubbard countered. "Let them see what's it's like to earn money for a job well done—a job not assigned by a teacher or a parent. It'll do them good. Give them a sense of pride."

Eventually, Jane capitulated. It was nearly impossible to say no to Mrs. Hubbard.

"Time to bake the scones," Mrs. Hubbard said, rising to her feet and smoothing her apron, which was embroidered with tiny pink and white teapots. "And since a handful of herbalists have checked in early, I've added cheddar and chive biscuits to the tea menu, so I'll have to make those as well."

It never failed to amaze Jane that Mrs. Hubbard, who rarely left the kitchen, was able to keep tabs on the goings-on at Storyton Hall. It didn't hurt that the majority of the employees fed her the choicest tidbits of gossip in exchange for a piece of shortbread or a slice of Victoria sponge.

"Maybe I shouldn't have taken the day off," Jane mused aloud. "I wonder who else has arrived early."

"Tammy said that she'd seen their group's president alighting from one of our cars just as she was heading out on her hike this morning. She didn't want to delay her walk, so she didn't stop to say hello. One of her closest friends, a photographer named Kira Grace, is also en route. She's very eager to explore the trails around Storyton." Mrs. Hubbard's jovial face suddenly clouded over. "And the *other* early arrival showed up just before you and the boys came into the kitchen. Billy carried her bags to her room." She lowered her voice. "Apparently, her luggage—and there was quite a bit of it—gave off a nasty odor."

Jane was surprised by the note of disapproval in Mrs. Hubbard's voice. It was most uncharacteristic of the jolly cook.

"Do you know this guest?" Jane asked.

Mrs. Hubbard scowled. "It was Constance Meredith."

Jane frowned. The name was familiar, but she'd reviewed so many names recently in reference to both the upcoming wedding and The Medieval Herbalists booking that they'd all begun to blend together.

"You'd probably recognize her by her *stage name*." Mrs. Hubbard's note of disapproval had morphed into outright disdain. "Does the Poison Princess ring a bell?"

"Ah, the Poison Princess!" Jane smiled. "According to Mr. Mason, the group president, she's their most famous member. She's served as an expert witness on dozens of murder trials, advised physicians, toured the world giving lectures on poisonous plants, and appeared on several television shows dealing with illusive medical diagnoses." Jane's smile faded as she examined Mrs. Hubbard's troubled expression. "You're worried. Why?"

Mrs. Hubbard twisted the corner of her apron and pulled a face. "At first, I was thrilled to learn that the Poison Princess was staying at Storyton Hall. As you know, I hardly ever use the computer, but I went into Mr. Sinclair's office and asked him to pull up her website. The more I read, the more I disliked the woman. I also watched some video clips and they made my skin crawl. She's as cold as the White Witch of Narnia. You should hear how gleefully she describes the manner in which certain poisonous plants affect people—she truly admires their power to injure or to kill. And one only has to watch her for a few minutes to tell that she didn't give a fig about the fate of the poor souls who came into contact with these plants."

"Maybe it's all for show," Jane suggested.

Raising her index finger, Mrs. Hubbard said, "She bears watching, Jane. Trust me."

Jane reached out and took Mrs. Hubbard's hand. "After what happened here during the Romancing the Reader convention, I wouldn't dream of ignoring your instincts. I'll keep a close eye on her. I promise."

"There's something else."

"Yes?" Jane asked, feeling an inexplicable sense of dread.

Mrs. Hubbard squeezed Jane's hand for emphasis. "Don't let that witch within a mile of my kitchens. Or near any food, for that matter. She knows a hundred different ways to kill someone using plants. And many of those plants are now growing right outside our back door."

TWO

As much as Jane wanted to view Mrs. Hubbard's behavior as purely theatrical, she didn't dare. Ever since Uncle Aloysius and Aunt Octavia had informed her that Edwin Alcott was a notorious book thief, Jane had started to doubt her own ability to form character judgments.

Edwin's secret profession wasn't the only thing that had turned Jane into a more suspicious person. As the Guardian of Storyton Hall, she was responsible for protecting the hidden library located in the tallest tower. And if a duplicitous potential lover and an invaluable collection of books, documents, and scrolls weren't enough to keep Jane on alert all the time, the fact that several murders had occurred at Storyton Hall since she'd become the resort's manager certainly had.

"That's over with now," she told herself en route to her office. "This week is all about nature lovers. History buffs, gardeners, and foodies. What could be more peaceful than a bunch of events attended by people who spend their free time studying, growing, and using herbs?"

And yet Jane felt compelled to visit Constance Meredith's website. At first glance, the site was unremarkable. The moss green background and black font were easy on the eye, and there was a banner that said THE POISON PRINCESS, surrounded by delicate roses. Constance's photograph, which revealed her to be a raven-haired beauty with pale skin and dark, impenetrable eyes, looked more like a Broadway headshot than the photograph of a renowned botanist. Jane reasoned that with Constance's numerous television appearances, she probably saw herself as the botanical version of Dr. Oz. To capitalize on that image, she marketed herself as a celebrity professor.

Jane clicked on a link called "Poison Plants by Zone" and was startled when the roses around the banner turned from pink to brown and the thorns grew dangerously sharp and pointy. A quote floated to the top of the screen.

> *Within the infant rind of this weak flower*
> *Poison hath residence and medicine power.*

"Shakespeare," Jane said and tried to recall which play. She could picture a portly friar explaining that the flower in his hand had the power to heal or to kill. "The flower had the power to poison," she murmured. "It foreshadowed the doom of two young lovers. *Romeo and Juliet.*"

Scrolling farther down the page, Jane found several video clips of the Poison Princess at work. One showed her reviewing a patient's mysterious medical symptoms with a physician. Mrs. Hubbard was right. Constance Meredith described the symptoms, some of which were quite gruesome, with ill-disguised zeal. She didn't seem to care a whit about the person who'd been poisoned. In another clip, she discussed her tendency to travel with at least a dozen deadly plants in her possession.

"It's not enough to show someone a slide of a plant," the Poison Princess said. Her confident tone held a hint of condescension, but she was undeniably captivating. "Consider the difference between seeing a photograph of a cobra and having a cobra on the ground at your feet. The difference is significant." Constance gave a little laugh and Jane shuddered at the analogy. Was Constance Meredith a fan of all biological organisms that produced toxins, poisons, or venom?

"Plants are living things," Constance continued. "I endeavor to give my audience an appreciation of their beauty, scent, and power."

"Oh boy," Jane muttered. She exited the website, pushed back her desk chair, and flung open her office door. It was her intention to march straight into the Henry James Library and ask Sinclair for a copy of the background check he'd run on Constance Meredith. The head librarian would have paperwork waiting for Jane's perusal on all The Medieval Herbalists, but she couldn't enter a public space in dirty jeans and a soiled T-shirt emblazoned with BOOK LOVERS NEVER GO TO BED ALONE.

At home, Jane discovered a note on the kitchen counter. The brief missive informed her that the twins had gone fishing with Uncle Aloysius.

Jane smiled at the picture of the fish in the note's margin. She loved it when Fitz and Hem spent time with her great-uncle, for he always entertained them with tales from his boyhood. Having never known a father, seeing as theirs died in a car accident before they were born, Fitz and Hem looked on Uncle Aloysius as their model of what it was to be a man. A Southern gentleman of impeccable principles and a kindly demeanor, Jane couldn't have asked for a better example. Of course, there was no shortage of gentlemen tutors at Storyton Hall. Butterworth, Sinclair, and Lachlan also contributed to the twins' upbringing, and Jane counted herself lucky that her sons were surrounded by father figures who not only cared for them, but were also willing to lay down their lives for them.

Jane showered and changed into a navy blue sundress. She pinned her strawberry blond curls into a loose twist and then returned to the manor house. Having expected the boys to be long gone, she was surprised to hear Fitz's voice echo down the lobby. This was followed by a shrill shout by Hem. Jane sighed in annoyance. The twins were breaking two rules. They weren't to loiter in public areas without permission, and when they did visit these areas, they were supposed to speak in hushed tones.

"Use your Sunday school voices," Jane had told them. Now she couldn't help wondering if they were behaving during Sunday school.

Fitz caught sight of Jane and, clearly hoping to reach her before Hem, sprinted to her side. "Mom! Guess what?"

"Would *you* like to guess how many rules you've broken?" Jane asked in reply, her eyes steely with disapproval.

Fitz deflated. "Uncle Aloysius said we could come to the front to meet Mr. Hughes. He gave us free tickets to the rubber duck race!"

"Lower your voice, Fitzgerald," Jane admonished sharply. "And I do *not* want to see you run in this lobby again or you'll be sitting in your room instead of watching the duck race, do you hear me?"

Chastised, Fitz nodded. "I'm sorry. I was just really excited because I saved my allowance to buy a ticket, so now I can pick *two* ducks. Hem can too."

Jane glanced down at her son. A few seconds ago, his face had been shining with happiness. The light had dimmed a little, but it was still there. Despite his transgressions, Jane realized that she'd rather see the gleam in his eye than have him be contrite. The rubber duck race was new to Storyton, and the staff had been talking about it with childlike glee ever since the local paper had printed a contest inviting people to name the ducks.

"Tell me about this Mr. Hughes," Jane whispered conspiratorially. "Does he hint at which duck is the fastest?"

Fitz's glimmer reappeared. "*No.* He said that the winner would be decided by the currents and Lady Luck." After a moment's hesitation, Fitz asked, "Is she real, Mom?"

Jane laughed. "No, honey. So Mr. Hughes gave you tickets to the race? That was very kind of him, especially since tickets don't go on sale until tomorrow."

"Well, it's *his* race after all!" Fitz declared.

"Yes, Mr. Hughes is the proprietor of Storyton Outfitters, the village's newest business. I've been so looking forward to meeting him." Jane proceeded down the lobby. Fitz marched at her side, waving his ticket in the air as though he were in a parade.

Mr. Hughes was a tall man in his mid-sixties with salt-and-pepper hair and blue eyes that reminded Jane of mountain lakes. Judging from his weathered skin and the lines etched into his face like a road map of his journeys, Mr. Hughes preferred to spend his time in the open air.

He shook hands with a firm grip, and his smile was genuine and warm. "I was just telling your great-uncle how much I enjoyed speaking with Mr. Lachlan in person. We've talked on the phone many times over the past few months, but neither of us are phone people. That's my wife's department." He chuckled. "Anyway, Mr. Lachlan and I have worked out an arrangement that will be mutually beneficial. I believe this is the start of an excellent friendship and partnership between Storyton Hall and Storyton Outfitters."

Jane was delighted by this news. When Lachlan, whose full name was actually Iain Landon Lachlan, the head of the activities department, first heard that an experienced sportsman planned to open a shop on the outskirts of the village featuring fishing, hiking, and camping equipment, he'd become very animated. It was Lachlan's hope that he and the new owner of Storyton Outfitters could work together to provide Storyton's guests with the opportunity to take half- or full-day fishing excursions, and it seemed as though his wish had been fulfilled.

"I know my uncle has probably told you how thrilled he is to welcome another fisherman to Storyton, Mr. Hughes," Jane said. "But I'd love to invite you and your wife to dinner one night next week. After all, we're neighbors now."

"Please call me Phil. Sandi—that's my wife—made me promise to tell you that she'd like you and the boys to come for lunch after The Medieval Herbalists have cleared out." He shrugged helplessly. "So you two ladies will have to get together and mark your calendars. I just go where I'm told."

Jane laughed. "Fair enough. I'll see her tomorrow at the duck race, right?"

"And for all The Medieval Herbalist events," Phil said. "She's one of them. In fact, that's how we heard about Storyton. When the notice went out about the meeting, Sandi started reading up on the place. At first, I thought we shouldn't come . . ."

At this moment, Uncle Aloysius seemed to suffer a brief coughing fit. "Boys, would you go fetch me a glass of water? I have a tickle just below my Adam's apple. Take your time and don't spill."

When the twins were a safe distance away, Uncle Aloysius looked at Phil and said, "You were concerned about the resort's unsavory history."

Phil nodded. "I was. Not Sandi. She was intrigued by this place the second she saw it online. Before I knew it, we were packing our bags and driving here for a weekend stay. I don't think we even finished walking to the other end of the village before Sandi had decided this was where she wanted us to live out our golden years. We signed the contract on the building by the river before we left on Monday and the rest is history."

"The entire village will be at tomorrow's duck race. The other merchants have decided to close early and we're going down to a minimum number of staff during the event so our employees can also attend," Jane said. She didn't want to dwell on the tragic events of the past. Even though those events had brought the media flocking to Storyton Hall and had increased their bookings by two hundred percent, Jane didn't want the resort to flourish because people had met their untimely end under its roof. She wanted it to thrive because it was a book lover's paradise.

The twins returned with a glass of water for Uncle Aloysius, who stared at it blankly for a second before recalling his throat tickle. After feigning another small coughing attack, he drank down the water and bustled the boys and Phil out the front door.

"The fish are waiting, Jane!" he called back over his shoulder. "Phil only has an hour or two to spare, so must we be off." He touched the brim of his fishing hat in farewell and gestured at the twins to hurry into the idling Rolls-Royce sedan.

"It was a pleasure to meet you, Jane. See you at the duck race!" Phil waved and then hurried down the steps to the car.

Butterworth, Storyton's butler, watched the Rolls pull away and ease down the gravel drive.

"What do you make of Mr. Hughes?" Jane asked him.

"I believe he's cut from the right cloth," Butterworth replied. "Like Mr. Sinclair, Mr. Sterling, Mr. Lachlan, and myself, Mr. Hughes is former military. He was an environmental science officer for the army."

"The only war he'll be waging will be against Uncle Aloysius—the battle over who lands the bigger fish," Jane said. She was about to comment on the extraordinary circumstances that had led Phil and Sandi Hughes to hang their shingle in Storyton Village, but the arrival of a new guest distracted her.

Butterworth's gaze was also fixed on the woman who alighted from the vintage Rolls-Royce Silver Shadow. She wore baggy green trousers, a filmy white peasant blouse, and bug-eye sunglasses. A long braid of copper-colored hair swung over one shoulder as she bent to collect her belongings from the backseat.

"Excuse me, ma'am." Billy the bellhop darted outside and hurried to the car, tipping his cap at the lady guest as he made for the trunk and her luggage. She flashed him a bright smile and jogged up the steps leading to the massive oak doors as though she couldn't wait to get inside.

As for Butterworth, he slowly pivoted in order to collect a silver tray bearing a linen cocktail napkin and a single champagne flute. He kept a printout of guest arrivals in his breast pocket and Sterling had apparently delivered this guest right on time. Jane backed away from the main doors to allow the butler to greet their new guest properly.

"Madame." Butterworth proffered the tray when the woman was in the vestibule. "Welcome to Storyton Hall. I hope your journey over the mountain was a pleasant one."

"It was absolutely breathtaking!" she exclaimed. She accepted the champagne and took a fortifying slurp. After gazing around the lobby with evident delight, she turned back to Butterworth. "Yes! Breathtaking! Dozens of red-tailed hawks swooped through the clouds! And the trees! They stretched on and on. An undulating sea of green."

"It is a most verdant landscape," Butterworth agreed politely, though Jane could tell that he was eyeing their new guest with suspicion, as though she might suddenly burst into song. Or worse, embrace him.

However, the woman, who had a camera bag dangling from one shoulder and a portfolio case hanging from the other, merely gesticulated with both arms. "I felt like I was entering another world traveling here. A place where people are unfettered—as light as leaves!" She thrust both arms into the air and champagne splattered on the rug and speckled Jane's ballet flats. The woman gasped and apologized for her clumsiness. Dropping all of her things, she began to dab at the beads of moisture with her cocktail napkin.

"Please, Madame." Butterworth intervened by placing a firm hand on her elbow. "Do not trouble yourself. Many guests are overwhelmed upon their initial arrival, so we are quite accustomed to mishaps, I can assure you. Miss Jane will escort you to the reception desk." He started to bend over. "If you need assistance with your, er . . ."

To Jane's astonishment, Butterworth faltered. Butterworth *never* faltered. His speech and movements were as fluid as running water. But when Jane glanced down at the rug, she understood what had shocked the unflappable butler.

Several photographs had escaped from the woman's portfolio case and Jane stared at them in disbelief. Unless her eyes were deceiving her, she was seeing close-up images of female body parts. They'd been distorted somehow, but that's what they looked like to Jane.

What I'd give for a fig leaf, she thought.

Dropping to her knees, she carefully pushed the photographs back into the case before any passersby could see them. With flushed cheeks, she faced her guest and beckoned toward the check-in area. "If you'd follow me, Ms. . . ."

"Kira Grace. Free spirit by nature, photographer by trade."

The name was familiar, and Jane knew that she'd just met another Medieval Herbalist. "My great-aunt is an admirer of yours."

"I never get tired of hearing that," Kira said happily, and Jane wondered if the photographer was always so effervescent. "Tell her that I brought prints to sell. I always sell out during our annual meetings. Year after year, rumors about the erotic nature of my work circulate through the hotel, and when the other guests finally get curious enough—and brave enough—they come find me!" She let loose a tinkling laugh.

Claude Mason had booked the Great Gatsby Ballroom so that the herbalists could put on a small medieval fair on Sunday afternoon. Jane had pictured tables covered with handmade soaps and scented satchels. Too late, she realized she should have vetted the herbalists' wares. How would her guests react when they saw Kira's photographs? And what of the villagers? They were bound to walk up to Storyton Hall following church services and a large midday meal. What would they think of her erotic prints?

Jane thought about the photographs she'd seen. If Kira was interested in herbs, then surely her work reflected her passion. "Forgive me, but I'm not well versed in photography. How do you create erotic images using plants?"

"Ever heard of Georgia O'Keeffe?" Kira asked and Jane nodded in understanding. The photograph she'd seen had featured a close-up of a plant part, not a human female body part.

Still, Jane wondered what the other herbalists had sold at previous fairs. She didn't want to hear that the Poison Princess was hocking packs of belladonna seeds to children after the fact, so she asked Kira to describe some of the items her friends would be putting up for sale in a few days' time.

"Oh, lovely things!" Kira cried in response. "Perfume, lotion, insect repellent, candles, honey, spices, jewelry . . ."

"What about Ms. Meredith?"

Something in Kira's face shifted. She tried to keep her smile from slipping, but failed. "She'll have copies of her book to sign. And she also sells pamphlets on regional poisonous plants. How to recognize them and what to do if you, your child, or your pet has accidentally ingested one—that sort of thing."

Jane relaxed. Mr. Green at The Potter's Shed had similar pamphlets on a display rack in his shop. Of course, his were free. She shared this detail with Kira.

"Well, your Mr. Green probably doesn't need to maintain

the lifestyle of a *princess*." Kira's tone sharpened dramatically. "You'd think she was *real royalty* because she's been on TV. Big deal! I've had shows in major art galleries across the world. You'd think she was the only celebrity among us—the way people fawn over her. And while she laps up their admiration, she *feels* nothing for them. Not even the ones she takes to bed." Kira raised her hands and shook her head. "No, no. I will *not* allow negativity to taint my time here." She closed her eyes and exhaled, and when she opened them again, her smiled had returned. "I can't wait to see my room! If it's as gorgeous as this lobby, I'll be in heaven!"

Recognizing her cue, Jane left Kira in the capable hands of the desk clerk while she fetched the brass room key from the key cabinet. No sooner had Kira headed for the elevator banks than two more female guests arrived.

The first woman looked like a Parisian runway model. Tall and slim, she had high cheekbones, full lips, and deep blue eyes with a hint of violet. Her blond hair was gathered into a loose bun, leaving several wisps to frame her lovely face.

"That must be our bride," Sue, the desk clerk, whispered. "She has that glow."

Jane nodded in agreement. "She does indeed. She's Victoria Billingsley. The woman beside her must be her sister and maid of honor, Hannah. Hannah is also a Medieval Herbalist, so for the first time ever, our wedding guests and special event guests are nearly interchangeable."

Hannah was easily a foot shorter and sixty pounds heavier than Victoria. She walked with a pronounced slouch to her shoulders. Her hair, which was the same hue as her sister's, was parted in the middle and hung over her face like a pair of curtains. She kept her gaze on the carpet, only glancing up when Victoria pointed at something.

"I think Hannah's limping," Sue said quietly. Her brows were knit with motherly concern. "Is she injured?"

Jane turned to Sue. "When Victoria and I spoke on the

phone, she told me that Hannah was born with a spinal deformity. Hannah has undergone numerous back and neck surgeries throughout her life. She suffers from chronic pain, so we must do our best to make her comfortable."

Sue put a hand over her heart. "That poor child. If Storyton Hall can help other guests escape their troubles, it can help this young lady too. I'll let the staff know to give her the star treatment."

"I know you'll make the Billingsley ladies feel right at home," Jane said and moved forward to greet the bride-to-be and her sister.

Ignoring Jane's outstretched hand, Victoria hugged her instead. "After all you've done to help me, I feel like you're part of the family! Besides, I'm a hugger. Hannah isn't."

"It's lovely to meet you." Jane applied gentle pressure to Hannah's hand, which was cold and covered with pigment. "You have such long, graceful fingers," Jane said. "Like those of a pianist. Or a painter."

Hannah blushed, clearly touched by the compliment. "I love music, but I don't play an instrument. When I was younger, I wanted to play the harp, but I couldn't take the weight . . ." The color in her cheeks deepened.

"My sister has other talents," Victoria declared proudly. "I brag about her whenever I have the chance. She restores antique art. Anything that was hand-colored. Drawings, maps, book illustrations. But her real love is botanicals."

"I can see why you joined The Medieval Herbalists," Jane said.

"I'm the secretary," Hannah said, meeting Jane's eye for the first time. "I put together our newsletters, moderate our listserv, and maintain our website. It's a ton of work, but I love it."

Victoria nudged her sister playfully in the side. "You should modify your title. Instead of going by secretary, you should go by patron saint. You should get a portion of the member dues for everything you do. No one else spends their free time toiling away on projects for the good of the group."

"They're my friends," Hannah protested.

Her sister immediately relented. "You're right. They're the reason we're here." Victoria smiled at Jane. "I had no clue where to have my wedding until Hannah showed me where she was going for her annual meeting. When I saw the photos of the Henry James Library, the Jane Austen Drawing Room, and the Agatha Christie Tea Room, I knew I had to be married here—in a place filled with books. It has everything I love inside and everything my sister loves outside."

"And the groom?" Jane asked. "Does he share your enthusiasm?"

Victoria gave a sheepish shrug. "Carson's just happy that I made a decision! Often, it's the woman who's in a rush to get married, but not me. Carson and I are both in our late twenties, and I thought we'd travel around and have some adventures before settling down, but Carson was ready to take the next step, so here we are."

To Jane, this didn't sound like a ringing endorsement for marriage. Judging from Hannah's pinched expression, she didn't think so either.

"Well, until your wedding night, you and Hannah are booked in our Secret Garden Suite." Jane said hurriedly. Marriage counseling was not in her job description. "The suite has two bedrooms and a sitting room, and a private garden with a patio area."

"See? You can paint in your pajamas while I read in my pajamas. It'll be just like being at home, but better," Victoria said, and the sisters exchanged smiles.

Watching them, Jane smiled too. Their fondness for each

other moved her, and she couldn't help thinking of Fitz and Hem. She hoped her sons would be as close as these sisters when they were grown.

As Jane escorted Victoria and Hannah to the reception desk, she explained that the lobby was becoming more and more crowded because it was almost teatime.

"People line up early," Jane said. "Though I don't know why. Mrs. Hubbard would never allow one of the menu items to run out."

Victoria clapped. "I love tea! And cake! Let's hurry and check in, Hannah Banana. I want to try one of everything!"

Hannah hesitated. "Can't we go when most of the other guests are done?"

"And settle for the leftovers?" Victoria asked before immediately softening her tone. "What does it matter if they stare? You'll never see these people again. By tomorrow, you'll be among mostly friends."

"You don't know what it's like, Via. You've always been beautiful," Hannah said with remarkable calm. "It gets really old. The feeling of eyes on me. That's why I stay at home. I'm just tired of it, okay?"

Victoria put an arm around her sister's waist. "Okay, Banana Boat. I get it. Why don't I grab plates for both of us and bring them back to our room? That way—"

"There's no need," Jane cut in smoothly. "I'll have Mrs. Hubbard make a tray of the choicest selections and have it delivered to your room. Along with a pot of tea, of course. You can enjoy your tea service in your private garden."

Hannah flashed her a grateful smile. "That sounds really nice."

Leaving the sisters with Sue, Jane popped into the kitchen to make the arrangements. When she was done, she wound her way through the staff corridors until she reached the Agatha Christie Tea Room. As anticipated, over a dozen eager guests were already waiting in the hallway.

Jane made her way down the line, chatting briefly with each guest. When she finally reached the end, she encountered a family of four. The parents were both dressed in tennis whites and had their eyes locked on the door to the Agatha Christie Tea Room. Their two teenage daughters were slouched against the paneled wall at a deliberate distance from their parents. They twisted pink earbuds around their fingers and studied the tea menu with marked disdain.

"The only thing that doesn't sound gross is the strawberry shortcake," the first girl said in a sluggish drawl. "I'm gonna have, like, four pieces."

"Me too." The second girl's speech was equally lethargic, as though she found it too taxing to enunciate. "The heifers ahead of us can't afford the extra calories anyway. We'll be doing them a favor."

Jane's eyes widened over this rude remark. She looked to see if the girl's parents had heard her, but they were busy whispering to each other.

At that moment, Victoria and Hannah crossed the lobby en route to the western wing and the Secret Garden Suite.

"Oh my gawd! Check her out!" The first girl pointed at Hannah. "I had no idea that the Hunchback of Notre Dame moved to Virginia."

The second girl sniggered. "It's more like *Beauty and the Beast on Ice*. Without the ice."

Both girls burst into giggles.

Jane glowered at them, but they were as oblivious to her presence as their parents were to their inexcusable behavior.

"Someone should tell the management that the gargoyles belong on the *outside* of the hotel," one of the girls said and let loose a shriek.

Fuming, Jane turned on her heel and hurried into the tea room. Gathering the wait staff around the delectable spread of cakes, cookies, sandwiches, scones, and tarts, she pointed at the strawberry shortcake and said, "Two teenage girls are about to enter this room. They're both wearing pink earbuds. No matter what it takes, I don't want either girl to receive a single piece of this cake. Not even a crumb. Do you understand?"

When the staff responded with blank stares, Jane quickly told them about Hannah's condition and how the girls had belittled her with their cutting remarks.

"We'll see to it, Miss Jane," one of the waiters said through lips tight with anger.

Jane lingered just long enough to watch, with no small amount of satisfaction, as the same waiter whisked the platter of strawberry shortcake into the kitchen the moment after the guest in front of the girls had helped himself to a generous slice.

Seeing the girls standing at the buffet table with their mouths unhinged and their foreheads furrowed in shock and indignation, Jane thought, *Who looks like a pair of gargoyles now?*

THREE

Even though the following day was a Thursday, it had a beginning-of-a-weekend feel. Jane suspected the atmosphere had something to do with the fact that tickets for Storyton's inaugural rubber duck race would be available for purchase when Storyton Outfitters opened its doors for the first time that morning.

According to the ad in the paper, participants could bet on a favorite duck as if they were betting on a horse at the racetrack. Storyton Outfitters was not only providing prizes to three winners, but also donating half the race profits to the Virginia Conservation Network.

"We moved to Storyton because we love nature," Phil Hughes was quoted as saying. "As residents and business owners, Sandi and I want to do our part to keep our rivers unpolluted and our mountains litter free. This is one of the most beautiful places in the country, and we'd like to preserve its beauty."

Jane was prevented from reading the rest of the article because Hem's fingers curled over the edge of the paper, crinkling the words until they were illegible. "Can we go now?"

"Is your room clean?" Jane asked.

Behind Hem, Fitz saluted. "Shipshape, Captain!"

Jane tossed the paper on the kitchen counter and glanced at her watch. There was still plenty of time to bike into the village and select their ducks. "Mr. Hughes is the only official captain in Storyton that I know of, and I bet he wouldn't approve of dirty clothes stuffed under the bed or pushed into the closet."

The boys gave her guileless stares.

"I can predict what I'll be doing when we get home," Jane murmured, realizing that the twins had undoubtedly scooped everything off the floor and shoved it into the laundry basket in the hall closet. Still, they'd fulfilled their end of the bargain, so she ruffled their hair and said, "We can go now."

"Race you to the shed!" Hem shouted, and with a bang of the front door, they were gone.

Jane followed at a more sedate pace. After collecting water bottles and her handbag, she headed to the large shed where the staff and family bicycles were stored. She loaded her items into her bike basket and pedaled to the end of the long driveway, where she knew the twins would be waiting.

She insisted on taking the lead whenever they biked into town. For most of the trip, the road took them through the quiet countryside with its tree-covered hills and cornfields. They passed fields of wildflowers, rolling pastures dotted with grazing cows, and a chestnut pony who never failed to meet them by the fence, hoping for a lump of sugar or a snack of sliced apples or carrots. Despite their rush to get to Storyton Outfitters, the boys stopped to give the pony his treat and were rewarded with a whinny of gratitude as they rode off again.

Jane slowed her pace as she approached the final bend

before the bridge. Even though a sign had been erected warning of its sharpness, the curve took visitors by surprise. Dozens of tourists riding rental bikes from Spokes either ignored the sign's warning or didn't respond to it in time. These sorry souls ended up in the thicket of blackberry bushes if they were lucky or slamming into a tree if they weren't. Dubbed Broken Arm Bend by the locals, that bit of road had the village's only doctor stocking fiberglass for casts all year long.

When Fitz and Hem spotted the sign, they shouted the poem one of the village children had made up to commemorate the danger of the infamous curve.

Broken Arm Bend,
Where rides come to an end,
In screams and scrapes.
Yes, your bones will mend,
But it would have been better
If you'd used your brakes!

Jane laughed. Hem and Fitz's classmates were constantly revising the poem. By now, there had to be a dozen different versions.

"Where are we parking?" Fitz yelled as their tires rattled over the wooden bridge.

"The Cheshire Cat," Jane called back over her shoulder. She'd already asked her friend Betty if she and the boys could stow their bikes in the pub's garage. With nearly all of the villagers, the majority of Storyton Hall's staff and guests, and visitors from over the mountain attending the duck race, every parking spot and bike rack would be needed.

"Come in!" Betty Carmichael beckoned from the back entrance of Storyton's pub. "Bob and I made special drinks for the kids today. Would you be my taste testers, boys?"

Fitz and Hem were more than happy to comply and Betty

told them to sit at the bar. They rested their forearms on the polished wood and watched her as she placed paper coasters in front of them.

"Bob calls this the Fluffy Ducky." Betty took a plastic pitcher from the cooler and filled two mason jars with a pale yellow liquid. Sticking a straw into each jar, she set the drinks down with a flourish. "The adults will have their own version," she said to Jane. "The Fuzzy Duck."

"Is it like a Fuzzy Navel?" Jane asked.

"Something like that," Betty replied with a wink and then focused on the boys again. "Well, gentlemen. What's the verdict?"

"Delicious!" Hem cried.

Fitz pointed at his mason jar. "Awesome! What is it?"

"Promise not to give away the secret ingredients?" Betty held out her pinkie.

Fitz and Hem took turns exchanging pinkie promises with her.

"Canned pineapple and nonfat yogurt. That's all," Betty said. "Sweet, healthy, and refreshing. Bob built a little rolling cart just for today's race. We have coolers filled with Fluffy Ducky and hope to sell lots of smoothies while the sun is shining. Later, when the race is over, we plan to serve more hot and thirsty customers here in the pub."

"If I didn't *really* want to buy a duck race ticket, I'd pay for a Fuzzy Duck, Mrs. Carmichael," Fitz said. "No matter how much you charged, it'd be worth it."

"You're such a charmer." Betty beamed at him. "Have you decided which duck to pick?"

Fitz nodded. "But I'm not saying. Neither is Hem. We think it's luckier not to tell."

"Fair enough." Betty looked at Jane. "What about you?"

"I want to see what their costumes look like first—get a vibe for each one before I choose," Jane said. "Did you and Bob already buy your tickets?"

"Bob did, but I'm torn between two ducks. Maybe you can help me decide which one to pick."

Hem slung an arm around his brother. "You should bet on both of them, Mrs. Carmichael. Two is always better than one."

Laughing, Betty scooped up their mason jars and plunked them in the sink. "Well said, Master Steward. Let's go, gentlemen. We're off to the races!"

The party of four walked back across the bridge to the two-story stone house Phil and Sandi Hughes had converted into Storyton Outfitters. Like many Storyton merchants, the Hugheses had set aside the ground floor for their business while the kitchen and second floor made up their living quarters. However, Storyton Outfitters didn't fill its front garden with flowers, sculptures, or comfortable benches, but with kayaks and canoes.

"Cool!" Fitz ran his hand along an orange kayak. "Can we try these, Mom?"

"Maybe later in the summer," Jane said. "I'll have to see what options the captain has for children."

She reached for a painted oar, which served as a door handle, and tugged. The moment the door opened, the sounds of children shouting, "Captain Phil! Captain Phil!" came tumbling out.

Glancing over shelves of camping and fishing gear, Jane saw kids of all ages mobbing the checkout counter at the back of the shop. In their eagerness to purchase rubber duck race tickets, they'd forgone everything they'd been taught about good manners. Not only were they shouting, but they were pushing and shoving one another as well.

Suddenly, the blast of a boat horn cut through their clamor. Every child covered his or her ears and froze in place.

"That's better." Phil Hughes touched the brim of his blue fisherman's cap. "I'm Captain Phil. Welcome to my shop. I'd be glad to sell tickets to any lady or gentleman who can stand straight and tall in an orderly line. If you can't, I'd be just as glad to toss you into the river with the ducks."

Several adults chuckled at this, but the children immediately began forming a line. They'd recognized the indisputable authority in Captain Phil's voice.

"The names of the twenty ducks are listed here." Captain Phil pointed to a chalkboard. "Their photographs are next to their names. The real ducks are in a special container waiting to be taken to the river."

A little girl standing in the middle of the line raised her hand. "Captain Phil? Did you decorate the ducks?"

"No, miss. The costumes and paint jobs are the handiwork of Mrs. Hughes. You'll meet her at the starting line." He smiled at his first customer. "Yes, sir. May I help you?"

"A ticket for Frankenduck, please," said a small boy. "Green's my favorite color."

Jane told the twins to join the line and then turned to Betty. "I want to study the photographs before I pick my lucky duck, and I can't see them from back here."

"Me either," Betty said. "Oh, look! Mabel and Mrs. Pratt are heading for the chalkboard too."

Mabel Wimberly and Eugenia Pratt were fellow members of the Cover Girls, the book club Jane held in her home. Mabel owned La Grande Dame, a clothing and fabric shop, and was known throughout the valley for her skill as a seamstress and dress designer. As for Mrs. Pratt, she was mostly known for her propensity to gossip.

"Hello, ladies!" Jane greeted her friends warmly.

"Howdy, gals. Is this the cutest thing you've ever seen?" Mabel gestured at the board. "Sandi Hughes is a creative genius. Get a load of these costumes."

Jane and Betty moved as close to the board as they could without blocking the view of the children now waiting patiently in line. As Jane's eye moved down the list of names, she began to grin. By the time she reached the twentieth name, she was smiling in childlike delight.

"These are so clever!" She glanced over at Phil Hughes and found him watching her. He seemed pleased by her response to the board. "I'm thrilled to discover that you and Sandi are bibliophiles."

"Guilty as charged," Phil said. "When we first talked about having the race, I tossed out Moby Duck as a joke, but Sandi loved the idea of giving the ducks literary names. Minutes later, she was on the phone with the Storyton paper, setting up the contest calling for duck names. Here we are, nineteen ducks later."

"I'd like Katniss Everduck, please," said a teenage girl and laid her money on the counter.

"Excuse me." Captain Phil touched his fisherman's tap in deference to Jane and then turned his attention back to his customers.

"Which yellow darling has caught your eye, Jane?" Mrs. Pratt asked. "I'm choosing Ducktor Zhivago. How can I resist a duck with a fur hat and mustache? He also reminds me of one of my all-time favorite books. Some of those Russian novelists really knew how to blend epic tragedy and romance."

"The movie was wonderful too," Mabel said.

While her friends launched into a discussion of the film's high points, most of which featured Omar Sharif's smoldering eyes, Jane reread the list of duck names and tried to make a decision:

The Ducks of Storyton

1. Quack and the Beanstalk
2. Ganduck the Wizard
3. "Bill" Shakespeare
4. Ducktor Zhivago

5. Quacktain Hook
6. Quackenezer Scrooge
7. Duckelberry Finn
8. Katniss Everduck
9. Peeta Mallard
10. Quack in the Hat
11. Frankenduck
12. Jane Eggyre
13. Pippi Longducking
14. Nurse Quatchet
15. Sherduck Holmes
16. James Pond
17. Lisbeak Salander
18. Duckter Jekyll
19. Moby Duck
20. Count Quackula

"I'm putting all my eggs in James Pond's basket," said a familiar voice from behind Jane. Eloise Alcott, Jane's best friend, joined the other Cover Girls and began studying the board with an amused expression. "How could I go wrong with a pistol-toting duck in a white dinner jacket? Besides, James Pond always gets his man."

"He could end up swimming in circles around all the lady ducks and come in last," teased Phoebe Doyle, the owner of Canvas Creamery and another Cover Girl.

Violet Osborne, the final book club member to join her friends at the chalkboard, pointed at Lisbeak Salander. "As a professional stylist, I declare that she has the hippest hair. Not only does that duck have a spiked Mohawk, but she also has piercings and a dragon tattoo. She's going to leave all the other ducks crying in her wake."

"I'm going with Pippi Longducking." Jane said. "She was my one of my favorite book characters when I was little.

And just look at those pigtails. They're sure to help her stay balanced as she zooms down the river."

Eloise arched her brows. "I was positive you'd want Jane Eggyre. Especially with that cute blue bonnet and the book tucked under her wing."

Jane shook her head. "Too predictable."

Laughing, the Cover Girls took their places in line.

"I'm really looking forward to our book discussion with The Medieval Herbalists," Eloise told Jane. "But I'm a little intimidated too. Our Cover Girl meetings are relaxed and low-key. We share a meal, have a few cocktails, and talk about the book. There are no rules and we all respect one another's opinions. Most importantly, we have a good time."

"Are you worried that we won't have a good time with our guests?" Jane asked.

Eloise shrugged. "I just hope they don't respond to the books we chose with an analytical, academic manner. It's possible to dissect novels in a way that takes all the feeling out of them."

"I've already met three Medieval Herbalists and they don't seem stuffy. In fact, there's a photographer who might focus solely on the sex scenes in *Outlander* and ignore all the references to herbal medicine."

"Did you mention something about sex?" Mrs. Pratt whispered excitedly.

Jane and Eloise exchanged a quick grin, before Jane said, "I was talking about Kira Grace."

Mrs. Pratt nodded knowingly. "I have a copy of her book, *PolliNation*. That woman has the ability to turn a simple flower stamen into a—"

"Yes," Jane cut in smoothly. "I saw an example of her work yesterday. As did Butterworth."

"Oh, my." Mrs. Pratt giggled. "I can just picture his facial expression." She mimicked Butterworth's look of stern disapproval.

Jane was about to scold her friend for making fun of Butterworth when she realized that it was her turn to buy a ticket.

"Pippi Longducking, please," she told Captain Phil.

He instructed her to put her name and phone number on two tickets with matching numbers. "You keep one and I drop the second in Pippi's fish bowl. If she wins the race, we'll pick a random name from the fishbowl and that person wins the grand prize. If she comes in second, a winner gets the second-place prize, and so on."

"I'm not sure what I'd do with a kayak, so I hope someone with more free time and better balance wins the grand prize." Jane took her ticket and stepped aside to allow Eloise to purchase her ticket.

Once all the Cover Girls had their tickets, they rejoined Fitz and Hem outside. By this time, a large crowd had congregated on both sides of Storyton River.

"Look at all these people!" Jane exclaimed softly.

"I'd better run," Betty said. "Bob should be pushing the drink cart to the bridge right about now and he'll be wondering where I've gone. See you at book club!"

After she hurried off, the twins asked Jane if they could watch the race with their friends.

"Yes. You can meet me at the finish line, where Uncle Aloysius and Aunt Octavia will be sitting. Watch out for toddlers or little old ladies in your rush to follow the ducks." Jane raised a warning finger. "There are tons of Storyton guests at this event, so mind your manners."

"What your mom is trying to say is don't push anyone into the water," Eloise added with a playful wink. "Even if they act like jerks because their duck is in the lead."

Jane elbowed her best friend. "Don't give them any ideas."

The boys told their mother they'd behave and were off like a shot, nearly barreling into an elderly man using a walker.

Jane rolled her eyes in exasperation. "At least Sinclair,

Lachlan, and the Hogg brothers are officiating. With those five gentlemen spread out along the route, the twins can't get into too much trouble."

Eloise shook her head. "You're bound to regret those words. Come on, Mrs. Pratt is saving us a spot by the riverbank. See how she's sticking her elbows out? She looks like a flustered hen!"

Arm in arm, Jane and Eloise squeezed in next to Mrs. Pratt and peered up at the bridge. They saw Bob Carmichael's drink cart with its bright blue umbrella, and next to the cart, a woman wearing a yellow Storyton Outfitter's T-shirt. Jane recognized the green font and the logo, a canoe paddle crossed over a fishing pole, because Captain Phil was wearing an identical shirt.

The woman raised a bullhorn to her lips. "Welcome, everyone!" Her voice floated down from the bridge. "Welcome to Storyton's inaugural rubber duck race!"

The crowd cheered.

"I'm Sandi Hughes. Most of you have probably already met my husband, Captain Phil. Today is a very special day for us. We're celebrating the grand opening of our business, Storyton Outfitters, which is a dream come true for Captain Phil, but we're also the newest members of this beautiful and charming community, which is a dream come true for both of us."

This elicited even more cheers and applause.

"And now, according to the Casio Pro Tek watch on my wrist—a prize I'll soon be presenting to the third-place winner—it's two minutes to four." Sandi leaned over the bridge railing and pointed down at the river. "As you can see, the ducks are lined up and ready to swim. As soon as Captain Phil releases the netting, the ducks are free! The first duck to cross the finish line just shy of Broken Arm Bend is our winner. Please do not interfere with the racers or throw anything in the water. The three prize drawings will take place at Storyton Outfitters after the race. Good luck, have fun, and thank you for coming today!"

Captain Phil waded into the river and gave a short blast of his air horn. "Count down with me!" he shouted.

Jane looked at the twenty ducks bobbing up in the current and felt a thrill of excitement. She glanced at the opposite bank and saw Tammy Kota standing with a short man who bore an uncanny resemblance to Benjamin Franklin. Jane recognized the man as Claude Mason, the president of The Medieval Herbalists. Spotting Jane, Vivian waved and then turned to speak to her companion. After a brief pause, Claude smiled and waved too. Jane waved back, feeling a kinship with all those around her.

"One!" Phil began.

The crowd instantly joined in. "Two!"

"I feel like a child at a magic show. Or the circus," murmured Mrs. Pratt. She clasped her hands as though in prayer. "At my age, it's ridiculous to be this invested in a rubber duck."

And yet, she bellowed "Three!" along with everyone else and gave a triumphant whoop when the netting fell and the ducks were freed.

People surged downriver en masse, and Jane was relieved that the gentle current kept the ducks at a leisurely pace and allowed the spectators to get a head start. Of course, some of the attendees were waiting in chairs by the finish line. Uncle Aloysius and Aunt Octavia were among this group, as were several of their octogenarian friends.

As Jane walked close on Eloise's heels, she saw Victoria and Hannah Billingsley on the path ahead. Hannah's pace was even slower than that of the floating ducks, and people were politely skirting around her. Jane felt a stab of sympathy for the younger woman. With every step, Hannah's body swayed back and forth, and though her sister offered her arm more than once, Hannah refused to accept Victoria's assistance.

At least people aren't staring at Hannah, Jane thought.

She'd almost caught up to the Billingsley sisters when the current grew stronger and the ducks started to move downstream with more alacrity.

"Come on, James Pond!" Eloise shouted. "Go, go, go!"

Similar cries echoed over the water.

"Look!" a child nearby called out. "The Quack in the Hat is upside down! Can he win with his butt?"

The innocent question drew a roar of laughter from the crowd. Jane squinted at the yellow specks in the river until she saw that the duck with the red and white stovepipe hat and red bow tie was now floating with his head underwater. Though his progress hadn't been halted, the sudden reversal of his body had put him in last place, and the people who'd picked him to win were crestfallen.

"Flip over, Quack!" they pleaded. "Get your head above water!"

Bill Shakespeare was having problems too. A stick had become lodged between his wing and his quill pen and now, instead of floating straight, he was spinning around in circles.

"The Bard of Avon is creating his own whirlpool. A tempest, if you will," Mabel said with a chortle.

Jane was too distracted by the sight of Hannah veering off the path toward a large tree to respond to Mabel's comment. When Hannah reached the tree, she leaned heavily against its trunk and made waving motions at Victoria, indicating that her sister should go on without her. Victoria put her hands on her hips and refused to budge.

By the time Jane caught up with the siblings, the current had increased and the ducks were now floating so swiftly that the excitement among the spectators had reached a fever pitch.

"Pippi's in the lead!" Mrs. Pratt shrieked. And then, "Jane? Aren't you coming?"

"Go on. I'll catch up." Unaware that she was doing so, Jane mimicked Hannah's gesture.

When her friends had moved off, Jane approached the two sisters. "Is there room at this tree for a third?" Jane smiled briefly at Victoria, but focused her attention on Hannah.

"I just need to catch my breath," Hannah said without conviction. Her face was drawn and her eyes were glassy. Having had to bring the twins to Doc Lydgate for stitches half a dozen times, Jane recognized the expression. Hannah was in pain.

"Would you like a ride back to Storyton Hall?" Jane asked softly. "Sterling, our head chauffeur, has a car parked in the village. Forgive me for being blunt, Ms. Billingsley, but you don't look well."

Victoria opened her mouth to protest, but Hannah put her hand on her sister's arm. "If it's not too much trouble, I'd be glad for a ride. My back's really hurting. I forgot to bring my body pillow from home, so I didn't sleep well last night."

"I'm sorry to hear that," Jane said. "I'll speak with our head housekeeper after the race. She'll come up with a substitute for your body pillow, even if that means sewing four of our regular pillows together. If that makes you comfortable, we'll do it."

Jane retreated a few steps, called Sterling, and told him where to meet the Billingsley sisters. "Have Mrs. Hubbard and Mrs. Templeton put their heads together to see what they can do to help Ms. Billingsley."

The last group of spectators was passing by Jane and the Billingsley sisters when Sterling appeared and offered Hannah his arm. "Your chariot awaits, milady."

When Hannah hesitated, Sterling whispered, "Please, miss. My boss is watching."

Though she knew she was being manipulated, Hannah complied. Keeping her eyes on the ground, she leaned heavily on Sterling as the trio made their way to the car. While Sterling got Hannah settled, Victoria turned and mouthed a silent "thank you" to Jane. She smiled in reply and hurried to catch up to her friends.

Jogging along the riverbank, she heard the crowd noise escalate.

The ducks must be close to the finish line, she thought and broke into a full run.

By the time she could see the chute Captain Phil had constructed to force the ducks into single file as they approached the finish line, a victor had already been declared. Jane couldn't hear which duck had nabbed the top spot because the spectators were still rooting for their ducks to claim second and third place.

Jane wound her way through a knot of riveted onlookers until she reached Uncle Aloysius and Aunt Octavia. Aunt Octavia sat in her chair like a queen on her throne. Her feet rested on a tufted footstool, she held a pair of mother-of-pearl opera glasses in front of her eyes, and a bag of popcorn was balanced on her expansive lap. Uncle Aloysius, in contrast, was standing at the river's edge, shouting for Quackenezer Scrooge to "swim like the Dickens."

Suddenly, he whooped in triumph and turned to exchange a high-five with a companion. Unfortunately, the friend missed Aloysius's outstretched hand and knocked his beloved fishing hat right off his head. It landed in the water and was immediately whisked away by the current.

"Sinclair!" Aloysius cried out in alarm, but his cries were swallowed by the surrounding cacophony and Sinclair continued to gesture at a group of children who were in danger of going for an impromptu swim if they continued to jostle one another.

Jane hurried over to her uncle. "Don't worry. I'll get it where the river bottlenecks."

"My sweet Octavia gave me that hat," he said with the forlorn expression of a child who's lost his favorite toy. "Every hook and fly has a story."

"I won't come back without it," Jane promised. "Keep an eye on the twins for me."

And she was off again, running along the river trail.

As the river curved away from the village, the trail grew steeper. It wasn't long before Jane was breathing heavily. She glanced at the water, hoping that her uncle's hat would be directed toward the bank by a stray current, but it floated steadily downstream.

By the time the river narrowed and a cluster of rocks created a logjam of leaves, branches, and other natural debris along the eastern bank, Jane had a stitch in her side. Luckily, the tip of a pointy stick had snagged her uncle's hat, so Jane kicked off her shoes, rolled up her trouser legs, and waded in after it.

Mud squelched between her toes and she wobbled awkwardly over the slick stones and the riverbed. The cool water rushed around her calves, and then her knees, when she finally grabbed hold of her uncle's hat.

That's when she saw the body drifting in the flotsam.

"God," Jane whispered in horror and splashed toward the body. Instinct told her she could do nothing to help. The person was floating facedown, but she rushed forward as fast as she could despite this knowledge.

Shoving her uncle's hat on her head, she reached for the woman's shoulders. A cloud of copper hair fanned out from the center of her head like sunrays and tiny fish darted away as Jane strained to flip the woman over. She was inordinately heavy.

When her face was finally turned to the sun, it was a grotesque mask of bloated white skin. A dark leaf was plastered over one eye and specks of dirt clung to her lips and cheeks.

Jane stood in the river, numb with shock, and cradled the dead body of a Storyton Hall guest.

FOUR

Jane couldn't believe she was holding the lifeless corpse of Kira Grace.

Kira, who'd been bubbling over with energy the previous day. A woman with dancing eyes and laughter in her voice. A woman who seemed on the verge of skipping instead of walking.

But death had robbed her of her effervescence. She was now heavy—weighed down by sodden, mud-covered clothes and wet, clotted hair.

Jane couldn't stop staring into Kira's eyes.

They were opaque and looked to be covered with a bluish film, like the eyes of a newborn kitten. Kira's eyes reflected nothing. They were horrifying and pitiful at the same time.

"I have to get you out." Jane's voice was little more than a hoarse whisper, but it sounded far too loud in this bend in the river—this place where Kira's body had gotten stuck with the rest of the debris.

Jane took a moment to gather her resolve. She touched the hat perched on her head, and her fingertips brushed the silky threads of one of her uncle's flies. The hat reminded her that people were waiting for her upriver. If she didn't return soon, the twins might come looking for her.

She shook her head. She didn't want her boys to see the dead woman. Or for anyone else to see her, for that matter. Only the Fins (the group of men who worked at Storyton Hall and used their vast and secret talents to protect the Seward Family), Doc Lydgate, or someone from the sheriff's department should be privy to the sight.

Fearing that she'd already wasted too much time, Jane slid her forearms around Kira's waist and tugged. She expected the dead woman to obediently drift sideways toward the bank as directed. Instead, the body rolled to the right and dipped below the surface, as though unseen hands were holding her and refused to let go.

Jane bent down until her chest was nearly touching Kira's chest. Repositioning her arms so that they were now behind the dead woman's back, she yanked upward. A putrid odor rose from the corpse and Jane nearly gagged, but she hung on. Locked in her gruesome embrace, Jane closed her eyes, clenched her jaw, and pulled with all her might.

She heard a muted tear and the dead woman's weight shifted so abruptly that Jane was thrown off-balance. She reeled, felt her foot slide on a sharply angled rock, and fell backward.

As the water closed over her head, she made a grab for her uncle's hat. Her fingers had just closed around the brim when something touched her cheek. Opening her eyes underwater, Jane saw a swollen, milk white hand lunging toward her. It seemed to close over her face, blocking out the light.

Startled, Jane sucked in a mouthful of water. Her confused lungs contracted and she spluttered violently. She kicked her legs and pushed upward, fighting to get her head above the surface.

And then someone was lifting her up from behind. Someone with incredible strength pulled her halfway out of the water with one yank, but Jane was unable to focus on her rescuer until she'd expelled the water from her lungs.

"I thought you were an accomplished swimmer," said a male voice in a tone of either mockery or amusement.

Jane swung around to find Edwin Alcott standing chest-deep in Storyton River, and her initial shock over the sight of Kira's body and over the touch of the dead woman's hand instantly turned to anger. Reaching out, she thumped Edwin on the chest. Three times. As hard as she could. "I don't need your help!" She pointed at Kira. "*She* does!"

Edwin didn't so much as flinch. "That woman is beyond anyone's help. Take my arm, and once you're on dry land, I'll go back for her."

He held out his elbow, but Jane ignored it. After making sure her uncle's hat was still in place, she half swam, half waded to the bank. She was being churlish, she knew, but she didn't care. As far as she was concerned, she didn't owe Edwin Alcott a thing. Not even common courtesy.

Edwin waited until Jane was completely out of the water before approaching Kira's body. He then studied the scene for several minutes. His eyes scanned the corpse and the debris surrounding it. Apparently satisfied that there was no information to be gleaned from the clogged jumble of twigs and leaves, he glanced back over his shoulder as though retracing the possible path the currents could have carried the dead woman.

Finally, when Jane was on the verge of shouting at him to hurry, Edwin scooped Kira up in his arms and lifted her from the water without the slightest trace of revulsion.

He laid her body gingerly on the grass and looked at Jane. "Do you know her?"

"She's one of our guests," Jane replied tersely.

With a nod, Edwin stripped off his black T-shirt, wrung

out as much water as he could, and then gently placed it over Kira's face. "Do you want to stay with her while I get help or would you prefer to go?"

What Jane wanted to do most was slap Edwin. After that, she wanted to grip him by the shoulders and shake him. She wanted him to explain where he'd been for the past four months and why he hadn't called or written. But she refused to show him how much he'd hurt her with his silence, so she pushed a lock of wet hair off her forehead and said, "I'd be grateful if you'd call Doc Lydgate. Do you have a cell phone on you?"

"No. I only use mine when I'm abroad," Edwin said. "As a rule, I dislike such gadgets. I realize that I'm in the minority, but I don't believe they've done much to advance society. I'll run to the doc's office."

"Please be as quick as you can." Jane pointed up river. "I don't want my sons to come searching for me and encounter a dead body."

With a dip of his chin, Edwin turned and sprinted toward Storyton Village. Jane was tempted to watch him run. She could easily imagine how the muscles in his long, lean back would move, or how the sweep of dark hair falling across his forehead would lift and lower like a raven's wing, but she refused to look. Instead, she took off her uncle's hat and put it on a flat rock in the sun to dry. She then knelt in the grass and sat vigil over Kira Grace.

As the minutes ticked by, question after question surfaced in her mind. The steady gurgle of the river provided no answers. Neither did Kira's inert form.

"How did you end up in there?" Jane asked nonetheless. "And how long were you in the water?"

Hours, Jane silently replied on Kira's behalf. It was obvious that the deterioration of Kira's skin and the excessive bloating of her extremities hadn't occurred within the last hour or so. The famed photographer had been floating in Storyton River for a long time.

But why? Jane thought, fearing the answer to this question above all the others.

It wasn't Edwin who returned with Doc Lydgate, but Sterling.

"Knowing you might be tied up here for a spell, the doc had the foresight to call over to Storyton Hall requesting a car for Masters Fitz and Hem. I took the liberty of running the boys home," he told Jane. "Mrs. Hubbard promised to keep an eye on them."

At the mention of the twins, Doc Lydgate grinned. "How are my favorite patients? Not getting into too much mischief yet, eh? But the summer has just begun." Chuckling, he squeezed Jane's hand and then turned to the body on the grass. "What have we here?"

"I found her in the river," Jane said by way of explanation.

Kneeling, the doc removed Edwin's shirt. Without the slightest change of expression, he reached into his leather satchel and withdrew a pair of latex gloves, a tongue depressor, and a pen-sized exam light. After shining the light in Kira's eyes, Doc Lydgate used the tongue depressor to carefully pry open her mouth. He focused the light on her tongue, grunted once, and then sat back on his heels.

"Mr. Sterling, would you call Sheriff Evans? He'll want to see this lady before she's moved."

Jane felt a ripple of dread move up her spine. "Didn't she drown? Or did you find something else?"

Doc Lydgate nodded solemnly. "I'm afraid so. Do you know her, my dear?"

"She's a guest of Storyton Hall. Her name is Kira Grace." Jane stared at Kira's pale hand in disbelief. "She's only just arrived. I can't imagine how she ended up . . ." She trailed off, distracted by the sound of Sterling speaking into his cell phone.

"I'm sorry that you had to find her this way. It must have been quite a shock." Doc Lydgate rose to his feet and gave

Jane a long look of appraisal. "Mr. Alcott told me how he came upon you in the river. Are you feeling faint or unwell in any way?"

"Other than wet clothes and wounded pride, I'm fine." Jane smiled to show her gratitude, but her smile quickly vanished. "What did you see, Doc? When you opened her mouth—what did you see?"

"Discoloration of the tongue. Not a typical symptom of drowning. It's also not a result of the young woman having been in the water for an inordinate period of time. I don't have a great deal of experience in these matters, but I'm certain this is not a result of putrefaction or any other cause but the one I suspect."

Jane grew very still. "Which is?"

Removing his gloves, Doc Lydgate stroked the white whiskers of his beard and stared forlornly at Kira. "Poison."

A groan escaped through Jane's lips, and her entire body sagged. However, she only allowed fear and worry to rule her emotions for a brief moment before she regained control. By the time Doc Lydgate turned his attention back to her, she was completely composed.

"That's terrible," she said. Multiple scenarios were unfolding in her mind, each more disturbing than the last. "Yesterday, Ms. Grace seemed taken with the idea of setting out early to explore the hills surrounding the village. Could she have ingested something unknowingly?"

The doc shrugged. "She could have eaten raw wild mushrooms, though I'm not sure that's what happened in this case." He gave Jane a paternal pat on the shoulder. "Don't worry. Once she's over the mountain, they'll test her stomach contents and check her blood work—they'll find the answer quickly enough."

It wouldn't be quickly enough for Jane. Kira Grace was a Medieval Herbalist. She knew her plants. It was highly unlikely that she'd accidentally eat anything poisonous while out hiking.

Exactly where did you go? Jane wondered. *And did anyone else see you?*

"When will the sheriff arrive?" she asked Sterling.

"By now, it should be less than ten minutes. Miss Jane, would you like me to go back to Storyton and fetch you a change of clothes?"

Jane glanced down at her wet shirt and pants. "No. I'll stay like this until Ms. Grace has been seen to."

"Why should you be uncomfortable?" Doc Lydgate's voice held a trace of reprimand. "You're not responsible for the well-being of every guest. They're not children, and this is not your fault."

"Ms. Grace is my responsibility," Jane replied. "Like the rest of my guests, she came to Storyton Hall to escape the noise and stress of today's high-speed, hi-tech world. My guests trust me to provide them with a reader's sanctuary. A sanctuary implies a place that is both peaceful and safe. I failed to provide that for Ms. Grace, but I won't fail her again. I'll wait, just as I am, to ensure that she is removed in a dignified manner."

"This lady didn't die at the resort, so you're not culpable," Doc Lydgate pointed out, but Jane was no longer listening. She had returned to the moment when she'd last seen Kira Grace. She remembered how Kira had carried her portfolio case over one shoulder and her camera case over the other.

Where is her camera now? Jane's gaze traveled upriver before moving to the hills behind the village. If the camera wasn't in Kira's guest room, it could be anywhere.

When Jane looked back at Doc Lydgate again, he was busy replacing Edwin's T-shirt over Kira's face.

"Mr. Alcott wanted to accompany me, but I wouldn't let him," the doc said, snapping his case shut. "There was a large line forming outside his café and I saw no sense in his losing business when I could find my own way. He seemed very disappointed when I refused him. I assume he was eager to see you, Jane—" Mercifully, the slamming of car doors distracted Doc Lydgate, and less than a minute later, the sheriff and two deputies joined them on the riverbank.

"Ms. Steward." Sheriff Evans touched the brim of his hat before shaking hands with Sterling and Doc Lydgate. Evans, a fair-haired, stocky man in his mid-fifties, had been the sheriff for over twenty years and was well respected throughout the region.

With his deputies standing several feet behind him, Sheriff Evans hooked his thumbs under his utility belt and stared down at Kira's body. "All right, Doc. Would you explain what you found in layman's terms?" Before Doc Lydgate could speak, however, the sheriff put a hand on his arm to stay him. "One moment, Doc." After surveying the scene, he looked at his deputies. "Deputy Phelps, while the doc and I are talking, I'd like you to walk along the bank—see if anything catches your eye. Deputy Emory, please take a brief statement from Ms. Steward. We'll get her complete account later."

Jane shot a quick glance at Sterling, wordlessly signaling that he should listen in on the conversation between Evans and Doc Lydgate, and he sidled closer to Kira's body with the light, noiseless tread of a cat.

Deputy Emory opened a small notebook and uncapped her pen. She stuck the cap behind her ear, where it nestled in her auburn hair, and gave Jane an encouraging smile. Jane had gotten to know the female deputy a little bit last winter, but she was surprised anew by how young and fresh-faced she was. With her creamy skin and bluebird eyes, she looked like she should be playing one of Austen's or Brontë's heroines on television instead of standing in the heat in her drab brown uniform. "What made you come to this part of the river?" Deputy Emory began.

Jane reviewed her movements, doing her best to recall as many details as possible. Deputy Emory listened attentively and took copious notes, despite the fact that Jane would have to repeat the same information during her formal interview at the station at a later time.

When Jane had finished her narrative, the young deputy closed her notebook and darted a quick glance at Kira's body. "I've seen her work," she said in a soft voice. "I couldn't choose between my two favorite fields in college, so I opted for a double major in criminal justice and art history. One of my art classes was called 'The Feminist Art Movement.' We studied Georgia O' Keefe, Eva Hesse, Yoko Ono, Kira Grace, and more. Ms. Grace is known for her evocative photographs, but I love her shots of bees at work. Have you seen them?"

Jane shook her head.

"Did you get everything you need from Ms. Steward?" Sheriff Evans asked from behind Deputy Emory. "I'm sure she's ready to go home and change clothes."

Deputy Emory gave Jane an apologetic smile. "Yes, sir."

"Was Ms. Grace staying at the resort by herself or did she have a companion?" the sheriff asked Jane.

"She traveled alone, but she's part of a group called The Medieval Herbalists," Jane answered. "We have over thirty members staying with us. Some are here with their spouses. Others are unattached. Ms. Grace was one of several members who booked a single room."

The sheriff opened his mouth to say something else when a series of high-pitched beeps cut through the air. It was the sound of a large vehicle reversing. Kira Grace's ride had arrived.

Deputy Phelps jogged up the rise to meet the driver and his assistant. Satisfied that his deputy was handling the situation, Sheriff Evans turned to Jane again. "I'd like to see Ms. Grace's room," he said. "I'll be at Storyton Hall as soon as I can. Until then, don't let anyone enter her room. In fact, it would be best if you carried on as if nothing unusual had happened." He raised his hands, obviously expecting an argument from Jane. "If another guest is responsible for this woman's death, let him believe he's gotten away with murder. Just for the time being. You see, I don't want him to get spooked and run. Let him, or her, indulge in your glorious afternoon tea service. Let him sip cups of Earl Grey and nibble cucumber sandwiches and cake. With every passing minute, he'll relax a little more. He might just make a mistake and reveal himself."

Two men carrying a stretcher appeared on the path alongside the river. Jane looked from them to the body on the grass. "It doesn't seem right." She was unable to disguise her anger. "Why should a murderer devour raspberry cream scones or sit in Milton's Gardens when a woman who was so filled with vitality lies there with a damp T-shirt over her face?" Now it was Jane's turn to raise her hands to stop the sheriff from arguing. "I know it's necessary, but that doesn't mean I have to like it."

"Understood." Sheriff Evans tipped his hat again, said she was free to go, and moved to speak with the men bearing the stretcher.

Jane and Sterling left the professionals to their work. To the casual observer, it would appear as though Jane's part in the drama was mostly done, but nothing could be further from the truth.

The moment they were alone in the car heading back to Storyton Hall, Jane and Sterling began plotting their next move.

"We'll search Kira's room first," Jane declared as soon as Sterling eased the Rolls onto the road. "If there's a killer under our roof, we need to discover that person's identity immediately."

"I agree." Sterling rolled down the window and made a minor adjustment to his side mirror. "I've already let the rest of the Fins know what's going on. We'll have to search Ms. Grace's room swiftly and carefully. It won't take the sheriff long to transfer her body."

"We have a hotel filled with plant experts. If we find out that Kira was given poison that came from a local plant . . ." She trailed off, recalling what Mrs. Hubbard had said about the Poison Princess.

Sterling remained silent, waiting for her to continue.

Jane shook her head. "There's no sense jumping to conclusions. I just hope we find a tangible clue in Kira's room."

Sterling drove without speaking for a full minute, but as Storyton Hall's massive wrought iron gates came into view, he scratched the back of his neck—a sign that he wasn't entirely comfortable with the subject he was about to raise— and said, "I heard you tell the doc that you were fine, but are you? With Mr. Alcott's abrupt return—"

"I'm glad he came along when he did, as I was having trouble getting Kira out of the water," Jane said in a neutral tone and then abruptly punched the seat. "Actually, I wish he could have stayed longer. I would love to have demonstrated a few of my martial arts maneuvers on him."

The corners of Sterling's mouth twitched. "If he'd seen your board-breaking sessions, he might have been more communicative over the past few months."

Jane couldn't find any humor in the situation. Between the discovery of Kira's body and Edwin's unexpected reappearance, the merriment she'd felt biking into town for the duck race had been replaced by a feeling of gloom.

As the Rolls passed through the open gates, which were carved with Storyton Hall's motto in Latin, Jane considered the translation, *Their story is our story.* She'd heard it hundreds of times, of course. And yet its meaning seemed to change with every season.

I must discover your story, Kira, Jane thought, her resolve to seek justice for the plucky photographer banishing her despondency.

For once, Sterling didn't bother garaging the car. He parked behind the kitchen and followed Jane through the staff doorway. Butterworth was waiting on the other side, a brass room key resting in his white-gloved hand.

"Where's Sinclair?" she asked, taking the key.

"Making extra copies of the background checks he ran on The Medieval Herbalists," Butterworth said as the trio made their way down the staff corridor. "He'll meet us after we've finished searching Ms. Grace's room."

That left one Fin without an assignment. "And Lachlan?"

"Mr. Sterling used his cell phone to identify the GPS coordinates of the bend in the river where you found Ms. Grace." Butterworth ascended the staff stairway first, his patent leather shoes echoing on the cold stone. After many years of servants traveling up and down carrying laundry, wood for fireplaces, food trays, and more, the stairs had become concave. By now, as Jane's employees literally followed in the footsteps of the former servants, the stone was smooth and shiny with use.

Jane loved these stairs and the history they represented, just as she loved every other part of the Stewards' ancestral house and would do anything in her power to protect it and those who called it home.

Kira's room was on the second floor overlooking Milton's Gardens. Jane made sure no other guests were nearby before knocking, which she did out of habit, and then hastily unlocked the door.

Inside, the room was in a state of complete disarray.

Kira's clothes were everywhere. A Japanese silk robe

was draped over the lamp, a pair of jeans and a batik blouse had been tossed on the reading chair, a nightgown lay in a heap just outside the bathroom, and all the towels had been used and dumped on the writing desk. Kira had piled several art magazines and a book called *A Poultice for a Healer* by Caroline Roe on top of the towels. Tennis shoes, sandals, and a pair of silver pumps were scattered across the floor and a straw hat had been deposited on the bedside table.

"Did anything make it into the closet?" Sterling wanted to know.

"You can check after you put these on." Butterworth held out a pair of latex gloves. "Miss Jane."

Jane pulled on her gloves while continuing to scan the room. "I guess Kira had more important things to do than tidy up."

The bed had been made at some point during the morning and was the only neat thing about Kira's room. The house-keeping staff had done their best to vacuum, dust, and straighten, but because Storyton's employees were told never to touch a guest's personal belongings unless absolutely necessary, they'd left Kira's clothes, books, scarves, socks, shoes, hats, and jewelry just as they were.

Butterworth walked over to the chest of drawers. A black stocking foot hung from the top drawer, and when the butler opened it, the stocking fell to the floor and a jumble of undergarments seemed to swell from the cavity. Scowling, Butterworth pinched up the stocking between his thumb and forefinger and pushed it back into the heap of lingerie.

"'And this mess is so big,'" he grumbled. "'And so deep and so tall. We cannot pick it up. There is no way at all!'"

Despite the gravity of their situation, Jane laughed. "I don't think I've ever heard you quote Dr. Seuss before."

Sterling, who'd been inside the walk-in closet, reappeared holding Kira's portfolio case. "Which book is he citing?"

"*Cat in the Hat*," Jane said. "The twins never cared for

that story. Even though they knew everything would be okay in the end and that the children's house would be cleaned up before their parents came home, the boys got so anxious about the increasing mess—especially when Thing One and Thing Two showed up. It's a stressful book for some kids."

Sterling put the portfolio case on the bed and stepped back to allow Jane to open it. "There was no camera in the closet?" she asked.

He shook his head. "Just her suitcase and two cocktail dresses. She actually hung them on hangers."

Butterworth, who was still examining the contents of the chest of drawers, grunted.

"Could you take a peek in the bathroom while I look through this?" Jane reached for the zipper on Kira's case. For a moment, there was only the sound of the zipper teeth parting, and Jane paused. Somehow, she felt that the contents of Kira's case were far more intimate than the contents of her drawers, closet, or cosmetic bag. Jane had only met the woman once, but even from that brief encounter, she could tell that Kira had been passionate about her work.

Butterworth came over to the bed carrying Kira's handbag—an enormous Vera Bradley tote. "I think I should put a towel down before emptying the contents," he murmured and proceeded to do so. Jane watched as he upended the bag and a cascade of tissues, lotions, lip balm, pens, film canisters, receipts, and finally, a wallet came tumbling out.

"Nothing unusual in here," Sterling said, standing on the threshold between the bedroom and the bathroom. "She was a fan of plant-based products and sunscreen." He flicked his gaze at Butterworth. "You might have a stroke if you go in there."

Butterworth grunted again and pulled a card out of Kira's wallet. "Mr. Sterling, would you take an image of Ms. Grace's Social Security card? It will speed things along later on if we have reason to look into her financial affairs."

Sterling fished his cell phone from his pocket while Jane opened the portfolio case.

At first, she saw prints that were similar to the ones she'd seen yesterday. There were at least a dozen color photos focusing on a particular part of a flower. In each case, the image resembled a human female's reproductive organ. These photographs were all neatly aligned in plastic folders, as were the next group, which featured plants. Jane almost flipped past them, assuming there was nothing interesting about the detailed shots of foliage or stems, when she spotted an insect on one of the photographs. It looked like a green beetle and had blended in so perfectly with the plant leaf that Jane had initially missed it. All the images in the series contained camouflaged insects.

"Did Ms. Grace use her art to convey her own need to hide?" Jane wondered aloud. "Was she scared? Did she have a secret to keep?"

When she flipped to the next section of prints, she gasped. This series had nothing whatsoever to do with plants. It showed the most celebrated member of The Medieval Herbalists in a state of partial undress, locked in the embrace of a silver-haired man with a very tanned torso.

"It's the Poison Princess," Jane said. She pointed at a small band of gold on the third finger of the man's left hand. "It looks like she was captured fooling around with a married man."

"Perhaps Ms. Grace intended to blackmail one or both of these individuals, but her plan—" Sterling began.

"Backfired," Jane finished for him. "Maybe she left this morning for a meeting in a secluded place, taking one of the damning photographs with her, when suddenly the tables were turned. The blackmailer became the victim. And she ended up paying the ultimate price."

FIVE

Sterling looked at his phone screen. "The guests are starting to return from the duck race."

Jane nodded. She didn't have much time to decide what to do with the information they'd discovered. "Butterworth, you'd better go back to your post. Please escort the sheriff and his team through the rear door and the staff corridors. There's no need for the rest of the guests to learn of Ms. Grace's demise until absolutely necessary."

As Butterworth slipped from the room, Sterling gestured at the portfolio. "Should I replace this or leave it for the sheriff to find?"

"Forward images of the incriminating photographs to Sinclair first," Jane said. "His first priority should be identifying Constance Meredith's lover."

"And what about Constance?" Sterling asked while snapping photos with his phone. "Did you see her at the duck race?"

Jane searched her memory, but the only Medieval Herbalists she'd noticed were Sandi Hughes, Vivian Ash, Claude Mason, and Hannah Billingsley.

"I didn't see her," she answered. "However, if Constance went into town, her name will appear on a passenger list. She doesn't strike me as the type to have arranged bicycle rental through Spokes. Not when a vintage Rolls-Royce and a driver in livery is at her disposal."

"I'll scan the clipboards in the garage before meeting you back in the surveillance room. If we're lucky, we can deliver Ms. Grace's killer into the hands of the sheriff before tea service is over."

Jane opened the door, waited for Sterling to step out into the hallway, and then cast a quick glance back into the room. Despite Kira's untidiness, it was still a lovely, welcoming space. The summer sun streamed through the tall windows and warmed the cozy reading chair and footstool. Jane was saddened to think that Kira wouldn't have a chance to peruse her books or magazines in that chair. It was easy to picture her sipping tea and nibbling Mrs. Hubbard's homemade short-bread cookies while she flipped pages. Jane could envision Kira's feet encased in the polka-dot slipper socks she'd seen in the dresser drawer and could imagine her wriggling her toes in delight as she dunked a cookie into her tea.

But your own actions ruined any chances of that, Jane thought, silently berating Kira. *Were you desperate for money? Or were you just plain greedy?*

She remembered Kira's expression at the mention of Constance Meredith's name. Kira had clearly disliked her fellow group member. Perhaps the dislike was mutual. And if Kira did something to threaten the success the Poison Princess currently enjoyed, Jane didn't think Constance would stand passively by.

All conjecture, Jane thought as she closed the door and locked it. To Sterling, she said, "I hope things turn out as you say, but somehow, I don't feel that lucky."

Sterling looked contrite.

Jane touched his arm. "Don't mind me. It's just that I

caught a glimpse of myself in the mirror a moment ago and I really need to get cleaned up. I can't let our guests see me like this." She handed Sterling her great-uncle's fishing hat. "Give this to a bellhop, would you? At least I was able to rescue something today."

As they descended the staff stairwell, Sterling shot her a brief glance. "I would have warned you about Mr. Alcott had I known he was back. He must have returned to the village—"

"Like a thief in the night?" Jane allowed a hint of anger to creep into her voice. "I hear that's one of his many skills. Sneaking into places." She shook her head to stop herself from focusing on Edwin's secret identity—the one that identified him as a famous book thief called The Templar. "I might be furious with him, but I'm glad he showed up when he did. He was able to get Kira out of the water and fetch Doc Lydgate. His timing was fortunate."

"I doubt Mr. Alcott was at that bend in the river by chance," Sterling grumbled. "When you separated from the crowd to chase after your uncle's hat, Mr. Alcott probably saw an opportunity to speak with you in private." A gleam appeared in Sterling's eyes. "He must have been surprised to see that the object you were trying to retrieve from the water was a far cry from a fishing hat."

"If he was surprised, he hid it well," Jane said. "I did a terrible job concealing how I felt, even though I'd mentally rehearsed how I'd react when I saw Edwin Alcott again. I was going to be the picture of courtesy. But cool and distant. Untouchable."

Sterling raised his brows. "And?"

"I didn't exactly pull it off."

By this point they'd reached the rear exit. Sterling was just about to head to the garage when he turned back to Jane and said, "We Fins swore an oath to protect you, and we're more than willing to teach this man a lesson about what it means to trifle with your feelings, Miss Jane."

Jane smiled. "I shouldn't have mentioned Mr. Alcott. Sometimes I forget that I have highly trained personal bodyguards, all of whom happen to dote on me and defend my honor as they would their own kid sister. And while I'm not former CIA or a retired Army Ranger and have never worked as an analyst in Her Majesty's Secret Service, I am learning to hold my own."

Sterling nodded. "You are developing skills, Miss Jane, but you are no match for the likes of Mr. Alcott."

Jane stared at him. "What makes you say that? He's a book thief, not a trained assassin." She glared at Sterling. "Please tell me I was *not* falling in love with a hit man."

"Falling in love?" Sterling looked taken aback.

Cheeks burning, Jane mumbled something about needing a shower and dashed outside. As she hurried behind the loading dock, she heard the sound of the twins' laughter.

"I'm home, boys!" she called. "Did you have fun at the duck race?"

"We can't talk now, Mom!" Hem shouted back. "We're working!"

"Yeah, we're on the clock!" Fitz added, doing his best to sound macho.

Stifling a laugh, Jane continued toward home, all thoughts of Edwin Alcott temporarily banished. Hearing the twins laboring in Mrs. Hubbard's kitchen garden had reminded Jane of why she needed to get cleaned up in the first place. She'd gotten wet while trying to pull Kira's body out of the water. Right about now, her friends would be lining up outside the Agatha Christie Tea Room. Would any of The Medieval Herbalists notice Kira's absence?

Jane took a quick shower and changed into her cornflower blue dress. After forcing her damp strawberry blond curls into a tight braid, she dabbed on tinted lip gloss and added blush to her cheeks before hurrying back to the manor house again.

She found Sinclair in the surveillance room, pacing in front of the bank of monitors like a restless cat.

"There you are," he said upon seeing Jane.

"I couldn't risk being seen looking like a drowned rat." Jane gestured at the papers in Sinclair's hand. "Did you identify Constance's lover?"

Sinclair nodded. "Nico Scannavini. He's in the perfume business. His family has turned plants into scents for the past two hundred years. Nico is the younger son. The older brother, Matteo, makes all the decisions while Nico flits around the world attending conferences, movie premieres, car races, and the like." He showed Jane a color printout featuring a row of glass bottles with decorative labels. "Elements is a niche company. They produce artisan perfumes using all-natural, botanical ingredients."

"Pretty," Jane said. Sinclair flipped to a second page and passed it to her. It was an article from an Italian newspaper and showed the man Jane recognized cozying up to two very tall, very thin blondes. "Nico obviously likes the ladies."

"Yes," Sinclair agreed. "There are dozens of photographs of him in the company of attractive women. However, they are always taken as a means of promotion and the parties involved are always fully clothed."

Jane examined several images. "In other words, the pictures Kira took are far more incriminating because she *caught* Nico cheating on his wife." Jane looked at Sinclair. "What's Nico's wife like? And is she here in Storyton?"

"Unlike her Italian-born husband, Michelle Scannavini is an American. She was hired as a chemist in Elements' New York plant, which is also where Nico Scannavini's office is located. The two met, had a whirlwind courtship, and were married. Mrs. Scannavini accompanies her husband on all his trips." Sinclair rubbed his chin. "And even though both of the Scannavinis are Medieval Herbalists,

Nico, it would appear, joined simply to earn brownie points with his parents. They are Elements board members and history buffs. Michelle, on the other hand, is genuinely interested in herbs and their chemical makeup and loves to study how they were used throughout the ages."

"Which means she would have been busy attending all the scheduled events during last year's retreat," Jane said. "Leaving Nico free to sneak off for trysts with Constance."

Sinclair frowned in disapproval. "That's what I would assume."

"Another possibility is that Michelle already knew about the affair," Jane mused aloud. "Maybe she forgave her husband. Maybe she wasn't going to allow Kira to expose him. Either that, or she wasn't going to let Kira's blackmail tarnish the company's reputation. Michelle could also be a suspect."

"She could," Sinclair agreed.

Jane sank into a chair, the printout of the perfume bottles on her lap. "I don't know, Sinclair. The world has become such a jaded place. Even if Nico's philandering became public, would the news really impact Elements' bottom line? He just doesn't seem that important. Looking at these other articles, he only manages to get media attention by being in proximity to famous people." She shrugged. "Still, Sheriff Evans will have to question both Nico and Michelle."

"As well as Ms. Meredith," Sinclair said. "Fortunately, all three suspects have already returned and headed directly for the tea room."

Jane considered what to do next. "After we escort the sheriff to Kira's room, where he'll discover the incriminating photographs, we can arrange for him to interview the three suspects in one of the conference rooms. If we handle this correctly, we might not have to issue an announcement that a woman died under mysterious circumstances until tomorrow."

"I believe that the rest of The Medieval Herbalists will notice that four of their members have gone missing," Sinclair said.

"Especially since tonight is the blindfolded taste test competition hosted by Mrs. Hubbard." Jane groaned. "How will I explain this to our special guests?"

Sinclair put a hand on her shoulder. "I don't think it'll be your place to do so, Miss Jane. The crime did not occur within these walls or on our grounds, remember? The sheriff is up for reelection this year, so he's bound to handle every nuance of this case. And while he's welcomed our assistance in the past, we can't assume that he'll welcome it now."

Jane touched the tip of her finger to the screen showing a view of the long driveway. At that moment, two sheriff's cruisers were rolling over the gravel. Because most of the guests were in the tea room or lounging by the Jules Verne Pool, no other vehicles were in motion.

"Good. They're parking by the loading dock," she said. "And Butterworth's at the door, waiting for them."

"I should keep an eye on our suspects until the sheriff sends for them. When that time arrives—" Sinclair was interrupted by a sharp knock on the door.

Jane leapt to her feet.

Landon Lachlan entered the room. His cheeks glistened with sweat, and the wave of sandy-colored hair falling across his forehead was damp. The Storyton Mews T-shirt he'd designed last spring, which featured a falcon flying over the manor house, was plastered to his muscular chest. The new head of recreation had been at Storyton for half a year now, but his novelty hadn't worn off with the female staff members. His shy smile, bright blue eyes, and rugged, out-doorsman appearance had instantly charmed the ladies of the village and the Hall alike. However, it was Lachlan's introverted nature that lent him an air of mystery. Lachlan suffered from post-traumatic stress disorder and, in general, preferred the company of raptors to people. His unpredictable behavior only increased his appeal with the local women, and they endlessly whispered about him in the stores and in Tresses, Violet's beauty salon. However, he had eyes for only one woman, and that was Eloise.

Wiping his face with a handkerchief, Lachlan gave Jane an apologetic look. "Sorry. I didn't want to waste time getting cleaned up."

"Don't worry about it," she said. "You should have seen me earlier. I was a frightful sight. Did you find anything?"

Lachlan nodded. "A tire track leading from the river to the road. It was faded, but I followed it up the rise."

"A single tire track?" Sinclair sounded perplexed. Then, he brightened. "Ah! From a wheelbarrow?"

This elicited another nod from Lachlan. "I think the killer pulled a truck to the side of the road, unloaded the wheelbarrow, and took Ms. Grace's body out of the passenger seat. The killer pushed her down the bank and dumped her in the water. It was early and the grass was wet, so the tire left a depression. I found another divot right at the river's edge too. That would have come from the metal encasing the front tire, which would have bit into the ground as the killer tipped the wheelbarrow forward and the weight of Ms. Grace's body bore down."

This was a lengthy speech for Lachlan, and he seemed more spent from talking than from tracking. Reaching behind her, Jane poured him a glass of water from the water cooler and handed it to him. She waited until he drank several swallows before asking, "Was this spot far from where I found her?"

"Not very," Lachlan replied. "My guess is that the killer knew about the duck race. There was no reason anyone would walk to the place where the river bottlenecks. They'd be focused on the action near the bridge. And even if someone did, the killer probably felt safe. He had hours to put between himself and the place where he dumped the body."

Sinclair rubbed his chin, his brows furrowed. "Why bring her to the river? If the killer knew about the duck race, he took a risk in bringing her to that location. Why not leave her body in the woods?" He fixed his attention on Jane. "Isn't that where Ms. Grace was headed this morning? The trails behind the village?"

"That's what she told me. However, if blackmail was her goal, she might have been lying about her destination. Maybe she was heading somewhere else entirely." Jane turned to Lachlan. "I don't know how you found those tracks. I didn't see a thing, and I don't think Deputy Phelps did either. Thank you."

Lachlan reddened slightly. "I'm not much of a car guy, but the truck tires seemed to belong to a smaller truck. I took a photo of the marks the right tire made in the dirt in the side of the road. It's only a partial imprint, but Mr. Sterling might recognize the type of tire."

Jane rubbed her temples. "The killer doesn't sound like one of our guests. They all come to Storyton by train. A Storyton Hall driver meets them at the station. After that, it's a forty-five-minute drive through mountainous terrain to our resort. Without knowing someone with a truck, how can one of the three suspects in our tea room be a killer?"

"I could be wrong," Lachlan said quietly. "Tracking is guesswork. Instinct. It's not a science."

"And Gavin says there's none better than you when it comes down to it." Sinclair clapped Lachlan on the shoulder. "We're just not seeing the whole picture yet." He pulled his phone out of his pocket and examined the screen. "Mr. Butterworth is escorting the sheriff to your office, Miss Jane. Sheriff Evans would like to question the suspects immediately."

Jane's stomach lurched at this news, but she didn't let her anxiety show. "Sinclair, please tell Mr. and Mrs. Scannavini that I'd like a word with them after tea. Ask them to remain in the Agatha Christie Tea Room. As for Ms. Meredith, ask her to wait for me on the back terrace."

Sinclair understood Jane's plan at once. "Mr. Butterworth can watch over Mr. and Mrs. Scannavini while I keep Ms. Meredith company. I can show her some of the books I pulled from the stacks for The Medieval Herbalists. Perhaps she'll be suitably distracted until it's her turn to be questioned by the sheriff."

"Are you going to tell Sheriff Evans about my wheelbarrow theory?" Lachlan asked Jane when Sinclair was gone.

Jane shook her head. "No. And it isn't because I don't have faith in your abilities. I do. I just don't want to muddy the waters where Sheriff Evans is concerned. As for us? We need to continue investigating independently. If the sheriff makes an arrest, we'd better be sure he has the right man or woman. After all, these people are our guests. Until we're completely convinced one of them is a murderer, we must be their advocates."

"I'll get with Mr. Sterling right away," Lachlan said. At the doorway, he paused. "I admire your desire to protect the guests, Miss Jane, but experience has taught me to keep my guard up at all times, especially when it comes to strangers. We shouldn't trust our guests, because people are rarely what they seem. There's the side people present to the world and the dozens of other sides they keep to themselves. Even with background checks and security cameras, there's still plenty our guests can hide from us."

An image of Edwin flashed in Jane's mind, but this was not the time to dwell on his duplicity.

"You're right." She smiled at Lachlan, who'd spoken more in the past ten minutes than he had all week, and followed him out of the room. "I won't let my deep-rooted Southern hospitality override my caution, though I am hoping it'll help sway the sheriff into doing things my way."

Sheriff Evans had been in Jane's office for all of two minutes before Jane realized that he wasn't going to be influenced by offers of tea and cake, an outpouring of courtesy, or anything else.

Declining the guest chair across from Jane's desk, he stood with his hands on his utility belt and announced his intention to speak with her three guests posthaste. He also wanted to meet with all three of them at the same time.

"As of this moment, I'm viewing Ms. Meredith and Mr. and Mrs. Scannavini as persons of interest. Until I receive confirmation that Ms. Grace was poisoned, I don't have a murder case. I have an accidental drowning. I expect those results tomorrow afternoon at best—Monday at the latest—seeing as I called in a favor. Therefore, anything your guests share with me will be voluntary. Right now, I'd like to establish a timeline for each of them for this morning."

"But why are you speaking with them as a group?" Jane asked.

"To see how they react," Sheriff Evans explained. "This will be our only opportunity to witness how they react to the news. Will they point fingers? Get upset? Say things they might not have said had they not been taken by surprise? Because the second I let them out of that tea room, the whole resort will know that Ms. Grace is dead."

Jane swallowed hard. This was not how she wanted the summer weekend to start. She wanted people to stroll through Milton's Gardens, sip champagne cocktails on the terrace, and dance on the back lawn. She didn't want the hallways filled with whispers of fear and excitement. However, Jane realized that there was little point in delaying the inevitable. And unless someone confessed to killing Kira Grace, the news of her passing wouldn't alter the course of either investigation—the sheriff's nor Jane's.

Squaring her shoulders, Jane met the sheriff's direct gaze and said, "I insist on being present for this interview, regardless of its informal nature. These three individuals need someone to serve as their representative. Besides, I can't protect my staff or the rest of my guests if I'm kept in the dark."

Sherriff Evans was on the verge of responding when the

intercom button on Jane's phone lit up and a front desk clerk said, "Sorry to interrupt, Miss Jane, but Mr. Butterworth wanted you to know that Mr. and Mrs. Scannavini are waiting for you in the Agatha Christie Tea Room."

Jane pushed the talk button. "Would you ask Mr. Sinclair to escort Ms. Meredith there as well? Thank you, Sue."

"I can see there's no use in arguing." The sheriff signaled to his deputies to follow Jane out of her office, through the staff corridors, and through a narrow doorway leading into the hallway near the tea room.

Most people, when unexpectedly confronted by members of law enforcement, act nervous. Or at the very least, subdued. Not Constance Meredith.

At the sight of Sheriff Evans, she rose to her feet and extended a limp hand, as though the sheriff ought to plant a kiss on it. "Do you need my assistance with a case?"

Her question clearly threw the sheriff off balance and Michelle Scannavini offered her own response. "Not *every* man enters a room looking for you."

"Most do," Constance countered without averting her gaze from the sheriff.

Nico Scannavini, who sat next to his wife, seemed preoccupied with polishing his watch face with a napkin.

"I'm here to talk to all of you about Kira Grace," the sheriff said, recovering. He gave Meredith's hand a brief and formal shake and then asked her to join the Scannavinis at their table.

Michelle sighed in annoyance and scooted her chair farther away from Constance's and closer to her husband's. As for Nico, he kept his eyes on his watch.

Jane took a seat near the table, making it appear as though she were siding with her guests. However, she positioned herself so that she could closely watch all of them.

"I'll begin with you, Ms. Meredith." Evans spread his hands in a friendly, open manner. "When did you last see Kira Grace?"

His body language failed to conceal the directness of his question, and Constance arched her pencil-drawn brows. "This sounds an awful lot like the opening to a murder investigation."

"Please answer the question," the sheriff said.

Constance smiled and leaned back in her chair. Jane recalled how unnerved she'd been while viewing the video clips on the Poison Princess's website. Constance Meredith was even more unsettling in person. Not only did she possess a confident, almost predatory air, but she also seemed to derive pleasure from the discomfort of others. She stared at Sheriff Evans, allowing the silence to stretch until it became awkward. Everyone else in the room began to fidget. Except for Butterworth, that is. He stood as rigid as a yeoman warder.

"Ms. Meredith?" the sheriff prompted with admirable calm.

"All right, I'll play along," she relented. "I saw Kira last night. I was entering the Ian Fleming Lounge just as she was leaving. It was going on eleven. I'm a creature of the night, you see." Her eyes flashed.

Again, her comment seemed to throw Sheriff Evans off his game, but he blinked and continued his questioning. "And today?"

Constance shook her head. "Never saw her. I slept until nine and enjoyed a late breakfast in my room while I caught up on e-mails. After that, I had a video chat with my agent. Around noon, I had a driver take me into the village. I wanted to pop into the bookstore, but it was closed, so I ended up in a charming café instead. You can ask the owner about me. I'm quite positive that I made an impression on him." She smiled like a cat whose just been given a saucer of cream.

"Thank you." Sheriff Evans turned to the Scannavinis. "Mrs. Scannavini? When did you last see Ms. Grace?"

"A year ago," Michelle said simply.

Nico raised his index finger. "Same here. My wife and I arrived at Storyton around eight last night and went straight to our room. We're still trying to get over our jet lag from a recent trip to Paris. We renewed our vows last week." He reached for her hand and she surrendered it to him. The couple held each other's eyes for a long moment and Jane saw true affection in their gaze.

Constance yawned loudly and rudely, and the movement wasn't lost on the Scannavinis.

"I know about your fling with Nico," Michelle said, swiveling to face Constance. "He told me everything. I have no idea what he saw in you, but it was a one-night stand and it's in the past. So focus your wiles elsewhere, because I'd like to enjoy this retreat." Having delivered her message, Michelle turned to Sheriff Evans. "This morning, Nico and I also had a late breakfast. We were in the Madame Bovary Dining Room. We were so late that we almost missed the start of the duck race, but a driver was able to get us to the village in time." She spread her hands, repeating the sheriff's opening gesture. "We've answered your questions. Now it's time for you to answer ours. Where is Kira and why did you chose to speak with the three of us in particular?"

"Because the sheriff wanted us to supply him with our alibis. That way, he can check them," Constance declared with a sniff of condescension. "Which can only mean one thing. Kira Grace is dead."

Nico started. "Dead?"

"Yes," Constance said, her eyes shining. "And I doubt her death was an accident. I'd bet you my collection of antique herbals that Kira was murdered, and that *we're* the suspects." She sat back in her chair with an eager grin, as though she couldn't wait for the process to continue.

Watching her, Jane couldn't decide if the Poison Princess was a skilled actress or a psychopath, but she was leaning toward the latter.

SIX

Sheriff Evans realized that he was losing control of the interview, and he swiftly explained that Kira was found in Storyton River and that her death was being viewed as an accidental drowning. After informing the three guests that the investigation was ongoing and admonishing them about spreading rumors, he released them.

"The news will be all over the resort by suppertime," Jane said the moment they were gone.

"It can't be helped." Sheriff Evans gestured for Deputy Emory's notebook. "Their movements should be easy to confirm. Your drivers keep logs, correct?" At Jane's nod, Evans went on. "And your kitchen staff would have records of the room service delivery, right?"

Jane's nod was more impatient this time. "Yes, yes. Mr. Butterworth can help you collect the records. Now, if you'll excuse me, I should speak to the president of The Medieval Herbalists. I'd prefer his group to hear of Ms. Grace's death from me rather than Ms. Meredith or the Scannavinis." Pausing by the door, she gave the sheriff a plaintive look. "Will you share the lab results as soon as you get them? If Ms. Grace was poisoned, I need to know immediately. After all, I'm hosting a group of thirty-odd experts in herb lore."

Evans understood the gravity of Jane's comment. "I will inform you. In the meantime, keep your eyes and ears open. Call me if anything raises your suspicions."

Leaving Butterworth to assist the sheriff, Jane went in search of Claude Mason. Luckily, Billy the Bellhop had spotted the older man entering the Henry James Library. Jane found him standing shoulder to shoulder with Sinclair.

"It's magnificent," Claude was saying. "Many museums and academic institutions show a complete lack of representation when it comes to the subject of medieval herb lore. Frankly, I'm surprised by the depth of your collection."

"We cater to guests with an amazing variety of interests," Sinclair said, clearly pleased by Claude's enthusiasm. "Also, we've been amassing material for hundreds of years. It helps to have a seemingly endless amount of shelf space."

Claude chuckled and went on to ask Sinclair a question about provenance.

Jane hated to interrupt, as she knew that Sinclair had taken great pains to organize a special display on medieval plants. And for the first time in the history of the Steward Family, an item from Storyton's secret collection was being shown to the public. Of course, none of the guests were aware that the illuminated manuscript Sinclair kept locked in a glass case next to his desk numbered among the hundreds of rare and wonderful literary treasures housed in a windowless turret room.

And while people could look at the manuscript, only Sinclair could touch it. Even Claude, who was a museum curator and was experienced in handling fragile and priceless items, wasn't invited to slip on a pair of white gloves and run his fingers over the beautiful pages. Instead, he stood with his hands clasped behind his back, his eyes drinking in the curves of the illuminated capital letters and the delicate floral designs in the margins.

"I'm sorry to bother you," Jane said softly and both men turned.

The light from Sinclair's lamp reflected off Claude's spectacles and he lowered his chin to get a better look at Jane. "Ah, Ms. Steward. I was just admiring your marvelous manuscript. It's not often that our members have the chance to see an original twelfth-century herbal. You've already made our visit memorable, and it's just begun."

Claude's cheeks dimpled when he smiled, and again, Jane was reminded of Ben Franklin. Knowing she was about to make this sweet man's visit unforgettable in a most unpleasant manner, she reached for his arm. "Would you sit with me for a moment?"

Though surprised by the request, Claude was too much of a gentleman to refuse. "Of course."

Jane led him to a pair of wing chairs by the windows. The chairs were angled toward each other, lending her the privacy she needed. "I'm sorry to be the bearer of bad news, but Ms. Grace was found in the river a little while ago." Jane hesitated for a second before continuing. "I'm afraid she's dead."

"What?" Claude's bushy eyebrows crinkled in confusion. "Kira? How could that be?"

"This must come as a terrible shock," Jane said gently. "But I also wanted you to know that the sheriff's department is conducting an investigation. At this time, Ms. Grace's death is being viewed as an accidental drowning."

Claude ran his hand over his shiny pate and released a long, slow breath. "I can't believe it. I just saw her yesterday, and she was in fine spirits. Like always. 'Full of piss and vinegar,' as she used to say." He shook his head. "I'm a conservative man by nature, and I admit that there were times I found Kira's exuberance a bit irritating. But overall, she was refreshing. In my line of work, people tend to be serious. Studious. Quiet as church mice. Kira was the opposite. She was colorful and noisy. She laughed without hindrance—loud and often."

Jane nodded to show that she was listening, but Claude lapsed into silence. His gaze moved to the windows and traveled over the Lewis Carroll Croquet Lawn until he was staring at the blue-green hills surrounding the resort.

"I can't fathom how she ended up in the river," he said at last.

"Ms. Grace set out from Storyton Hall early this morning intent on hiking the trails behind the village. I don't know how she turned up where she did," Jane replied honestly.

Claude rubbed his hands together as though he felt chilled. "During our retreats, I advise our members to hike in pairs, but Kira often preferred to go out alone. She didn't like to work in front of an audience. She explained this to our group once." He frowned and Jane had the sense that it was important to him to recall the exact words. "She said that photography was very intimate. An adulation of nature. It was the only time she felt self-conscious."

"As the group's president, I'm turning to you for guidance," Jane said softly. "Should we cancel this evening's taste-testing contest out of respect for Kira's passing?"

This question seemed to agitate Claude. He rose from his chair and began moving in a slow circle around it. "I don't think she'd want us to," he said. "And since we're dining as a group on the back terrace this evening, we could use that time together to express our grief. We could share stories about Kira and raise glasses to her memory."

Jane smiled. "That's a lovely idea." Again, she hesitated. She wanted to be sure that Claude understood what the next day or two held in store for The Medieval Herbalists. Not only would they have to go on with their scheduled events without Kira—and that included Victoria Billingsley's wedding—but they also needed to be prepared to face scrutiny by the sheriff's department.

Claude was astute enough to realize that Jane wasn't quite finished. Forcing himself to be still, he waited for her to continue.

"You should probably warn your members that they will be questioned. While this is routine when someone has died unexpectedly, it can be an unnerving experience," Jane said. "Sheriff Evans has already spoken with three Medieval Herbalists, but he may want to talk with the rest of the group tomorrow."

"I think the sheriff will find us a cooperative bunch," Claude said. "We'll do anything in our power to help find out what happened to Kira."

Unless one of you killed her, Jane thought harshly.

"Thank you for being so frank and so sensitive, Ms. Steward." Claude stole a glance at his watch. "Can you get a message to The Medieval Herbalists? I'd like to gather on the terrace earlier than we'd originally planned. I'm thinking an impromptu Irish wake is in order."

"I'll have the desk clerks call their guest rooms right away." Jane got to her feet. "What time would you like them to arrive?"

Claude shared his vision for the evening and then left the library. After phoning the front desk from Sinclair's office, Jane went to the kitchen to check on the twins.

They were no longer in the garden, but perched on stools at a work counter, devouring open-faced peanut butter and jelly sandwiches. They'd been given milk to drink, and their glass tumblers were marred with grimy fingerprints. As she drew closer to her boys, she saw that their hands were probably their cleanest parts. Their arms were covered with garden soil and their fingernails were rimmed with dirt. Their clothes were stained, and they both had dirt smeared on their cheeks, noses, and foreheads.

Fitz looked up from his sandwich and smiled. "Guess what? We worked for almost *two hours*!"

"That's why we're starving!" Hem added proudly.

Jane touched his head and discovered that his hair was also coated in a layer of dirt. "Was rolling around in the garden bed part of your job?"

Hem shook off her hand. "*No!* We were weeding and watering—just like Mrs. Hubbard asked us to."

"There were tons of weeds too," Fitz said, jumping in to support his brother. "We even pulled out the hard ones. The dandelions and those grasses that go way under the ground."

Hem nodded. "They have white roots, so Fitz and I pretended they were snakes sent by Voldemort. Voldemort can talk to snakes, remember?"

"I do," Jane said.

"Some of them went *really* deep!" Fitz lowered his left hand toward the floor. "We had to keep digging and digging to get them out."

At that moment, Mrs. Hubbard appeared with a plate of chocolate chip cookies. "Oh, Jane! You should see how much progress the boys made in my garden. I can't tell you how impressed I am by their efforts." She gestured at the sandwiches. "Don't worry about this ruining their supper. They'll gobble up every crumb. Men who work out in the sun burn lots of fuel. Isn't that right, gentlemen?"

The boys murmured a low assent, trying to sound as adult as possible.

Mrs. Hubbard beamed at them and lowered the plate of cookies, but Jane's hand darted out and blocked the boys' fingers before they could make contact with the treats. "We'll save those for dessert, Mrs. Hubbard. I believe these *gentlemen* could use a long, hot shower with lots of soap."

This statement elicited a series of groans.

"Can't we just jump in the pool?" Hem asked.

"And scare off the guests with the dirt cloud you'd create

in the water?" Jane retorted. "No. Besides, Voldemort's snakes probably made you a little itchy, didn't they? I always feel kind of prickly after I've pulled out lots of different weeds."

Fitz and Hem dropped their gazes to their forearms. "Will soap help?" Fitz asked.

"I have a special soap just for gardeners," Mrs. Hubbard announced. "Finish your sandwiches and I'll be back in a tick."

Jane refilled the twins' glasses and watched them polish off the rest of their snack in record time.

Mrs. Hubbard returned several minutes later with a plastic bag containing a single bar of soap, which she proffered to Jane. "Don't use this on your faces, boys. It's too harsh. But this will get the dirt and grime off your hands and arms."

Opening the bag, Jane examined the soap. "It smells wonderful."

"Lemongrass and basil," Mrs. Hubbard said. "Tammy makes it specifically for gardeners. She'll be selling a whole range of soaps at the fair on Sunday, and I plan on stocking up. That woman is truly gifted." She splayed her hands. "I wash these mitts so many times per day that my skin felt like an onion peel, but not anymore. Tammy gave me a sample of her moisturizing soap, which is made of avocado and almond oil, vitamin E, and honey. Now my hands are like a baby's bottom."

"Ew!" The twins giggled.

"Go on, you two." Mrs. Hubbard pulled a dishrag from her apron pocket and made a shooing motion at the twins. "I need to get my staff busy with supper preparations and I have *my* event to prep for as well. I can't have two dirty men in my kitchen with all that needs to be done."

Thrilled over being called dirty men, the boys hopped down from their stools and carried their plates to the sink. Jane gave the soap to Fitz and watched the twins dart out through the back doorway.

"They won't go near the bathtub until I threaten them. They'll be distracted by a dozen things on the way back to the house, mark my words," she told Mrs. Hubbard. "I'll need to make sure they don't flounce on the sofa in their current condition, but before I head home, there's something you should know."

Mrs. Hubbard tucked the dishrag back into her pocket and smiled. "Yes, dear?"

Once Mrs. Hubbard heard about Kira's death, the news would be spread throughout Storyton Hall like the wind, but it couldn't be helped. Mrs. Hubbard was hosting an event for The Medieval Herbalists and Jane couldn't predict what condition the participants would be in after their impromptu Irish wake. The least she could do was warn her head cook what she had in store.

Mrs. Hubbard's eyes grew round as pie plates when she heard of Kira's death, but instantly narrowed at the mention of Constance Meredith's name.

"Of course the sheriff's checking *her* alibi!" she exclaimed triumphantly. "Didn't I tell you that there was something off about that woman?"

"Ms. Meredith is not a suspect. She's a guest, and should be treated like any other guest," Jane said with a hint of reproach. Remembering her own reaction to the Poison Princess, she added, "To be completely honest, my first impression of her wasn't very favorable. But you and I are professionals in the hospitality business, and it's our job to make every guest feel like we'd bend over backward for them. Even if we can't stand the person."

"Oh, I can pretend to like Ms. Meredith," Mrs. Hubbard said. "There'll be a big, Cheshire Cat smile on my face when I feed her a spoonful of ground pinecone during tonight's game."

Jane gaped. "You wouldn't!"

Mrs. Hubbard gave a noncommittal shrug. "Actually, I don't think I can count pinecones as an herb. However, there *are* several foul-tasting samples on my list. Who's to say the Poison Princess won't end up trying all of them?"

"There's no sense borrowing trouble. We have enough of that already," Jane said and left.

Much later, Jane stood on the back terrace, glancing up at the star-pocked sky. A warm breeze bearing the scents of honeysuckle, wild rose, and Confederate jasmine ruffled the hem of her dress. The evening was so lovely that it seemed incongruent with Claude's impromptu wake.

Per Jane's request, the staff had moved The Medieval Herbalists' tables away from the other diners. Extra tealight candles had been scattered across the white tablecloths and a sprig of rosemary, the herb representing remembrance, had been entwined around each napkin ring.

Having left the twins in the care of her great-aunt and -uncle, Jane circulated around the terrace. She tried to remain unobtrusive. Listening. This way, she could make sure her guests had everything they needed.

And what The Medieval Herbalists seemed to require was wine. Bottles and bottles of it. They also ate copious amounts of pasta primavera and homemade bread dipped in olive oil, which Jane hoped would serve as a sponge for some of the alcohol.

The group members, along with their overwhelmed spouses and partners, toasted Kira a dozen times. They told stories about her and alternated between laughter and tears. At times, they grew very loud. And then, a moment later, someone would whisper poetry from the Middle Ages. Jane recognized a few snippets from Dante, but not the lines about being laid to rest under the grass by a poet named Marie de France.

As she watched from her place behind a column, she observed the faces of The Medieval Herbalists. Butterworth, who'd been trained to interpret body language, had been schooling Jane in this inexact science, and while she tried to put her new skills to use now, she found she couldn't. There were just too many people. Plus, the candlelight transformed their features, making them simultaneously more beautiful and more grotesque.

"Any telltale signs?" Sinclair asked, creeping up behind her.

Jane shook her head. "They seem to genuinely enjoy being together. Everyone has had something kind to say about Kira. Even Constance Meredith. Though her anecdote centered more on her own finer attributes than on Kira's, it was still positive." She sighed. "The only complaints I've heard about Kira were her refusal to adhere to a dress code and that she could be as rambunctious as a child."

Sinclair looked skeptical. "If those are the worst things that can be said of her, then either Ms. Grace never offended her fellow herb lovers, or those who truly disliked her know how to conceal their feelings."

"But the three most likely suspects are in the clear," Jane said. "The sheriff was able to establish a timeline for all of them based on our record keeping. Unless Constance or one of the Scannavinis gave Kira a slow-acting poison the night before she died, they're innocent."

A waiter approached Claude and moved to refill his glass, but Claude smiled and waved him off.

"The wine has been flowing freely since six o'clock," Jane whispered. "I was hoping it might encourage a few confessions, but all it's done is inspire the recitation of poetry."

As if compelled by her words, Claude got to his feet and tapped the side of his glass with his fork. The assembly fell silent.

"Every year, Hannah Billingsley produces the itinerary for our annual retreat. These lovely, handmade booklets always commence with a poem. This year, Hannah chose 'From Homer's Hymn to Earth: Mother of All,' by Percy Shelley. I won't read it all—just a few lines with which to close our meal and our memorial to Kira. Shelley does a far better job than I ever could in saying farewell to one of our own, and Kira would have loved this imagery." He cleared his throat and adjusted his spectacles. When he next spoke, his voice was hushed and reverent.

> *O universal mother, who dost keep*
> *From everlasting thy foundations deep,*
> *Eldest of things, Great Earth, I sing of thee!*
>
> *With bloom-inwoven dance and happy song,*
> *On the soft flowers the meadow-grass among,*
> *Leap round them sporting—such delights by thee*
> *Are given, rich Power, revered Divinity.*
>
> *Mother of gods, thou Wife of starry Heaven,*
> *Farewell! be thou propitious, and be given*
> *A happy life for this brief melody,*
> *Nor thou nor other songs shall unremembered be.*

Vivian Ash, who was sitting next to Claude, stood up and raised her glass. "To Kira."

One by one, The Medieval Herbalists followed suit. They toasted Kira once more before putting their napkins on the table and heading inside for their taste-test contest. With one exception. A woman with brown hair heavily threaded with filaments of gray moved in the opposite direction, descending the stairs and slipping behind the hedgerow into Milton's Gardens.

"I'm going to see what Tammy's up to," Jane told Sinclair. "Would you monitor the tasting contest? You'll have to keep an eye on Mrs. Hubbard along with the herbalists. If you don't, she might feed Constance a mouthful of chopped earthworm mixed with fennel. Or fly wings tossed in cumin."

Sinclair grinned. "I'd rather like to see that. The woman is insufferable. After criticizing the layout of the Henry

James Library, she proceeded to lecture me on the short-comings of our toxicology collection. When I informed her that the majority of those books were in the Isak Dinesen Safari Room, she groused about the inefficiency of housing our books in different rooms."

"Constance has a toxic personality—to use a term she'd understand—but she's still our guest," Jane reminded Sinclair before hurrying into the garden after the dark-haired woman.

Several couples were strolling along the gravel paths, and Jane couldn't help wondering how Victoria Billingsley felt about her forthcoming wedding. Had a pall been cast over her big day because of Kira's death? Even though Victoria hadn't been close to Kira, she obviously thought highly enough of The Medieval Herbalists to invite them to her wedding.

Or did she do that just for Hannah? Jane silently mused.

Jane was so lost in thought that she nearly passed by the woman she'd set out to find.

"Hello," she said softly. She didn't want to startle the solitary figure on the bench beneath the wisteria-covered arbor. "Not in the mood to be blindfolded?"

"By the right man, sure. But to taste mustard seeds or basil leaves? That's not my idea of dessert. I'd rather have a piece of chocolate cake," Tammy said.

Jane laughed and gestured at the bench. "May I join you?"

At Jane's nod, Tammy touched a leaf on the wisteria vine. "If I lived here, I'd wake up every day and pinch myself. It's so beautiful. It's nice in Tennessee too, but this place is pure heaven. I just can't believe Kira won't get a chance to experience all the fun things you have lined up for us. It won't be the same without her."

Seeing the tears pool in Tammy's eyes, Jane reached for the other woman's hand. "I'm sorry. Were you two close?"

"We were. Kira was the only person in the group I kept in touch with all year long. We'd e-mail and even talk on the phone every now and then. She didn't look down on me like some of the others do. I don't have a bunch of degrees on my wall, but Kira respected my craft." She raised Jane's hand to her nose and sniffed. "Ah, you used my gardener's soap."

Jane smiled. "It worked perfectly. Even my boys liked it and that's saying something. They usually avoid soap like the plague."

Pleased, Tammy released Jane's hand and gave it a pat. "Send your boys to my table during Sunday's fair. I'll give them samples of my favorite products."

"What other products do you make?" Tammy's wares genuinely fascinated Jane, but that wasn't the only reason she asked about them. She was also hoping to distract Tammy from her grief for a few moments.

"Soap, scrubs, body wash, lotion, lip gloss, insect repellant, essential oils, and a household cleaner or two."

Jane waved her arm, indicating the garden. "All plant-based? Amazing. Your entire group is talented. Your unique products. Kira's photographs. Vivian's renovations. And you all seem to get along so well. Has it always been that way?"

Tammy looked up at the stars. "We've had our squabbles, but they're few and far between. Probably because we're a bunch of tree huggers. We hang out in greenhouses and gardens. We go on long hikes and drink herbal tea. That's why this thing with Kira—I can't wrap my head around it. I don't get how she could accidentally drown. She was a good swimmer!" She stared intently at Jane. "Did the sheriff tell you anything else? Anything that would help me make more sense of this? Did she trip and fall—get knocked unconscious before she went in the river? Please. I need to know. This doesn't *feel* right to me."

Jane couldn't tell Tammy that her instincts were correct. She had to let Sheriff Evans handle things, but her heart ached for Tammy. She and Kira had obviously shared a genuine friendship. Of all The Medieval Herbalists, Tammy was the only person who was unable to move on—to go inside and attend the next event. Her grief was more acute. Jane could sense it in the air surrounding Tammy. It draped around her shoulders like a heavy shawl. If it had a color, it would be the hue of the sky during a winter rainstorm.

"Would you like a cup of tea?" Jane asked Tammy. "Or could I find you something made of chocolate? There's always a fresh supply in our kitchens, and while I can't answer your questions, I can offer you comfort food."

Tammy managed a wan smile. "No, thanks. I suppose I'll watch the contest after all. It'll make me feel better if Constance guesses wrong. She can't stand to be wrong."

"Is it hard to hang out with a celebrity?"

"Nah," Tammy said. "Constance knows that I'm just as smart as she is when it comes to poisons. She has book learning, but I have hands-on experience with the plants and herbs used during medieval times. I can't diagnose people like she does, though. I like hearing about her cases and she likes talking to me about plant care. Constance is all right when you get her alone." Tammy plucked a wisteria blossom off the vine and held it in her palm. "Over time, this flower has had many meanings. Endurance, clinging love, the releasing of burdens. Tonight, you helped me release a burden. Thank you."

Tammy walked away, but Jane stayed where she was. It was so peaceful on that bench, watching the sky deepen from cobalt to dark violet, that she did not want to leave.

"'The moon looks upon many night flowers,'" a voice said from behind the hedge and Edwin stepped out onto the path. "'The night flowers see but one moon.'"

Jane's heart hammered in surprise, but she kept her cool. "Are you quoting poetry?"

"Jean Ingelow," Edwin said, approaching Jane slowly, warily. "I hadn't planned on borrowing the poet's lines. I came to give you this, but you look so beautiful—like Rossetti's painting of Helen of Troy. Men would go to war over you too, Jane Steward."

Anger coursed through Jane's body. She opened her mouth to flay Edwin with her tongue. To rebuke him for daring to compliment her now, after ignoring her for so long. But she never got the chance.

Edwin closed the distance between them, tossed something on the bench, and cupped Jane's chin in his hand. Tilting her head upward, he kissed her. Though it was a brief kiss, it was still forceful and hungry.

And when Jane pushed him away, Edwin grabbed her by the shoulders and whispered in her ear, "Read this. I want you to understand what I am."

Then he released her. Pinching off a wisteria flower, he set it on top of what Jane assumed was a book wrapped in brown paper. "In Japanese legend, which is older than the Victorian language of flowers, a maiden waited for her lover under a wisteria vine," Edwin said. "Through many heartaches and trials, she never wavered. She endured. She was a woman like no other woman. She was like you, Jane."

And with that, Edwin Alcott melted into the shadows, leaving Jane alone with clenched fists and the fire of his kiss on her lips.

SEVEN

Jane knocked on the twins' bathroom door, reminded
Hem to wash his hair, and then sank down on the edge of
her bed. Holding the package Edwin had given her in both
hands, she took a deep breath and removed the brown paper.

"What's that?" Fitz asked. He sat in Jane's bathroom, holding
a comic in one hand and an egg timer in the other. His pajamas,
which resembled a Hogwarts uniform, were on the floor. Jane's
white bath mat was covered in dirt from Fitz's soiled clothes.

"A journal maybe. There's no title or author on the cover."
Jane walked into the bathroom and showed Fitz the camel-
colored leather.

Fitz pointed at the cover's elaborate engravings. "What
are those shapes?"

"This looks like a cross worn by a group of men called
the Knights Templar," Jane said, pointing at the cross with
two intersecting beams of equal length. "These two men riding the horses must be knights. They're wearing armor and
have lances. Aunt Octavia gave you a medieval castle play
set, so you know what lances are, right?"

"Lances are okay, but Hem and I like other weapons better." The egg timer stopped ticking and abruptly sounded its alarm. "Hem!" Fitz shouted. "My turn!"

Jane heard vigorous splashing from down the hall and imagined brown water sloshing over the edge of the tub to coat the floor.

"You should see the water!" Hem yelled. "It looks like chocolate milk!"

Fitz scooped up his pajamas and hurried into the hall. "Show me!"

"Wait until I get a towel!"

There was a click as Hem unlocked the door and let his brother in.

"Cool." Fitz sounded impressed. "Put some in a cup. That way, when I'm done, we can see whose water was darker."

Grinning, Jane returned to examining Edwin's book. She gently opened the supple cover, noted the marbleized end paper, and turned two blank pages until she reached a single line of text stating, "The Diary of Lionel E. Alcott, 1876."

The words had likely been written using a metal dip pen. The original black ink had faded with time, but Jane had no trouble reading the opening lines. They described Lionel's preparation to embark on a long journey to recover a valuable treasure.

"You too, eh?" Jane scowled at the page. Were all the men in Edwin's family thieves? Had Edwin read this dairy as a boy and, influenced by Lionel's adventures, decided to follow in his relative's footsteps? Had the Alcott men been recruited by some maniacal secret society? Or were they independent agents—mercenaries who stole rare and priceless books in exchange for monetary gain and for the thrill of the hunt?

Jane didn't make much progress with Lionel's diary that night. There was supper to prepare, laundry to do, a Harry Potter audiobook to play, and after the twins were asleep, e-mails to read and schedules to review.

By the time she put on her nightgown, it was almost eleven. And though her body was tired, her mind wouldn't quiet down. She kept revisiting the moment when she'd turned Kira's body over in the river and that ghostly, bloated face had stared up at her.

This calls for medicinal wine, she thought and tiptoed downstairs to the kitchen. She took the glass and her cell phone out to the garden and dialed Eloise's number.

"Are you still up?" she whispered.

"Of course," Eloise said. "I'm reading. What else would a single, thirty-something bookstore owner be doing on a Thursday evening? My hot dates with a certain shy and sexy but very busy falconer are few and far between, so I'm getting my thrills by burning through the latest Jade Lee novel instead."

Jane smiled. "Do you have a glass of wine to help you drown your sorrows?"

"Only the finest vintage—straight from the box." Eloise laughed. "Actually, that's not true. I have a lovely chilled dessert wine from Italy. Edwin gave it to me. I didn't know whether to accept or bludgeon him with the bottle." She took a breath. "Oh, Jane! I was afraid to call you. What if you didn't want to be my friend anymore?"

"Because of Edwin?" Jane asked in astonishment.

"He's been a total cad," Eloise exclaimed softly. "You haven't said a word, but I know you. He hurt you with his disappearing act. He does this all the time, and while I'm used to him jetting off without a word, you're not. I warned you about him. He's my brother and I love him. He does have admirable qualities, but his faults are hard to overlook. And he's so damned secretive!"

Jane was about to ask Eloise if she'd ever heard of Lionel Alcott when she decided against it. She didn't want to talk about Lionel. Or Edwin. Not until she'd read Lionel's book and had a chance to see for herself if the diary explained anything about Edwin's double life. "Your brother doesn't seem to operate like other people," Jane said eventually. "But nothing he did or might do would ever interfere with our friendship. You're like a sister to me. Which is why I called you. I can't stop thinking about—"

"Oh, Lord!" Eloise cried in dismay. "Here I am going on about Landon and Edwin and I totally forgot to ask if the rumor Mrs. Pratt is spreading about a drowned Storyton Hall guest is true."

"It's true," Jane said. "I found Kira Grace in Storyton River."

Eloise groaned. "You poor thing. Tell me everything."

Eloise was an excellent listener, and Jane held nothing back. She even told her best friend of Doc Lydgate's suspicions that Kira had been poisoned. When she was finished, she felt better for having let it all out.

"If the sheriff has to wait until Monday for the lab results, then I think the Cover Girls should get involved," Eloise said. "We could use our book discussion as an opportunity to get to know The Medieval Herbalists better—maybe ask them a subtle question or two."

Jane considered the idea. "It couldn't hurt. Maybe we'll learn that they're not quite as chummy as Claude Mason would have me believe. I keep coming back to those photos Kira took of Constance and Nico. What if this wasn't Kira's first attempt at blackmail? What if she's done it before?"

"A member other than Constance or the Scannavinis *must* have had it out for her," Eloise declared firmly. "Otherwise, you wouldn't have found her floating in the river."

The next day was jam-packed with activities and arrivals. Sheriff Evans appeared when the halls and corridors were still hushed and established himself in the William Faulkner Conference Room. He started his first interview at six thirty and, according to Sinclair, was focusing on each Medieval Herbalist's relationship with Kira Grace, as well as their movements the morning of the duck race. By the time breakfast was finished, every member had been interviewed.

Evans met with Jane in her office and explained that it would take a few hours to organize and check on the members' statements.

"Can they go on their scheduled nature hike in the meantime?" Jane asked.

The sheriff hesitated. "We can't let thirty people wander into the hills without supervision. One of them might be a murderer, after all. Who's leading the group?"

"Tom Green," Jane answered.

Evans grunted. Tom Green was a mild-mannered man of small stature. With his shaggy hair and gentle ways, he often reminded Jane of a Hobbit. "Mr. Lachlan will be going too," she quickly added. "He's a retired Army Ranger."

"I want one of my people there as well," Evans had said. "I'll send a deputy in plainclothes. Someone the members haven't seen before. You can say he's on your staff."

Jane agreed, and by the time Tom Green showed up to lead The Medieval Herbalists, a Deputy Mills was standing with Lachlan. As for Tom, he looked every inch the seasoned hiker in his cargo pants, brown T-shirt, and worn boots. He also held a walking stick in his right hand. The stick had clearly seen much use. The hand-carved flowers and ivy vines encircling its shaft had become so smooth in places that they glistened beneath the light of the lobby chandeliers.

"Thank you for recommending me to these folks," Tom said. "I've been hoping to rub shoulders with them for years." He lowered his voice to a conspiratorial whisper. "I've wanted to apply for membership, but I've been too intimidated. They're all so accomplished, and I'm just a guy who runs a plant store in a tiny town."

"You're not 'just' anything," Jane protested. "Besides, you should be proud of The Potter's Shed. Even people with brown thumbs are able to grow things with your help. And I bet you impress master gardeners as well. You have some unusual specimens in your greenhouse."

At that moment, Claude Mason and a large contingent of Medieval Herbalists exited from the Madame Bovary Dining Room, heading straight for Jane and Tom. Tom shot them a worried glance. "Not unusual enough for this lot, I'm afraid," he muttered.

By the time the hikers had gathered around Tom, he was smiling brightly again, and Jane put his momentary lapse of good humor down to nervousness.

The group set off—minus Hannah Billingsley, Jane noticed—at a leisurely pace with Lachlan and Deputy Mills in tow. The two men were charged with carrying water and healthy snacks, and while Lachlan looked like he could hike the entire Appalachian Trail without difficulty, Mills was clearly out of shape.

With the group gone and Butterworth seeing to the sheriff's needs, Jane was able to focus on wedding preparations. The groom's family would be trickling in from Richmond throughout the afternoon, and Jane wanted to assure them that she and her staff had everything ready for tomorrow's celebration.

Victoria and her future husband, Carson, had decided against a rehearsal dinner. Victoria told Jane that she planned to spend the better part of Saturday lounging by the Jules Verne Pool. As for Carson, he'd booked a fishing excursion with Captain Phil for his groomsmen and would be away from the resort for hours. Jane fervently hoped that the couple's evening wedding could still be magical, despite what had happened to Kira. However, it all depended on what Sheriff Evans and his team discovered today.

One of the most important elements of the Billingsley-Earle wedding was the food, so Jane visited the kitchens, where Mrs. Hubbard was already working on the cake.

Jane poured herself a cup of coffee and sat on a stool. She loved to watch Mrs. Hubbard bake. The cakes she made for tea were lovely and delicious, but her wedding cakes were works of art. Jane kept a scrapbook with photographs of every cake and proudly produced this album whenever prospective brides were touring Storyton Hall.

"What's in Victoria Billingsley's dream cake?" Jane asked.

Mrs. Hubbard, who'd just finished pouring batter into a cake pan, offered Jane a spoon to lick. "Perks of the job, my dear. Can you guess which flavor I've added?"

Jane grinned. "Is this like last night's taste contest?"

"Without the blindfold." Mrs. Hubbard filled a second cake pan. "It was great fun too. I think it helped that the contestants were a bit tipsy. There was plenty of laughter and no one seemed to mind when they got an answer wrong, which didn't happen often. Those folks know their herbs."

Jane licked the spoon clean. "And the Poison Princess? She survived?"

Mrs. Hubbard shrugged. "I gave her a taste of fennel and another of cloves. She could have had it much worse." She put her hands on her hips. "Well?"

"Almonds?" Jane guessed.

"Correct!" Mrs. Hubbard cried. "Because Victoria wanted a Hildegard-themed wedding feast, I needed to use the ingredients from, oh, when did Hildegard start writing her book?"

Jane tried to recall the biographical details of Hildegard Von Bingen's life. Hildegard, renowned among herbalists for her knowledge of plant lore, had been born in Germany in 1098. She became a nun at the age of fifteen. Her order followed the Rule of Saint Benedict, and Hildegard proved to be a wise and gifted healer.

"I think she worked on her book from 1141 to 1151," Jane said. She pointed at the cake pans. "You told me that you were using herbs mentioned in Hildegard's *Physica*, but I didn't realize the wedding cake was included as well. I guess that rules out any chance of a chocolate mouse filling."

Mrs. Hubbard nodded. "Which is fine with Victoria. She's not a fan of chocolate. Can you imagine?"

"No," Jane admitted. "My life requires copious amounts of tea, coffee, books, and chocolate. And not necessarily in that order." Jane searched the counter and noted a lack of decorating tools and supports for the tiers. "Where are your pillars and other goodies?"

"Don't need them. This won't be a traditional wedding cake. We're serving multiple cakes, but they won't be frosted or covered with the usual fondant decorations. To stay true to the food in Hildegard's book, I've created a sugar-honey glaze and sugared violets."

Jane smiled. "It certainly won't look like a traditional wedding cake, but then again, this wedding meal is one for the ages. Which reminds me. I'd better make sure the front desk has the menus printed."

"You can set your mind at ease about the tea treats for your book discussion. Everything will be ready and waiting in the Daphne du Maurier Parlor."

"Thank you." Jane kissed her head cook on the cheek. "You are the heart of Storyton Hall."

Mrs. Hubbard's face dimpled with pleasure. "I'm just the enticing aroma flowing through its corridors. You're its heart, dear. You and those boys. Now, get going before you make me cry in the batter. It wouldn't do for me to add extra salt to this cake."

When Lachlan returned from the hike, he immediately requested a meeting with Jane. She was having lunch with the twins and Aunt Octavia, but told Butterworth to send Lachlan up to her aunt's apartments.

"He's been hiking all morning, so he'll probably be worried that he isn't presentable," Jane said.

Aunt Octavia dismissed this notion with a wave. "It's a good thing I ordered extra sandwiches. Aloysius is in the village, seeing if any of the merchants heard the other herbalists talking about Ms. Grace before she, ah, went into the river."

"Is that the only reason he went into town?" Jane asked dubiously.

Aunt Octavia shrugged. "He might pay a visit to Mr. Alcott. I couldn't say."

The twins perked up at the sound of Edwin's surname. "Mr. Alcott's back?" Hem asked. "Can we visit him, Mom?"

"He told us that he'd bring us something cool." Fitz's eyes gleamed.

Jane hid her frown behind her napkin.

"Mr. Alcott has a café to run," Octavia reminded the twins. "You'll have to wait until he has time to spare. As for cool things, why don't you take a peek in the office?"

The boys tossed their napkins on their plates and were about to rush off when Aunt Octavia cleared her throat. The noise stopped them in their tracks. "May we be excused?" they meekly asked.

"Yes," she replied just as someone knocked on her apartment door. After rearranging her pink and black leopard-print housedress, she called, "Come in, Mr. Lachlan!"

The door opened and Muffet Cat shot into the living room. The portly tuxedo made a beeline for Aunt Octavia, jumped onto her lap, and meowed.

"I didn't know he could move that fast," Lachlan said.

"He must be half starved!" Aunt Octavia declared and fished a handful treats from her pocket. Muffet Cat wolfed them down and curled up on Octavia's lap.

"Please sit at the table," Octavia said to Lachlan. "And don't protest. It's just a chair. Tell us about the hike, and then dig into those sandwiches. Mrs. Hubbard made egg salad with cress as well as ham and brie with apples."

Defeated by Octavia's clout, Lachlan took a seat. "Unless they were all pretending, the members really do get along. Constance Meredith is the prickliest of the bunch. She's definitely the most pretentious, but I guess the rest of the group is used to her. Eventually, she stopped talking about herself and focused on the plants. When she did that, she became likable. She got excited about finding this plant called snakeroot. She told another woman—Tammy—that the root is poisonous. If ingested in large doses, it can cause internal injuries, paralysis, or death. Tammy explained that although snakeroot was once used to counteract snake venom, its rhizome is now being harvested as a diuretic."

Aunt Octavia, who'd been petting Muffet Cat until his rumbling purrs filled the room, grew still. "There were no arguments? No one pointed fingers or whispered when they believed to be out of earshot?"

"The only unusual exchange occurred between Claude Mason and Tom Green."

"Tom?" Jane repeated in surprise.

"We were taking our midway break when Mr. Mason pulled Tom aside," Lachlan said. "The others were sitting on a group of rocks in the shade, eating the snacks we'd brought and listening to Vivian Ash talk about her most recent renovation project. I crept around the rocks and got close to the two men. Mr. Green looked uncomfortable and I caught a few phrases. They don't make much sense to me, but maybe you'll understand them better, Miss Jane."

Jane nodded in encouragement. "Go on."

"Mr. Mason mentioned a druid, and Mr. Green literally flinched at the sound of the word. He shook his head in refusal and said 'recluse' and 'potentially dangerous.'" Lachlan gazed into the middle distance, recalling the scene. "Mr. Mason persisted. He put his arm around Mr. Green's shoulder and murmured something. It impressed Mr. Green. He had this expression—like a kid standing in front of a toy store window."

"Membership," Jane said. "I bet Claude offered Tom membership in exchange for . . ." She looked at her great-aunt. "Have you ever heard of a druid in the area?"

"As a matter of fact, I have." Aunt Octavia's mouth curved into a smug grin. "You need to talk to Tobias Hogg. When Pig Newton was sick back in May, Tobias feared that he couldn't be saved."

Jane made a sympathetic noise. "I remember how upset Tobias was, and the vet over the mountain didn't think there was much hope."

"Tobias tried everything. He got a second opinion. After that, he scoured the Internet for home remedies, and one of the housekeepers said that he'd sought the help of a druid. Some wild man living in the hills between Storyton and the next town."

"Am I always the last person to hear about everything?" Jane couldn't hide her exasperation. "A druid? Seriously?" She glanced from her great-aunt to Lachlan, who responded with a perplexed shrug. "All right. I'll call Mr. Hogg right now."

However, Tobias Hogg had taken the day off to enjoy a summer picnic with his girlfriend, Barbara Jewel, the famous romance novelist.

"I'll see if the Cover Girls can discover anything before our book discussion," Jane said. "For once, Mrs. Pratt's propensity for gossip might come in handy."

Eugenia Pratt loved being the center of attention. She sat on the divan in the Daphne du Maurier Parlor like a queen awaiting the adulation of her subjects.

"Well?" Mabel prompted, elbowing Mrs. Pratt in the side. "Don't add theatrical pauses. Just tell us about this druid!"

Mrs. Pratt scowled. "There's a certain way to tell a tale, you know."

"Have you ever *seen* him?" Phoebe asked impatiently.

Anna, who was admiring the tea spread, turned to her friend. "How does one recognize a druid? It's not like he'd walk through town wearing a robe and carrying a staff."

"I also picture him with a long beard and an owl on his shoulder," Violet added.

Sensing that she was losing her audience, Mrs. Pratt waved her hands. "No one has seen him. Except Tom Green. Apparently, Tom serves as the druid's go-between. He buys whatever staples the druid can't produce and leaves them somewhere in the woods."

Jane couldn't believe her ears. "And what does the druid use as payment? Daisy chains? Salves and tinctures in unmarked bottles?"

"No one knows," Mrs. Pratt said, enjoying the discussion immensely. "But Tom has procured medicines from him for years. Dozens of people have used the druid's holistic cures. Word has it that the man has cured a variety of ailments from warts to the flu with far better success than the doctors over the mountain. Apparently, he has a concoction that works wonders on sore joints."

"Made from herbs, no doubt. No wonder The Medieval Herbalists are intrigued." Jane took a moment to absorb this information. "But how would they have found out about this man? Or have known that Tom served as the druid's errand boy?"

Eloise nodded. "Exactly. I've lived here for years and never heard a single whisper about a druid. How is that possible?"

"His customers won't speak openly about him," Mrs. Pratt informed her friends. "The druid fiercely guards his privacy. If Tom hears anyone talking about the druid or his medicine, that person is permanently cut off."

"This is too bizarre," Jane said. She was about to ask Mrs. Pratt another question when the sounds of voices in the hall made her stop. "Don't mention the druid. Just focus on getting to know these people better. The spouses or partners aren't attending this event, so the group will be more intimate."

Jane moved to the doorway to welcome the herbalists. They all appeared to be in good spirits and seemed to have rested since their hike.

"I think you're the healthiest group we've ever had at Storyton Hall," Jane said.

"We won't be if we keep eating like this." Laughing, Vivian Ash pointed at the tea spread. "Miniature beef pies! And salmon with parsley, dill, and scallions. I wasn't even hungry until I got here, but now I want one of everything."

Eloise smiled at her. "We have plenty of material to discuss, so load your plates."

From that point, Eloise took over. The event had been Eloise's brainchild. As soon as she'd heard about the retreat, she'd e-mailed Claude Mason and suggested that his group read *Outlander* by Diana Gabaldon, *A Poultice for a Healer* by Caroline Roe, *Matilda Bone* by Karen Cushman, and any book in the Harry Potter series mentioning mandrakes prior to their arrival at Storyton. Claude had been delighted by her proposal.

"Let's start with a game," Eloise announced now. "Each Cover Girl has dug up—sorry, I couldn't resist the pun—a literary quote including an herb. If you can name the source, you'll win a prize."

Michelle Scanavanni clapped. "How fun!"

"Can you win more than one prize?" Constance asked.

Eloise seemed taken aback by the question. "How about this? If you win two, why not give your extra to a friend?"

"Good idea." Sandi Hughes nodded approvingly.

"Phoebe, why don't you go first?" Eloise pointed at her friend. "Phoebe runs the Canvas Creamery, so if you need a fantastic espresso drink or frozen treat, she's your girl. And if you want to see the raciest sculptures in town, check out her *back* garden."

Tammy looked at Phoebe. "I've heard about your book babes. Aren't they oversized nudes made from recycled materials?" A shadow of sadness entered her eyes. "Kira would have loved those. And this. She was always up for a game. Please, go on."

Phoebe gave her a warm smile and opened her notebook. "Who said, 'There's rosemary, that's for remembrance; pray you, love, remember'?"

Hands shot into the air. Phoebe called on an attractive man in his early forties.

"John will get *all* of these," Constance whined.

"The quote is spoken by Ophelia in Act 4, Scene 5, of Shakespeare's *Hamlet*," John said a trifle sheepishly. "And I won't raise my hand again. It's not fair. I'm an English professor."

"Congratulations on winning a free drink on me." Phoebe gave the professor an appreciative once-over.

Several more rounds passed before it was Jane's turn. "Mine contains two deadly plant references and my prize is a gift certificate for a free falconry lesson for you and a friend with Mr. Lachlan. Of course, you are all scheduled for an introductory lesson, but this will be a far more hands-on experience."

This created a great deal of excited whispering and Jane had to wait a moment before reading her lines. "'Neither twist Wolfs-bane, tight-rooted, for its poisonous wine; Nor suffer thy pale forehead to be kiss'd by nightshade.'"

Jane called on several people. After incorrect guesses of William Blake, Robert Frost, and William Wordsworth, Hannah Billingsley raised her hand. She'd chosen a seat in the corner of the room by the fireplace and had been so quiet that it was possible to forget that she was there, but Jane crossed her fingers behind her back in hopes that Hannah had the answer. She thought the younger woman would be delighted to stroke the feathers of a Cooper's hawk or feel the weight of a peregrine falcon as it perched on her forearm.

Jane pointed at her, and Hannah softly said, "Is it Keats? I think it is."

"Yes." Jane clapped and the other Cover Girls followed suit. Hannah blushed with pleasure.

The quote contest proved to be the perfect icebreaker, and by the time Eloise asked her first book discussion question, The Medieval Herbalists were clearly enjoying themselves.

An hour quickly turned into two, and the kitchen staff replenished the food and hot water. A few people, including Constance Meredith, ordered cocktails. As the afternoon faded into evening, she seemed to grow more and more congenial. At one point, she even ordered a round of mint juleps for everyone.

By her third drink, however, she began to exhibit signs of restlessness.

"J.K. Rowling's depictions of the mandrake were my favorite," she said in response to Eloise's final question on memorable scenes. "She did her medieval folklore research."

Anna cocked her head. "Well, I didn't. Would you explain the folklore?"

Constance swelled like a puffer fish. "Certainly. In the Harry Potter books, the characters must wear earmuffs when they uproot a mandrake. Otherwise, the plant's screams would kill them. This dates back to a genuine belief that the mandrake root was a demon—a living creature—and that the person who removed it from the ground would either be murdered by its scream or cast into a pit of Hell."

"Good Lord!" Mabel exclaimed.

"People solved this dilemma by tying the mandrake plant to a dog," Constance said, a wicked glimmer in her eyes.

"They'd whip the dog until it ran, thus pulling up the root and incurring the curse. Once the animal was dead, its owner would collect the root."

Violet looked stricken. "What a horrible legend. Dogs aren't disposable!"

"The mandrake root has an anthropomorphic appearance," Constance said. "Once you've seen one in person, you'll understand why people living in a superstitious world would fear it. Luckily for everyone here, I'll have several on display at Sunday's fair. I *am* a root short, seeing as I generously gave a lovely specimen to a pair of inquisitive boys. Twins, I think."

Jane took several steps toward Constance. "When?"

Constance shrugged. "Before I came here. I ran into these two boys talking about a kitchen garden. I rarely meet children who express an interest in herbs, so I rewarded them for being refreshingly different."

"Did you warn them of its dangers?" Jane asked in what resembled a low growl.

"Why? I don't expect them to eat it," Constance replied defensively.

Raising the index finger of her right hand, Jane brought it very close to Constance's heavily made-up face. "The next time you give my sons poisonous presents, you will find yourself walking to the train station. Do I make myself clear?"

Constance was about to argue, but she must have seen the transformation in Jane. Gone was the congenial resort manager. Another woman had taken her place. This woman was a mother, a fighter, and a protector.

"Yes," she whispered petulantly.

Jane shot Eloise a look to convey that she should wrap up the event and left the room. The second she was in the hallway, she broke into a run.

EIGHT

In the lobby, Jane nearly collided with Sheriff Evans.
She mumbled a harried "excuse me" and tried to maneuver
around him, but he reached out and grabbed her arm.

"Your sons are okay," he assured her. "Were you after this?"
He held up a plastic bag containing a brown, man-shaped root.

Jane took the bag and stared at the object within. "You
got that from my boys?"

"Mr. Lachlan saw them playing with the root and took
it away," the sheriff said. "Your sons were quite vocal in
their indignation, and their complaints drew the attention
of Deputy Emory. When Emory overheard Mr. Lachlan use
the word 'poisonous,' she felt compelled to investigate. Mr.
Lachlan turned the root over to us."

Now that she knew the twins were safe, Jane's anger
over Constance Meredith's foolishness—or deliberate
maliciousness—redoubled. "That woman!" Jane fumed. "I
should press charges against her!"

"According to Emory, your boys were wearing earmuffs,"
the sheriff explained. "They'd buried the root at the edge of

the kitchen garden and had action figures positioned around it. When one boy pulled the mandrake root out of the ground, the other would knock over the action figures and howl as if they'd died an agonizing death."

Jane understood at once. "They were playing herbology class."

"What?" Evans frowned in confusion.

"It's a Harry Potter thing," Jane said, her gaze still fixed on the root.

The mandrake root definitely had an anthropomorphic shape. It was all too easy to envision two arms, two legs, a trunk, and a head, albeit these were somewhat bulbous and misshapen. There were even depressions on one side of the "head," and Jane could envision a grotesque face staring back at her. As she continued to inspect the mandrake, she saw raw white spots where smaller pieces of root had been snipped off.

"The Poison Princess trimmed this root to make it look more like the plant described in medieval folklore," Jane said, showing the cuts to Sheriff Evans. "*That woman!*"

"You have every right to be upset," the sheriff said soothingly. "However, Ms. Meredith has not broken any laws. I checked. Anyone may buy, cultivate, or distribute mandrake, despite the fact that it's poisonous."

Jane glared at the sheriff. "I would kick her out of Storyton Hall before sundown if there wasn't an ongoing murder investigation!"

"Speaking of which, I have preliminary results from Ms. Grace's toxicology test. Would you like an update as you check on your sons?" Evans kindly asked. "Mr. Lachlan is letting them feed his birds to make up for 'ratting them out,' as he put it."

"I do want to lay eyes on the boys," Jane said. "Irrational as that is."

Evans put a hand on Jane's shoulder. "It's a parent's prerogative to worry."

Flashing him a smile, Jane led the sheriff to the garage where the John Deere Gator carts were parked. "If we drive, we'll get there faster and have more privacy while we talk," she said.

The moment Jane cleared the driveway and hit the wooded trail, she accelerated. She continued picking up speed until the trees zipped past.

"Was Kira poisoned?" Jane asked once Storyton Hall had receded into the distance.

"Yes!" Evans had to raise his voice over the noise of the Gator's motor and the rush of air. "However, we need tests to determine what type. The medical examiner did discover a puncture wound at the base of Kira's neck."

Jane slowed the cart. "A puncture wound? As in, from a syringe?"

"Exactly." Evans sounded impressed. "It could easily have been overlooked. Ms. Grace's hair covered the injection spot."

Storyton Mews came into view and Jane stopped the cart and turned to the sheriff. "So it's definitely murder."

Removing a folded piece of paper from his shirt pocket, Evans handed it to Jane. "This list reflects those individuals who had an opportunity to kill Ms. Grace. We still have no obvious motive."

Jane examined the names. "It's not a very long list."

"I'd like to search their guest rooms immediately. Depending on what we find, I may also conduct additional interviews," the sheriff said. "Right after you see your sons."

Jane promised to be quick. "I want this case solved as badly as you do," she said in a hushed voice as she parked next to the building. "I only wish we knew which poison had been injected into Kira. Liquefied mandrake root, for example."

"Ms. Meredith is in the clear," the sheriff reminded her.

"Yes, I know." Jane was unable to hide her disappointment.

The mews were quiet. No visitors were permitted after five, as Lachlan liked to be alone with the birds before settling them down for the evening.

The most recent additions to the Storyton Mews, a peregrine falcon named Horus and a merlin named Cillian, were not tame enough to hunt on their own. Though Lachlan allowed them to go on short flights each morning, they kept close to the mews because they knew an easy meal awaited them there.

Freyja, the Cooper's hawk Lachlan had snuck into his cottage last winter, and the reason there now was a falconry program at Storyton Hall, had advanced in her training to the point where she could bring down smaller birds. For the most part, however, the raptors' diet consisted of frozen chicks. And while Mrs. Hubbard had eventually forgiven Lachlan for giving her the shock of her life when she'd accidentally opened a box stamped PERISHABLE to find a supply of day-old chicks inside, she insisted that the mews be equipped with its own freezer.

As Jane approached, it was clear that the twins had just finished doling out supper for Cillian, for one of Lachlan's boxes was on the ground in front of the merlin's mew. Hearing the Gator, Lachlan returned Cillian to his perch, locked the door, and hustled over to Jane.

"I'm so sorry, Miss Jane," he said, twisting his heavy leather gloves in his hands. "I had no idea she would give them such a thing. I should have been watching."

Lachlan was genuinely distressed. Once, Jane had had reservations about employing a man suffering from PTSD, but she soon realized how foolish she was being. Lachlan, who was as loyal and courageous as a lion, didn't have any more demons than she did. He just couldn't hide the fact that he was battling them as well as others could.

"You did nothing wrong," Jane said gently. "I'm their mother, and *I* wasn't watching. We can't always be there. What matters is that you spotted the danger and you removed it. Thank you, Landon." She used his first name for emphasis.

Though Jane was tempted to squeeze his forearm, she refrained. She sensed that he wouldn't welcome her touch just then. However, she did see him relax a little. "They've all but forgotten the root," he whispered conspiratorially. "And I think Cillian's starting to get used to them. It's a good start. He's the only bird who still freaks out around kids."

"Well, if he can tolerate Fitz and Hem, he can handle visits from the Tasmanian Devil and a troupe of whirling dervishes." Jane spent a few minutes visiting with her sons. While the sheriff was busy admiring the raptors, she quickly updated Lachlan on the status of the investigation.

"Tell Sinclair that I'd like an in-depth report on Ms. Grace brought to my great-aunt and -uncle's apartments. I want all the Fins to join me there. It's time for us to determine the killer's motive." She glanced over her shoulder to where Sheriff Evans stood reading the information plaque on Cooper's hawks. "Just in case he doesn't."

The Medieval Herbalists lacking solid alibis for the estimated time of Kira's death included Hannah Billingsley, Claude Mason, and Tammy Kota. Also, Sherriff Evans wasn't completely satisfied by the statements provided by Phil and Sandi Hughes, considering they were each other's alibis.

None of the herbalists staying at Storyton were upset when Sheriff Evans informed them that he intended to search their rooms.

"Go right ahead," Tammy said. "My life is an open book. Some of the pages, and their illustrations, might make you blush, but I've got nothing to hide." With a wink, she offered the sheriff her room key.

Evans assigned her room to Deputy Mills.

"Do I have to watch?" Tammy asked Jane. "I'd rather sit in your gazebo with a glass of wine and meditate for a spell."

Jane granted Tammy permission to leave. As the sheriff distributed other assignments, she made her own. A Fin would supervise each search. And though Sheriff Evans had no idea that Storyton Hall's butler, head librarian, or head chauffeur were far more than accommodating staff members, Jane knew nothing would escape their sharp-eyed glances or acute hearing.

However, by the time Jane, the Fins, Uncle Aloysius, and Aunt Octavia reconvened, nothing useful had been discovered.

"Not a single piece of dirty laundry was brought to light," Sterling said.

"Mrs. Pimpernel would disagree." Butterworth sniffed. "Ms. Kota's room was in a deplorable state. It bore a remarkable resemblance to a gypsy encampment."

Jane, who'd taken an instant liking to Tammy, said, "That sounds rather fun." Turning to Sinclair, she gestured at the stack of papers on the coffee table. "I hope you've had more success."

"Not much, I fear." Sinclair quickly distributed a packet to each person. "Kira Grace didn't have expensive tastes. She was not a spendthrift. Hers is not a history tainted by avarice. For most of her life, she lived quite modestly. When her career took off and she finally began making a little money, she didn't know what to do with it. Unfortunately, she entrusted it all to a man she knew back in college. This man was running a Ponzi scheme. He went to jail, but not before Ms. Grace lost all of her assets. She was forced to declare bankruptcy."

Jane shook her head. She'd been having a difficult time

understanding why Kira had taken the damning photographs of Constance Meredith and Nico Scannavini, but now her motives were clear. "So the victim of a financial crime turned to blackmail. She must have been desperate."

"Ms. Grace was actually homeless for a time," Sinclair said. "That doesn't excuse her from making a very poor decision, but after conducting extensive research, I've come to believe that this was her first blackmail attempt."

"What about all those clothes in her room?" Jane asked. "How did she buy those if she was broke?"

Aunt Octavia looked alarmed. "What of her hotel bill? How did she plan on paying for this weekend's expenses?"

Sinclair brandished another stack of papers. "She was doing the credit card shuffle."

Uncle Aloysius growled. As a rule, he distrusted credit card companies and paid for purchases via cash or check. Every time he read an article or heard a news report featuring credit card debt, fraud, or outrageous interest rates, he'd launch into a monologue on how these companies preyed on hardworking Americans.

From under the table, Jane heard a feline growl and knew Muffet Cat was responding to the noise Uncle Aloysius had made.

"The bastards! Forgive my language, ladies, but it's true," her uncle railed. "People think they need to carry a balance on their credit cards to establish a credit rating. They believe it's wise to increase their credit limit. The fancy platinum cards tempt them. They don't read the fine print. Suddenly, a nasty annual fee appears on their statement along with a whopping interest rate. Multiply that monthly bill by several cards and—"

"All right, Aloysius." Aunt Octavia silenced her husband with a look.

Jane focused on Sinclair again. "If what you're saying is true—and we have no way of confirming that Kira didn't attempt extortion before this weekend—then our best motive just went out the window." She turned to Lachlan. "After hiking with the herbalists this morning, your impression was that they genuinely like one another. And they liked Kira."

"We certainly lack the usual motives for murder," Butterworth said. "Money, revenge, envy, a crime of passion, et cetera. However, an injection of lethal poison to the back of the head reeks of cowardice. The murderer didn't wish to see his victim's face."

"A cowardly and callous killer," Jane said. "The way he loaded Kira in a wheelbarrow and dumped her in the river showed how little respect he had for her body."

Sterling, who'd been silent up to this point, suddenly jerked in his chair. "What if the crime *was* about money? Ms. Grace set out on a solo hike. With her camera. We already know she had the means to blackmail her fellow herbalists, but perhaps she was gathering evidence on someone *else* that morning. Someone who could provide her with a bigger payoff. If so, there would be no need to approach her friends."

"There's only one person I can think of with a secret that might lead to murder," Aunt Octavia said gruffly.

Jane's blood turned cold as she met her aunt's dauntless gaze. "Edwin Alcott."

"We know so little about him, Jane," Uncle Aloysius said, trying to soften the blow with a kind look. "Only that he's called The Templar and is a notorious book thief. And while he did return one of the missing pages from our Gutenberg Bible, we can't say what his motives are or who employs him. Can we?"

"No," Jane replied. "But Edwin gave me a book to read. A diary. He told me that it would help me understand who he was and what he did."

A host of raised brows followed this announcement.

"We should still be suspicious of him, of course, but I

wanted you to know that he believes the diary will clarify things," she quickly added. "I also think we need to see how Edwin interacts with the other Medieval Herbalists. *If* Kira was aware of his *other* profession, who's to say she was the only one?"

"How do you plan to bring the wolf among the sheep?" Aunt Octavia asked.

At that moment, Muffet Cat rubbed against Jane's leg, signaling that he wanted to jump up. She pushed back her chair and he vaulted onto her lap. Stroking Muffet Cat's fur, Jane felt like an Ian Fleming villain as she declared, "I'm going to ask Mr. Alcott to be my date at tonight's wedding feast."

When Jane stopped by Victoria and Hannah's guest room to deliver their floral bouquets for the wedding, she found Hannah in tears.

"Is she all right?" Jane whispered from the threshold.

Victoria, a vision of effortless beauty in a strapless white gown with a sweetheart neckline, moss green sash, and sweeping train, pulled Jane into the room. "Now that the time has come, she's scared. Change can be scary, but she'll be just fine. She has her work, her friends, her garden, and her darling cats." She turned to face her sister. "Besides, it's not like we won't see each other again. Nothing could ever keep us apart. You're the light of my life, Banana Puddin'."

"Don't call me that." Hannah sniffed.

Jane slowly approached Hannah. "You look lovely."

Hannah wiped her wet cheeks. "I do like my dress. It's the same hue as Via's sash." She held out her bare arms and suddenly began to panic. "My jacket! Where's my jacket?"

"You have to stop hiding, Hannah." Victoria's voice was steely. "Ms. Steward won't run out of the room screaming because you have a hump and scars. When are you going to see yourself as more than the shape of your spine? When are you going to give someone other than me a chance to know the real and wonderful you?"

Hannah dropped her gaze and her sister crossed the room and grabbed her hands. "You are whip smart, amazingly funny, and supercool. I was incredibly lucky to have had you to myself after we lost Mom, but I can't leave this room and start the next chapter of my life until I know that you'll at least *try* to show people how awesome you are."

Victoria waited for her sister to answer. When she didn't, Jane looked at Hannah. "Does she always call you Banana something?"

Hannah managed a small laugh. "Yes, damn it. Ever since we were kids. Our mom started it. She had a whole song about me. If there was a dessert made with bananas, it was in that song. Bananas Foster, banana cake, banana cream pie—you name it. My mom was clever with rhymes. Via was a teenager when Mom died, but she remembers every line to that song. She remembers everything about our mother. She wouldn't let me throw away a single thing that belonged to her. She kept it all. Even locks of her hair and hospital ID bands. When Via loves someone, she loves them forever."

"I hope Carson realizes what a gem he's about to claim." Jane offered Victoria her bridal nosegay. She then pointed at one of the tiny white flowers in the bouquet. "I know you have a marigold posy, Hannah, but I could pin a few of these in your hair. Having a few of your sister's flowers might help you feel . . . connected during the ceremony."

Victoria beamed at her. "I love that idea. Are they chamomile flowers, Hannah? What do they mean?"

"Healing and protection," Hannah said. "In medieval times, they were strewn over floors to give rooms a pleasant odor. They smell a bit like apples. *Not* bananas," she added very quickly and the sisters broke out in a fit of giggles.

That's better, Jane thought.

After using bobby pins to secure several white flowers in Hannah's hair, Jane left the sisters to their final preparations and went to the back terrace to meet Edwin.

Both the wedding ceremony and the medieval feast were being held in Milton's Gardens. In the summer twilight, the gardens were pure magic. The flowers were radiant with color. Floral scents perfumed the air and tiny white lights twinkled around the arbors and lampposts. As a wedding surprise, Jane had also strung the entire gazebo with white lights so that the bride and groom could share their first dance as man and wife on their own private dance floor.

"Why she picked marigold garlands for the ends of the chair rows is beyond me. What's wrong with magnolia or gardenia flowers with greens?" Jane heard someone grumble and turned to find Carson's mother standing a few feet away.

"Carson said that Victoria wanted their wedding to have some medieval traditions. He doesn't care about the ceremony. He just wants her to be happy," Carson's father responded evenly. "I think the garlands are festive."

Carson's mother grunted. "They'll keep the deer away, that's for sure."

"Mosquitoes too," said Vivian Ash. She smiled at the older couple, winked at Jane, and continued walking toward the garden.

"Victoria has strange friends," Carson's mother said sourly.

"I believe they're Hannah's friends," her husband pointed out.

His wife grunted again. "That's strange too. Why doesn't Victoria have her own? Why is she so wrapped up in her sister's life? It's not normal. I hope she doesn't plan to spend all of her time visiting that Hannah after she's married. Victoria will have a very large house to run, and with Carson focused on work, he'll need a wife who can manage things at home. She can't dash off to play therapist to her sister every time someone calls Hannah a name or gawks at that crooked back of hers." She sighed. "I wish Carson had listened to me and asked Victoria to have genetic testing done before he gave her that expensive ring. No testing and no prenup. Our only son could be pissing away the legacy we worked so hard to establish. Forgive me if I don't feel celebratory."

"Deirdre, this is not the time or the place," her husband said in a clipped voice. "Carson loves Victoria, and in about fifteen minutes, she's going to be our daughter-in-law. If you can't pretend to enjoy yourself, then fake it. Do it for your son."

As Carson's parents descended the stairs to the gardens, Sinclair appeared next to Jane and whispered, "What a piece of work. Do you suppose Victoria knows what her future mother-in-law is like?"

Jane smiled. "I think Victoria can hold her own. She certainly got her way when it came to the wedding itself."

Sinclair looked thoughtful. "Her choices seem to have been based on what would please her sister. It's very generous for a bride to share every aspect of her wedding day."

"Maybe Victoria fears that Hannah won't have a wedding, so she included her sister in every facet of her own wedding day," Jane said. "Theirs is a rare bond, Sinclair. I just hope Hannah can adjust to Victoria becoming Mrs. Carson Earle."

"Victoria could probably move Hannah into a wing of their house and Carson wouldn't even notice. The Earles control a pharmaceutical empire, and Victoria's starter home is the size of Monticello."

Having visited Thomas Jefferson's stately mansion several times, Jane recalled that the house was around eleven thousand square feet. She whistled. "That explains why the Earles are footing the bill for the wedding. How do you know all these details?"

"I decided to do further research into every member's financial status," Sinclair said. "Hannah Billingsley lives frugally and raises no red flags. Victoria, a medical librarian with a comfortable income, is about to enter a markedly different tax bracket."

"A librarian?" Jane couldn't hide her surprise. "No kidding."

"We don't all wear spectacles, suits, and bow ties," Sinclair said.

Jane hooked her arm through Sinclair's. "And none look like Sean Connery's James Bond but you." She shook her head in disgust. "I can't believe Mrs. Earle is worried about genes. Victoria's kind, smart, and gorgeous. What more does the woman want?"

"The ceremony is about to start, so I should get to my point." Sinclair produced a slip of paper from his breast pocket. "These Medieval Herbalists are living paycheck to paycheck. Or in Ms. Kota's case, craft fair to craft fair."

Jane's heart sank. "Do we have any reason to suspect her?" She read the second name on the list. "Not the Hugheses too!"

"I'm afraid so. They spent most of their earnings on their mortgage and college and graduate school tuition for their three children. Sandi then took an early retirement to care for her ailing father. Not long afterward, they had to dip into their retirement fund to cover nursing home costs for Phil's mother. The Hugheses have sunk every last penny into Storyton Outfitters."

"They might face financial hardship, but neither Tammy nor the Hugheses would profit from killing Kira," Jane said. "If Kira discovered a secret worthy of blackmail, then I think it was far more serious than a low savings account balance."

Sinclair reclaimed the list and tucked it in his pocket. "I concur." His eyes slid to the right. "Speaking of secrets, your date has arrived. Were you able to finish Lionel Alcott's diary?"

"I'm halfway through," Jane said. "So far, it's only left me with more questions. And more doubts."

"Let your instincts be your guide," Sinclair advised before retreating inside.

Edwin Alcott appeared at the foot of the terrace steps. He stared up at Jane and smiled the rakish smile that had once made her blood rush to her ears. The sight of him still had an effect on her, but it was no longer as powerful.

He is the most alluring, elusive, and deceitful man I've ever known, she thought. Remembering how he'd kissed her in the garden, she felt her body temperature rise by several degrees. She thought of Emily Dickinson's line, *The Heart wants what it wants—or else it does not care*, and reminded herself that she was on a mission that far outweighed the irrational desires of her heart.

"You look like you're made of starlight," Edwin said, taking her hand. "You'll outshine the bride."

Jane didn't think her champagne-colored dress, which was fairly conservative, merited such a compliment, but she thanked Edwin and held out her arm. "We'll watch the ceremony from the back. During the final reading, I'll have to sneak off to check on the food."

"Ah, the Hildegard feast," said Edwin. "Not one's typical wedding fare, but with Mrs. Hubbard in charge, it's bound to be a success."

"Are you familiar with Hildegard?" Jane asked. She couldn't help being impressed, despite the fact that Edwin had once told her that his reading tastes were extremely varied.

Edwin nodded. "I've read her *Physica*."

"The original version?"

Jane had only been joking, but Edwin flashed an enigmatic grin. "Did you finish the diary?" he whispered as they approached the marigold-covered arch that Victoria would pass under. The wedding guests, who were all seated and waiting for the bride to appear, were engaged in a bout of hushed and enthusiastic pre-ceremony chatter.

"I read a good bit," Jane whispered back. "But it's done nothing to make things clearer. I still have no idea who, or what, you are."

"You must finish it to understand," Edwin said. "Still, I'd like to speak with you alone at some point this evening. There are things I need to say and I don't want to be overheard."

Jane recalled how Edwin had suddenly appeared after she'd discovered Kira's body in Storyton River. Why had he really been following her that day?

She was just about to ask him this question when the delicate, fairylike sound of harp music floated into the air. The guests fell quiet and Jane pulled Edwin off the path.

Victoria and Hannah walked slowly down the garden path. Victoria was all smiles and confidence, while Hannah focused on the marigold petals being flattened beneath her silver ballet flats.

When they reached the arch, Victoria stopped and turned to her sister. She kissed Hannah on the cheek, embraced her, and then proceeded under the arch and up the makeshift aisle on her own. As soon as she was close to a beaming Carson, he took her hand. She returned his smile, but not before casting a final backward glance at her sister.

The ceremony was short and sweet. One of Carson's friends read from Corinthians, and Claude Mason recited a medieval love poem called, "Joyous in Love, I make my aim." The band of musicians the Earles had hired delighted the younger guests with a medieval rendition of The Cure's "Lovesong."

"Never thought I'd hear that melody from a mandolin," Edwin said. "It's quite beautiful."

Jane thought the whole ceremony was unique and beautiful. The flower-studded garden, the perfumed air, and the purpling sky formed the perfect backdrop. And yet she couldn't help feeling sorry for Hannah. She sat near the arch, a forced smile plastered to her face, and held on to her nose-gay as though for dear life.

"I need to go now," Jane said. "I'll meet you after the meal's been served."

It was highly irregular for Jane to sit with the wedding guests, but Victoria had been so insistent that Jane had even-tually agreed. In the end, she was glad she did, for it was one of the most splendid meals she'd ever eaten.

After serving wine sprinkled with violets, the waitstaff brought out leek soup and rye rolls baked with garlic and thyme. Following the soup was a salad of prickly lettuce, celery, parsley, and cress. The entrées included lamb and lentil stew, pan-fried catfish flavored with coriander and cumin, and beef ribs in a wine, currant, and onion sauce. The side dishes were carrots with cumin and squash baked with garlic and cheese. For dessert, the guests were treated to Mrs. Hub-bard's delicious wedding cakes as well as plantains drizzled in cinnamon, nutmeg, and honey and an apple, almond, and ginger compote.

The feast was a huge hit with both The Medieval Herb-alists and the groom's family and friends. Mrs. Hubbard's excellent food and a seemingly endless supply of wine had all the guests smiling and laughing. Jane watched them and felt contentment flow over her like a warm wind.

By the time the dancing started, she had begun to believe that everything might be all right—that love, friendship, and goodness would triumph over evil.

Edwin was just about to ask her to join him for a waltz on the grass when Butterworth suddenly appeared at her side.

"You must come at once," he whispered urgently into her ear. "The rare herbal Sinclair put on display in the Henry James Library has been stolen."

Jane threw Edwin a brief, distrustful glance before calmly

rising to her feet and following Butterworth away from the festivities.

As she hurried through the flower-covered arch on her way back to Storyton Hall, she yanked off a single marigold flower. She then crushed the blossom until it was nothing but yellow dust in her fist.

NINE

In the Henry James Library, Sinclair was despon-dently staring at the empty display case.

Though Jane practically tiptoed across the carpet, he heard her approach and raised his eyes to meet hers. "Your uncle will never allow you to auction an item from the secret library now. Forgive me, Miss Jane."

Jane was crushed. She'd been trying to convince Uncle Aloysius to let her sell one or two of the more obscure treasures housed in the temperature-controlled attic turret. Building the Storyton Mews and retiling the Jules Verne Pool had eaten up all the profits from the Romancing the Reader event, and Jane had so many projects tacked to the Hopes and Dreams board in her office that there wasn't room for more. She wanted to restore the folly and the orchards, create more walking trails through the woods, open a second boutique, and buy paddleboats for the lake. Above all else, she wanted Storyton Hall to have a world-class spa.

Jane gazed at the velvet-lined display case in despair. "Uncle Aloysius had his doubts about my taking that herbal from the secret library, but you know how I feel about all those books, scrolls, and documents being sealed away up there, and I finally convinced him that sharing these works is the right thing to do."

"And I agree wholeheartedly," Sinclair said. "Except for the materials with harmful or destructive content, of course. Those should remain in their locked drawers. There are many others, however, too splendid and wonderful to be kept in the dark."

"Stories are meant to be shared," Jane insisted. "No writer ever picked up a pen hoping that no one would see the results of his or her labors."

Sinclair indicated a distant bookshelf. "A personal diary might be the exception to that rule."

At the mention of a diary, Jane thought of Edwin. He hadn't left her side all evening. Could he have been responsible for the theft?

"The lock was picked?" she asked Sinclair.

"Yes," he answered. And then, "I thought a sturdy lock, combined with my presence, would be a sufficient deterrent against theft."

Jane leaned over and examined the glass. "I don't see any fingerprints. I suppose the thief wore gloves. Is Sterling reviewing video footage?"

"As we speak." Sinclair laced his hands together. "Miss Jane, I believe I was in my office when the theft occurred. The Henry James Library doesn't close until nine, so the main door stood open. Naturally, I wanted to be available for those guests not attending the wedding, but as the evening wore on, it became clear that I was unlikely to receive any patrons. Therefore, I entered my office to continue work on a list of plants that can be successfully made into lethal, injectable poisons."

"Sinclair." Jane walked around the barren case and took the head librarian's hands. "This is not your fault. We're not equipped with motion detectors or laser sensors. It's bad enough that we have cameras recording the activities in our public areas. Whoever stole that herbal will appear on the hallway feed. Unless they were aware of the camera. In that case, they could have timed their departure from the library to avoid being captured on film. Still, we should be able to see who entered from the back terrace—" She abruptly stopped. Dread seeped into her bones like a winter mist dampening the ground. "When did you last see the book intact in its case?"

"Moments before I spoke with you on the terrace."

Squeezing his hands a little tighter, Jane asked, "And when you returned to the library?"

"I didn't look at the case, Miss Jane," Sinclair admitted miserably. "Nothing seemed amiss, and I was intent on continuing my research."

"The thief could be Edwin, then. I'm sure he's adept at lock picking. He could have taken the book and hidden it somewhere until after the wedding," Jane said. She released Sinclair's hands because her own arms felt too leaden to hold up.

"This is not my handiwork, I can assure you. I wouldn't have been so sloppy," a low voice said from behind them.

Jane swung around to see Edwin squatting by the case. "I believe the culprit entered sometime during the wedding feast."

"How can you tell?" Sinclair asked.

Edwin indicated a tiny orange petal on the carpet. It was well camouflaged by the red and yellow floral designs in the wool carpet, but with Edwin pointing it out, Jane had no trouble identifying its source.

"A marigold petal," she said, recalling the blossom she'd crushed in her fist.

"There's also a strong hint of cumin in the air, which wouldn't have come from you, Jane, because you partook of dessert." Edwin stood up. "The thief didn't. He or she ate the catfish or carrots before entering the library to commit the crime." He glanced between Sinclair and Jane. "Is the book very valuable?"

"A twelfth-century herbal. Intact. Completely original. Magnificent illumination." Sinclair never spoke in staccato, and Jane shot him a concerned look.

Edwin, on the other hand, nodded gravely. "A rare treasure, indeed. But hope is not lost. The culprit left the wedding feast during a specific time period, entered the resort, and then returned to the feast after stealing—and supposedly stashing—the herbal. You have a camera feed for the back terrace and another for the hallway outside the library, so you should have no trouble identifying the most likely suspects."

"You've scoped out our camera locations quite thoroughly," Jane said accusingly.

Edwin shrugged. "An occupational hazard." Keeping his gaze fixed on Jane's face, he gestured at the lock. "May I take a closer look?"

To Jane's surprise, Sinclair produced a pair of gloves from his desk drawer and offered them to Edwin. "Would a magnifying glass be useful?"

"It would," Edwin said. "And a flashlight, if you have one." Sinclair fetched both from his desk.

"Would you mind pointing the beam at the lock?" Edwin asked and Sinclair instantly complied.

Jane couldn't believe what she was seeing. Why was Sinclair allowing Edwin to investigate?

Why am I allowing this? she silently wondered. But she knew the answer. She wanted to give Edwin a chance to either incriminate or exonerate himself. She wanted to know now, before another second passed, if Edwin Alcott would dare to steal a book from Storyton Hall.

So she made no move to stop Edwin as he held the magnifying glass over the lock. "Scratches everywhere. This was the work of an amateur. The thief was flustered. Rushed." Edwin returned the glass and the gloves to Sinclair. "No professional would have left this lock with a bit of metal from a lock-picking tool lodged inside. He would have simply pocketed the lock and left. Add that mistake to the flower petal and the telltale aroma, and the conclusion is that you're dealing with an individual who is either desperate for funds or coveted that particular book."

Jane and Sinclair exchanged concerned looks. Edwin's description could fit any number of Medieval Herbalists.

"If you'd just stolen a priceless book from this library, where would you stash it?" Jane asked Edwin.

His expression became pensive. "Not outdoors. It's far too humid. The safest place would be among other books. In another reading room perhaps. The real question is how does the thief plan to get the book off your property? He can't pack a twelfth-century herbal in his suitcase and hope for the best."

At the very thought of this, Jane felt her face flush with anger. "No one will be leaving without having every inch of their belongings searched. There's more at stake here than the book itself. I have plans . . ." She trailed off, too angry to continue.

Edwin reached for her hand. "I'll do anything in my power to help retrieve the stolen herbal. But I won't be of much use if you can't trust me. Please, Jane. Grant me ten minutes. Alone."

"Not now," Jane said, pulling her hand free. "I need to review the video footage."

"I could watch the feed too, but you can't allow that because I'm not above suspicion. Please, Jane," Edwin persisted. "Ten minutes. If I haven't convinced you after that, I'll leave. And I won't breathe a word about the missing book."

At a loss, Jane glanced at Sinclair and was astonished to see him dip his chin in a barely imperceptible nod. None of the Fins trusted Edwin Alcott, and Jane knew they'd be glad if he never stepped foot inside Storyton Hall again. And yet Sinclair, who was the closest thing Jane had to a father other than Uncle Aloysius, was encouraging her to hear Edwin out.

"All right," she told Edwin. "Sinclair, I'll meet you in the security office in twenty minutes."

"Where are you going?" Sinclair wanted to know. It was Jane's job to protect the secret library, but as a Fin, Sinclair was responsible for keeping the Guardian of Storyton Hall safe. Though he was willing to give Edwin a chance, he wasn't going to trust the man until Jane did.

Jane's mouth twitched. "To sit in my garden. I saw Muffet Cat headed that way, and he's an excellent judge of character."

Edwin groaned. "I should have saved a piece of catfish from supper."

Ignoring the jest, Jane led Edwin outside. It was only when they were safely hidden behind the tall hedge of Milton's Gardens that she said, "I was close to trusting you before you went away. When you failed to communicate with me during your absence, doubt crept in."

Edwin's expression was solemn. "And your other feelings? The warmer ones? Were they as fleeting as your trust? A passing fancy?"

If his intent had been to provoke her, he succeeded in spades. Jane stopped and rounded on him. "*You* played with my heart like it was made of clay. I'm a widow in my thirties with two sons! I can't indulge in *fleeting* emotions. I don't *have* flings or *passing fancies*." She performed a mock curtsy as she repeated this phrase. "I never came close to falling for another man since William died. Until you came along. I didn't want to have feelings for you, but I did all the same. Look where *that* got me!"

Edwin seized her hand again. "I couldn't contact you. I thought about you every hour. Every minute. I was afraid this would happen, but I had no control over my situation. I swear to you, Jane. I never meant to hurt you."

"You *couldn't* contact me?" Jane stared at him in disbelief. "Why not? Was there no cell phone service in Shanghai? No Internet in Istanbul? Was there a stamp shortage in Palermo or—"

"I was being held captive," Edwin interrupted. "I was a prisoner."

For the first time since his return, Jane really looked at Edwin. When she stood very still and studied him, she realized that his face had the pallid, drawn, and slightly gaunt appearance of someone who hasn't been exposed to sunlight or fresh air for too long. She'd seen that look on guests visiting Storyton Hall. Guests who'd been trapped in cubicles or windowless offices for weeks on end. Guests who'd been ill and had spent fitful days in a hospital bed. These people came to Storyton to rest and read, but they also came to walk in the gardens, to play croquet on the lawn, and to breathe the mountain air. They came to have their bellies warmed by homemade food and to have their spirits restored by bookcase after bookcase of stories and by the pristine beauty of their surroundings.

Jane felt a lump form in her throat. Perhaps Edwin didn't deserve her pity. After all, he was a thief who'd undoubtedly been caught in the act of stealing, so why did the idea of his being locked in a lightless cell cause her such grief?

"Edwin," she whispered hoarsely, touching his cheek. "Is any book worth imprisonment?"

Closing his eyes, he covered her hand with his own. "Let me explain. Please."

Jane led him to the wooden bench at the far end of her garden. She loved this spot. Vines of morning glories bloomed on a trellis behind the bench, and on temperate evenings such as this, she liked to sit and read while bees, butterflies, and hummingbirds busied themselves among the heart-shaped leaves and purple-blue flowers.

Edwin joined her on the bench and withdrew his hand. "I'm called The Templar because the men in my family have been Templars since the Order was founded. Not every Alcott male. Only those who've felt the calling. What do you know of the Templars, Jane?"

"I read up on them after I heard your nickname for the first time," Jane admitted. "The Templars were formed by a French nobleman who wanted to protect pilgrims journeying to Jerusalem. These people were being robbed, injured, or attacked en route to the Holy City, so Hugues de Payens and a group of fellow knights pledged to surrender their worldly goods and devote their lives to ensure safe passage for anyone on a pilgrimage to Jerusalem." She paused, waiting for Edwin to interject or add to her narrative. When he didn't, she continued. "The Templars received the blessing of the Pope and were later supported by both kings and popes. The order was involved in the Crusades, some of which were successful campaigns while others were not. Following a terrible defeat in the final Crusade, Pope Clement the Fifth decreed that the Templars were to be disbanded, and many brave and devout men were tortured or executed as heretics."

"A solid summary," Edwin said approvingly. "But there is much more to the Templars than can ever be found online or in books. We have many divisions and many secrets. And each faction has its own goals and treasures."

Jane thought of Lionel Alcott's diary. "Your great-grandfather was pursuing one of these treasures, wasn't he? In his diary, he talks about his long sea voyage and how he traveled by cart and by camel. He never says where he's going or what he hopes to retrieve." She shook her head. "I've read plenty of fantastical stories about the legendary treasures of the Templars, but those tales remind me of Indiana Jones movie plots. I know there are people who believe that the Templars have the Holy Grail, King Arthur's sword, mountains of gold, and priceless religious relics hidden away in some secret location, but I've never been one of those people."

"That's because the Templars didn't place value in gold. To them, the greatest treasure was knowledge," Edwin said. "Our order was actually established several years before Hugues de Payens came along. The goal of the original Templars was to preserve sacred knowledge. Not just Christian materials, but materials from all faiths. The founders, one of whom was an ancestor of mine, believed there was value in every sacred text. They believed there would only be peace between cultures if the knowledge contained within these ancient texts was combined. To them, this union of all faiths was the only path to enlightenment. I know it sounds a little flaky to our modern ears, but they truly believed this. This philosophy also compelled them to preserve certain secular writings too, especially in the fields of medicine and science."

Jane was fascinated. "I'd never heard this version of their history."

"As time passed and the Templars gained fame for their banking and fighting skills, only a handful of men devoted to the order's *original* purpose remained." Edwin said trying to complete his speech as quickly as possible. "After the persecution of the Templars in the fourteenth century, this splinter cell, for lack of a better term, was thought to have been completely eradicated."

Having read multiple volumes about the Inquisition in her lifetime, Jane knew that the extermination of these men was likely brutal and inhumane. "But why?" she asked. "What threat did the Templars pose?"

"They were a highly trained fighting force under no ruler's authority. They controlled large parcels of land, had multiple strongholds scattered across Britain and Europe's mainland, and both monarchs and powerful noblemen owed them huge sums of money. By getting rid of the Templars, these men could absolve themselves of debt, put aside any worry over being attacked by an independent army, and reclaim the lands they'd once donated to the Templars. And so they did."

Even though these events had occurred hundreds of years ago, Jane felt inexplicably sad. "These knights gave up all they had to protect innocent travelers, but in the end, they were treated like criminals. Worse. They were treated like traitors."

"It's more complicated than that, but I don't have time to go into detail now. Suffice it to say, my order was not eradicated during the reign of Pope Clement. We simply went underground. Our name has changed throughout the centuries, but our mission remains the same. Lionel Alcott's mission. My mission. I swore an oath to preserve rare and important materials like your Gutenberg Bible. Several months ago, I mailed you a missing page because your Bible needs to be made whole. I then returned to the Middle East to recover another page, but I underestimated the security system in a sheik's compound. Let's just say that this sheik did not appreciate my sudden appearance in his pleasure garden."

A corner of Edwin's mouth twitched, but Jane found nothing amusing about his capture. "I didn't ask you to take such a risk. Why didn't you just tell me your plans before jetting back across the ocean?"

Edwin shook his head. "Because it wasn't about you, Jane. I got a lead from a reliable source about one of the missing pages, and I had to respond. It's my calling." He unknotted his black tie and roughly yanked it off. He then swiftly unbuttoned the top five buttons of his white dress shirt and pulled down the left side to reveal a tattoo on his chest, an inch away from his heart. Jane half expected to see a Templar cross, but Edwin's tattoo was a tree. A tree that grew both above and below the earth. "You have your symbol and I have mine," he said. "This tree represents the belief that knowledge can unite all cultures."

Involuntarily, the fingers of Jane's right hand moved toward the swell of her left breast, where Sinclair had tattooed her with the mark of a Guardian: an owl with a scroll clasped in its talons. Edwin had seen it the night he and Jane had danced alone in the Great Gatsby Ballroom. He'd lowered her in a dip and the movement had caused her gown to slip, showing more décolletage than Jane had wanted to reveal that evening. It had also bared part of her owl tattoo. At the time, Jane wasn't sure if Edwin had seen the owl. Now she knew that not only had he seen it, but he'd also recognized it.

Suddenly, the few inches of bench separating them felt like a thousand feet. "How much do you know?"

"Everything," he said. "Other than a detailed catalog of the treasures in your secret library, that is. I know where the library is located, and I can imagine, having seen the long chain you wear around your neck nearly every day, how one could gain access to the library turret." Edwin smiled at her and Jane tensed. Was this all a ploy to get her key? "Don't worry," he said soothingly. "I don't intend to *steal* from your collection. Quite the opposite. My goal is to *add* items to it. And if I can, to restore damaged or incomplete materials."

"Why us? Why not help a museum?" Jane asked. "Why commit crimes for . . ." She trailed off, studying him. "Whom *do* you work for?"

"I do help museums. Universities and libraries too. As long as they have someone to finance a mission," Edwin said nonchalantly. "But I steal from such institutions as well. No person or place is off limits. I'd rob the Queen of England if she had a page of your Gutenberg Bible."

Jane frowned. "I don't understand."

"My aim is to make the scrolls, documents, and books whole again. To bring the fragments together," Edwin explained while buttoning his shirt.

"And who deserves to own a restored item?" Jane wanted to know.

Edwin gazed up at the sky and sighed mournfully. "Therein lies the rub. Not many. The individuals in my order. Guardians like yourself. A few librarians and a rare curator or two. Everyone else can be bought, so no one else is trustworthy."

Jane's head was spinning. She still wasn't sure if Edwin was a good guy or not. His explanation sounded implausible. And yet her own story was equally unbelievable. If someone had told her a year ago that there was a secret library containing rare and priceless works in the highest turret of Storyton Hall, Jane would have assumed the person was drunk or had read far too many fantasy novels. But the secret library *was* fantastical. It was like passing through C.S. Lewis's magical wardrobe into a treasure trove that writers like J.R.R. Tolkien, Enid Blyton, Robin Sloan, and J.K. Rowling could only imagine.

"How do you know about things that are *supposed* to be secret?" Jane asked with an edge of steel to her tone. She felt naked and vulnerable sitting next to this man who possessed more knowledge about the Steward family than he had a right to possess.

"Storyton Hall is a stronghold," Edwin said reverently. "My order was delivering materials to this sanctuary long before Walter Edgerton Steward dismantled his manor house in the English countryside and rebuilt it here." Edwin held Jane's gaze for a moment before glancing at his watch. "My time is up."

Jane jumped to her feet and walked behind the bench. Tracing the silky petals on a morning glory blossom, she tried to organize her tumultuous thoughts. Finally, she said,

"Our goals aren't the same, Edwin. You want to hide these works while I want to share them. People record their thoughts intending for them to be read. Words. Stories. Ideas. Personal histories. They belong to everyone. No one has the right to decide who is worthy of possessing them."

"Have you spoken to your great-uncle about this?" Edwin asked sharply.

There was no point in lying, so Jane said, "Yes, and he was open to putting the herbal on display. If that was a success, my next move was going to be contacting Sotheby's about auctioning a few items. I have dreams for Storyton Hall. Dreams that require money. If I sell a couple of books, those books will finally be read, *and* my coffers might be filled to the point where I can make some significant changes around here." She turned to face Edwin again. "So you see, we're not exactly compatible."

Smiling, he got to his feet and came around the bench until he was standing very close to her. "By all means, hock an obscure poem or an English Bible. But you can't sell a rare incunabulum, a Gutenberg Bible that isn't supposed to exist, or an undiscovered Shakespeare play."

Jane stiffened. Did Edwin know about the play in their secret collection or was he guessing?

"If you put such an item up for sale, every book thief in the world would descend on Storyton. The precious works you vowed to protect would be at the mercy of the worst kind of scum—men who steal for monetary gain. They don't care about books, Jane. They'd rip pages right out of the binding if it meant increasing their profits."

Jane grimaced.

"I'm nothing like them." Edwin put his hands on her shoulders. "I want to preserve books. To restore them. And despite the minor mishap during my last mission, I was able to retrieve four missing pages from your Bible. I believe that leaves only four more for me to find."

Jane was astonished. "You'd search for the rest, even after what happened?"

"I've seen the inside of a number of cells." He grinned. "Unlike the thief who stole your herbal, I'm quite adept at lock picking." He traced her jawline with the tip of his index finger and his grin vanished. "I want to restore an important book, Jane, but I also want to show your family and the men pledged to defend you that I'm not a louse. I didn't return to Storyton last year by chance. I was instructed to do so by my order and I was furious. I saw it as a punishment for failing to fulfill a mission. I met you on the street a few days after my return. Do you remember?"

Jane would never forget a moment of that day. In her mind, she saw Edwin racing by her on horseback as he tried to stop a spooked mare whose rider had lost consciousness. Eventually, Edwin had seized the mare's bridle and brought her to a halt. The young lady was taken to Doc Lydgate's while Edwin searched for someone to identify her. The first person he'd run into had been Jane. He'd been brusque and agitated and she'd been shocked by both his rudeness and his inexplicable allure.

"I remember," she whispered, her hands moving to his waist.

"I'd never seen a more beautiful woman. And you were fearless. You immediately took charge and were so protective of that stranger. I could tell that you were a woman of courage and conviction. A rare woman. And when I discovered you were the sole heir of Storyton Hall, I knew that you would one day be named its Guardian. So my penance became a boon. Because of you, Jane. Because you are everything I have ever wanted and everything I could ever hope for. And now you know what I am." His hand traveled down the curve of her neck and followed the slope of her shoulder, raising gooseflesh along her skin. "I am yours, if you'll have me."

Jane knew that she could not enter into a relationship with a thief. She couldn't allow herself to love a man who jetted around the world stealing rare books while pretending to run a café in Storyton. His own sister believed that he was a part-time travel writer. How could Jane lie to her best friend? To her sons?

And yet Jane's heart disregarded these arguments. All her heart knew was how much it had missed this man. Her body had missed his touch. She had missed his wry smile. Talking books with him. Watching him interact with the twins. She'd missed the chance to know him better, and she didn't want to miss another moment.

"I don't see how this is going to work," she whispered. "But right now, I don't care. Just kiss me, Edwin. Show me what you thought about while you were in that prison."

His smile was wolfish. "I don't think we have time for that, but I'll do my best to convince you that my mind, body, and soul were completely fixed on you."

For several minutes, Jane forgot about the theft of the herbal, Kira's death, and the ongoing wedding. There was only Edwin. The taste of his mouth and the touch of his hands on her body. She wanted to stay in this garden with him for the rest of the night, but she didn't have that luxury.

Gently, she pulled away. "We need to go back," she said, raking her fingers through her tangled hair. "It's almost time for the bride and groom's send-off and I have a thief to catch."

"Let me help you." Edwin tucked a wayward curl behind Jane's ear.

Jane became very still. "I won't grant you access to our secret collection."

"I wouldn't dream of asking you," Edwin said solemnly. "Your vow is as sacred as mine. And nearly as ancient. I only ask to be of service to you. Like a knight to his lady." And with that, he bent over her hand and kissed it.

It was such a theatrical gesture that Jane broke out in a laugh.

"What? Too much?" Edwin asked.

"Definitely," Jane said and laughed again. "Come on, Sir Alcott."

They headed for the garden gate, where they found Muffet Cat proudly guarding the corpse of a large mole.

"Well done," Edwin said approvingly, and Muffet Cat arched his back, rubbed up against the gate, and purred. "Does this mean I've passed his character test?"

"Either that or he smells catfish," Jane said, stepping over the dead rodent and hurrying toward the lights of Storyton Hall.

TEN

As Jane and Edwin approached Milton's Gardens, they heard raucous cheers erupt from the other side of the hedge.

"Oh dear," Jane said. "I think we just missed the tossing of the bridal bouquet."

Edwin understood her concern. "And the send-off of the bride and groom."

"Maybe the party won't break up right away," Jane said hopefully. "Many guests continue to eat, drink, and dance once the newly married couple have left the reception."

However, when the boisterous shouts faded, the band did not resume playing.

"We should split up." Jane felt her panic rise. "The thief might retrieve the book on the way back to his or her room."

"Tell me which of the herbalists is missing so I can search for them," Edwin said.

Entering the clearing where the feast had taken place, Jane saw that the majority of the guests were dispersing. Only Carson's friends were continuing to celebrate. They'd carried glasses and several bottles of wine into the gazebo and looked to be settling in for at least another hour or two of revelry.

"The herbalists are gone," Jane said miserably. "Except for Hannah. She's sharing a bench with Tom Green. Do you see them? There, in that secluded little nook opposite the sundial."

Edwin peered into the gloom. "I believe he's comforting her."

"Poor Hannah," Jane whispered. "But I have to leave her in Tom's hands. With all the herbalists gone, I now need to meet with—" She was going to use the word "staff" when she suddenly wondered if Edwin knew about the Fins as well.

Edwin took Jane by the elbow and gently turned her to face him. As though answering her unspoken question, he said, "Ask Mr. Sinclair about the origin of his order. Perhaps you'll understand why he was willing to give me a chance. I know you're not ready to trust me yet, so I'll stay away until you are." He leaned in and brushed her lips with a feather-light kiss. "I'm not sure if a man with so many secrets has a right to fall in love. But when I met you—a woman who is my equal and, in many aspects, my better—I dared to hope that it was possible. I dared to hope that I'd found the woman I'd been searching for my entire life." He released her. "You should go, but if the Fins are concerned about my skulking around the resort, please tell them that I'm looking for the herbal."

At the mention of the missing book, Jane snapped back to reality. She felt as though Edwin had been using his words and his kiss to cast a spell over her, and she wasn't ready to succumb to his charms. There was far too much information for her to process about Edwin Alcott, so she stepped away from him and whispered, "Good night."

Without looking back, Jane hurried into Storyton Hall. There were only two Medieval Herbalists in the lobby.

Though Constance Meredith and Tammy Kota were standing next to a floral arrangement opposite the elevator bay,
they were in no apparent rush to return to their guest rooms.
Both women had flushed cheeks and were speaking to each
other in low tones.

Jane decided to wish both ladies a pleasant evening and
proceed to the security room. In her current mood, she
couldn't trust herself to be cordial to the Poison Princess,
and she was eager to hear whether Sterling had finished
compiling a list of suspects based on which Medieval Herbalists had left the wedding reception to enter Storyton Hall
after the entrees had been served.

"Ms. Steward!" Tammy called out upon seeing Jane.
"Could you help us out?"

Constance murmured something to Tammy, but Tammy
ignored her.

Tammy beckoned to Jane. "I need to tell someone else
about this or I won't be able to sleep."

"Why won't you listen to me?" Constance was clearly
put out. "It was just the booze talking. That little man just
wants to be noticed. He's trying to impress us. I've met
hundreds of people like him. They're a dime a dozen, especially in dead-end towns like this." Constance released an
exasperated sigh. "But if it makes you feel better, then tell
the lady of the manor. As for me, I'm turning in. Claude
promised us that *extra* excursion tomorrow."

Wriggling her eyebrows in a taunting manner, Constance
crossed the hallway and pushed the elevator call button.
When the elevator doors opened, Jane indulged in a brief
fantasy in which she struck Constance with a flying sidekick,
propelling her into the cab with such force that she would
slam into the back wall before crumpling to the floor in a
heap. Instead, she turned to Tammy and asked, "Which little
man is Ms. Meredith referring to? Mr. Green?"

Tammy caught the note of disapproval in Jane's voice.

"Connie doesn't mean to cause offense. She's lacking in people skills, but she's a good egg."

Jane scowled. "She gave a mandrake root to my sons earlier today. They're seven, so forgive me for not being a fan of hers." She shifted impatiently, something she rarely did in front of guests. "What is it you wanted to tell me about Mr. Green?"

"Well, like I said, he'd been drinking pretty steadily all night, so it's hard for me to judge if what he told me is true, but . . ." she trailed off and waved her hands as though attempting to erase her words. "Let me start from the beginning. I went to sit with Mr. Green after dessert because he seemed lonely. And sad. He was staring into his wineglass like he could read the future in it, and he didn't care for what he saw."

Jane frowned. "That doesn't sound like Tom."

"During our hike, Claude pressured him to take us to the druid," Tammy said. "He could have told Claude no, but Claude promised him automatic membership if Tom agreed to lead us to the druid's garden. It's supposed to be wonderful. We even volunteered to be blindfolded."

Despite her concern over the stolen book, Jane was intrigued. "Did Tom agree?"

"Yes. We're going tomorrow." Tammy couldn't conceal her eagerness. "We're not supposed to tell anyone about the visit. We're supposed to act like we're heading into the village to shop and have lunch, but what we'll really be doing is meeting at Mr. Green's plant store for a trip into the hills." She smiled. "Claude would blow a gasket if he knew I was sharing this with you, but I know I can trust you, Ms. Steward. I'm good at reading people and you give off a very positive vibe."

"Thank you," Jane said, returning Tammy's smile. "And I understand why a visit to the druid's garden would appeal to your group. But why is Tom glum? Has the druid refused to see you?"

Tammy seemed surprised by the question. "You know,

I got the sense that Mr. Green wasn't planning to ask his permission. He was simply going to show up with us. Maybe that's what troubling him, but there was something else. Something unrelated to the druid stuff. Mr. Green kept telling me how sorry he was for my loss. Referring to Kira, of course. None of us had mentioned her because we were trying to focus on Victoria and on keeping things positive for her wedding. But after a few glasses of wine, this man who never even knew Kira couldn't stop saying her name. It was unnerving."

Does Tom know something about Kira's murder? Jane wondered

"I'm not any pointing fingers," Tammy was quick to add. "I chatted with Mr. Green during our hike and he seems like a sweet guy, but if I didn't know better, I'd say he felt guilty about something. I'm sure it's because he agreed to take us to the druid— we heard how much the fellow covets his privacy. Still, I wish Mr. Green hadn't mentioned Kira so often. It was weird."

Jane laid a hand over Tammy's. "Maybe Tom was looking for an outlet for some grief of his own. I can't say for certain—I'm grabbing at straws—but what if he suffered a loss too and was hoping that by bringing up Kira, he could share his feelings with you? You're kind and approachable, Tammy, so I could see why he would have chosen to make himself vulnerable to you."

Tammy looked stricken. "But I didn't give him the chance. I kept changing the subject because I didn't want the atmosphere to turn heavy."

"Which was the right call," Jane assured her. "For Victoria's sake. If it's any comfort, Tom and Hannah are sitting on a garden bench this very moment. I suspect Tom will find all the compassion he needs from Hannah and vice versa."

"The universe has ways of working things out," Tammy said, instantly brightening. "Thank you. *Now* I can sleep!"

Jane hesitated. She was tempted to ask Tammy about the missing book, but decided against it. Instead, she said, "You might not believe this, but I've never seen the druid. In truth, I hadn't even heard of him until your group arrived."

Tammy was clearly astonished. "You're kidding me!"

"In light of what happened to Kira, I believe it's important for me to meet him," Jane said gravely. "I'm not insinuating that the druid had anything to do with her death, but to those of us at Storyton Hall, he's an enigma, and we want to be able to say that we followed every possible lead." Tammy looked doubtful, so Jane pressed on. "It would just be me, following from a distance. If there's nothing suspicious to be seen, I'll leave and no one will be the wiser. I know you don't want me to tell Sheriff Evans about the hike, but I have to do all I can to seek justice for Kira. You want that too, don't you?"

Tears pooled in Tammy's eyes. "You'll have to be really careful. Mr. Green warned us that he'd call off the whole thing if we didn't follow his rules to the letter."

"He'll have no idea I'm there," Jane promised. She was about to bid Tammy goodnight when she suddenly thought to ask, "How *did* your group hear about this druid? He's such a guarded secret in these parts. Thousands of visitors have come through Storyton without learning of his existence, so how is it that The Medieval Herbalists knew about him?"

"The first whisper I heard of a druid was on our hike," Tammy said. "Connie told me about him on the way back to the resort. She was bubbling over with excitement."

The grandfather clock in the lobby began to ring out the hour. The deep, low notes reverberated through the vast space. To Jane, the sound was unusually ominous. Time was not on her side. In two days, The Medieval Herbalists were scheduled to leave. The sheriff couldn't hold them all without sufficient cause, and unless Jane and the Fins discovered evidence to incriminate a specific person, one of them was going to get away with murder.

"Why was Ms. Meredith excited?" Jane asked as she escorted Tammy to the elevator bay.

Tammy pressed the call button and said, "Because the druid is supposed to have a secret garden. A walled garden filled with all sorts of the most wondrous—and most deadly—poisonous plants."

Jane burst into the security room. Slamming the door shut behind her, she searched the faces of the men who'd turned to look at her.

"Please tell me that you found the thief and I have one less thing to worry about," she said.

"I'm afraid not, Miss Jane." Butterworth gestured at the empty chair next to his. "However, we've narrowed down the suspects to three individuals."

Hearing this manageable number, Jane felt a surge of hope. "And they are?"

"Mr. Mason, Captain Hughes, and Ms. Kota."

Jane groaned. She genuinely liked all three of those people. "Why couldn't Ms. Meredith's name be on that list?"

"Disappointing, I know," Sinclair said. "And we can't ignore the fact that Captain Hughes and Ms. Kota appear on another list."

Sinclair was referring to his research into the financial health of each of the Medieval Herbalists. Both Phil and Tammy were short on funds and, therefore, had a powerful motive to steal a rare book.

Butterworth indicated the wall of television screens. "Those three guests had the opportunity to enter the library, steal the herbal, stash it elsewhere, and return to the wedding reception."

"Because the herbal is such a small book, it could easily fit in the waist band of a gentleman's pants or in a ladies' handbag," Sinclair said mournfully. "We'll search the closest reading rooms when we're finished here. Mr. Lachlan has already checked the lobby restrooms."

Jane tried to imagine where she might hide a valuable book until she could secret it away from the resort. "How will the thief get the herbal out of Storyton Hall? Surely, he or she expects us to search every scrap of luggage following the theft of such a valuable book."

"Unless he doesn't have luggage." Sterling pointed at a still shot of Captain Phil. "Storyton's newest resident wouldn't need to stash the herbal. He could simply leave it in his jacket pocket until he arrives at home."

"*If* the captain is our thief, he'll have to figure out how to sell a stolen rare book," Sinclair said. "That is no simple task. Any book dealer worth his salt will want a record of the book's provenance."

"All three of our suspects face the same challenge. None of them can just list the book on eBay and hope for the best. Selling it will take careful planning," Jane said. "I think we need to place a call to Storyton's post mistress as soon as she opens for business on Monday."

Butterworth grunted in approval. "Good thinking, Miss Jane. Mr. Mason or Ms. Kota might mail the book to avoid being caught with it on their person."

"What about Captain Hughes?" Sterling asked. "He'll be much harder to investigate."

Jane had no ready answer for this problem. She and the Fins exchanged doleful looks until Sinclair drew their attention to the calendar affixed to the wall near the door. It showed a photograph of a man sitting in a rowboat in the lake behind the resort. He was stretched out across the length of the boat with his hat covering his face and a book splayed on his chest. His fishing pole dangled unattended in the water. It was a scene of utmost relaxation. A languid summer day with no responsibilities. No meetings to attend. No phone calls or e-mails to answer. Just a man succumbing to the sun warming his skin and the gentle rocking of a boat. A man napping away the afternoon. A man without a care in the world. How Jane envied him.

"Thoreau said something like, 'Men go fishing all of their lives without knowing that it is not fish they are after,'" Sinclair said. "Perhaps your great-uncle is best suited to the task of investigating the captain. From what I've heard, a compatible fishing partner must read his mate's moods. He must know when to talk and when to be quiet. Your uncle has fished for most of his life. He claims to be able to judge a man based on the lures he uses."

"In that case, we should line up all the Medieval Herbalists and subject them to an inspection by either Muffet Cat or Uncle Aloysius. Why didn't we think of this before? The murderer could already be behind bars," Jane groused, but immediately regretted her behavior. "Forgive me, Sinclair. I'm angry, overwhelmed, and tired. Sending my uncle to speak with Captain Phil is an excellent idea." She turned to Lachlan. "He won't be the only one spending time outdoors tomorrow. You and I are going hiking in the morning."

Confused, Lachlan reached for his phone. "Did the herbalists schedule a last-minute excursion?"

"You could say that," Jane said. "Tom Green is taking them to see the druid. According to Tammy Kota, it's supposed to be a secret. She only told me because Tom was acting a bit odd toward the end of the wedding feast. He'd had too much to drink and kept mentioning Kira's name. I tried to put Tammy's concerns to rest by making up a theory about Tom processing a loss of his own, but I don't believe that. What if the wine allowed his real emotions to come through? And what if that emotion was guilt?"

"The tire tracks," Lachlan said, his gaze on Sterling. "Could Mr. Green's delivery van be a match?"

Sterling stared at him. "Tom Green? A murderer?" Jane could see his entire body stiffen in protest over the idea.

"I'll look into it. Of course I will. It's just that Tom's been delivering flowers to Storyton Hall for over a decade. He's a soft-spoken, amiable guy." Sterling glanced at Sinclair. "We've done background checks on all the locals. Nothing in Tom Green's history has raised concerns before, has it?"

"No," Sinclair said. "Mr. Butterworth? Has Mr. Green's body language altered as of late?"

"On one occasion. When he returned from hiking with the herbalists, he looked like a different man." Butterworth said. "The Mr. Green from that morning was in high spirits. His face was bright with anticipation and his head was held high. The man who came back to Storyton Hall focused his gaze on the ground. His eyes were dull. His gait was hesitant and his shoulders drooped. It wasn't because he was physically fatigued either. Mr. Green was troubled and we know why. He was offered membership into a society he was most eager to join in exchange for taking the herbalists to the druid."

Jane pressed her fingers to her throbbing temples. She was ready to take some aspirin and call it a night. Sensing her need, Sterling opened a desk drawer and took out a bottle of ibuprofen. After swallowing several tablets, Jane outlined her plan. "Tomorrow, Lachlan and I will follow the herbalists into the hills behind the village. Lachlan should have no difficulty tracking a group of their size." She gave Lachlan an encouraging smile. "While we're gone, there's still so much to be done. Sterling, will you examine the tires on Tom's truck?" At Sterling's nod, Jane turned to Butterworth. "You and Sinclair can search the guest and reading rooms for the missing herbal. I don't expect you to find it, but we have to try."

Butterworth inclined his head. "Agreed."

Finally, Jane looked at Sinclair. "Edwin Alcott has offered his assistance. Since I'm not sure if I can trust him, I declined for now, but he told me to ask about the origin of the Fins."

"I thought he might," Sinclair said.

"Why?" Jane asked, wishing the pills she had taken would work faster.

Sinclair spread his hands. "Because the Fins were once Templars. Like the Freemasons, the Fins separated from the Templars to pursue a different mission. Our forefathers and Mr. Alcott's forefathers were allies. That's what he wants you to know."

"A link from centuries ago doesn't mean that we should trust him," Butterworth muttered.

"Only Miss Jane can make that decision," Sinclair said.

Jane thanked each of the Fins for their tireless work and then informed them that she was through with making decisions for the day. "I need to rest," she told them. "Not only do I have to hike for who knows how many miles to find this mystical druid, but I also have to tell Uncle Aloysius that the very first book I took from the secret library to share with the public has been stolen."

"Would you like me to walk you home?" Lachlan asked politely.

"Thank you, but I prefer to be alone," Jane said. "Part of me hopes that someone will jump out of the bushes and attack me. It's been frustrating enough to make so little progress in solving Kira's murder and now, someone dares to steal a book from our library—!" Too irate to continue, she twisted the doorknob and flung open the door. "Let's just say I'm spoiling for a fight."

The next morning, after the twins polished off a breakfast of strawberry pancakes topped with banana slices, they prepared to attend the early church service with Aunt Octavia and Uncle Aloysius.

"Why aren't you coming with us, Mom?" Fitz asked, eyeing his mother's green T-shirt and cargo pants.

"I have to work," Jane answered. "Be good in Sunday School. A little bird told me that a new shipment of audio books is supposed to arrive at Run for Cover on Monday. I believe one of them is the next book in the Harry Potter series."

Hem bounced on his heels and then elbowed his brother. "Do you think we have enough money?"

Fitz closed his eyes and performed some mental calculations, his lips moving as he pictured the crumpled dollar bills and loose change on the top of his bureau. "It depends how much we put in the offering plate," he whispered to Hem.

Though Jane was tempted to intervene, she wanted to see what decision her sons would arrive at without her influence.

"We can't give less because we want something," Hem whispered after a long pause.

Fitz looked disappointed, but nodded his head in agreement. Suddenly, he brightened. "Maybe we could ask Mrs. Hubbard to pay us early. I bet she would."

"That isn't a good idea," Jane said gently. "If you spend money that you haven't earned yet, then you might not do your best work."

Hem was affronted. "We would so!"

"Yeah," Fitz added with a scowl. "We like the garden!"

Jane tried not to smile. "It's wonderful that you're both taking such pride in your work. It really is. So let's do this: Keep your offering the same and, if I hear a good report from Aunt Octavia about Sunday School, I'll lend you the money for the Harry Potter audiobook. You can pay me back on Friday after you collect your hard-earned dollars from Mrs. Hubbard."

"Isn't that the same thing as spending money we haven't earned?" Hem asked.

"There's a difference between getting a payday advance from an employer and a loan from your mother," Jane said. Seeing the baffled expression on the twins' faces, she threw back her head and laughed. "I'll explain these tricky financial terms another time. Come on, we don't want to keep Aunt Octavia waiting."

As the little family headed outside, Fitz stopped by the garden gate to collect a plastic bucket.

Jane peered in at the contents. The bucket was stuffed with dandelions. The plants were slightly shriveled, but not dead because their roots were soaking in several inches of muddy water.

"What are you doing with this?" she asked.

"We're bringing the dandelions to Pig Newton," Fitz said. "For his Sunday supper."

Jane took the bucket from him, as she didn't want the dirty water to slosh out of the bucket and onto his church pants. She shooed the boys through the gate. "You two run ahead. Get your wiggles out!"

Fitz scooped a stick off the ground and pointed it at Hem. "I'm going to turn you into a newt!" He shouted some nonsense words followed by a shrill squeaking sound.

"Oh, yeah?" Hem grabbed his own stick and parried the attack with more nonsense words and a low, rumbling noise. "I'll block your spell with an instant fog!"

Watching her two sons race across the wide swath of green lawn, Jane felt, for just a moment, that all was right with the world.

Two hours later, Jane leaned against the trunk of a black oak tree and drank thirstily from her water bottle. She and Lachlan had been hiking for over an hour, moving steadily south by southeast. Because they had climbed up and up into the hills, Jane felt as though they were traveling north, so she was completely turned around.

For a time, there had been a clear path. The villagers maintained several miles of walking trails, but those were all on lower elevations.

The lack of trails didn't bother Lachlan one bit. He continued to surge forward, pointing out broken branches and crushed plants left in the wake of Tom Green and The Medieval Herbalists.

At the beginning of their hike, Lachlan had offered Jane a walking stick. She'd refused it at first, having never needed one before, but he'd insisted that she take it.

"It's a good thing to carry in the summer," Lachlan said, pressing the stick into Jane's hand. "There are snakes in these woods. Thorns too. Not to mention poison ivy, poison sumac, and dozens of spider webs. Once we leave the trail, we'll be doing plenty of bushwhacking. You'll be glad of this stick at that point. Trust me."

Jane had been glad of the stick. She'd already used it to keep a seemingly endless supply of brambles and cobwebs away from her face and hair.

Now, Jane leaned on it as she climbed over a cluster of uneven rocks. Ahead of her, Lachlan suddenly stopped and peered down at the ground.

"What is it?" Jane asked. She tried not to sound out of breath, but she was having a hard time keeping pace with Lachlan.

"Someone is riding a horse," he said.

Jane looked from the pile of droppings to Lachlan. "It must be Hannah. She could never make this hike on foot."

"This guy's garden must be a sight to behold for these herbalists to go through this much trouble. I know they garden and take nature walks, but this is a completely different kind of hike." Lachlan squinted up the hill. "People like them don't venture into the wild."

Because she sensed that he was right, and because she needed to conserve her oxygen, Jane said nothing. For a time, they descended instead of climbing, and just when Jane felt there would be no end to their hike, Lachlan raised his hand in a fist and halted. He then sank to his knees and put his finger to his lips. He then used his free hand to point at a clearing up ahead. They'd found the druid.

Her fatigue forgotten, Jane took a pair of binoculars out of her backpack and peered through them. She saw a log cabin with a front porch facing a large vegetable garden. The cabin appeared well built and tidy. There were two wooden rocking chairs on the porch and the morning breeze tickled a tuneless melody from a bamboo wind chime. Firewood was stacked neatly along one side of the house and chickens scratched at the ground around an enclosed coop.

The Medieval Herbalists were nowhere in sight. Other than the chickens, Jane didn't see another living creature until Tom Green abruptly exited the cabin through the front door. A second man was close at his heels. If Jane had expected the druid to sport a lush beard, a robe, and a cowl, she was to be disappointed. This man was clean-shaven and wore jeans and a T-shirt. Judging from his red face and dramatic gesticulations, he was also very angry.

Tom wheeled around to face the druid.

The two men were now only inches apart.

Jane inhaled sharply. "Good Lord!" she whispered to Lachlan. "The druid looks just like Tom. If I didn't know better, I'd say they were . . ." she trailed off, lowering her binoculars in shock. "Brothers."

ELEVEN

"The druid's taller, but he looks like an older version of Tom," Lachlan whispered.

"A much older version," Jane said. "The druid has lots of gray in his hair and beard. I don't think they're brothers. Maybe father and son."

The druid was shouting now. Jane couldn't make out the words, but his meaning was clear enough. Judging by his red face and the direction in which he pointed, he wanted Tom to take the herbalists and go. With a final yell, he turned his back on Tom and stormed into his cabin.

Tom threw his arms up in defeat. He then crossed the yard and headed down a path descending through a tall field of grass.

"According to the survey maps I found in the library, there should be a stream at the end of that path," Lachlan said. "I can see why the druid built his homestead here. It's a good location for horticulture, there's a fresh water supply, and he even has a hot spring nearby for bathing."

"So he grows his own food, raises chickens, and produces

medicine. There are also several large sheds on the other side of his cabin." Jane swept the area with her binoculars. "I wonder what he keeps inside."

Lachlan jerked. "I don't know, but it's time for us to move. Here comes Ms. Billingsley. She's on a pony and the rest of her friends are right behind her."

Jane swung her binoculars around to where she'd last seen Tom. He was now back in the yard, waving for the herbalists to follow Hannah.

"That isn't one of Sam's ponies," Jane murmured. "He doesn't own a pinto."

"We didn't see a horse trailer by The Potter's Shed either," Lachlan said. "The pony must have been dropped off for Hannah and been tethered to the fence near the trail entrance. This was a highly coordinated excursion."

The pony began climbing the grassy embankment, heading directly for them. Lachlan elbowed Jane and pointed at a copse of trees to her right.

Jane grabbed her backpack and scurried in a half crouch until she was squatting behind a trunk. "What if they come this way?" she asked Lachlan.

"They won't," he assured her. "Too many stones. The pony might slip. Mr. Green will lead them to that break in the pine trees. The rise is gentler."

They watched Tom hurry around the pony's side and grab hold of its bridle.

"I was just starting to enjoy myself," Constance Meredith complained loudly. "What a treasure trove! And I had so many questions! Tammy did too. Why did we have to leave so suddenly?"

"I'm sorry, Ms. Meredith," Tom called back over his shoulder. "I warned you about this possibility. The druid doesn't welcome visitors to his home. You're lucky you were able to see as much as you did."

"We don't mean to sound ungrateful," Vivian Ash said.

"It's just so rare for us to meet someone with as much knowledge of the natural world as your friend, but it was very kind of you to arrange this excursion. It was a truly unforgettable event. Thank you."

From her hiding place, Jane couldn't see Tom's face, but she wondered if he still viewed the herbalists as being above him. Half of them were sulking, while the other half just looked exhausted. Especially Hannah. She was abnormally pale and Jane wondered if Hannah thought the trip was worth the pain she was undoubtedly feeling.

Lachlan was right. This group isn't used to hiking in the wilderness, Jane thought. *How will they find the energy to run the medieval fair later today?*

Tom headed exactly where Lachlan had predicted he'd go. Lachlan sat utterly still, watching, until the last herbalist was out of sight. He didn't speak at all. After tracking the group for another fifteen minutes, he finally whispered, "They're out of range."

It had been well over thirty minutes since the druid had kicked Tom and the herbalists off his land, and he had yet to reemerge from his cabin.

"What now?" Lachlan asked.

Jane was just about to say that she hadn't come all this way to leave without talking to the druid. She had to stand on his doorstep and see how he'd respond to Kira's name. She didn't have the chance to explain this to Lachlan, however, because at that moment, a muted scream of agony made her forget her plans.

"Where did that come from?" With her heart hammering in her chest, Jane glanced around. She pictured Hannah on the ground, having fallen off the pony and seriously hurting her back or neck.

Lachlan stood up. "The cabin," he said, reaching down to take Jane's hand. He hauled her to her feet and began to move. She followed, copying his slouched jog and the way his gaze darted left and right, constantly assessing their environment.

As they neared the cabin, another scream echoed from inside.

"He must in terrible pain," Jane said, ready to kick in the door and rush to the druid's aid. The sound was unlike anything she'd ever heard. It made her heart wrench to think that such a bestial howl came from a human being.

Lachlan clearly didn't feel the same way. He thrust his arm out to block her path. "An injured man is a dangerous man."

Jane stared into his haunted blue eyes and knew that while part of Landon Lachlan stood on the druid's front porch with her, the other part was back in Afghanistan or Iraq, reliving some covert operation. Reliving his own personal pain.

"We have to try to help him," she whispered.

Lachlan put his fingers to his lips and crossed the porch until his back was between the door and the window. Keeping his shoulder pressed against the wood, he cast a lightning-quick glance through the window. He then grabbed the door with one hand and beckoned Jane forward with the other.

"He's on the floor in the fetal position. His arms are crossed over his stomach," Lachlan whispered. "He's vomited. I don't think he has the strength to attack us, but be prepared to defend yourself in case I'm wrong. Remember your training. Keep your hands near your face and kick before you punch."

"Just get in there!" Jane cried and gave Lachlan a shove. He might be in Army Ranger mode, but she couldn't tolerate the pitiful groaning coming from the other side of the door.

Once inside the cabin, Lachlan kept his distance from the druid. He remained as tense as a threatened snake, but not Jane. She dropped to her knees next to the tortured man. "Sir? We're here to help. What can we do?"

The man's eyes were rolled so far back that the irises

were barely visible, giving him a ghastly, zombie-like appearance. He squeezed the lids shut and mouthed a word.

Jane couldn't hear, so she leaned in until her ear was close to the man's lips.

"Miss Jane," Lachlan warned but Jane hushed him.

"Char . . . coal," the man on the floor said in a half whisper, half moan. Unable to raise his hand, he pointed a crooked finger at a cabinet on the far side of the room.

Lachlan flung open the doors and began scanning the bottles, vials, and glass jars on the shelves. "Here!" He grabbed a plastic tub and showed it to Jane. "Activated charcoal."

"Tell me how to prepare it," Jane commanded.

Lachlan read the directions and Jane scrambled to fill a glass with water from the pitcher on the druid's kitchen table. She then mixed in the powered charcoal as quickly and thoroughly as possible. "Lift him up," she told Lachlan.

He got behind the druid and gently raised his shoulders. The man let out another shriek. Jane winced, but the hand holding the glass to the sick man's mouth didn't tremble. In her firmest mother's voice, she said, "Drink this. All of it."

The man tried. He swallowed once. "Arsenic," he croaked before Jane pressed the cup to his lips again. He managed a second swallow. However, his throat seemed to close and the third swallow came gurgling back out of his mouth. His eyes bulged and he stiffened in agony.

"What do we do?" Jane asked, her panic rising. "Either he chokes trying to drink this or the arsenic he ingested will kill him."

Lachlan locked eyes with her. "You have to get that into him. He's dying."

"I'm going to pour the charcoal into your mouth a little at a time," Jane said loudly, hoping the man could hear her through the pain. She nodded at Lachlan, who held the druid's head firmly in place while Jane opened his mouth and slowly emptied another two tablespoons of the mixture straight down his throat. His gag reflex kicked in and the muscles in his throat tightened. Black spittle flew across Jane's face. Without flinching, she continued to pour the contents into the druid's mouth, dribble by dribble.

By the time the glass was empty, black droplets were running down Jane's chin onto her T-shirt. She set the glass aside, wiped her face on her one dry sleeve, and took the man's hand. He began to thrash wildly. His grip became so powerful that Jane had to pull her hand away.

Lachlan did his best to hold the druid's head, but his entire body bucked and spasmed with such force that it became impossible.

And then, just as swiftly as the convulsions started, they stopped. The man lay on his braided rug, his eyes fixed on the ceiling, his blackened mouth stretched open in a soundless scream. He looked like a monster—a creature from a nightmare—until Lachlan leaned over and pushed the lids down over his sightless, lifeless eyes.

Jane sat back on her heels. She felt sick. The shock of the druid's abrupt and violent death combined with the odor of vomit and charcoal made her feel unbalanced. She focused on the weave of the rug under her hands and tried to breathe deeply through her mouth.

"Come away, Miss Jane." Lachlan eased her to her feet and led her outside. He settled her in a rocking chair on the front porch. He said nothing, but stood silently by her side, waiting for her to recover.

As for Jane, she stared across the druid's tidy yard to the break in the bushes where Tom Green had gone to fetch the herbalists. From this angle, she could see a clear path leading downhill.

To the walled garden, she thought. *The secret garden.*

The longer she stared at the green line of bushes, the better she felt.

"Poison," she said after what seemed like an eternity, though she'd only been outside for a few minutes.

"It looks that way." Lachlan studied her. He pulled a pair of latex gloves from his backpack and worked them onto his large hands. "I'm going to get a towel for your face."

He returned with a damp dishrag. The cool fabric felt wonderful against Jane's clammy skin. She cleaned herself up and then checked her reflection in the window behind the rocking chair. "You need to go for help," she said. "I'm assuming our cell phones are useless up here."

Lachlan nodded in confirmation. "We've crossed into the next county. Which means that this case won't fall in Storyton's jurisdiction."

"Then the Fins need to investigate first," Jane said. "Do you have more gloves?"

After giving her a pair, Lachlan dug out a bandanna from his pack. "Tie this over your mouth and nose," he said. "It'll help block the smell."

Leaving Jane to her preparations, he ran toward the largest shed. Jane snapped her gloves into place, tied the bandanna on, and moved to the cabin's doorway. The horrible scene laid out before her in the cabin's main room momentarily immobilized her, but she finally turned away and headed for the second room, which was a bedroom and storage loft. It was a comfortable space filled with ready-to-assemble furniture, two lamps, and a wardrobe. Jane had just opened the wardrobe and thumbed through some of the clothes when she heard the revving of an engine. Seconds later, Lachlan pulled up in front of the cabin riding a strange-looking motorcycle with large tires and a camouflage-design paint job.

Jane returned to the porch and pulled down her bandanna.

"The perfect hunter's bike," Lachlan said, patting the seat appreciatively. "Or vehicle for a man who wants to move about with stealth. This bike is designed to go off-road and is fairly quiet. It's not cheap either. Neither is the fully loaded ATV the druid has in that shed. I saw tracks leading south. I think this guy went over the mountain fairly regularly. I'm going to follow the tracks until I get a signal on my phone. I'll be back as soon as I can." He hesitated. "Will you be okay? I don't like to leave you."

"I'll be fine," Jane assured him. "There's something you need to do before you return." She held out her hand. "May I borrow your phone?"

Lachlan passed it over and waited for Jane to duck back into the cabin. When she reemerged, she showed him the photo she'd taken. It was of the small safe she'd found at the bottom of the druid's wardrobe. "It's locked, but we need to find out what's inside. I think we can conclude that either Tom Green or an herbalist poisoned the druid. But why? Because of what's locked in this safe? Because he murdered Kira? Hopefully, I'll have more answers by the time you come back, but if none of the Fins can crack this lock, then you'll have to ask for help."

"Who can break into a . . ." Lachlan understood before he even finished his sentence. "Edwin Alcott."

"I have no choice but to trust him." Jane prepared to replace the bandanna over her mouth and nose. "Be careful."

Lachlan pointed at the door. "Lock that behind you. I'll be as quick as I can."

Jane watched him go. When she reentered the cabin, she ignored his command. Instead, she left the door ajar and opened all the windows. She wanted the mountain air to sweep the foul stench out of the cabin, and she also took comfort in the outdoor noises. The birdsong and insect sawing. The squirrel chatter and the shrill cry of hawks. The sounds were so ordinary, so peaceful, compared to the sight of the druid's body as he lay, frozen in his final spasm, on the floor.

For the first time since her arrival, Jane really looked at

the main room. Like the bedroom, it contained several pieces of easy-assembly furniture, but it included a futon and a flat-screen television as well. There was also a gas stove, a sink, a refrigerator, and a coffeemaker, so the druid had his creature comforts.

And a powerful generator or two, Jane thought. Recalling what Lachlan had said about the druid's vehicles, the question of the druid's income now rose to the forefront of her mind.

She continued to scan the room, keeping her gaze off the dead man, until a white clamshell take-out box on the kitchen table caught her attention. Sleeves of identical boxes could be found in both the kitchens of Storyton Hall and in the Rudyard Kipling Café.

"Please, no," Jane whispered, opening the lid.

A fork sat in the middle of the box. There were several crumbs stuck to the fork and to the bottom of the box, but that was all. Jane raised the box to her nose and sniffed. She smelled honey. And more faintly, almonds.

"No, no," Jane repeated, lowering the box to the table again. She had little doubt that she'd just inhaled the sweet aroma of Victoria and Carson's wedding cake.

The take-out box was the only sign that the druid had recently eaten. Aside from an empty water glass next to the box, the rest of the kitchen was neat as a pin.

Jane turned from the table to the dead man. She studied him for a long moment, wondering who carried a piece of poisoned cake all the way from Storyton Hall. And why. She considered the common thread linking all of them: Tom, the druid, and The Medieval Herbalists, and could only come up with a single word.

"Plants," she murmured to the room. Her voice sounded too loud in the dead man's presence, and she regretted having spoken.

Suddenly, she wanted a name to attach to the body on

the floor, so she returned to her search by opening the large cabinet on the back wall. This was filled with homeopathic medicines, which were carefully labeled and arranged alphabetically. To Jane, they looked innocuous enough and seemed to focus on minor injuries or the relief of aches and pains. Next, she moved to a small desk and rifled through the drawers. The druid's house was oddly free of personal effects. There were no photographs, letters, bills, or the kind of minutiae that usually ended up in a desk drawer. Jane couldn't find a driver's license or a single identifying document. She paused, wondering if it was possible to drop off the grid in their modern world. Could this man truly not have a post office box or bank account?

Maybe his safe is filled with cash, she thought. *If so, how is he earning it?*

She was convinced the answer also involved plants.

Leaving the cabin, Jane made her way to the row of sheds. Lachlan had left the door to the first open wide, and Jane saw the ATV he'd mentioned, along with a workbench, a pegboard loaded with tools, an assortment of gardening supplies, and a row of red gasoline jugs. The space could have belonged to any number of men.

The contents of the next shed gave weight to Jane's theory that the druid did more with his plants than create homeopathic medicines. The entire space was devoted to the growing of seedlings, the grinding of plants into powder, and the packing of powder into airtight plastic tubs.

"Illegal drugs?" Jane wondered aloud.

Picking up one of the tubs—which she estimated held about thirty ounces—she unscrewed the lid and discovered a coarse green powder mixed with clumps of green- and yellow-hued seeds. At that moment, she remembered Lachlan saying that the druid had chosen an ideal place to grow crops.

What if that crop is marijuana?

Replacing the tub, Jane decided to investigate the secret

garden. She had to know if the secret had nothing to do with rare and poisonous herbs and everything to do with the cultivation of illegal plants.

She headed for the path Tom had taken to fetch the herbalists. For the first time, she felt as though she were trespassing. There was something especially intimate about the narrow trail leading downhill. In other circumstances, Jane might have noticed how the tall grass flanking the path was dotted with Queen Anne's lace and thistles, or seen the bee boxes at the edge of the clearing, but her gaze was fixed on the high, ivy-covered brick wall waiting at the end of the trail. And on the wooden door in the middle of the wall.

Jane paused in front of the door, thinking of how often she'd envied the little girl in the Francis Hodgson Burnett novel. Of how often she'd wished that she'd had a secret garden of her own to play in. The druid's door reminded her of the entryway to that storybook garden. Its polished wood looked thick and sturdy and it boasted a large keyhole. Luckily, Jane didn't need the key to enter. It had already been unlocked to allow entry to Tom and the herbalists.

Now it's my turn to see what mysteries are hidden on the other side of this door, Jane thought.

She pushed it open and nervously peered around its edge.

What she saw was an ordinary garden. At least, that's what it appeared to be to Jane. The garden was laid out in a large square with shade-loving plants around the perimeter and plants in need of full sun in the center. These central beds were divided into four additional squares of equal size, and at the heart of the garden, perched on a low stone pedestal, was the statue of a monk or a saint. Jane studied the sculpture. It was well weathered and she couldn't tell what the bearded man held in his right hand—a leaf or a bowl perhaps—but he carried a bouquet of flowers in his left.

"*You* don't seem threatening at any rate," Jane said to the monk. Though his face was solemn, it wasn't unkind. It was as though the sculptor had caught him during a moment of deep contemplation.

There were no places to sit and contemplate in this garden. Other than the dirt paths, plants occupied every available inch. The druid clearly had a green thumb. Every plant looked robust and the air was perfumed by a host of unfamiliar smells. Jane was accustomed to the scents floating around Storyton Hall—honeysuckle, roses, Confederate jasmine, boxwood, magnolia, gardenia, and lilies. Not only were the scents in the druid's garden unfamiliar, but most of the plants were also.

Jane recognized a few. She picked out rhododendron nestled against the western wall as well as foxglove, catmint, and jimsonweed. The sight of the jimsonweed was surprising. Though it produced a lovely white flower, Jane couldn't imagine why anyone would deliberately grow such a poisonous plant.

That's why the Poison Princess was so keen on coming, though, she reminded herself. *She couldn't wait to see his collection of poisonous plants.*

"You're all deadly, aren't you?" Jane spun in a circle and tried to count how many different species the druid was growing.

She stopped counting after the second bed. It was obvious that the man had planted anything he could grow in the western Virginia climate.

And what he can't grow outdoors is undoubtedly inside the last shed, she thought wryly.

The existence of the poisonous plants, as fascinating and unnerving as they might be, still didn't explain how the druid earned a living. He grew much of his own food and probably hunted for game, but there were plenty of other items in his cabin that had been purchased using currency other than herbal medicine. Jane didn't care how good the druid's remedies were supposed to be. No one had given him an off-road vehicle or a flat-screen television as payment.

Jane continued walking through the garden until she came to the door on the opposite side. She grabbed the handle and pushed, but this door was locked.

"Damn."

Turning to face the garden, Jane wondered what the druid had on the other side of that door. What secret had he been unwilling to share with the herbalists?

And is Tom Green a party to this secret?

Jane trudged back to the druid's cabin. Her feet felt heavy. Now that the shock of the druid's death had worn off, hunger, thirst, and fatigue set in. Along with these were the bevy of unanswered questions concerning the druid, Tom, and the herbalists. Jane had been searching for well over an hour and she was no closer to knowing why one of them had poisoned the reclusive healer.

In the doorway of the cabin, she stared at the druid's body. She was reticent to enter the room again, even though the fresh mountain air had dispelled the worst of the noxious odors.

"I'm sorry," she whispered, tiptoeing toward the corpse.

No matter what this man was guilty of, Jane didn't like leaving him exposed. She wished she could take the blanket from his bed and cover him with it, but this was a crime scene and she'd already marred it enough by searching the druid's possessions.

She wasn't finished with her search either. She hadn't found a skeleton key while examining his things, which meant that it was probably on his person.

"Sorry," Jane repeated as she patted the man's front pockets. Feeling despicable, she slid her hands under his buttocks in order to check his back pockets. They, too, were empty.

Jane touched the chain around her neck. The chain was so long that the locket containing the key to Storyton's secret library hung between her breasts. Steeling herself, Jane slipped her fingers under the druid's collar. His shirt was damp with sweat and saliva, but she refused to pull back. And when she touched a length of leather cord, she felt a surge of hope. She tugged at the cord until she'd exposed a brass skeleton key.

After pulling the key and its leather cord over the druid's head, she ran out of the cabin. She was eager to be back in the fresh air, so she kept running all the way to the locked door in the druid's garden.

The key was a perfect fit. On the other side of the door, she found a path leading to the stream. There was some fishing equipment, including a bucket and a net, but that was all. Across the stream, however, Jane saw a large expanse of cleared land. And growing on that land was a plant Jane instantly recognized.

"Cannabis," she declared triumphantly.

Finally, something made sense. The druid was involved in the cultivation and sale of marijuana. Surely that explained both his income and his desire for privacy.

But it did not readily explain why one of The Medieval Herbalists had killed him.

Hearing the distant whine of an engine, Jane shoved the key in her pocket. She backtracked through the garden and crouched behind a bush near the cabin. As soon as she recognized Lachlan on the druid's motorcycle, she relaxed. She'd barely stepped out into the open before a second off-road motorbike pulled alongside Lachlan's.

Edwin Alcott removed his black helmet and quickly dismounted. Taking Jane by the elbows, he glanced at her soiled shirt. He then searched her face, his dark eyes full of concern. "Are you okay?"

"Yes." She smiled. She was undeniably glad to see him.

He returned the smile. "We brought you water, food, and a clean shirt."

Jane thanked him before gesturing at the cabin. "I hope

you can get into this safe. I think I've solved part of the riddle, but the biggest piece of the puzzle is still missing."

Edwin removed a bag from the back of his bike and followed Jane and Lachlan inside. He paused in the main room, taking in the pungent odor, the charcoal-spattered rug, and the sorry state of the dead man's corpse. "No one should die like that. No one."

Jane nodded solemnly and then showed him to the safe. He immediately set to work cracking it. She watched him while she drank water and ate the sandwich Mrs. Hubbard had packed for her. Standing in the druid's bedroom, she didn't have much of an appetite, but she made herself eat so she'd have the energy to handle what promised to be a stressful afternoon.

She'd just finished her lunch when Edwin whispered, "Gotcha," and the safe lock disengaged with a loud click.

Edwin moved aside to allow Jane to examine the contents. There were stacks of cash—mostly fifties and hundreds—a file folder stuffed with papers, and sitting on top of all these, a camera. A camera with a strap featuring a unicorn and floral design reminiscent of a famous medieval tapestry.

Kira's camera.

TWELVE

"This is Kira's." Jane reached for the camera. "I recognize the strap."

Edwin followed her gaze. "The design looks like a sample of the medieval unicorn tapestries."

Jane was too intent on their discovery to confirm Edwin's theory. "Did the druid kill Kira?" she asked instead. "Did he catch her photographing his special crop on the other side of the river? He clearly has dozens of poisonous plants at his disposal. And he owns the second half of the murder weapon too. I saw a box of syringes in the same cabinet where he keeps his homeopathic medicines."

"Ms. Grace attached her zoom lens," Edwin said. "She must have hoped to take photos without being noticed, but failed. Are there any images on there?"

Jane examined the Canon camera. It had more bells and whistles than the digital camera she used, but she was able to locate the power button. She pressed it, and though the LCD screen came to life, there was only a brief flash of light before the screen went dark again.

"It needs to be charged," Lachlan said. "The cable is still in Ms. Grace's room."

"Then we're taking this with us." Jane put the camera aside and returned her attention to the safe's interior. After removing the file folder, she swiveled to allow Lachlan and Edwin to view its contents.

Opening to the first document, she frowned in puzzlement. The paper appeared to have been written in code. The only thing Jane understood was that she was looking at a detailed list of items and quantities.

"Is this an inventory of his medicines?" she asked the two men.

Edwin motioned for Jane to proceed, and she flipped to the next document. "It's nearly identical," he said. "Maybe they're order forms."

"These codes could represent customers, I guess." Jane continued to study the sheet. "How could a backwoods farmer fulfill these orders on a regular basis? I know you two haven't seen the size of his current crop yet, but it doesn't seem possible."

The folder contained half a dozen such sheets.

Jane couldn't decipher a single line. "Unless Sterling or Sinclair can decode one of these before we leave, we'll have to take a sample with us along with the camera. I can't wait for the cops from over the mountain to process the evidence. We need to catch the killer now. Today!"

As if echoing the rumble in her voice, the sound of multiple engines floated through the open window.

Jane leafed through the rest of the documents. Under the coded lists, there was an assortment of recipes for creating herbal medicines. Though the instructions for preparing each medicine and its recommended dosage had been written out in layman's terms, the ingredients were once again in code.

"Wait." Edwin stopped Jane from turning to the next

page. "The code in this headache remedy also appears on the order forms. I believe it's an ingredient."

Jane pulled out a random list and laid it next to the headache remedy. "You're right. A. Bell is written on both sheets. So if A. Bell isn't a person, it must be a plant."

"*Atropa belladonna*," said Sinclair from the doorway. "Otherwise known as deadly nightshade." He brandished a book called *The Poison Garden* and smiled at Jane. "We needn't always have a satellite signal to find the answers to our questions. Thankfully, the information in some books never goes out of date."

Sinclair looked so prim and proper in his white Oxford shirt and blue and yellow bow tie that Jane found herself smiling back at him. "I'm glad that you've come."

Nodding deferentially at Edwin, Sinclair said, "I see that your efforts were successful, Mr. Alcott. Well done." His gaze then landed on the camera near Jane's hip. "Ms. Grace found her way to this place? I wonder how she accomplished such a feat."

"I don't know how she heard about the druid, and I can't imagine anyone finding his house on their own, but somehow, she and the druid interacted," Jane said sadly.

"How did any of The Medieval Herbalists learn of his existence? The man was clearly off the grid," Sinclair said. "We'll pay Mr. Green a visit as soon as we're finished. He must be hiding something." He gestured at the folder. "May I?"

"Of course," Jane said.

Sinclair spread out the lists and recipes on the druid's bed. "He wrote the instructions for mixing the herbal medicines a long time ago," said the observant librarian. "See how the paper has yellowed. The lists are newer. They were written on lined notebook paper."

Jane joined Sinclair by the bed. "What are Sterling and Butterworth doing?"

"After Mr. Sterling compares the ATV tires to the tracks

found near Storyton River, he'll photograph the contents of each shed. Mr. Butterworth is examining the druid's body. When he's done, he'll search the yard and gardens."

"I'm going to check out the marijuana plants," Lachlan said.

Sinclair watched Lachlan leave before turning back to Jane. "The druid was cultivating cannabis?"

"That and more," Jane replied darkly. "Look at all these codes. But I don't get how his operation worked. Who places regular orders for deadly nightshade? Or this?" She pointed at a recipe for curing migraines and menstrual cramping. "What's C. Mac?"

Sinclair paged through the glossary of his book. "*Conium maculatum*. Water hemlock."

"Hemlock? Do all of the druid's remedies include poison?" Jane asked incredulously.

"Maybe he only used trace amounts," Edwin said, showing Sinclair a prescription for treating gout and arthritis pain. "What about this one?"

Sinclair consulted the glossary again. "That code stands for sassafras."

"Even though the druid used a poisonous plant to create an ointment, it doesn't necessarily mean his medicines were harmful," Edwin said. "They weren't FDA-approved, but it's possible they were still efficacious."

Jane glared at him. "He was hardly practicing the Hippocratic oath when he killed Kira! He's been hiding up here for years growing deadly plants and mixing concoctions, which he sells to our neighbors. He was a drug dealer. I don't care if the marijuana growing across the river was meant for medicinal purposes. I don't care if he successfully treated hundreds of people. He had Kira's camera locked in a safe along with stacks of cash. He was *not* some mystical hermit healer or saint." She looked away from Edwin. She wasn't really angry with him. She was more frustrated by the fact that the mystery of Kira's death kept growing more complex. "Where does Tom fit into this? What terrible secrets is he hiding?"

"I think it's time we found out why Mr. Green was so troubled during last night's wedding reception," Sinclair said gravely.

Edwin looked at Sinclair. "Were you able to recover the missing herbal?"

"I'm afraid not. We searched the guest rooms belonging to Ms. Kota and Ms. Billingsley, but found nothing suspicious."

"I don't want Captain Phil to be the thief." Jane waved her arm to indicate the adjacent room. "It's hard enough to learn that Tom Green worked as middleman to a drug dealer. *Tom!* He's been delivering flowers to Storyton Hall since before I became manager. I'm very fond of him . . ."

Edwin touched her hand. "There are multiple layers to every person's story. Unexpected plot twists. Sudden tragedies. People don't always make the right choice. We're all flawed. Tom included. We should give him a chance to explain himself."

"Should we?" Jane snapped. Kira's death, the stolen herbal, and the druid's poisoning had taken their toll. Despite the weight of her burdens, she felt hollow.

In the middle of this tense moment, Sterling appeared in the doorway. "The tire tracks don't match. Mr. Butterworth and I have concluded that the druid had been testing combinations of innocuous and poisonous plants. There's a chemistry lab in the largest shed, and we found several notebooks detailing his experiments. Multiple entries ended with a notation of 'Delivered to E.P.' followed by a date. It's always E.P., and the oldest entry dates back fifteen years."

"I feel like we're in an episode of *Breaking Bad*," Jane muttered. "Did you take a notebook? I may have to show one to Tom."

Sterling produced a spiral notebook with a green cover from the messenger bag slung over his shoulder. "We left everything else in place. There's nothing more to learn here and we shouldn't delay reporting the druid's death any longer." His gaze shifted from Jane to Lachlan.

"I'll wait for the authorities," Lachlan volunteered.

Jane knew it would be very stressful for Lachlan to deal with the police from over the mountain. He'd be forced to answer a barrage of questions and would spend hours in an interview room. The scenario was bound to trigger his anxieties.

"No," she said decisively. "You need to get me to The Potter's Shed. Quickly. Sterling can handle things at this end."

"I'll take you to Tom's on my bike," Edwin said. "It's the fastest way."

Sinclair nodded. "Mr. Alcott is correct. Because we drove Storyton Hall Gators, we took the trail leading over the mountain and must return the same way."

"I'm going with Edwin," Jane said. "I'll meet the rest of you back at Storyton Hall after I speak with Tom."

Outside, Edwin gave Jane a spare helmet. He mounted the bike and gestured for her to get on. Without hesitating, she straddled the seat and pressed her body against Edwin's.

"Wrap your arms around my waist!" he yelled over the engine. "It's going to be a bouncy ride. Lean when I lean. If you get scared, tap my shoulder and I'll slow down."

"Not going to happen," Jane shouted back. "I'm too angry to be scared."

Edwin pushed his visor down, put the bike into gear, and accelerated. Startled, Jane gasped. From that point onward, she was too focused on the terrain and on echoing the movements of Edwin's body to make a sound. She kept waiting for the bike to skid out from under them, but Edwin skillfully forged a trail back toward Storyton.

Jane was grateful for Edwin's helmet, as its face shield

provided her with complete protection. She was also glad that she still wore Lachlan's bandanna around her neck. More than once, the thin fabric had kept her skin from being scratched by brambles or tall blades of wild grass. Unfortunately, there was nothing to save her bare arms from being marked by whip-thin branches or prickly plants.

By the time they reached the walking trail leading to Storyton Village, Jane felt as though every vertebra in her spine had been jostled loose. She hadn't even realized how tightly she'd been clinging to Edwin until he pulled the motorcycle in front of The Potter's Shed. When Jane dropped her arms, they were trembling from exertion.

Edwin removed his helmet and dismounted. He then offered Jane his hand and helped her off the bike. "Have you ridden many motorcycles?"

"That was my first," Jane said. "And I feel like my brain is still rattling around inside my skull."

"You did really well." Edwin smiled at her. "I liked your holding on to me like that. I almost wish we had farther to go."

Jane looked at him for a long moment. Finally, she said, "That was the only part of the ride I enjoyed. Maybe, when we're done here, you could take me home."

"It would be my honor."

Reclaiming her hand, Jane took in the flowerbeds surrounding Tom Green's garden shop. The blooms made her think of the floral design on Kira's camera, and her anger flared. She marched up the front walk with the straight-backed, purposeful stride of a soldier heading into battle.

Inside the shop, which was blissfully cool, Tom was wrapping a bouquet of gerbera daisies for a female customer. He smiled at the lady and thanked her for her patronage, but the moment she turned away, his smile vanished. He looked exhausted. By the time Tom saw Jane, it was too late to hide his weariness.

"Are you alone or is your assistant here?" Jane demanded without preamble.

Tom was clearly surprised by her brusque tone. She'd never spoken to him like that before. He cast an anxious glance at Edwin and then said, "She's on break. I think she went to The Pickled Pig to do a little shopping."

"Good," Jane said. "Is there someplace we can talk without being disturbed?"

"What's this about?" Tom asked.

Ignoring his question, Jane pointed at the doorway behind Tom. "How about your office? That way, you'll know if a customer comes in."

"All right," Tom said after a brief hesitation. Beckoning for Jane and Edwin to follow, he stepped into the next room. "Please excuse the mess." He hurried to shift cardboard boxes and papers from the surface of a chair to the top of his desk.

Jane sank into the metal folding chair without waiting for an invitation. Edwin declined the desk chair. Instead, he leaned against the wall, his arms folded over his chest. His posture was both relaxed and intimidating, and Tom shot another nervous glance in his direction before settling across the desk from Jane.

"I followed your little group this morning," Jane said, gazing steadily at Tom. "To the druid's cabin."

Tom grew pale. "You did?"

"Who is he, Tom? A relative of yours, obviously." Jane deliberately spoke of the druid in the present tense. "I could see the resemblance. Is he your father?"

Tom's eyes swept around the room, as though in search of an escape route. "I don't see—"

"You led a group of my guests to the druid," Jane cut it sharply. "I know it was by their request, but I saw his secret garden. I also saw the crop across the river and what he keeps inside his sheds."

Hearing this, Tom cringed. He pulled his hands close to his chest and hunched inward. It was a protective gesture that made the small man appear even smaller. "I only wanted to—"

"Impress them? I understand," Jane said, softening her voice. "Is the druid your father, Tom?"

Tom didn't reply.

"For years, you've supplied the village and our resort with beautiful plants and flowers. But you've procured other products for our neighbors as well, haven't you? Like drugs. *Illegal* drugs." Jane shook her head. "How could you put people at risk like that?"

"I didn't!" Tom protested heatedly. "You've got it all wrong. You see, some of the villagers are barely squeaking by. They can't afford health care or the high prices of certain traditional medications. That's how this whole enterprise got started. During the last recession, I asked my dad to help these folks. He was once a board-certified physician. He also knew his way around lab equipment from when he worked at a teaching hospital before entering private practice. I was pretty sure he could create some of the medicines people needed, and he did. It's not against the law to make and sell herbal medicines, and he's able to reproduce the same medicines you or I might find at Storyton Pharmacy."

Jane had learned two significant facts from Tom's speech. She now knew that the druid was Tom's father and that he'd been a doctor. "What's your dad's name?" she asked.

"Andrew." Tom released a heavy sigh. "Please don't tell anyone. He's already mad at me for bringing The Medieval Herbalists to his home."

Jane spread her hands. "I can understand why he wouldn't welcome visitors. *I* certainly wouldn't want people poking around my place if I were growing and selling cannabis."

"What are you talking about?" Tom jumped out of his chair. "He's growing wild hemp! *You're* thinking of *Cannabis sativa*. That plant is bred for its potent glands. It has the trichomes, which allow people to get high. *That's* marijuana. What my dad grows only contains trace amounts of THC. It's actually called ditchweed and is an established crop in nearly every industrial country except ours. A useful plant for its oils and fiber, but because it's marijuana's cousin, it's eradicated everywhere."

"So it's also illegal."

"Only because our government is obtuse." Tom dropped back into his seat with a frustrated sigh. "Wild hemp can be used to produce environmentally friendly fuel, paper, fabric, and food. My dad uses the seeds to make flour. It would be a great alterative to plastic. Items made from wild hemp wouldn't clog up our landfills!" Tom's face became flushed with indignation. "Until the late 1930s, lots of American farmers grew this crop. Guess the gurus in charge of agriculture were smarter back then. Now the DEA wastes tons of money running around the country killing ditchweed because it looks like the 'bad' cannabis plant. And even though the 'bad' plant is legal in some states, government agencies continue to destroy thousands of useful wild hemp plants. Which is why I call them obtuse."

Jane realized that she'd leapt to a conclusion about what she'd seen. Feeling abashed, she wondered what other erroneous assumptions she'd made about Tom's father.

She looked down at her hands and tried to find the words to broach the subject of the druid's death. After storming into Tom's shop and demanding that he answer her questions, it seemed cruel to now tell him that his father had been poisoned. Cruel and harshly abrupt. And yet she had no choice. One of her guests was a murderer and Jane had to learn that person's identity. Two people had been killed within a matter of days, and as much as Jane wanted to show Tom compassion, she didn't have time to be delicate.

In search of encouragement, Jane met Edwin's eyes. He responded with a slight nod. He understood that the moment had come for her to ask Tom the more important question of all.

"Forgive me," Jane said to Tom. "I obviously can't tell the difference between the two varieties, and I should have asked for clarification before jumping to a conclusion. You know more about plants than anyone I've ever met."

"Until your recent guests arrived," Tom muttered unhappily.

Jane shook her head. "No. They might be more knowledgeable about which herbs were used during medieval times, but you know about our indigenous plants *and* the symbolism behind hundreds of plants and flowers. Most of all, you have a gift when it comes to matching flowers to people. You have a good sense of people, Tom Green. And that's why I'm asking you to help me find out what happened to Kira Grace."

Tom's anger drained away. He dropped his gaze, but not before Jane caught the haunted look in his eyes. "That poor woman," he whispered. "I wish I could help, but I don't know anything."

"I don't believe you." Jane's voice was low and gentle. "I think you're trying to protect your father, which I understand. But Tom, you kept mentioning Kira's name at the wedding. The other herbalists noticed. Your remorse over Kira's loss makes no sense unless you played a part in her death. Or you know someone else who did."

"I didn't hurt her!" Tom was obviously horrified by the idea. "I could never hurt someone. I'm . . . I don't have that in me."

"Does your father?" Jane waited a long moment for Tom to respond. When he didn't, she said, "He owns syringes. He has access to dozens of lethal plants. Kira didn't drown, Tom. Someone injected poison into her neck. Right here." Pivoting, Jane swept her strawberry blond braid to the side and put her fingertips on the hair at the base of her skull.

Without turning around, she said, "Kira's attacker couldn't face her. He needed to get rid of her, but he didn't want to watch her die."

Jane stayed very still, her hand pressed to her head. Finally, she spun around and studied Tom's face. It was twisted in anguish, and in that moment, Jane saw flashes of how Tom's father had looked as the poison he'd ingested assaulted him with wave after wave of unbearable pain.

"Tell me, Tom," she whispered. "What happened between Kira and your dad?"

Tom said nothing for a full minute and Jane feared that he wouldn't speak, but then, he drew in a shuddering breath and said, "I think she went to see him. She must have followed me. I was listening to music—sometimes I do that on the trip up the mountain—so I didn't hear her walking behind me. I never see anyone else on the trails when I'm out. I'm out and about way too early for most people, but I'd overslept the day of the duck race."

Jane waited. When Tom didn't continue, she scooted her chair closer to his. She gave him an encouraging smile. "You're doing great. Go on."

"One second." Tom stood up and shuffled into the adjacent room. He maintained his hunched posture, keeping his arms close to his chest as though he wished he were a turtle and could withdraw into a protective shell.

Edwin stopped leaning against the wall and moved to the doorway to watch Tom. Jane stayed put. She sensed that Tom would only resume his narrative if she remained composed.

He reentered the room clutching a handful of herbs in his right hand. "Thyme," he said as he sat back down. "For courage and strength."

"I could use some of that," Jane said.

Tom immediately offered her a sprig, and she inhaled the pleasant fragrance.

"I don't know why my dad chose to become a hermit,"

Tom continued, his eyes locked on the cluster of thyme in his hand. "My mom left without so much as a note when I was a baby and my dad sent me to live with his mother in Harrisonburg. Soon after, he took off too. My granny was a wonderful woman. She taught me just about everything I know about plants. I never heard from my dad the whole time I lived with her."

Jane thought of her sons growing up without knowing the love of either parent and felt tears prick her eyes. Tom didn't notice. His own eyes had gone glassy as he became lost in his memories. "My dad contacted me right after Granny died. She'd left me everything. Her house, her car, and some money. Dad called from a pay phone and recommended I move to Storyton. He said he was living nearby and would come see me once I was settled. I was really lonely without Granny and I'd always dreamed of reuniting with one of my parents, so I moved." Tom smiled nostalgically. "I loved Storyton from the first. Everyone I met was welcoming. I noticed that there wasn't a place for people to buy flowers and plants, so I opened The Potter's Shed. The night after my Grand Opening, my dad knocked on my kitchen door."

"And you finally got to know him." Jane said, her heart aching for Tom. How would he cope when he learned that his father was dead? That he'd been murdered? She couldn't stop a single tear from escaping, but she hurriedly wiped it away and waited for Tom to continue.

Tom responded to Jane's comment with a shrug. "I got to know him as much as he'd let me. He would never tell me why he bolted when I was a kid or why he lived like a hermit up in the hills. He'd only say that he left me with Granny for my own protection. I asked him if he'd committed a crime. I thought it might be tax evasion or something like that, but he refused to answer. Granny told me that he'd been a doctor. That's why I was willing to sell his medicines. And they *do* help people. I've seen how they help."

"I'm sure you have," Jane said soothingly.

"He also works on developing new medicines," Tom added with a hint of pride. "I don't know who pays him to do the research. Over the years, I've stopped asking because he won't tell me. I tried searching for clues about him on the Internet, but I don't think Green is his real surname. It might not be my name either, but it's the only one I have." Tom gave Jane a hapless shrug. "Eventually, I stopped searching. I figured he'd tell me in his own time. I'm content knowing he's close by. We share meals several times a month. We talk about plants and my customers. We have a good relationship."

"Or at least you did until Kira came along," Jane said quietly.

The brightness that had illuminated Tom's face when he'd spoken of his father disappeared. He nodded in misery. "My dad *never* comes to Storyton, but I think he came down from his cabin to borrow my truck. Years ago, I gave him a set of keys to my house—just in case he needed a place to stay during bad weather or in an emergency. I keep the keys to both my delivery van and my pickup on a hook by the kitchen door. I hardly ever drive the truck. It's pretty old and I only use it for trips over the mountain. I park it out behind the greenhouse." He looked at Jane. "The day of the duck race, I noticed that it wasn't parked exactly where I'd left it. It had been moved."

"So after that, and after you heard about Kira's being found in Storyton River, did you ask your father about her?"

"Why would I?" Tom asked. His caustic tone was so out of character that Jane flinched. "What could he possibly have to do with the death of a Storyton Hall guest?"

Jane didn't reply. She simply waited while Tom brought the thyme to his nose and breathed in. Eventually, he sighed and resumed his narrative. "Lately, my dad has been acting stranger than ever. Super paranoid. I don't know what compelled me, but I mentioned the herbalists to him. And Kira. All he would say was that he borrowed my truck to pick up supplies that wouldn't fit in his ATV. I wanted to believe him. I would never have sprung the whole group on him this morning if I did, but I *needed* to see for myself if there was something tying him to the herbalists."

At last, they'd come to the heart of the matter. "Was there?"

Tom shrugged again. "I don't know. He flew off the handle when I arrived with them. He vowed to lock himself in his cabin until we were gone. He said that . . ." Tom swallowed hard. "He'd never trust me again. That I'd betrayed the one thing he valued most. His privacy."

Jane reached for the small man's hand and discovered that it was shaking. "No one could blame you, Tom. There have been holes in your family history for your entire life. Anyone would want to fill those gaps."

"My dad says the past is irrelevant. Only the present matters," Tom mumbled. "He'll never forgive me for what I did, and it was all for nothing." He looked at Jane. "I didn't discover any connection between my dad and The Medieval Herbalists. All I did was alienate him. So like I said, I can't help you."

Jane squeezed his hand. "You've been very helpful. I only have one more question, and it's important." She kept her eyes locked on his. "Who brought the piece of wedding cake to your father?"

Tom frowned in confusion. "The cake? Why does that matter?"

"Please." Jane's voice was a soft plea. "It matters very much."

After casting a brief glance at Edwin, as though searching his face for clues, Tom turned back to Jane. "It was Hannah," he said simply. "She gave him the cake."

THIRTEEN

"Hannah?" Jane couldn't help repeating the name.
"Are you sure she wasn't carrying it for someone else in the group since she was on horseback?"

Tom shook his head. "When I spoke to her the night before, we talked about lots of things, including the arrangements I'd made for her to travel to my dad's. When I told her that the druid had a sweet tooth, Hannah said that she wanted to bring him a piece of wedding cake. She asked me to acquire a saddlebag big enough to hold the take-out box. I agreed. I knew my dad would appreciate the gesture—even if he was furious with me for leading the herbalists to his doorstep."

Though Jane believed Tom, she still struggled to accept the truth that Hannah had poisoned the druid.

No, not the druid. The man had a name. Andrew. And a son, she silently berated herself. And it was time for Jane to tell the son what had happened to his father.

She glanced down at Tom's hand and thought of the many floral arrangements he'd put together for the people of

Storyton. Of all the times had he'd used flowers to help his neighbors celebrate. And grieve.

Recognizing that she was about to break this quiet and humble man's heart, Jane placed her free hand over his. "I'm so sorry to tell you this." Jane looked directly into Tom's eyes. "But that piece of cake was poisoned. Lachlan and I found your father suffering the effects of its poison. We tried our best to save him." She swallowed the lump forming in her throat. "We failed. I'm really sorry, Tom, but your father is dead."

The news didn't register right away. Tom stared at Jane for several long seconds. The air in the room felt heavy with his numb silence.

Finally, his gaze slid to the window. It seemed as though seeing the blue-green hills on the other side of the glass allowed him to process the news. He slowly pulled his hand from Jane's grasp and, after dropping what remained of the crushed clump of thyme to the floor, he rose and shuffled over to the window.

The shock of what he'd just heard reverberated through his body. His legs seemed unwilling to carry the weight of his body, and when he managed to reach the windowsill, he clung to it as though he might fall should he let go.

"Poisoned," he whispered.

Jane could think of nothing that would bring Tom solace, but she desperately searched for the right words to soften the terrible blow she'd just delivered. For it was more than a blow. It was a wound. And it was so deep that it would never completely heal.

"Your father isn't alone," Jane said softly. "I want you to know that. Butterworth and Sinclair are with him. Lachlan too. They've called for help."

Tom turned away from the window. Without looking at Jane, he headed for the doorway. "I need to be with him."

"I have an off-road motorbike," Edwin said. "I can take you there."

Tom was out the door within seconds. Jane had only the chance to yell a hasty "Thank you" to Edwin before he too was gone.

The noise of Edwin's motorcycle had not yet faded when Tom's assistant returned from her break. She entered the shop humming dreamily, her hand closed around a frozen yogurt container.

"Excuse my humming, but I just had the most luscious snack at the Canvas Creamery. Ms. Doyle has a new flavor today. Peach Raspberry Cobbler. It has fresh fruit and real pieces of cobbler. It is *heavenly*!" She gave a little shudder of delight. "Are you here to see Mr. Green?"

"Actually, he had to step out." Jane tried to remember the woman's name, but failed. Tom handled the Storyton Hall deliveries, so Jane had only spoken with his assistant over the phone. She was a fairly recent hire from over the mountain, but Jane had a good feeling about her. "I doubt he'll be back before closing," she went on to say. "Do you have keys to the shop? Can you lock up when your shift is over?"

The woman studied Jane with a mixture of surprise and curiosity. "Yes, I can handle the closing duties. But please— is Mr. Green okay?"

Jane smiled. It was a testament to the woman's character that she asked after Tom's welfare instead of trying to satisfy her own curiosity. Because of this, Jane decided to be as forthright as possible. "Someone he cared about very much passed away. It was very sudden and Mr. Green is extremely upset. I don't think he'll be able to work for a few days. Can you cover for him?"

"Of course," the woman said. "I'm Gladys, by the way. You must be Ms. Steward. I never forget a voice."

"It'll be such a comfort to Tom knowing that The Potter's

Shed is in your capable hands," Jane said. "I must be going now too."

Jane headed for Run for Cover. She was also in need of comfort. She needed her best friend.

As she walked through the village, mechanically waving at familiar faces, Hannah's name kept echoing in her mind. Passing by a mother pushing a double stroller, Jane's gaze was drawn to the matching set of pink sunbonnets covering the heads of two baby girls.

For some reason, the sight of the infants reminded Jane of how Hannah's green dress had matched the green sash on Victoria's wedding gown. The sisters had seemed to be in sync from the moment they'd arrived at Storyton Hall. Was Hannah so broken up by Victoria's marriage and the idea of being separated from her that she'd become unhinged and decided to commit murder?

That's ridiculous, Jane thought. *There must be a reason Hannah chose the druid.*

Jane pulled out her phone and called Sinclair. Her call went straight to voice mail, and she assumed that he and the other Fins were still too high in the hills to get reception. She left a detailed message saying that Hannah had killed Tom's father and that she needed to be watched until the police from over the mountain took her into custody.

"Hannah's arrest will destroy Victoria," Jane muttered as she placed her foot on the first stone on a path of word stones winding through Eloise's front garden. The word protruding from beneath her hiking boot was "promise." Hadn't Victoria made Hannah promise that she would make more of an effort to come out of her shell following her wedding to Carson? Skipping over "friendship" and "honesty," Jane paused on "hope," before hurrying into the bookshop.

Eloise, who was rearranging a display of gardening books near the front counter, stopped what she was doing the moment she saw Jane.

"What it is?" she asked, reaching out with both arms.

Jane stepped into her friend's embrace and was instantly soothed by her touch and the familiar scent of her lavender soap.

"Come on. Let's go back to the kitchen." Eloise preceded Jane through the store. She immediately went to the cupboard and retrieved a bottle of whiskey and a pair of coffee mugs. "The bells hanging from my door will ring if a customer enters, so I'm all yours until they do. I stock this brand of whiskey for Edwin. Judging by the price, it must be decent stuff." She poured a finger's worth into one of the mugs. "Drink this down. I'm going to brew a pot of strong coffee. You look totally done in."

Jane swallowed the whiskey without argument. It burned her mouth and throat, but did much to chase the hollow feeling from the pit of her stomach. Eloise poured another splash into the mug.

"I don't need any more," Jane protested.

"This is for your coffee. Trust me, you need it. And a heaping spoonful of sugar too." Eloise pushed a tin of shortbread cookies next to Jane's mug and turned to make the coffee. When the machine began gurgling, she sat across from Jane and waited.

"I shouldn't even be here," Jane said. "One of my guests is a murderer. I should have gone straight to Sheriff Evans, but I need a few minutes. I just need to sit for a minute and"—she looked at her friend—"I don't know how I'll be able to close my eyes tonight, Eloise. I've never watched someone die before. And in such agony. It was horrible."

Eloise pointed at her mug. "Drink that."

Jane complied. This time, the whiskey's warmth spread through the rest of her body and helped her focus. "Can you dial the sheriff's office for me?" she asked Eloise, indicating the phone on the counter next to the coffeemaker.

Eloise got up, punched in the numbers, and told the

person at the other end that she needed to speak to Sheriff Evans. There was a pause, and then Eloise went on to say that she had urgent information regarding the Kira Grace. After passing the phone to Jane, she filled their mugs with coffee and grabbed a pitcher of cream from the fridge.

"Sheriff, this is Jane Steward," Jane said when Evans came on the line. "I've just come from an isolated cabin in the hills to the southeast of Storyton. The cabin is actually located in the next county and belongs to Tom Green's father. He was known to some of the locals as the druid, but his first name was Andrew. He was once a physician—of what specialty I couldn't say." She watched Eloise pour cream into her coffee. The tiny eddies of white in the dark brown liquid swirled violently until Eloise blended them with a spoon. "I'm calling because I followed The Medieval Herbalists to the druid's cabin this morning. It was supposed to be a covert venture, so I stayed hidden. After the group left, I heard screams coming from inside the cabin. I rushed in to find the druid writhing in pain. He indicated that he'd been poisoned and signaled for me to administer a dose of activated charcoal. I tried to get the charcoal into him, but his throat swelled and he . . ." Suddenly, Jane was back in the cabin. Her shirt was covered with black spittle, and panic threatened to overwhelm her.

Eloise squeezed her arm, and Jane returned to the moment.

"Ms. Steward?" Evans asked. "Are you there?"

"I couldn't save him, Sheriff. The druid is dead," Jane finally managed to say. "Mr. Sterling called the police and is waiting at the crime scene. I wanted you to know two things straightaway. First, it's possible that Hannah Billingsley poisoned the druid. She brought him a piece of her sister's wedding cake, and minutes after eating it, he died. When I was with him, he was able to speak the word 'arsenic.'"

There was a pause as the sheriff took all of this in. "Where is Ms. Billingsley now?"

"I would guess she's resting in her room at Storyton Hall," Jane said. "She rode a horse to the druid's place, and it clearly caused her discomfort. Her face was etched with pain."

"I'll head over to Storyton Hall and wait for the police with you. What was the second thing you wanted to tell me?" Evans asked.

Jane, who'd just taken a sip of Eloise's wonderful coffee, lowered her mug to the table. "I found Kira's camera in the druid's cabin, and I have it with me now. I am well aware that the camera belongs to a crime scene, but Kira's death is still unresolved. I have to see what's on that camera. So do you, Sheriff. The battery needs to be recharged, and the charger is in Kira's guest room. As soon as we see what images Kira was taking, the police can have her camera. I didn't leave fingerprints either, because I used a rag to handle it," she lied.

"Ms. Steward, I cannot condone—"

"I know, but what's done is done," Jane interrupted. "If you don't mind picking me up at Run for Cover, I'll tell you why I believe Andrew Green murdered Kira Grace."

The sheriff grunted. "I'll be out front in five minutes."

Eloise poured Jane's coffee into a take-out cup and then started turning out lights inside the bookshop.

"What are you doing?" Jane asked.

"Closing early," Eloise said. "You've been through hell already, and I'm not about to let you go through another second of misery alone. You need someone to lean on and that person is me!"

With a flourish, Eloise flipped the sign in her display window from OPEN to CLOSED. Pressing the take-out cup into Jane's hand, she shooed her friend outside and shut the front door. The bells dangling from the hinges let out a merry tinkle.

Jane and Eloise walked through her garden to the sidewalk to wait for the sheriff.

While Eloise craned her neck, searching for the brown cruiser among the other car traffic, Jane took her hand. "Virginia Woolf knew just how I feel when she said, 'Some people go to priests; others to poetry; I to my friends.' I should have gone straight to the sheriff's office, but after these last few days, I needed to see a friendly face. Your face."

"You should have asked for help long before this," Eloise chided.

"Believe it or not, I asked Edwin." Jane lifted her eyes to the hills. "He gave me a ride on that off-road bike of his."

Eloise started. "Good Lord, I knew you were brave, but I had no idea you were *that* brave! I've seen him zoom off on that thing. He's totally reckless."

"He wasn't this time," Jane said. "He did his best by me, Eloise. I think . . . he's trying."

Eloise smiled. "If anyone can bring him around, it's you. Oh! Here's the sheriff. If he asks, tell him I'm coming along for moral support."

Sheriff Evans had dozens of questions for Jane, none of which involved Eloise. Jane answered robotically, her body pressed against the cool leather of the cruiser's backseat, her thoughts turned toward home. Toward Hannah.

In the passenger seat, Deputy Emory's head was bent over her notebook. She didn't contribute to the conversation, but Jane was secretly pleased that Evans had chosen her to accompany him over his other deputies.

"Please pull around to the loading dock," Jane directed the sheriff as Storyton Hall's massive iron gates came into view. "It won't be long before scandal descends on the resort, but there's no need to alarm the guests prematurely. I intend to plug in Kira's camera first. Next, I'll locate Hannah, though I'm fairly confident she'll be in her room. The herbalists are supposed to host a medieval fair in two hours' time. I bet they're all resting from this morning's hike and wondering how they'll ever drum up the energy to decorate tables in the Great Gatsby Ballroom and hock wares to a crowd of villagers and fellow guests."

Evans glanced at Jane in the rearview mirror. "I've made assurances to the Alleghany police that I would secure the suspect's room. If you believe Ms. Billingsley used arsenic to poison the druid, ah, Dr. Green, then the poison may still be in her possession."

Jane knew it wasn't. After all, the Fins had already examined every inch of Hannah's room in their search for the missing antique herbal. If she'd had arsenic tucked away among her things, surely the Fins would have spotted it.

Unless it was in a perfume bottle or some other type of makeup container, Jane thought ruefully. The Fins had been looking for a book. They wouldn't have expended energy inspecting Hannah's cosmetics.

"I want to be there," Jane said, suddenly changing her plan. "I'll have Eloise see to Kira's camera. We'll have to wait a bit for the battery to charge anyway, so I should go to Hannah's room with you."

As Jane knocked on Hannah's door, she felt a wave of sadness wash over her. She liked Hannah and still couldn't picture her as a murderer. She also couldn't imagine how the young woman, whose life had been defined by bouts of chronic pain, would survive behind bars.

"She's not answering," Jane whispered to Sheriff Evans and Deputy Emory.

After knocking once more, Jane pressed her ear against the thick wood and listened. Hearing no sounds from within the room, she used Mrs. Templeton's master key to let herself in.

"God, no!" she cried, seeing Hannah's inert body on the bed.

She raced into the room, the sheriff on her heels.

"Don't touch anything," Evans commanded. He held his palm close to Hannah's mouth. Her lips were parted and her eyes were closed. Her skin had a waxen, sickly cast.

Jane tried to read the sheriff's expression. "Is she alive?"

"Yes, she's breathing." Evans pressed his fingers to the inside of Hannah's wrist. After locating her pulse, he followed the second hand on his watch. "Her pulse is slow," he said when he was finished counting. "She might have taken something."

Deputy Emory glanced at her superior. "An overdose? Should I call for an ambulance?"

"Let's check the bathroom before we make that call," the sheriff said. "This may be more of a drug-induced sleep than an overdose. Her pulse is slow, but not thready or weak. If I hadn't just completed that refresher course for first responders, I wouldn't be able to tell the difference."

Her panic ebbing, Jane hurried into the bathroom, where she found several pill bottles. "I see Vicodin, Flexeril, and ibuprofen," she called out. After quickly scanning the usages and side effects listed on the label of each prescription drug, Jane added, "Vicodin and Flexeril can cause drowsiness. Vicodin's an opiate and Flexeril is a muscle relaxant. If Hannah took both of those drugs at once, it would explain her condition."

"You said that she appeared to be in considerable pain earlier today, so that explanation is very plausible," the sheriff said, joining Jane in the bathroom. "Still, we'll call the paramedics, as I'd rather err on the side of caution. Emory? You got that?" Evans directed his voice toward the bedroom, but his gaze was fixed on the pill bottles lined up to the right of the sink.

"Yes, sir."

"I'll have Billy keep an eye out for the EMTs and the police. I'm going to see if Kira's camera battery has charged long enough to show us anything," Jane said, backing out of the bathroom.

Eloise had been entrusted with the job of locating Kira's wall charger and transferring the battery from the camera to the charger. After promising Sheriff Evans that she would touch only those items, Eloise was given permission to enter Kira's room.

"Send for me immediately if the images reveal anything pertinent," Evans commanded as Jane moved toward the door. "Having to share evidence is going to complicate matters as it is, and things are bound to become less friendly when my crime-fighting colleagues learn where the camera was found. So I'd like to see any relevant pictures for myself before the Alleghany cops take the camera."

Jane hesitated long enough to glance at Hannah's face. "What if Hannah knew of Kira's plans to visit the druid? Maybe she and Kira were closer than I thought. Why else would someone with a bad back and neck endure such a painful trip on horseback to see him if not to seek revenge for a friend's murder?"

"If they were such close friends, then why wouldn't Ms. Billingsley come to me with her suspicions?" Evans asked. "Why throw her life away?" He shook his head. "No, there's something more to this killing. Something we're not seeing."

Jane had to agree. It didn't make sense for Hannah to wait for the group excursion to avenge Kira's death. What if that excursion had never come about? What if Tom had turned them down?

"EMTs are en route," Deputy Emory said, snapping Jane out of her reverie.

"I'll send Eloise if there's any news," Jane promised and left the room.

The carpeted corridor was quiet and Jane ducked into the staff stairwell, thankful to have avoided running into one of Hannah's fellow herbalists. Or worse, her sister.

How will I find the words to tell Victoria what Hannah did? Jane wondered, climbing the worn stone stairs to the next level. For she knew this task must fall to her. She couldn't leave such a delicate matter to a member of the Alleghany police. Victoria's world was about to unravel. The least Jane could do was sit next to her, woman to woman, and speak to her with genuine compassion as she explained that Hannah would probably be accused of poisoning the man known as the druid.

"At least Victoria has Carson. She won't be alone in her pain."

In Kira's room, Eloise was bent over Kira's camera. As per Jane's request, she'd donned a pair of housekeeper's gloves and had plugged the camera battery into its wall charger. She now stood staring intently at it, as though willing it to charge faster.

"Is it working?" Jane asked.

"According to that orange light, it's charging," said Eloise. "I wanted to give the battery enough time to allow for a quick glimpse at her images. However, I have no idea how many she took. Her memory card is capable of holding over a thousand."

Jane frowned. "We have neither the time nor the battery life to scan that many. Maybe we can view thumbnails or search images by date and time. Either way, it's now or never. Stick the battery back in and let's see the world through Kira's eyes."

Eloise fitted the battery into the bottom of the camera and turned the camera on. She pressed the menu button and was able to scroll down a list of images by date from oldest to newest.

"It looks like she took over a hundred photos the day of the duck race," Jane said, watching Eloise click on the first image. It was a close-up of a ladybug climbing the stalk of a Queen Anne's lace wildflower. "Zip through these nature shots. They're pretty, but they won't tell us why she was killed."

Eloise pushed an arrow button and the images flashed past. And then, the first image of the druid's cabin appeared on the camera's LCD screen. "Is this his house?" Eloise asked. "The druid's?"

"Yes," Jane said.

Kira had used her camera to document the druid's homestead in its entirety. She'd included dozens of shots of the interior of the sheds as well as the poisonous plants growing in the walled garden. The druid must have been preoccupied inside his house because Kira continued on her self-guided tour and photographed the wild hemp crop without being interrupted.

"Here are the money shots!" Eloise exclaimed, pointing at the hemp. "Do you think Kira knew the druid was growing marijuana all along? Was she planning to blackmail him after she took photos of his crop?"

Jane shook her head. "It's not marijuana, but a plant called ditchweed. Also known as wild hemp. It doesn't have the same mind-altering effects, though it's still illegal to cultivate."

Eloise gaped at the image in surprise. "Well, that shows how useless I am as a botanist. And there goes my blackmail theory too. However, Kira wouldn't have made the same mistake. She knew her plants, so let's see where she goes next."

Judging by Kira's photographs, which were now fewer and far between, she'd retraced her steps through the garden and had focused her sights on the cabin's interior. The living room, to be specific. Having just been there that morning, Jane guessed that Kira had crouched behind a bush near one of the side windows. From that vantage point, she'd then taken dozens of images of the druid.

"Whoa," Eloise whispered. "This is stalker behavior. There are twenty shots of the man drinking a glass of water."

Jane murmured in agreement. Not only had Kira snapped hundreds of images of the druid conducting mundane tasks, but she'd also captured his face from every angle. "I know she had a zoom lens, but some of these images are *really* close up. He must have heard the clicking of the camera."

"Why did she want so many different angles of his face?" Eloise shook her head in puzzlement. "To prove that he actually existed and wasn't just a legend?"

"Kira needed money," Jane said. "She was going to show these photographs to someone as leverage. But who?" She made a hurry-up gesture. "We'd better finish scanning in case the battery dies again."

Eloise pressed a button and the image jumped from the druid reaching for a jar from his medicine cupboard to him unscrewing the lid from that same jar. The next photograph showed him filling a syringe with the liquid stored in the jar.

"Good Lord!" Jane cried. "Kira photographed her own murder weapon."

There were two more images in which the druid put on a baseball cap and headed for the front door of the cabin before the stream of photographs came to an end and the screen went dark.

"She must have turned and run at that point," Eloise said. "Or tried to hide."

Jane couldn't take her eyes off the black camera screen. "Either way, she failed. The druid hit her with a rock or heavy branch. Once she was down, he pushed the needle into the back of her neck and released whatever poisonous plant extract was in that jar. He snatched up her camera and locked it in his safe. That done, he strapped her body on his ATV and got her down the mountain to Tom's truck. He loaded her into the passenger seat, drove her to Storyton River, and dumped her in."

"How could anyone be that cruel?" Eloise shook her head in disgust.

Grabbing a tissue from the nightstand, Jane hit the camera's menu button. She brought up the image of the druid filling the syringe and stared intently at it. "Tom said that his father was once a practicing physician. Maybe Andrew Green had to abandon his son and literally flee for the hills because Kira wasn't the first person he killed. Maybe he helped other people die well before their time. Maybe the man that the people of Storyton mistakenly believed was some gentle, nature-loving, hippie healer was really a fugitive. If so, and if what Kira caught on camera helps bring justice to an old case, or cases, then Kira's death might mean something."

Eloise touched the camera. "No matter what happens, her *life* meant something. Every photograph is part of her story. And now I feel like her story has been woven into mine. It's just like reading a book. The author shares something with us in the telling. Kira shared the hidden side of herself through her photography. And this time, she showed us someone else's secret side as well." She looked at the camera screen and frowned. "We're losing the battery charge again."

"You'd better plug it back in," Jane said. "I'll tell the sheriff what we saw. If Hannah's still asleep, I'm going to spend a few minutes with the twins. I need a respite from this madness. Do you mind staying here? I can have a tray sent up."

Eloise grimaced. "Seeing that syringe robbed me of my appetite. You know how much I hate the sight of needles. Just don't forget about me. If you get too busy in Hannah's room, you can always send Lachlan after the camera."

This elicited a smile from Jane before she took a final glance at the camera screen, which had gone completely black. Her smile slowly faded and she hurried from the room.

FOURTEEN

Knowing she had a little time before the paramedics arrived, Jane hurried to her aunt and uncle's apartments to see her sons.

"I ordered a tea trolley." Aunt Octavia ushered Jane into her library. "You look like you could use a cup."

Jane nodded in agreement. A cup of strong tea would help her to think straight. Even on scorching summer days, she enjoyed hot tea. It was partially the tradition of afternoon tea that Jane found so enjoyable. Just taking a few moments to sit for a spell—to pour tea into a porcelain cup or spread jam over a warm scone—these slow, deliberate actions were soothing. Of course, the daily ritual was secondary compared to the tastes of the rich tea and sweet, buttery pastries. The combination of the two, or any number of Mrs. Hubbard's delectable sandwiches or desserts, produced such a state of bliss that Jane consistently felt her cares ebbing away during the twenty-minute break she took around three o'clock each day.

Taking a seat at the library table, Jane accepted a cup of

tea and said, "I can't stay long. Have the boys been behaving?"

"They've been perfect cherubs. I'll call them in after we've had a chance to talk." Her aunt studied her. "What's going on downstairs? I heard that we have unwanted visitors again."

One day, Jane would have to find out how her aunt was able to discover what went on in every corner of Storyton Hall without having to leave her living room. In a low voice, Jane gave her a quick recap of her day.

Aunt Octavia responded by gesturing for the bowl of clotted cream. "My diet be damned. The sheriff *and* the police? We'll be all the over the news again."

"At least the murders didn't occur on our property," Jane said feebly.

"That won't spare us!" Aunt Octavia threw her hands into the air. "Every headline will scream out how a Storyton Hall guest poisoned a local healer. You'll see."

Jane drank more tea. The hot, strong liquid gave her a measure of solace. "The local healer poisoned a Storyton Hall guest first. The police will have to collect enough evidence to prove that Andrew Green killed Kira Grace, but I saw the photographs stored on Kira's camera. I believe the lab results will validate the incriminating action captured by that photo, which was of the druid loading poison into his syringe. A poison that ended up in Kira's bloodstream."

Aunt Octavia, who's been voraciously chewing a jam-and-clotted-cream-covered scone while Jane had been speaking, swallowed and daintily dabbed her mouth with a linen napkin. "You don't know why he murdered her or why Hannah murdered him?"

"No," Jane said, putting her teacup in its saucer. "Which is why I should be going. If the paramedics revive Hannah, I need to be in the room. I also want to be the one to tell Victoria that her sister is a murder suspect."

"A new bride shouldn't have to experience such anguish." Aunt Octavia made a clicking noise with her tongue. "It isn't right."

Jane didn't want to dwell on the subject. Absently, she placed a scone on her plate and split it in half with her knife. "I haven't had the chance to ask until now, but did Uncle Aloysius have any luck on his fishing expedition with Captain Phil?"

"He caught enough trout to feed the entire kitchen staff, but he learned nothing of the whereabouts of the missing herbal," Jane's aunt replied.

At that moment, the twins appeared in the doorway.

"Mom!" they cried in unison. And then, "Tea!"

"Come on in," Jane said with a smile.

Hem dropped into a chair, whisked his napkin onto his lap, and helped himself to three scones. "We were good at Sunday school."

Jane pointed at his plate. "Though I'm very glad to hear it, two scones are plenty. Give one to your brother."

Fitz held out his plate and, in his best Cockney accent, said, "Thanks, guv'na."

"Please, gentlemen." Aunt Octavia held out her hands. "No more dialects for today. Your mother only has a few minutes to spare, so let's make the most of it. Why don't you tell her your plans for after teatime?"

Jane shot her aunt a grateful look.

"Mrs. Templeton has a big surprise for us!" Hem declared.

Fitz swallowed a bite of scone with alacrity and added, "She cleaned out one of the old servants' rooms, which has been full of a bunch of junk—"

"Like broken mops and stuff," Hem interjected helpfully.

"And she's going to show us how to make a giant fort out of sheets," Fitz said, finishing his thought.

The boys exchanged excited glances and chewed with equal fervor.

"That sounds really cool." Jane could imagine her sons

spending hours in their cotton fortress. "Will it be a maze with a Minotaur in the center or a restful place where you'll play games or read?" The tea and the presence of her family were proving to be a balm to her frayed emotions and taxed body. It seemed like days ago, not hours, that she'd parted company with her sons so that they could go to church and she could join Lachlan for a grueling hike into the hills.

"Maybe both," Fitz said. "What do you think, Hem?"

"Every fort should have a monster guard," Hem said. "It won't hurt us, of course. Only bad guys." A twinkle entered his eyes. "Hey! We could use that broken broom!"

Fitz nodded. "Yeah! And that rake too. For claws!"

Gulping down the rest of their sugary tea, they turned to their mother and, in unison, asked, "May we be excused?"

"Sure. Have fun." Jane longed to pull both boys to her and hug them tightly, but if she did that, she might alert them that something was wrong. Her sons were perceptive, and she'd rather they spent the rest of the afternoon in a small room building a sheet fort than watching troops of uniformed men and women march in and out of Storyton Hall. "See you at home for supper."

The boys paused to give Aunt Octavia a lightning-quick kiss on her wrinkled cheek. She pretended to shoo them away as though they were annoying her, but the second they were out of earshot, she picked up her teacup and, beaming, murmured, "See what I mean? Cherubim."

"Did they really receive a good report from their Sunday school teacher?" Jane asked. She put her napkin on the table. Though it was time for her to go, she was reluctant to leave.

"Well, her exact words were that their behavior was 'improved over last week.'"

Jane frowned. "That isn't saying much. Hem turned his cotton ball lamb into the three-headed dog from the first Harry Potter book. Their Sunday school teacher, who isn't familiar with the world of Harry Potter, was *not* amused."

"That doesn't sound so terrible."

"That's only the half of it," Jane went on. "Fitz fed his lamb to Hem's dog and at least three little girls in their class burst into tears."

Aunt Octavia sniggered.

"Don't encourage them," Jane admonished as she stood up. "I'd better go. I'll give you an update as soon as I can."

"Good luck, sweetheart. You can handle this." Aunt Octavia squeezed Jane's hand. The touch warmed her as she walked back down the cool servants' stairs toward Hannah's room and to what Jane fervently hoped would be the end of days of questions, confusion, and fear.

Sheriff Evans met her just inside the door. "Were you able to view the images on Ms. Grace's camera?"

Jane looked over his shoulder to where three paramedics crouched over Hannah's body.

"Yes," she said. "One of them shows the druid filling a syringe from a bottle in his medicine cupboard. If we could zoom in on the bottle, I'm positive that it would identify which poisonous plant extract he injected into Kira's neck." The sheriff opened his mouth to ask Jane another question, but she beat him to the punch. "What's Hannah's status?"

Evans gestured at each EMT in turn. "Hancock is administering fluids, Carilion just finished taking vitals, and Radford is about to break out the smelling salts. Those should bring Ms. Billingsley around, especially since she started stirring before the paramedics arrived. It's like she sensed she wasn't alone anymore but couldn't quite rouse herself from the trance the drugs had put her under."

The female paramedic named Radford held something under Hannah's nose. Within seconds, Hannah's eyes flew open and she pulled her covers up to her chin. She kicked out with both legs, trying to clear the space around her bed, and swung her head from left to right, her startled gaze traveling from unfamiliar face to unfamiliar face.

"Hannah!" Jane rushed toward the bed. "It's okay. These people are here to help you. You had too much medicine. You gave us quite a scare."

Jane knelt by the bed and reached for Hannah's hand, but Hannah snatched it away and turned her face to the ceiling. Her eyes rolled in their sockets, revealing so much white that she looked like a panicked horse.

"It's all right, ma'am," Radford said calmly. "We're giving you fluids because you were dehydrated. You'll be just fine."

"I'm not going anywhere. You can't take me anywhere!" Hannah tried to pull the IV out of her arm, but Hancock caught her wrist to stop her from doing so and she bucked in protest.

Carilion approached Sheriff Evans. "She might injure herself, Sheriff. I recommend transferring her to the gurney and using restraints."

Having overheard this, Jane leaned close to Hannah. "If you don't calm down, they're going to restrain you. Do you want that? Of course you don't. Please, Hannah. Calm down. Try to focus on my face. If you calm down, I'll call Victoria for you. Would you like me to call Victoria?"

At the sound of her sister's name, Hannah began nodding feverishly. "I need Via. Get me Via."

"I will," Jane whispered. She pushed her hands in a downward motion. "But you must lie still and let the paramedics treat you. If you do that, I'll pick up the phone on your bedside table and dial your sister's room. You can watch me. Deal?"

This time, Hannah was slow to nod. Her gaze had slid away from Jane and back to the crowd of people in her room. When her eyes met Jane's again, they were filled with distrust.

"Sheriff Evans? Could you ask some of our visitors to step out of Ms. Billingsley's room?" Jane's imperious tone made it clear that she was not making a request. "The circus atmosphere is obviously elevating her anxiety. She just woke from a deep slumber to find a group of strangers gathered around her bed. That would upset anyone." Jane darted an accusatory glance at Carilion. "Perhaps the three of us—you, me, and Ms. Radford—would be sufficient to see to her needs for now. Ms. Billingsley has agreed to receive the necessary treatment. In exchange, I've promised to send for her sister."

Jane didn't wait for the sheriff's response, but picked up the phone and dialed the Princess Bride Suite. The phone rang and rang, but no one answered.

Hannah, who'd been distracted by the departure of Deputy Emory and the other paramedics, now turned back to Jane with naked terror on her face.

"I'll call the front desk," Jane said hurriedly. "They can locate your sister."

Jane disconnected her call to the bridal suite and dialed zero. Sue answered with a cheerful, "Good afternoon, Ms. Billingsley. How can we be of service?"

"It's me, Sue," Jane said. "Ms. Billingsley is looking for her sister. She'd like Victoria to join her in her room. It's urgent."

"I just saw her heading for the Paperback Parlor!" Sue exclaimed. "I'll deliver the message myself."

"Your sister will be here in a few minutes." Jane replaced the phone in its cradle. "How are you feeling?"

Hannah eased her white-knuckle grip on her covers. "I'm thirsty."

Hearing this, the sheriff went into the bathroom to fill a glass with water. In his absence, and with the paramedic busy packing equipment into her kit, Jane was sorely tempted to ask Hannah why she'd poisoned Andrew Green. She could lean close to Hannah's ear and whisper the question very quietly. But Jane sensed—even if she possessed the callousness to ask this frightened, pain-riddled woman such a crucial question—that Hannah was incapable of replying.

Sheriff Evans returned with the water and gave it to Jane. "Do you want me to hold the glass?" Jane asked Hannah gently.

Hannah nodded weakly and took a sip. And then another.

Jane experienced a horrifying feeling of déjà vu. Only a few hours earlier, she'd held a glass of water mixed with activated charcoal to the druid's lips in an effort to coax the liquid down his swollen throat and counteract the effects of the arsenic he'd ingested.

Why? Jane was dying to ask Hannah. *Did you know that the druid was Kira's killer? If so, how did you find out? And why would you risk your entire future to avenge a friend's death? You and Kira weren't even close. Tammy is the only herbalist who deeply cared for Kira.*

If Jane were writing a novel, she'd reveal, in the denouement, that Hannah had been wearing a prosthetic hump all along. That her birth defect was a contrivance and she'd played the part of a chronic-pain sufferer in order to carry out the perfect murder. But Jane was not a novelist and Hannah's medical issues were very real. Jane also believed that Hannah had killed Andrew Green out of desperation. Why else would she deliberately subject herself to such agony? Or ruin the first day of her sister's marriage? And the most telling argument of all was the likelihood that she'd be caught.

Someone knocked on the door and Hannah cried, "Via!" in the shrill voice of a frightened child.

Jane rushed to let Victoria in, She barely managed to step aside as Victoria barreled into the room and knelt by her sister's side.

"What the hell is going on here?" she demanded angrily. "Why does my sister have an IV?" Victoria rounded on Jane. "What is the sheriff doing here? Don't your guests have the right to their privacy?"

Sheriff Evans cleared his throat and adopted an officious stance. He stood, feet spread hip-width apart, with his thumbs hooked under his weapon belt, and gazed steadily at Victoria. "Ms., uh . . ." He turned to Jane for help. Clearly, he'd forgotten Victoria's new surname.

"Mrs. Earle," Jane said.

"Mrs. Earle, your sister needed medical attention. She might have taken more than the recommended dosage of her prescribed medications. I can't say for certain, but she was barely conscious when we found her."

Victoria touched Hannah's forehead. "Oh, Banana. The thing this morning—it was too much for you."

"I'll be okay." Hannah managed a weak smile. "It was so pretty up in the hills, Via. I wish you could have been there."

"I know, puddin', but I'm here now. What can I get you?"

Hannah raised the arm attached with the IV. "I think I'm getting it already. Just don't let them take me to the hospital. I *was* hurting pretty badly when I got back from our trip and my pain meds weren't doing the job, so I took another dose."

"Is it possible that you opened the wrong bottle?" Victoria asked gently. "Could you have taken a Flexeril first followed by a Vicodin? Or the other way around?"

Keeping her eyes locked on her sister's, Hannah seemed to search her memory. "It's possible. I really don't know. I was nearly blind with pain."

"What is your pain level now, Ms. Billingsley?" Radford asked. "On a scale of one to ten, one being the lowest and ten being the highest."

Turning to the paramedic, Hannah said, "It's between a four and a five. And before you grow too concerned, I deal with that level on a daily basis. If you took an X-ray of my back, it would look like the aisle of a hardware store. I'm held together with rods, pins, plates, and screws. I spent so much of my life wearing a brace that I feel weird without it, and I've been stuck with so many needles that I could start my own IV." She paused for a breath. "Yes, I took the wrong pill, but I wasn't trying to kill myself or harm myself in any way. I was at a level nine at the time and my judgment was impaired. It won't happen again. I don't plan on riding a horse again. Ever. Please, let me sit with my sister in peace for a while. I'll remove the IV when the fluid bag is empty."

Radford started to protest when Sheriff Evans put a hand on her shoulder. "It's all right. Thank you, and thank your team for getting here so quickly. Deputy Emory will handle the paperwork and I'll check in with you later."

Shaking her head in confusion, annoyance over being dismissed, or a mixture of both, Radford collected her gear and left the room.

Though Hannah exhaled in relief, Victoria remained dissatisfied. "Despite my sister's medical issues, I don't understand why your presence was necessary, Sheriff."

"Perhaps she would prefer to explain that herself," the sheriff said. He took several steps back, giving the sisters their space, and Jane followed suit.

"Hannah?" Victoria took her sister's hand. "What's going on?"

The fearful expression returned to Hannah's face. "I don't know what he's talking about. I've been asleep since we got back." She darted a glance at the clock. "It's been over two hours. I have no idea what he means!"

Victoria studied her sister for a moment before caressing her hand and murmuring to her, "Okay, Banana. Okay, honey. I'm going to take these people to the patio and straighten this all out. We'll be right on the other side of the French doors."

"I'm afraid that's not how things are going to proceed," the sheriff said. He calmly pulled up a chair next to Hannah's bed. "You see, I've come to Storyton Hall ahead of the Alleghany police, and I don't expect them to be as patient with you as I've been, Ms. Billingsley. Kindly tell me one thing: Had you ever met or heard of Dr. Andrew Green before this morning?"

"Who's Andrew Green?" Hannah asked.

"The druid," Jane said.

Hannah glanced from Jane to the sheriff. "No. Of course not."

The sheriff spread his hands as though accepting her answer as an absolute truth. "All right. Did you bring the druid a piece of your sister's wedding cake?"

Hannah nodded, but shifted her gaze to Victoria. "It was packed in a take-out box and wrapped with string. I didn't get to see if he ate it, though. None of us were even able to meet him. Tom said that he was really angry that we'd invaded his privacy. We only had a chance to see his garden for a few minutes and then we had to leave." She released a resigned sigh. "I was in such pain by that point that it was probably a good thing that he kicked us out. If we'd stayed any longer, I might not have made it back."

"You're a tough cookie." Victoria tucked a damp tendril of hair behind Hannah's ear. Turning to Evans, she said, "What point are you dancing around, Sheriff? My sister never met this man until today and she brought him a piece of my wedding cake. Why are cops heading to Storyton Hall? You're not clarifying anything for me."

"I was hoping Ms. Billingsley wouldn't make this so difficult," the sheriff said, and Jane knew that she wouldn't have the chance to deliver the news to Victoria. Hannah and Victoria might be her guests, but crime was the sheriff's business, and he'd be the one working in conjunction with the police.

"Leave my sister alone." Victoria's voice was low and ominous. "I'm an Earle now. We're a very powerful Virginia family, and I think you've harassed her enough for one day."

The sheriff was the picture of composure as he said, "Dr. Green died shortly after ingesting the piece of cake your sister brought him. The Alleghany police have undoubtedly already begun running tests, but it's very likely they'll find traces of arsenic in the remains. Ms. Steward was with the doctor during his last moments, and she asserts that he was the victim of a fatal poisoning."

Victoria stood up and walked around Hannah's bed, putting herself between her sister and the lawman. "What are you implying, Sheriff?"

"I'm trying to prepare you for what's to come, Mrs. Earle. Officers will be arriving shortly to arrest your sister under suspicion of murder."

Hannah let out a bestial cry.

"Based on what hard proof?" Victoria asked acidly before making a visible effort to master her emotions. "Anyone could have tampered with that cake. Was the slice monitored since it was cut? Because if not, there is no evidence that my sister poisoned it. Where would she get arsenic in the first place?" She dismissed the notion with a wave of her hand. "This whole thing is absurd. I want you both to leave my sister's room this second. I'm calling my husband, and *he's* going to call his family's attorney."

During Victoria's speech, Jane had been watching Hannah for signs of guilt, but the only emotion she saw on the younger woman's face was fear.

"Can you help us sort this out?" Jane asked, directing her question to Hannah. "Did you pick up the cake in the kitchen or was it delivered to your room this morning?"

"Don't answer her, Hannah." Victoria's tone was sharp. "Wait for the lawyer."

But Hannah's eyes were already on Jane. "You've been kind to me, so I'll tell you."

"Hannah—" Victoria pleaded.

"I have nothing to hide," Hannah interrupted before pointing at the small refrigerator across the room. "I requested that fridge when I booked this room because I travel with ice packs. The freezer section is tiny, but it's big enough for my needs. Anyway, I boxed up a piece of cake last night and brought it back to my room. One of the waiters gave me the take-out box and the string. He even lined the bottom of the box with a paper doily."

Jane gave Hannah an encouraging nod. "When did you put the cake in the box?"

"Not long after I'd finished eating my piece. I knew we'd be visiting the druid the next morning because Tom had told me during dinner. He explained that he'd rented me a horse for the day so that I wouldn't be left behind." Her eyes grew moist. "No one's ever done anything like that for me. Except for you, Via. Tom also told me that the druid would love a slice of wedding cake. He rarely got to enjoy such a treat living way up in the hills."

"That was very thoughtful of you," Jane said and cast a quick glance at Sheriff Evans. She knew she'd run away with the interview, but he inclined his head, wordlessly signaling for her to continue. "And was the boxed piece of cake close at hand the rest of the night?"

Hannah pursed her lips in thought. "No. At one point, I went inside the hotel to use the ladies' room. And I also left it on the table when Tom and I decided to sit and talk on one of the garden benches."

"See!" Victoria cried triumphantly. "There were plenty of opportunities for another person to tamper with it."

Ignoring her, Jane pressed on, "I saw you and Tom chatting before I went inside for the evening. You seemed to be getting along really well. I'm glad, because Tom's a fine man." She hated to manipulate Hannah, but she had no choice. With a heavy sigh, she said, "I thought I knew him so well, but today, I learned that the druid was his father."

Hannah's mouth formed an O of surprise. "*What?*"

"I tracked Tom down today because I wanted to know why he kept mentioning Kira's name last night. After all, he hardly knew her." Jane focused intently on Hannah. "Did Tom tell you why he was so broken up about her death?"

Hannah twisted her sheets around her fingers. "I don't want to get him into trouble," she whispered.

Victoria was on her knees in a flash. "You need to tell us, Banana. You and Kira have known each other for years. You can't let her murder go unsolved."

Reaching for her water glass, Hannah took a long swallow. Still clutching the glass, she said, "Tom was worried that Kira might have visited the druid before she was killed. Tom was going to try to find out while the rest of us were looking at the garden of poisonous plants. He planned to pull the druid aside and ask him about Kira. With so many of us nearby, he wasn't concerned about his safety."

"Were you the only person who knew of this plan?" Jane asked.

"Yes," Hannah said. "Tom and I are alike in many ways. We understand solitude and the beauty of the natural world more than most. He was teased as a boy for being small and for growing up without parents. It wasn't quite the same experience as mine, but it made him sensitive. I guess you could say that I found a kindred spirit in him. And he in me. We trusted each other with stories of our pain . . . and a few secrets too."

At any other time, Jane would have found Hannah's revelation a source of joy, but all she could think about now was the take-out box containing the slice of cake sitting unattended at Hannah's place at the table.

"Did you notice the box at all?" Jane asked Victoria.

She shook her head. "Carson and I were so caught up visiting with guests that I barely sat down after we cut our cake. After sampling our piece, we went to the gazebo for our first dance. We didn't return to our seats until over an hour later."

"We'll have to speak with everyone else at that table," Sheriff Evans said.

Jane felt numb. Would the twists and turns of this day never cease? "If I remember correctly, there were a few

Medieval Herbalists seated there," she said. "As well as Tom Green."

Victoria stared at the sheriff. "This Mr. Green—he owns a plant shop, right? Which means that he has a supply of pesticides and fertilizers. I don't know much about medieval herbs, but in my job, I've come across multiple records of accidental poisoning from these sources."

"Did those cases involve arsenic?" Sheriff Evans wanted to know.

After hesitating just long enough to throw Hannah a look of distress, a look that spoke of her reluctance to incriminate her sister's new friend, Victoria said, "Each and every one."

FIFTEEN

While Jane had been preoccupied with Hannah and Victoria, the Fins had returned to Storyton Hall. Unfortunately, Jane didn't have the chance to speak with any of them because Sue from the front desk called Jane on her cell phone to tell her that the Alleghany police had arrived and were asking for her.

Jane had no prior experience with the police from the neighboring county, so she let Sheriff Evans take the lead. He and Jane stood in the main lobby, observed by a gaggle of curious guests, and made the necessary introductions.

The officer in charge was a man named McCullough. Jane had a good feeling about him—probably inspired by his unhurried air and his willingness to accept the sheriff's proposal that they all relocate to the large conference room in order to share information relevant to the case.

The party turned out to be a large one, consisting of Sheriff Evans and Deputy Emory, four Alleghany police officers, and Jane and Sinclair. Sterling had gone off to his lab to compare the rubbings he'd taken from the tire on Tom

Green's pickup truck with the marks found in the ground near the site where Kira's body was found. Lachlan was to interview the waitstaff on duty during the wedding to see if they remembered someone tampering with the piece of cake meant for the druid. As for Butterworth, he'd taken up his customary position by the front doors in an effort to create an atmosphere of normalcy.

Once everyone was seated, Sheriff Evans wasted no time outlining the details of Kira's case. "Until today, I had no concrete leads," he explained to his fellow lawmen. "We suspected Ms. Grace was engaged in extortion. Her financial status was dire and she may have turned to blackmail in the past. We can now conclude, judging from the images and timestamps on her camera, that she visited Andrew Green the day of her murder." He gestured at Sinclair. "This is Mr. Sinclair, the head librarian of Storyton Hall. He has a projector screen and will show you what we believe are Ms. Grace's final minutes on this earth as well as evidence indicating she was killed by Andrew Green."

Sinclair dimmed the lights and proceeded to scan through Kira's photographic tour of the druid's property. When he reached the most significant image, he paused the slideshow.

"This, gentleman, is likely the murder weapon to which Sheriff Evans referred," he said. "You can see that Dr. Green is filling a syringe from a jar. It wasn't possible to view the label from this image, so I blew it up. You can now read it quite clearly."

"Water hemlock?" Officer McCullough arched his brows. "Isn't that what the ancient Athenians made Socrates drink?"

"Yes, he was forced to commit suicide via poison hemlock," Sinclair said, noticeably impressed.

"The ME has yet to confirm our suspicions," Sheriff Evans cut in, "but I expect him to get back to us with his findings by day's end. Tomorrow at the latest. With our cases being so clearly linked, they should receive priority status."

Officer McCullough frowned. "Around here, that doesn't always mean much. Half of the department's on vacation." His gaze moved from the image onscreen to the sheriff. "Tell me something if you would. If the victim's camera wasn't found with her body, how did it end up in your hands?"

"I took it from the druid's cabin," Jane said before Evans could reply. "I knew it was wrong, but I think we have more important issues to address. For example, Andrew Green ingested a piece of cake laced with arsenic. This piece of cake was served at the Billingsley-Earle wedding, which occurred last night at Storyton Hall. The bride's sister, Hannah Billingsley, decided to bring a slice of cake to Andrew Green and asked a waiter for a take-out container. The next morning, she carried the cake from Storyton Hall to the druid's cabin."

"So why are we sitting around this table?" a young policeman asked McCullough. "The killer must be this Hannah Billingsley."

McCullough held up a finger, indicating patience. "Please continue, ma'am."

Jane looked at Sheriff Evans to see whether he wanted to take over, but he nodded to indicate that she could continue, so she did. "The sheriff and I were speaking with Ms. Billingsley shortly before your arrival. We'd also assumed that she was likely Andrew Green's poisoner. Our suspicions were increased when she didn't pick up the phone in her guest room or respond to repeated knocks on her door."

"What made you so certain she was inside?" McCullough wanted to know.

Jane was glad he'd asked this question, because it gave her an opportunity to describe Hannah's physical appearance and medical issues in advance of his meeting her.

"We learned that several people had the opportunity to lace that piece of cake with poison," Jane added after finishing up her summary of Hannah.

McCullough tented his fingers. "They're your guests, Ms. Steward. Do you suspect anyone in particular?"

"No," she confessed. "But I think the motive lies in the past. I believe the killer knew Andrew Green. Back when he was a practicing physician. Perhaps he hurt someone the poisoner cared about. Perhaps he hurt the poisoner. Maybe Kira Grace's wasn't the first life he deliberately brought to an end."

"There's another possibility," Sherriff Evans added. "This one excludes the herbalists and keeps the suspect list all in the family, so to speak. I'm talking about Andrew Green's son. Tom Green owns The Potter's Shed in Storyton. He led the herbalists on their hike this morning and was also a wedding guest. He had both the means and the opportunity to kill his father."

The sheriff went on to share what Victoria had told them about the case studies she'd come across involving arsenic and fertilizers and pesticides.

When Evans was finished, McCullough let out a whistle. "We have a ton of ground to cover. I hope I can count on your continued cooperation, Sheriff. And yours, Ms. Steward." After receiving assurance from both parties, McCullough turned to the officer seated to his right. "You and Anderson go pick up Green. Question him at the station. We'll interview everyone else here. It'll take too long to cart them back and forth."

"You're welcome to use this room as your center of operations," Jane said. "I'll have coffee, tea, and water sent in for your officers and the guests. Is there anything else I can do to help?"

"Yes." McCullough pointed at the screen. "I'd like that camera. Also, I'd prefer that no one leave the hotel without my permission. That goes for these Medieval Herbalists as well as any of the hotel staff involved with the preparation or serving of food at the wedding."

Jane didn't want her staff members living in the village to be detained past quitting time, so she requested they be interviewed first.

McCullough agreed. "They'll probably be eliminated right off," he told Jane as she headed for the door. "I'd also like copies of their employee files and I need to speak with your head cook!" he called after her.

Oh boy, Jane thought.

She found Mrs. Hubbard separating chilled homemade dough for dinner rolls.

"I don't care if he's the King of England!" she declared when Jane explained that a police officer needed to speak with her right away. "If I don't get this dough in the oven, there'll be no rolls for dinner! If it's so important, he can talk to me back here."

In the end, McCullough lost his patience and stormed into the kitchen.

"Didn't Ms. Steward tell you that I'm in the middle of a murder investigation?"

Mrs. Hubbard pointed at her ovens. "Time waits for no man, and neither does fresh bread. If I don't bake it now, our baskets won't be filled with the steaming hot, buttery rolls our guests love. Now that they're in, we can have a nice chat." She pulled out a stool. "Have a seat, dear. Would you like a piece of shortbread?"

And before McCullough could rebuff the offer, a plate of shortbread and a cup of tea appeared as though by magic in front of him.

Mrs. Hubbard sat opposite him and, smiling angelically, waited for him to speak. Jane took the empty stool to Mrs. Hubbard's left.

"Ma'am, could you tell me about the cake you made for the Billingsley-Earle wedding?" McCullough asked.

"Certainly!" Mrs. Hubbard exclaimed and began a lengthy recitation of her involvement in creating the Hildegard wedding feast.

McCullough shot Jane a confused glance, but she shook her head in warning and mouthed, "Don't ask."

"Could you recite the cake's ingredients?" he asked instead.

Mrs. Hubbard was delighted to oblige.

"So it contained almonds," McCullough murmured.

It suddenly dawned on Mrs. Hubbard that a policeman investigating a murder was keenly interested in the cakes she'd baked. Turning to Jane, she whispered, "What's this all about?"

"Someone used your beautiful cake to commit a terrible crime, Mrs. Hubbard. Officer McCullough is trying to discover who this person is."

Mrs. Hubbard's apple red cheeks paled. "I don't understand!"

"We think arsenic was added to a piece of cake," McCullough continued gently. "This would have been after the individual cakes were sliced and served. Hannah Billingsley requested a take-out box. Do you remember anyone from the waitstaff mentioning her wanting a piece of cake to take with her?"

"No!" Mrs. Hubbard cried. "I was swaying on my feet from exhaustion by that point. In fact, once the cakes were served, I practically crawled home and fell into bed."

Satisfied that Mrs. Hubbard had told him everything she knew, McCullough scooped up the shortbread, thanked her, and left.

Prior to entering Mrs. Hubbard's loud and fragrant domain, McCullough had questioned Storyton's waitstaff. Now it was time to interview the herbalists, and he made it clear that Jane was not invited to join him in the conference room.

Thus excluded, Jane headed to the Great Gatsby Ballroom, where she hung a sign announcing the postponement of the medieval fair until after dinner. She was just returning to her office to draft a message to the same effect, which could be printed, copied, and slipped under guest room doors by a pair of fleet-footed bellboys, when she was accosted by Mr. and Mrs. Earle.

"I can't believe you've allowed some Podunk police officer to treat your guests like criminals. You will rue the day you tangled with our family!" Mrs. Earle spat. "Neither my son nor my"—her face twisted as though she'd bitten into a piece of rotten fruit—"daughter-in-law will say one word without a lawyer present."

Jane plastered on her professional smile and said, "Officer McCullough is conducting a murder investigation. Had he chosen to do so, he could have carted every person in this resort to the police station for questioning. If you don't want your son or daughter-in-law to be interviewed without your attorney, that's your choice, but I would advise against referring to our local lawmen as Podunk. I assume you'd like to return to Richmond tomorrow."

"Our bags are already packed," Mrs. Earle scoffed. "The only tolerable thing about this place was the food, but now we have to worry about being poisoned!" She tapped the face of her gold Rolex. "No, missy, we'll be leaving the moment our attorney makes it clear to your *local lawmen* that Carson and Victoria had nothing to do with this nonsense. We have a company to run, for heaven's sake. We can't be stuck here with your sluggish Wi-Fi and your ridiculous antitechnology rules."

As much as Jane wanted to explain that the purpose of Storyton Hall's unique rules was to encourage an atmosphere of rest, relaxation, and reading, she sensed that her words would be wasted on Mrs. Earle. With a courteous smile still fixed on her face, Jane excused herself and exited the manor house, heading for home. She wanted to start dinner preparations before the twins returned from Aunt Octavia's.

Pushing open her garden gate, she reflected on her first meeting with Tammy Kota, and how she and the boys had peered up at her shadowy figure and taken her for a witch.

Who else have I completely misjudged? she wondered.

A dark-haired figure stood in the gloom beneath Jane's front door gable. A genuine smile sprang to her lips when she realized that the figure belonged to Edwin Alcott.

"Haven't you had enough drama for one day?" she asked.

"Apparently not." He grinned mischievously.

Sliding her key into her door, Jane paused to look at him. "How long have you been standing here?"

"Not long. When I stopped by Run for Cover and saw that Eloise had closed shop for the day, I got worried, so I took a few minutes to clean up and grab some provisions from the café before driving over." He gestured at a bag on the stoop. "I figured both you and Mrs. Hubbard have been through enough for one day. Besides, I made a promise to Fitzgerald and Hemingway and I'd like to make good on that promise."

Jane slipped her key into the lock and stepped inside. At once, the familiarity of her home wrapped around her like a chenille blanket. This was her haven. Her place of sanctuary. Her family's nest. Was she ready to invite Edwin to enter her most precious place again?

It's just dinner, she told herself.

Aloud she said, "The twins will be here soon. I called my aunt five minutes ago asking her to send them home, and those boys only have two speeds: fast and breakneck."

Edwin laughed. "Wouldn't you love to be young again? Every inch of my body is sore from riding that motorcycle. Ten years ago, it wouldn't have bothered me, but I'm feeling it in my back this evening." He held up his hands. "Don't worry. I can still heat up the food I didn't cook. My chef did all the work. I can only take credit as delivery boy." He carried the bag into Jane's kitchen. "Do you have any olive oil?"

When Hem and Fitz raced into the house a few minutes later, the aroma of garlic sautéing in butter was already wafting throughout the kitchen.

"Mr. Alcott!" Fitz shouted, his face lighting up like a small sun upon seeing Edwin standing at the stove, a red apron tied around his waist.

"You're back!" Hem cried giddily.

Edwin lowered the flame to a simmer just as both boys flung their arms around him.

He was clearly surprised by the show of affection, but quickly recovered and squeezed each twin in turn. "I think you've both grown a full inch since I last saw you."

"Really?" The boys exchanged happy looks.

"What are you cooking?" Hem asked, peering into the frying pan.

Edwin pointed at the oven. "Since the rest of the meal is warming up in there, I was going to sauté broccoli to round it off, but now that you two are here, I might let you gentlemen have a go at it. Why don't you wash your hands? I'll show you what to do."

While Edwin instructed the twins, Jane set the table. The oven timer beeped, and she plated the honey-glazed chicken skewers and grilled corn Edwin had brought from Daily Bread just as the three males finished cooking the broccoli.

As soon as they all sat down, the boys begged Edwin to talk of his travels. Jane hated to admit it, but she was just as eager to hear the details of his life away from Storyton.

Edwin didn't disappoint. He described the wares in the Turkish bazaars until Jane felt she could smell the fragrant spices or run her hands over a silk prayer rug. He spoke of men meeting in special cafés to smoke their hookah pipes and play games of backgammon on beautiful boards inlaid with mother-of-pearl.

"Many of their everyday things are so beautiful, so exquisitely made," Edwin said. "On cold winter days, I dream of their coffee." He smiled at the twins. "How you would love to explore the ruins of Pergamum and Ephesus. But for now, perhaps you'd be interested in solving a riddle. The answer will reveal a hidden treasure. How about it?"

If the twins leaned any closer to the table, their chins would soon hit their plates. "Yes!" they both cried.

Grinning, Edwin excused himself and opened the front door. He disappeared outside for a moment and then reentered the house carrying a plastic bag. "I tucked this behind a bush," he said to Jane. "Didn't want to ruin the surprise."

"You remembered to bring us something!" Hem clapped.

"Of course." Edwin presented each boy with a rectangular object wrapped in a thick layer of white tissue paper.

The boys tore off the paper and Jane silently prayed that Edwin hadn't given them anything fragile, but when she saw the edge of a wooden box, she relaxed.

"Whoa," Fitz breathed, running his fingers along the mother-of-pearl inlay on the box top. "Is this a backgammon game?"

"Like the men in Turkey play?" Hem added.

Edwin laughed. "No, though I will teach you how to play backgammon. It's a good game." He pointed at Hem's box. "These are puzzle boxes. They open, but not with a key. You must solve their riddle. When you do, you will find the treasure."

"Are they the same?" Hem asked.

"I don't think so," Fitz answered. "My flowers are different than yours. See?"

"That's right." Edwin said with a note of approval.

Hem looked at his brother. Very solemnly, he declared, "We won't solve this by acting like Harry Potter. We're going to have to think like Hermoine Granger."

Fitz nodded. "It's only for a little while." He then turned to Edwin. "Thank you, Mr. Alcott."

"Yeah, thanks!" Hem echoed. "These are so cool!"

"Take care of your plates before you start thinking like a girl," Jane teased.

Feigning a shudder, Fitz collected their dirty dishes while Hem carried their glasses to the kitchen sink and loaded them into the dishwasher.

"Cooties phase?" Edwin whispered.

"Big-time," Jane whispered back.

Having finished with their duties, the boys grabbed their boxes and darted upstairs.

"This might be the first time in history they forgot about dessert," Jane said.

"And I brought such an unusual one," Edwin said, producing a tin from the bottom of the plastic bag. "These are for you."

Jane took off the lid and peeled back a layer of wax paper, revealing pink, sugarcoated squares dotted with pistachios. "What are they?"

"Turkish delight.

"The candy the queen offered Edmund in *The Lion, The Witch, and The Wardrobe*?" Jane was astonished. "I've never seen it before." Her fingers hovered over a piece. "To think that Edmund betrayed his entire family in exchange for this treat."

Edwin shrugged. "To be fair, the queen's version was enchanted. This is the traditional version made with rosewater. Not magic."

Jane popped a candy in her mouth and chewed. It was gelatinous, extremely sweet, and had the consistency of a gumdrop except for the crunch of the roasted pistachio nut buried within its depths. Jane wasn't sure that she cared for the candy.

"They're not my favorite either," Edwin said with a laugh.

"But knowing how much you love books, I thought you'd like to try this candy. Just once."

"I'm glad I have. That was really thoughtful of you. And what you brought the boys—they'll never forget it." She took his hand. "I'd love to hear more about what you did and saw when you weren't a *special* guest of the sheik's, but I need to get back to Storyton Hall. Billy's coming to watch the boys and should be knocking on my door any second now."

Edwin pushed back his chair. "I understand. I also thought I'd peruse the fair. Have a casual chat with a few of the herbalists about books. Old books in particular. You're juggling enough as it is, and if I were a betting man—which I am—I'd wager that the book thief is feeling pretty confident about getting away with his crime in the midst of the chaos created by two murder investigations. Let me help you recover the missing herbal, Jane. This is what I do. It's who I am."

"The Templar," she said softly.

Edwin raised a warning finger. "Try not to bandy that name about in public."

The doorbell rang, interrupting Jane's airy laugh. It felt so good to smile and laugh with Edwin that Jane stepped close enough to kiss him on the mouth. The kiss was brief, but full of desire. And promise. "Thank you for everything you did today," she whispered.

"I'm not finished yet, sweet Jane." Edwin opened the front door and slipped outside with the liquid grace of a cat, leaving Billy blinking in surprise.

"The fair is a go," Billy told Jane as soon as he'd recovered. "The police didn't arrest any of the guests."

Jane could have hugged Billy for delivering this news, but she restrained herself. "Did all the herbalists get their tables ready in time?"

Billy nodded. "Yes, ma'am. They have some interesting stuff for sale too. I took a quick peek before I came over."

"I can only imagine," Jane said.

After saying good night to the twins, she left the house and called Sherriff Evans, who'd returned to the station.

"What's going on? Did the police leave?"

"For now," Evans said. "The ME wanted to review his preliminary results with McCullough. McCullough also wanted to talk to Tom Green. He collected statements from everyone who went on this morning's hike or had access to that piece of cake. All except Hannah Billingsley, that is. The younger Mrs. Earle forced her sister to lawyer up. She's claiming that her sister was coerced into speaking with the two of us while under the influence of medication. She also asserts that we violated Hannah's privacy."

Jane was shocked. "Victoria said that?"

"She's very angry."

"And she's extremely protective of her sister." Jane felt a prick of shame. "Consider how things looked from her viewpoint. She entered her sister's room to find three paramedics, the sheriff, and the resort manager encircling her frightened sister. I can't really blame Victoria for her reaction."

Jane heard another phone ring in the background. "I need to take this, Ms. Steward. I'm sure we'll talk later."

The medieval fair was a subdued event. Despite the upbeat instrumental music being piped into the ballroom through the overhead speakers, there was a distinct absence of enthusiasm among the vendors. Their lack of interest in describing their wares affected the shoppers, and few guests or villagers seemed inspired to reach for their wallets.

Jane made a beeline for Tammy's table and was relieved to find a small crowd gathered there. They were raptly listening to Tammy explain why her natural products were both more effective and healthier than those they could purchase in most stores.

"They're more expensive too," a man pointed out.

"That's true," Tammy agreed pleasantly. "But they'll last twice as long, so you get a better deal if you buy from me. Not only that, but by not supporting companies that use harmful ingredients or dump toxic chemicals into the earth, you really end up in a win-win situation. Hold out your hand, sir, and tell me if this bug spray smells nice."

Grudgingly, the man allowed Tammy to dab a little on his skin. He raised his hand to his nose, sniffed, and shrugged. "It's okay. I don't really care how I smell, though. I'm willing to stink like a garbage dump as long as the mosquitoes leave me alone. It's hell trying to fish when they're eating you alive."

"I know it works, so I'd like two bottles, please," Jane said loudly. "As well as two bars of that incredible gardener's soap and a jar of lavender bath salt."

"Coming right up!" No sooner had Tammy moved to bag Jane's selections than a lady guest started filling her arms with items from the table.

Realizing that she had an audience, the woman giggled. "I'm getting a head start on my Christmas shopping! I work in an office filled with women and we do Secret Santa exchanges every year. These soaps, essential oils, and scented satchels are the perfect size. And I won't have to stress over what to buy come December. I'll have unique and thoughtful gifts all ready to go."

"That's really smart," another woman said and scooped up a jar of eucalyptus-scented exfoliating scrub and a bottle of moisturizing body lotion.

Following a rush of sales, Tammy looked genuinely happy for the first time since Kira's death.

"You're beautiful when you smile," Jane said.

"I love what I do." Tammy started rearranging her wares. "It isn't about the money either. I love creating quality products, and I love matching people with the product they need most. It's a calling, and all the other things that happened this weekend almost made me forget how much I value my calling."

Jane saw the sorrow in the older woman's eyes. Tammy Kota was no killer. And Jane didn't believe she was a thief either. "I'm so sorry. About everything."

"I know you are, dear girl," Tammy said. "And I bear no ill will against the sheriff or the cops. They're just doing their jobs. What I can't understand is why anyone would kill the druid. Every plant he grew has two faces. A yin and a yang. Poison and healing. It just depends on the application."

"Perhaps the druid had two faces as well," Jane suggested.

Tammy grunted. "I'm sure he did. We all do, but some of us are better at hiding the less attractive one than others."

A customer approached the table and Jane moved off, her thoughts turning from the herbalists to Tom Green. As Jane strolled by Vivian's table and her books on garden conservation, and the Scannavinis' table with their bottles of perfumes, she considered how Tom had spent his entire life wondering what secret his father had fled from. Perhaps Andrew Green had carried the secret inside himself all along.

His other face, Jane thought. She stopped to stare at the twisted face of a dried mandrake root at the Poison Princess's booth. *Did Tom kill his father because he finally discovered the hidden side of the man he'd only partially known?*

As though in answer, her cell phone rang and Sheriff Evans's number surfaced on the bright screen.

Jane hurried out of the ballroom through a rear exit leading into a staff corridor and was immediately enveloped by cool air, dim lighting, and silence.

"I wanted you to hear the news directly from me," the sheriff said after Jane answered the call. His voice sounded raspy and thin, as though the long day and the burdens of his job had suddenly aged him. "Tom Green has been arrested on suspicion of murder. McCullough believes Tom had the strongest motive for killing Andrew Green."

Jane was gripping her phone so tightly that her knuckles had turned white. "Which was?"

"Money. His father had a safe filled with cash," Evans said.

SIXTEEN

Every part of Jane rebelled against the idea that Tom Green had killed his own father. She wasn't alone in her disbelief. The Fins also felt that the police had taken the wrong person into custody.

"Unfortunately, Mr. Green had means, opportunity, and in Officer's McCullough's eyes, motive." Sinclair said. "To secure Mr. Green's freedom, we must offer up the real killer. *If* the killer is still among us. Mr. Sterling? You've deduced that the tire mark embedded in the embankment near Storyton River on the day Ms. Grace's body was discovered is a match to the tire on Mr. Green's truck, correct?"

Sterling nodded. "Mr. Green's pickup is a 1985 Chevy C10. It wasn't hard to establish that the track belonged to one of the Goodyear tires from that truck."

Once again, Jane and the Fins had gathered in Uncle Aloysius's office. Jane, who'd been spinning her uncle's globe while she listened to the Fins exchange information, suddenly left her chair and approached the piece of slate containing the list of The Medieval Herbalists' names.

"The killer must be on this board." She jabbed at the slate. "And I believe we'll be closer to finding out who he or she is as soon as we hear from Butterworth."

Prior to convening in her uncle's office, Jane had sent Butterworth to speak with Claude Mason. "I don't care how you get the information out of him," she'd told the butler. "I need to know how he learned of the druid. Who was his source? Because that person may have had a connection to the man who was once known as Andrew Green, MD, and that fact will move their name to the top of our suspect list."

Until Butterworth reported back, Jane wanted to focus on the other herbalists. Picking up a stick of chalk, she drew a line through two names: Nico Scannavini and Michelle Scannavini. "This couple is in the clear. They skipped the wedding feast and the hike. According to Butterworth, they spent the morning hanging out by the Jules Verne Pool. Following that, they enjoyed an early lunch in the Rudyard Kipling Café."

"But why?" Lachlan frowned. "Why did they blow off what were bound to be two of their group's most unforgettable events?"

"I can answer that," Aunt Octavia said. She was comfortably settled in the wing chair closest to the window and was petting a comatose Muffet Cat in long, slow strokes from the top of his head to the tip of his tail. "According to the housekeeping staff, Mr. Scannavini and the Poison Princess had a fling during last year's retreat. Even though Mrs. Scannavini has forgiven her husband, it was very difficult for her to be in the same room with 'the tramp.'" Aunt Octavia held up a finger. "Mrs. Scannavini used a far more derogatory term, but I prefer not to repeat vulgarities. In any case, following your book club discussion, Jane, the couple elected to distance themselves from their fellow herbalists for the remainder of the retreat."

Uncle Aloysius shrugged. "Sounds reasonable to me. I

can certainly understand why Mrs. Scannavini wouldn't be able to enjoy herself in the company of her husband's former lover."

"Me too," Jane said. "Let's move on. I'm going to circle the names of the wedding guests who were seated at the bride and groom's table. These people had the best opportunity to add poison to the cake."

"Wouldn't one taste arsenic?" Aunt Octavia wanted to know. "I like to think my palette is discerning enough to detect a lethal dose of poison, even if it was mixed with lots of sugar." Her eyes gleamed and Jane guessed that her aunt was lost in a fantasy involving a very large slice of cake.

"I believe the arsenic was blended with honey and the mixture was drizzled over the entire piece," Sterling said. "The liquid would have soaked into the cake and the sweetness of the honey would have helped mask the slightly metallic taste of the arsenic. It isn't bitter like cyanide and can be disguised fairly easily."

Aunt Octavia sighed. "Poor Mrs. Hubbard. She'll never look at a wedding cake the same way again."

Though Jane adored Mrs. Hubbard, this was not the time to focus on her feelings. Turning back to the board, she asked, "Which of these herbalists could obtain arsenic?"

Before Sinclair could reply, the phone on the desk rang. "That'll be Mr. Butterworth." Sinclair passed the heavy rotary telephone to Jane.

"I've spoken with Mr. Mason who insisted that he couldn't remember which member had originally e-mailed him regarding the druid of Storyton," Butterworth began. "It was only when I threatened to recall Officer McCullough that Mr. Mason was suddenly able to clear the cobwebs from his mind and tell me what I wanted to know," Butterworth said in a self-satisfied tone.

"And?" Jane pressed.

"Hannah Billingsley first raised the subject." Butterworth

paused for a moment to allow this to sink in. "Ms. Billingsley wrote Mr. Mason that her sister, Victoria, had stumbled upon a document citing the existence of a holistic healer in Storyton, Virginia. At this point, the site for the next group retreat had not yet been chosen and Ms. Billingsley—Hannah, that is—proposed The Medieval Herbalists book a long weekend at Storyton Hall. She went on to suggest that they might look into paying a visit to this mysterious healer should the group end up at Storyton next summer."

"I can't believe it," Jane said, speaking into the mouthpiece while also addressing everyone else in the room. "Hannah also carried the poisoned piece of cake to Andrew Green. So is she the killer?"

"What's her motive?" Lachlan asked and then held out both hands. "I'm just playing devil's advocate."

Sinclair nodded in approval. "Having a theory challenged is the best way to view its strengths and its flaws."

"I don't see Kira's death as motive," Jane said. "I know that sounds callous, but it's Tammy who was Kira's friend, not Hannah. Why would Hannah risk her future and endure such physical pain to avenge the murder of an acquaintance?"

"She wouldn't," Uncle Aloysius declared. "But is there another person this young woman would have killed for? Someone she cares about who might have been hurt by Andrew Green in the past?"

Jane stared at him. "The person Hannah loves most is Victoria. Their bond is undeniably powerful. I felt it within minutes of meeting them. But what would have wounded Victoria so deeply . . ." She trailed off. Suddenly, she was standing in Victoria's guest room again. Victoria, resplendent in her wedding gown, was giving her older sister a pep talk. Jane remembered two details quite vividly. The first was putting flowers in Hannah's hair. The second was Hannah describing her sister's tendency to keep everything and anything associated with her late mother.

"You've had an epiphany," Aunt Octavia said.

Holding out a finger, Jane spoke into the earpiece. "Butterworth, could you use the computer in Sinclair's office to research Hannah Billingsley's mother? I'd like to know how she died."

"Certainly," Butterworth replied.

Jane put the phone down on her uncle's desk and then returned to the slate board. She circled Hannah's name twice and then glanced at Sterling, who knew more about chemicals than the rest of the assembly. "Hannah restores antique botanical prints and drawings. Would any of her art materials contain arsenic?"

"Certain pigments added to paint contain arsenic," Sterling said. "However, it would be extremely difficult to isolate the arsenic."

Sinclair, who'd been staring at the laptop screen, now looked at Sterling. "Ms. Billingsley is part of a large network of auction houses, antique dealers, and art gallery owners. She could acquire hazardous materials from another century. William Morris wallpaper containing toxic green paint would be easier to boil down to a liquid form than artist's paint from the tube, for example."

"It's possible, but one would still need some skill in chemistry to successfully produce enough milligrams of arsenic to kill a healthy adult male," Sterling said. He turned to Jane. "Why Hannah Billingsley? I thought you believed her to be innocent?"

"Because of the pain she endured in order to deliver that poisoned cake to Andrew Green." Jane now circled Victoria's name. "I no longer think his death is tied to Kira's murder. I think Hannah steered the herbalists to Storyton because she discovered that Dr. Green had something to do with her mother's passing. When I stopped by the bridal suite to deliver the wedding bouquets to the Billingsley sisters, I learned that their mother died of cancer. Victoria was a young girl when this happened, and growing up without a mom clearly marked her. I think Hannah did her best to fill her mother's shoes, but at what cost?" She paused. "Most of us see Victoria as the stronger sister, right?"

There were several murmurs of assent.

"Because she exudes self-confidence," Jane said. "She's self-possessed while Hannah is quiet and reserved. But I've seen another side of Hannah. She comes to life when she talks about herbs or her work. And I've witnessed the fierce love she bears for her sister. Like Tom, Hannah also had the means and the opportunity. The unanswered question is whether she had a valid motive or simply played the role of the unwitting courier for the real murderer."

At that moment, Butterworth appeared in the doorway. He stood like a soldier at attention. "Mrs. Janice Billingsley was experiencing flu-like symptoms and chronic fatigue," he announced somberly. "Eventually, she saw a physician and was informed that she had Stage 4 cancer. After being told that she had approximately three months to live, she was given several treatment options—which she refused as these were likely to prolong her suffering—and sent home."

"Damn cancer!" Uncle Aloysius muttered angrily. "Those poor girls."

Butterworth allowed for a moment of silence before continuing. "I thought I might have to gain access to Mrs. Billingsley's medical records, which would have cost us valuable time, but her name popped up in an article from the *Journal of Clinical Oncology*." He brandished the sheet of paper in his right hand. "This is a summary of the key points." Pointing at the slate board, he said, "I concur with your theory, Miss Jane. Hannah Billingsley killed Andrew Green as an act of revenge."

Aunt Octavia shifted in her chair, causing Muffet Cat to open his eyes halfway and cast his yellow-eyed glare at the person closest to him, which happened to be Jane. However,

Jane was too caught up in Butterworth's narrative to take note of the irritated feline.

"Would you explain what you found in that article?" Jane asked Butterworth.

Butterworth inclined his head. "According to a clinical research study, Mrs. Billingsley was one of hundreds of women diagnosed with cancer after taking a specific medicine during pregnancy. The medicine, Benetyne, was meant to relieve acute morning sickness."

Sterling frowned. "It caused cancer instead?"

Butterworth spread his hands in a gesture of helplessness. "The harmful side effects weren't immediately evident. In fact, the discovery of cancer among patients having used Benetyne for several months or for multiple pregnancies didn't present for years. The first sign that something was very wrong with this drug was the increase of birth defects in infants of mothers who used Benetyne."

Jane gasped. "Is that what happened to Hannah? All those surgeries? The braces and the pain? Her lifelong torment was because of this drug?"

"I believe so, yes," Butterworth said gravely. "Cervical kyphosis and other spine and neck issues were prevalent among the infants affected by the drug."

Aunt Octavia reached into her housedress for a lace handkerchief. "This is too horrible. Are you saying that because Hannah and Victoria's mother took a medicine to relieve the symptoms of morning sickness, she ended up delivering a baby girl with a birth defect? And, not too many years later, this same woman died a premature death—her body riddled with cancer?"

"Yes." Butterworth folded the sheet of paper in two and glanced at Sinclair. "There were a few obstetricians—not many, mind you—but a few, who continued to prescribe the drug even after word began to spread that it was unsafe."

"Why would someone do such a thing?" Jane cried.

Sterling sighed. "For the perks. This occurred two decades ago—before the relationship between prescribing doctors and pharmaceutical reps was regulated. The drug reps could offer physicians all kinds of incentives in exchange for writing prescriptions using their products. They'd give the doctors golf trips, cases of expensive wine, steak dinners at the finest restaurants, stock options, the latest equipment for his or her practice—the list goes on and on."

Aghast, Jane went quiet. So did everyone else. The silence in the room was heavy. Haunted. It was as though the ghosts of all the innocent women and children filled the space, mutely pleading for justice. Jane closed her eyes, and when she did, she saw Hannah in her maid of honor gown. Recalling the younger woman's embarrassment because the hump of her upper back had been exposed, Jane felt a sharp stab of grief on her behalf.

"Did you find out if Andrew Green was Janice Billingsley's obstetrician?" she whispered into the silence. "Is that why he had to abandon his child and start a new life as a recluse? Why he had to become a man with no identity? Because he continued to prescribe this drug after it was rumored to cause birth defects?"

"I don't know, but I suspect Mr. Sinclair is already searching for that answer." After exchanging nods with Sinclair, Butterworth moved to the slate. "There is another fact to consider, and that involves the pharmaceutical company responsible for manufacturing Benetyne."

Jane groaned. "Don't tell me . . ." But she knew what Butterworth would say before he spoke. She'd seen the initials E.P. in the druid's notebooks. She knew exactly which company Andrew Green had worked for—and had continued working for even after leaving his old life behind.

Butterworth touched Victoria's name, slightly smudging the V. "It was Earle Pharmaceuticals."

"There's your most logical source for the arsenic,"

Sterling said with confidence. "Arsenic compounds are used to wipe out certain cancer cells, aren't they, Mr. Sinclair?"

"One moment." Sinclair's hands fluttered over the keyboard like bird's wings. "You are correct, Mr. Sterling. Earle Pharmaceuticals produces one such drug created from arsenic compounds. There's a lengthy description of the tumor-fighting properties of this drug and an equally lengthy list of its potential side effects."

Uncle Aloysius cleared his throat. "Forgive me if I sound obtuse, but we don't think Victoria's young man smuggled arsenic from his company's lab per her request, do we?" He turned to his wife with a look of tenderness. "I know a boy will do just about anything for his girl, but would he steal poison for her? What sane reason could she possibly give for asking him to do such a thing?"

Jane leapt to her feet. "We're venturing into the realm of pure conjecture, and we have no time for that. I don't care how many attorneys the Earles keep on retainer. I'm going to have a talk with the blushing bride."

"A pair of Fins should accompany you," Sinclair said. "In the event things turn physical. At this hour, you're likely to encounter both newlyweds."

Lachlan had the quickest reflexes and Butterworth was the most adept at hand-to-hand combat, so these two formidable men flanked Jane as she knocked on the door to the Princess Bride Suite.

Carson cracked the door and peered out through the opening. "Seriously? Don't you think we've been disturbed enough for one day?"

"That depends," Jane said pleasantly. "You could invite us in for a friendly chat, or you could shut the door, and I will march straight to my office and dial the Alleghany police station. It's your choice."

Carson looked amused. "Really? Do you know how many times people have tried to get one over on me? I'm heir to the Earle Pharmaceutical empire. I was born with a BS meter, and it's going off right now. You're not going to call anyone."

Jane crossed her arms over her chest. "Your meter must have been malfunctioning for well over a year, because your wife has been keeping secrets from you." She leaned forward and raised her voice. "Isn't that true, Victoria?"

A flash of doubt crept into Carson's eyes, and he darted a glance to his left.

"Let them in or we'll never get any rest," Victoria grumbled. "But don't expect me to play the gracious hostess," she added as Jane, Butterworth, and Lachlan entered the spacious sitting room area of the bridal suite. Victoria was stretched out on one of two sofas perpendicular to the fireplace. She wore white sweatpants and an ivory sweater and held a glass of red wine in her hand.

"May I sit down?" Jane asked, indicating the sofa opposite Victoria's.

Instead of answering, Victoria waved at the bottle of wine on the coffee table. "I'm having a nightcap. Want to join me?"

"That would be lovely, thank you," Jane said, thinking that the newlyweds might relax their guard if she also imbibed.

After Butterworth did the honors, Jane toasted the health of the bride and groom. Carson took a tentative sip of the pinot noir, but not Victoria. She drank a deep swallow and then leaned back against the sofa cushions with an air of feigned nonchalance.

"I believe I understand why you and your sister hated Andrew Green. The man known locally as the druid." Jane spoke softly, keeping her gaze on the hearth as though it were wintertime and a stack of thick logs burned in the fireplace. "It was his fault, wasn't it? That your mother died of cancer. He gave her a harmful drug. Due to his blatant misconduct, you and your sister lost your mother at far too young an age. And because of one man's greed, Hannah also endured a lifetime of physical pain."

Jane stopped talking and let her words hang in the space between the sofas. Victoria drained the contents of her wineglass and reached for the bottle. Butterworth moved to perform his butler duties, but Jane shook her head to stop him.

"What the hell is she talking about?" Carson asked in a petulant tone. When Victoria didn't reply, but instead, raised the bottle to her lips and took a long pull of wine, he stared at her in open disapproval. "Via. Come on. We're not at a frat party."

"Don't call me that!" Victoria snapped. "Only my sister calls me that. I told you before. *She's* my only family."

Carson was clearly stung by the remark. "I'm your family too. I'm your husband!"

"Whatever," Victoria murmured and took another swig of wine.

Jane allowed the awkward silence to lengthen before she spoke again. "I grew up without knowing my parents. I had my great-aunt and -uncle, but I wasn't like the other kids and I felt the difference. There was a hole in the middle of my chest that was never filled. Not until I had kids of my own, that is. I'm sorry you had to feel that emptiness too. I'm sorry for both you and Hannah."

Slowly, Victoria turned her head to look at Jane. "You lost both parents?"

"I have no memory of either of them," Jane said sadly. "I had to rely on other people's memories. On letters and photographs. Do you remember your mom at all?"

"In flashes," Victoria whispered after a long pause. "I'm not sure if they're real or something I saw on TV." Tears welled in her eyes. "Green kept prescribing that drug *after* it was pulled from the market, you know. His deal with Earle Pharmaceuticals was just too sweet."

Carson, who was unaccustomed to being ignored, moved

to stand directly in front of Victoria, blocking her line of sight to Jane. Waving both hands in front of her face, he said, "Hello? Earth to Victoria. This is your husband speaking. The man you love. What the hell are you babbling about? Why are you talking about my company?"

Victoria sat up. Gingerly, she set the wine bottle on the coffee table and then released a long, slow sigh. "I'm sorry, Carson. I didn't mean for you to find out this quickly, but there's no avoiding it." She glanced up at him with a mixture of pity and contempt. "*Your* company is responsible for death, illness, and suffering. Because of a drug *your* company produced, my mother died prematurely and my sister spent her life in pain—both physical and emotional. Mine was just emotional, thanks very much."

"What—" Carson spluttered.

"Shut up," Victoria commanded. Her voice was like cold steel.

Carson reeled backward as though he'd been slapped.

Her eyes simmering with what Jane knew was a lifetime's worth of anger, Victoria pointed at a wing chair near the fireplace. "Sit there and be quiet. I need to speak with Ms. Steward." Without waiting to see if Carson would comply, Victoria fixed her gaze on Jane again. "I came across a study on Benetyne when I first starting working at the library. A med student needed material for a research paper on birth defects of the spine. Because of Hannah's condition, I was naturally curious about his topic and ended up reading most of the material he requested. Imagine my surprise when I learned about Benetyne. The dates of the drug's availability corresponded with my mother's pregnancies, so I did more digging. I found some old receipts in a box at home—my mom kept a file of drugstore receipts—and discovered that a Dr. Andrew Green had given her multiple prescriptions for Benetyne."

"Especially given the age gap between you and Hannah," Jane said.

Victoria balled her hands into fists. "Exactly! He would have seen Hannah. My mom had to bring her everywhere because she couldn't get anyone else to watch her. So that scumbag would have known what he'd done by prescribing Benetyne to my mom during her first pregnancy. And yet he prescribed it *again*. It's a miracle that I came out healthy."

"It is," Jane agreed, silently wondering how many other babies weren't as lucky. "Where was your father through all this, if you don't mind my asking?"

Looking aggrieved, Victoria picked up the wine bottle. She refilled her glass, but didn't drink from it. "He couldn't accept Hannah. He tried for a little while, but he and my mom divorced not long after I was born. He remarried and moved to California. We never heard from him again."

Jane fought to keep her emotions in check. It was difficult to listen to all that Hannah and Victoria had endured. She knew, at the end of Victoria's story, there would finally be an answer to why Andrew Green had been poisoned, but she now realized that the explanation would give her no comfort. No relief. This was a story about two little girls whose lives had been defined by the bad choices made by others. Those choices had continued to plague them until all they had left was each other. And a desire for revenge.

"After discovering that Andrew Green had prescribed the Benetyne, what did you do next?" Jane asked.

"I tried to hunt the bastard down," Victoria said sharply. "Of course, he was already off the grid by then. My next move was to seduce Carson in order to gain access to the Earle Pharmaceutical files. I figured it was a long shot, so imagine my surprise when not only did I find out that HR had a record on Green, but that it was still active."

Jane hadn't expected this. However, she was unable to

ask Victoria another question because Carson had bolted to his feet and was standing in front of his wife again. "You *used* me?"

"Sorry," Victoria said without much sincerity. "At night, I'd get on your computer after you were asleep to access company files. I learned that Green was on your payroll— that he'd signed a contract with Earle Pharmaceuticals before he fled to Storyton stating that he would continue the research he'd done during his academic days. This was before he went into private practice. He was studying pain management using poisonous plants."

"So?" Carson spat. "We have contracts with dozens of doctors and scientists. How do you think new medicines are invented?"

"Funny that neither you nor your parents mentioned knowing Dr. Green to the authorities," Jane said.

Carson sneered at her. "Our attorney advised us not to volunteer any information. Why should we?" He now directed his sneer at his bride. "*We're* not murderers."

"Yes, you are!" Victoria shouted. "Your family killed my mother! Your parents are the CEOs of a corrupt and immoral company. They suspected that Benetyne was responsible for birth defects, but they wanted to keep it on the market for as long as possible. They wanted to rake in a little more cash before they were forced to recall it. I *know* this because I found internal memos between your parents and the R and D department in your father's file cabinet. And you're no better. You're seeking FDA approval for a drug that has no business being manufactured. Pretending to be in love with such a shallow human being has been the hardest thing I've ever had to do in my life!"

"The only person you love is your troll of a sister!" Carson yelled.

Victoria nodded. "That's true. I doubt I could love any man. Between Green and my father, my trust in men was ruined from the start. Maybe a good man could have turned me around, but someone like you just made me more determined to set things right. I didn't have to marry you. I could have just strung you along until I had what I needed, but I wanted to make sure Hannah had plenty of money to live on if something happened to me. That's why I convinced you not to sign a prenup."

Butterworth began to edge closer to Carson. Lachlan also made his way deeper into the room and stood, tensed and ready to spring if necessary, behind Jane's sofa. Jane decided to ask Victoria a critical question before the fight between the newlyweds escalated into a full-blown brawl.

"Things are definitely clearer to me now," Jane said in a conversational tone. Her demeanor was so out of place that both Carson and Victoria looked at her. "I now know how you were able to tell Hannah where Storyton's druid was located. You found the information in Andrew Green's Human Resources file. Hannah then passed the information on to Claude Mason." Victoria gave a little shrug, which Jane read as assent and pressed on. "Did you get the arsenic from Earle Pharmaceuticals too?"

A veil fell over Victoria's features. She made a poor show of hiding a yawn behind her hand and then rose gracefully to her feet. "I'm sorry, but I've had enough for today. I'm going to bed."

"Not in that room, you're not!" Carson cried, pointing toward the bedroom suite.

Ignoring him, Victoria strolled into the room and shut the double doors behind her. She engaged the lock before Carson had a chance to wrap his hand around the brass handle.

"Open up this second!" he raged. When it was clear that his new wife had no intention of obeying, he swung around and glared at Jane. "You do it! Get a master key and unlock this damn door."

Butterworth stepped in front of Jane, shielding her with his body. "Mr. Earle. Mr. Lachlan and I will now escort you to another room." Carson's face grew ruddy with fury, but Butterworth didn't give him a chance to speak. Darting forward, he closed the distance between himself and the younger man in a flash. Towering over him, he whispered, "I will repeat myself once more. Mr. Lachlan and I will now escort you to another room. You can come willingly, or we can drag you out by your ankles. Which will it be, Mr. Earle?"

To Jane's relief, Carson left the Princess Bride Suite under his own steam.

As soon as the men were gone, Jane crossed to the writing desk and picked up the phone. Releasing a heavy sigh, she dialed the number for the Alleghany police.

When the officer on duty answered, Jane said, "I need to speak with Officer McCullough, please. Yes, it's urgent. He's arrested the wrong person for the murder of Andrew Green. The real killer is Hannah Billingsley, and she's here. At Storyton Hall."

SEVENTEEN

By the time Jane finally crawled into bed, it was so late that the night had already begun to morph into the next day and she felt sick with exhaustion.

After re-creating the scene from the bridal suite, Jane had watched McCullough and two other officers load Hannah, Victoria, and Carson into police cars. Carson had refused to ride in the same vehicle as his wife, though Victoria had been completely oblivious to his existence. She'd been far too preoccupied comforting her sister.

"I know you're scared," Jane had heard her whisper. "But by tomorrow morning, it'll be all over and everything will be okay. You'll see. Have I ever let you down before?"

Hannah had shaken her head, her eyes filled with doubt. Jane couldn't blame her. Not only was Victoria's statement cryptic and strange, but Hannah also had every reason to be terrified. She could no longer hide in her guest room. It was time for her to confess to her crime. She'd deliberately poisoned Andrew Green and her secrets were about to be laid bare.

Jane had watched a female officer gently help Hannah into the backseat of the cruiser before closing the door.

"We'll be in touch," she'd said, giving Jane a polite nod.

The police cars had eased away from Storyton Hall's entrance, their tires crunching over the gravel driveway as they headed for the massive iron gates. A few days ago, the three passengers in those cars had arrived as honored guests. Now, they were being taken over the mountain for questioning.

Jane, who'd been flanked by Fins, had stared at the red taillights until they'd receded into the blackness. When there'd been nothing left to see, she'd finally closed her dry, throbbing eyes. Still, the image of the red lights had remained imprinted on her inner lids.

"We all need to grab a few hours of sleep," she'd told the Fins and had gone home to find Billy sound asleep on her sofa. After laying a blanket over him, she'd trudged upstairs. She managed to kick off her shoes and climb under the blankets before she was pulled down into blissful oblivion.

It seemed as though she'd just closed her eyes when she felt a hand shaking her forearm and a high-pitched voice saying something about breakfast.

Jane tried to swat the offending hand away, but a second hand clamped onto her shoulder and another voice rambled on about a man and the doorbell. The persistence of both disturbances dragged her closer to wakefulness.

"I need . . . a few more minutes," Jane croaked without opening her eyes.

As though from a great distance, she heard whispering followed by the sounds of footsteps descending the stairs. And then, silence.

It was the silence that forced her into alertness.

Slowly, she dragged her sleep-heavy body out of bed, changed out of yesterday's clothes, pulled on a pair of yoga pants and a well-worn Virginia Tech tee, and downed three ibuprofen before heading downstairs to see what mischief the twins had gotten into.

Edwin was in the kitchen. He stood on one side of the island like a professor at a lectern while Hem and Fitz sat on stools on the opposite side, cracking eggs into mixing bowls.

"Eggcellent." Edwin said with the hint of a smile and, after a heartbeat, the twins giggled at his corny joke. Catching sight of Jane, Edwin's smile grew. "Good morning. We're making omelets. Would you like to place your order? We have an array of possible fillings." He waved a hand at the small glass bowls lined up on the island. "Bacon, feta, cheddar, mushrooms, tomatoes, scallions, ham, spinach, or avocado."

Never had Jane regretted her role as Guardian as much as that moment. She wanted to freeze time—to linger for an hour while Edwin showed her sons how to prepare her omelet. She wished she could calmly sit at the counter and watch them work. And then, after she was served, she could praise them over each and every bite of her breakfast.

"Three of my guests were taken in for questioning last night," she said to Edwin. "I need to shower and get to the main house as quickly as possible."

Edwin turned to the boys. "We'll make this a take-out order. Right, gentlemen?"

"Right!" the twins shouted.

"We'll be ready when you are," Edwin told Jane. "Master Hem, write down your mother's order. Master Fitz, prepare the frying pan."

The omelet smelled so delicious that Jane ate it while walking from her house to Storyton Hall.

The twins, fueled by eggs, bacon, and the idea of spending a morning at the Jules Verne Pool, said good-bye to Jane and Edwin and raced off.

"You always seem to know just when to show up on my doorstep," Jane said to Edwin.

Stopping, Edwin reached for the now-empty plate. His hands lingered on Jane's. "I know you have things to take care of, but I believe I know the identity of the book thief."

This was the last thing Jane had expected to hear. "You do?"

"Yes, and you'll be happy to hear that I don't think she ever intended to remove it from Storyton Hall. I believe she merely wanted to make sure that it was no longer on display." Edwin looked up, saw a couple strolling arm in arm in their direction, and steered Jane toward the entrance to Milton's Gardens.

"She?" Jane asked when they were completely alone once more.

Lowering his voice, Edwin continued to speak as they walked over the garden paths. Unlike the couple they'd just passed, there was an urgency to their gait and to their bent heads and rapid whispers. "Tammy Kota is responsible for the herbal's disappearance, and I believe she fully intends to return it before leaving Storyton."

This brought Jane to a dead halt. "Tammy? Why would she steal the book only to return it?"

"I think she was trying to keep it from harm. Last night, I did some research on your herbal. One of my contacts was able to help me discover exactly why that book was so valuable. It wasn't the description or drawings—though they are certainly wonderful—but one illumination in particular that made this herbal so unique. And for women living in the twelfth century, extremely dangerous," Edwin quickly explained.

Jane, who'd seen a number of materials in Storyton's secret library written for the sole purpose of denigrating, ridiculing, and even sterilizing women, felt her ire rising. "In what way?"

"The monk copying the original text changed a single entry in your herbal. On the page recommending how to stop blood loss in females, he added a snake to the illumination of the woman. This was to equate all women as Eve the Temptress, no doubt. But censoring the fairer sex wasn't enough for this monk. He changed the herb cited as well. I can't remember what the original plant was supposed to be, but this monk changed it to feverfew." Edwin's expression was stern. "Feverfew would increase the flow of blood. It would produce the opposite reaction as the original plant cited."

"That's reprehensible!" Jane cried.

"According to my source—another man of God—this monk's treachery was discovered and he was thrown out of the Benedictine Order. The book wasn't destroyed—probably because books were so precious back then. Despite its grievous and deliberate error, the herbal was kept hidden away until it ended up in the hands of a Steward."

Jane frowned. "But all the herbalists would have known that the herb recommended on that page was the wrong one, wouldn't they?"

"Only those proficient in Latin. The name of the herb is buried in the rest of the text," Edwin said. "The language restriction narrowed my suspect list to Claude, Constance, and Tammy. Tammy graduated from a Catholic high school where she won an award for her excellence in Latin. Also, she's the only person who knows the real Constance Meredith. Constance, whose mother was a missionary and died shortly after Constance was born. Her mother hemorrhaged, you see, and the doctor overseeing the delivery was completely inept. Especially compared to the village midwife. However, Constance's father wouldn't allow an untrained, native woman to treat his wife. As a result of his pigheadedness, she died."

"The doctor couldn't stop the bleeding?" Jane asked, feeling overwhelming sadness on Constance's behalf. Here was yet another child who grew up without a mother.

Edwin looked aggrieved. "The tale is unclear, but the

midwife told her children that the doctor gave Constance's mother the wrong medicine. Instead of saving her, it's possible that he hastened her death."

Jane sucked in a quick breath. "Just like the recommendation in our herbal."

"Exactly," Edwin said. "My theory is that Tammy didn't want Constance to see that page. She's probably Constance's only true friend among the herbalists."

We all keep parts of our stories hidden, Jane thought. *A chapter or two buried deeply within ourselves so that it can't hurt us anymore. But the words and images find a way to the light. They always find a way. Stories aren't meant to be hidden. Even the ugliest, most painful ones must be revealed or they'll rot inside of us like moldy pages.*

Jane took the breakfast plate from Edwin's hand and placed it on the ground. She then slid her arms around his back and pressed her head against his chest. "I don't know how you discovered all of this, but thank you. So much misery was carried to Storyton inside the hearts of this group of herbalists that I'd like to believe that at least one of them, Tammy, is different. Having spoken with her several times, I think she's earned the chance to prove her character." She pulled back and gave Edwin a small smile. "I don't expect Sinclair to be wild about this scheme."

"Nor do I." Edwin leaned in and gave Jane a tender kiss. "Do you want me to come in with you?"

"No, thanks, I've got this."

Edwin smiled. "I know you do. I'll be back for the final event. If it's still on, that is. I promised Eloise I'd go with her."

"The Poison Princess's lecture!" Jane exclaimed. "I haven't given it any thought. I'm not sure if there'll be anyone in the audience—not when everyone hears that Hannah Billingsley was arrested under suspicion of murder."

"Are you kidding? The whole village is coming." Edwin

ran a fingertip down Jane's cheek. "Everything's going to be all right. You'll see."

Scooping up her plate, Jane tried to hold on to Edwin's optimism, as well as the whisper of warmth on her skin, as she entered Storyton Hall.

Butterworth met her in the middle of the lobby.

"Coffee," he said, presenting her with a mug and relieving her of her dirty dish.

"Bless you." Jane closed her eyes, took a fortifying sip, and then met the butler's even stare. "Tell me. Are Mr. and Mrs. Earle raising hell yet?"

"They started carrying on at about half past six." Butterworth consulted his gold pocket watch. "By now, I imagine they're directing their rage at anyone wearing a police uniform. While they were waiting for a car to be brought around, Mrs. Earle informed me that the family attorney is being flown out by company helicopter and that we should expect to see her son and daughter-in-law freed by lunchtime."

Jane raised her brows. "I'm surprised she included Victoria in that statement."

"It was clearly a struggle," said Butterworth.

"I guess she doesn't care about Hannah's fate."

Butterworth merely grunted.

"Well, right or wrong, I do," Jane said. "And I can only imagine the discomfort she must be experiencing. I'm sure she's in dire need of her medication."

"That investigation is out of our hands now. We have another to solve before day's end," Butterworth reminded her.

Jane glanced down at her coffee cup and wondered if the Fins would find Edwin's story credible. "Actually," she began, but was unable to continue for she saw Tom Green pushing a rolling cart across the carpet. It was Tom's custom to replace the floral arrangements on Mondays, but Jane hadn't expected to see him today. If ever, considering all that had happened.

"Good morning, Mr. Green," Butterworth said as though this were an ordinary Monday.

Tom returned the greeting with evident relief and then gave Jane a hesitant smile. "I hear I have you to thank for my freedom," he said in his quiet voice. "But Hannah . . ." His shook his head, his eyes sliding away to lock on the floral arrangement made of sunflowers, delphinium, alstroemeria, yarrow, and daisy poms destined for the lobby's center table. "I just can't believe it."

"Did they tell you why she was arrested?" Jane asked.

"No," Tom replied.

Jane pointed at her coffee cup. "Let's sit down together over some coffee and I'll explain what I can." She gave him an encouraging smile and gestured at the row of silver coffee urns lined up on a rectangular table on the east side of the lobby.

Though she was more than ready for another hit of caffeine, her real motivation was to speak with Tom in private. The kind, quiet man had been hurt already, but Jane was about to add to his injuries. At least, when she wounded him, she would do it as gently as possible.

In her office, Jane invited Tom to sit in a guest chair. She then drew a second chair close to his. "My friend, I'm so sorry for all that you've been through. I'm also sorry for having doubted you in any way. Can you forgive me?"

Tom blinked in surprise. "I don't blame you or anyone else, Ms. Steward. You've always looked out for the people of Storyton and that's what you were doing when you came to talk to me at my shop. Someone was killed and you were trying to find out what happened. Even when the police took me in, you still keep searching for answers. Because of that, I'm here this morning, doing my job. So you see, there's nothing to forgive."

Jane waited a moment for Tom to take a sip of coffee. Then she said, "I don't think it was Hannah's intent to cause you grief. I really believe she likes you, Tom, and probably regrets having hurt you in any way. Unfortunately, her entire life has been colored by pain, and the source of her pain was your father."

"You found out who he was before he came to Storyton?" Tom lowered his coffee cup to Jane's desk and stared at her in astonishment.

"Yes," Jane whispered and proceeded to tell Tom all the terrible things his father had done.

He didn't interrupt her. Not once. He didn't make a sound or move during her somewhat stilted narrative. He kept his gaze locked on her face. The only sign that she was getting through to him was that he would occasionally flinch, as though some of her words had a shocking bite like the sting of a bee or a paper cut.

When she was finished, Jane laced her hands together. Again, she told Tom how sorry she was for how things had turned out and then she fell silent, giving him a chance to absorb all that she'd said.

"I always knew he had a dark secret." Tom spread his hands. "Why else would he have chosen to live the way he did? I wanted his crime to be tax evasion or something less, well, odious because it allowed us to have a relationship. I could have dug around. I could have pried. But I didn't. Deep down I knew I'd find something ugly."

"What made you so certain?"

Tom shrugged. "Because he left me. What kind of man abandons his child?"

Jane almost told Tom that Hannah's father had left her too, but decided against it. That painful truth was not hers to share.

"I also knew that he was working on formulas for a company. They paid him in cash. Off the books," Tom continued. "But I let myself be convinced that he was doing something good."

"Maybe he was," Jane said. "He was trying to produce new pain medications. Perhaps he meant to make amends."

Tom shook his head in dismissal. "Who knows what would have happened to his formulas once Earle Pharmaceuticals started manufacturing them? Nothing good would have come out of that partnership."

There was a light rap on Jane's door.

"Come in," Jane called, and Sue Ross poked her head in.

"The police are here," she said, her face pinched with worry. "They brought all three of our guests back. Mr. and Mrs. Earle have returned too. And a carload of lawyers."

Jane bolted to her feet. "Good Lord." She turned to Tom. "Will you be okay?"

He nodded. "I'd like to speak to Hannah, if they'll let me." His throat seemed to suddenly tighten around his words and he had to force them out. "I want to . . . I want her to know that I don't hate her."

Jane was already moving when Tom said these words. She was too focused on the abrupt return of Hannah, Victoria, and Carson to do more than give Tom a quick bob of her head.

Sterling was waiting for her on the other side of the reception desk. "Mr. Butterworth and Mr. Sinclair have managed to steer the recent arrivals into Shakespeare's Theater. Mrs. Earle—the older Mrs. Earle, that is—was causing such commotion that guests were starting to gather in the lobby to see what all the fuss was about."

"Who could blame them?" Jane asked wryly. "There's nothing like a bunch of armed policemen and an irate guest to get the blood flowing on a Monday morning. But I'll give Mrs. Earle credit for one thing: she must have retained the best defense attorney in the state to have managed the immediate release of Victoria, Carson, *and* Hannah."

As it turned out, the Earles' attorneys had argued that the Allegany Police Department didn't have sufficient evidence to hold his clients any longer. Especially since none of them had confessed to any wrongdoing.

Jane was floored to hear this. "Are you trying to tell me that both Hannah and Victoria denied knowing that the druid was Andrew Green, MD? The man who prescribed an unsafe medication to their mother?" she asked Officer McCullough in disbelief.

The two of them were standing at a distance from Jane's guests, who had been told to sit in the first row of seats and were being watched by a trio of stern-faced policemen.

"We went at them pretty hard, but there was a limit to how much we could push Ms. Billingsley," McCullough explained. "And the newlyweds wouldn't say a word. Not one. We can't take any chances, so right now, we have no confessions, no witnesses, and circumstantial evidence at best. With the Earles lawyering up, we were forced to back off. We need to go over every inch of Ms. Billingsley's room and the bridal suite and pray that we find traces of arsenic."

Picturing the thoroughness of the housekeeping staff, Jane suppressed a grimace. As reluctant as she was to do so, she had to find another way to prove that Hannah was responsible for Andrew Green's death, and quickly. Constance's lecture on poisons was scheduled to begin at one o'clock sharp. After that, the retreat would officially be over.

Jane spun around and spotted Tom loitering uncomfortably by the doorway.

"What are you thinking?" Sinclair asked, having silently appeared at her elbow.

"He's been through so much, but I believe that he can draw Hannah out. They made a connection the night of the wedding," Jane said. "I saw it."

Sinclair glanced from Tom to Hannah. "You must choose between seeing that justice is served and causing Mr. Green additional grief."

"Yes," Jane said morosely. "There really isn't a choice, is there?"

She walked to the doorway, took Tom by the hand, and led him over to where Hannah was sitting next to Victoria. Carson was seated with his parents and the family attorney. He had his back turned to his bride as though he couldn't stand the sight of her, but Victoria clearly didn't care. She and Hannah had their heads bent and their foreheads pressed together and looked, for just a moment, far younger than their age. On another day and in another setting, Jane could imagine them whispering about a secret dream or the cute boy who rode the same school bus.

The sisters were so absorbed with each other that they didn't realize that Jane and Tom were standing in front of them until Tom reached into his pocket, pulled out an object wrapped in tissue paper, and began to unwrap it.

Hannah glanced up just as Tom bent down to lay a single purple hyacinth in the palm of her hand, which she had resting in her lap.

Her eyes filled with tears. "For sorrow," she said in a voice that was barely above a whisper.

"And forgiveness," Tom repeated in the same soft tone.

"I knew you were a good man," Victoria said. She gave Tom such a sweet, sorrow-tinged smile that Jane felt a sharp twinge of anxiety. Clutching her sister's free hand, Victoria continued to look at Tom. "Hannah doesn't need your forgiveness though. I'm responsible for your father's death."

Hannah's body contracted in fear. "Via, *no!*"

Victoria nodded as tears slipped down her cheeks. "It's okay, Banana Cake. I knew this is how things would end up. I planned it this way. I'm just sorry that I had to involve you at all. I never meant for you to feel pain or to be scared, but I knew even if you experienced those things, it would only be for a little while."

The sisters were so focused on each other that they didn't

see Jane signal for Officer McCullough to come around behind their seats in order to listen to the rest of the conversation. They also didn't notice how Butterworth and Sterling were successfully distracting the Earles and their attorney by serving them coffee and an array of fresh, warm pastries. These items were wheeled into the theater on two carts and both the butler and head chauffeur made a great show of fawning over the infuriated guests.

"I knew it had to be you, of course," Hannah said. She was crying now too. "But why, Via? Why did you throw your life away to kill this man?"

Victoria ran her fingers as tenderly as a mother's over her sister's misshapen back. "Because he did this to you. Because he gave you every scar. It was his fault you needed all of those surgeries and the braces and the pills. He was responsible for you missing out on kickball games, gymnastics, tree climbing, boyfriends . . ." Victoria released a long, weary sigh. To Jane's ears, it was the sound of someone who was ready to lie down and rest. The sound of a person who was tired of keeping secrets. It was also the sound of a woman preparing to say good-bye to the person she loved most.

"How?" Hannah asked.

"He gave Mom a drug he shouldn't have been prescribing. He was a bad man, Banana. He was receiving kickbacks from Earle Pharmaceuticals, and he didn't want to stop receiving them." She took both of her sister's hands in hers, nearly crushing the hyacinth. "That drug killed Mom. It's why she got cancer."

Hannah sagged. Her entire body folded inward, and Victoria pulled Hannah toward her and gingerly held her. "I know," she whispered, smoothing her sister's hair. "It hurts. That's how I felt when I found out. And the hurt grew and grew."

"But now I'll lose you too!" Hannah cried, and Jane could see her gripping Victoria's arms so tightly that her hands were trembling.

"Never," Victoria said calmly. "You'll visit me. We'll write. And Tom will check on you. He'll make sure you're okay." She glanced up at Tom, her eyes pleading. "Won't you?"

Tom clasped his hands together and stood very tall. "I will. I promise."

Victoria smiled in relief. "There, you see. And I don't want you to worry about me. I'm tired, Hannah. I've been living with this rage for a long time. It's eaten away at me. It's left me incapable of caring about anyone or anything except for you. I couldn't stop myself once I learned the truth. It's all I thought about. It has totally consumed me."

"No." Hannah shook her head in denial.

"You have your work. You still have me. You have your old friends, and now, you have some new ones." This time, when Victoria looked up, she smiled at Jane. "Things will be a little different, but you're the strongest person I know. You'll survive this."

Hannah wrapped her arms around her sister and hugged her tightly. "You should have told me, Via. This wasn't the way to fix things."

"I had to," Victoria insisted. "I had to."

A miserable silence descended over the embracing women. The Earles, having finished making their selections from the pastry cart, returned to their seats.

The family attorney remained standing, holding a plate laden with half a dozen pastries. He must have sensed that something significant had occurred and he'd missed it, for he narrowed his eyes at Officer McCullough. "Are you questioning my client?" he demanded sharply.

"He hasn't said a word," Jane answered on behalf of the policeman. "Though I was just about to ask Victoria—forgive me if I don't call you Mrs. Earle, but it's my guess that you'd prefer not to be addressed as such—how she was able to transfer the arsenic to the cake."

"She's not going to speak to you," the attorney said. "She knows what best for her and that's to keep her mouth shut."

Victoria glared at him. "Why don't you sit down and stuff your own mouth with more of those pastries?" She turned to look at McCullough. "That man no longer represents me. Hannah will help me find a decent attorney later, but I'd like to answer Ms. Steward's question." Fixing her gaze on Jane again, Victoria said, "I'm sorry to have caused you distress. You've been nothing but kind to the two of us. I'll tell you anything you want to know."

"How did you poison the cake?" Jane asked.

"One of Hannah's history books showed me the way," Victoria said. "Mr. Sinclair. Are you familiar with the term *meli chloron?*"

"Roughly translated, it means 'golden honey,'" Sinclair replied. "Are you referring to the Greek General Xenophon's account of how his men were driven mad by poisoned honey?"

Victoria seemed pleased by Sinclair's knowledge. "Yes. Honey made from a species of rhododendron flower that causes hallucinations, seizures, and even death. This species is prevalent in Turkey, near the Black Sea, and I was able to procure a jar. I stole the arsenic from a lab at Earle Pharmaceuticals, of course. I made Carson take me there after hours and then drugged him with one of his own products so I could help myself to the arsenic. I used his ID badge and master key, and even though I ran into several maintenance workers, everyone knew me by then and I just pretended to be surprising Carson with a late dinner. I carried a take-out bag and wore a sexy dress to look the part."

"Have you no shame?" Mrs. Earle interjected contemptuously.

"What about you?" Victoria shot back. "If you and your board members had done the right thing years ago, none of this would have happened. You let people *die!* All in the name of your bottom line! How do you face yourself in the mirror each day?" She pointed at each Earle in turn. "How do any of you sleep at night?"

Victoria shook her head in disgust and then resumed her narrative concerning the honey. However, Mrs. Earle couldn't contain her wrath. Glowering at Victoria, she shouted, "I knew you were nothing but a—"

"This is *not* the time nor the place," Jane interjected. "If you cannot refrain from interrupting, Mr. Butterworth will escort you backstage."

Butterworth took a step toward Mrs. Earle, who squeaked in surprise and shock. She elbowed her husband, but he didn't seem inclined to take on the powerful-looking butler.

"The honey?" Jane prompted Victoria.

"I had it in a travel-sized shampoo bottle," she said. "Inside my little bridal purse. Hannah carried it for me. I poured the honey on the slice of cake Hannah had set aside for the man everyone called the druid. It only took a few seconds. I put the empty bottle back in my bag. Later that night, I washed it out with really hot water and tossed the bottle in the trash."

Tom, who'd stood very still while Victoria was speaking, now wiped a hand across his forehead. "It must have tasted very sweet. With all that honey."

"I'm sorry," Victoria said, and for the first time, Jane believed that she was finally regretting her actions. "I didn't mean to hurt you. You're a good person, I can tell. And I apologize to you too, Ms. Steward, for causing you grief." She turned to McCullough. "I'm ready now. I'd rather not string this part out. It's hard enough as it is."

McCullough dipped his chin. "I see no need to cuff you. If you'd just walk with me out front, we'll keep this nice and quiet."

"Thank you," Victoria said as Jane echoed the sentiment with her eyes. "Can my sister walk with us?"

McCullough allowed it, and the two sisters held hands through the lobby and down the steps to the waiting cruiser. Jane didn't want to watch their parting, but did so anyway.

Hannah stood alone in the driveway, her arms wrapped around her body, until the police cars were gone. And then Tom joined her. He returned the hyacinth she'd left behind in Shakespeare's Theater, and as she brought it to her nose to breathe in its scent, he spoke softly to her.

And when he offered her his hand to lead her back inside Storyton Hall, she gave him the smallest of smiles and took it.

EPILOGUE

For Jane, the rest of the day was a seemingly endless blur punctuated by the ringing of phones and a barrage of questions from curious guests.

The Earles were so anxious to get the ball rolling on Carson's legal separation from Victoria that they left Storyton in the company helicopter without even waiting for permission from the authorities.

As for Hannah, she seemed to grow in strength and confidence as the day progressed. By teatime, she'd hired a defense attorney to represent her sister and rented a small house in Alleghany County. She'd done none of these things on her own, however. Tom had advised her, driven her around, and done his best to comfort her.

When Jane noticed the pair seated at a table in the Agatha Christie Tea Room—a man and a woman on the verge of keeling over from exhaustion and grief, but still able to smile at each other—she believed that some higher power had brought them together. The thought warmed her heart.

By that time, most of The Medieval Herbalists had

checked out. Not the Poison Princess, of course. Though she'd already given her lecture to a packed theater, Constance Meredith wasn't going to leave when an army of television crews was about to descend on Storyton Hall.

And descend they did, because any story involving Earle Pharmaceuticals was a big story. By four in the afternoon, news vans were double-parked outside Storyton's iron gates. Jane and the Fins watched several early reports in the privacy of the security room and found them to be very similar. They focused their venom on the corrupt partnership between Earle Pharmaceuticals and physicians like Andrew Green. Kira's murder was also mentioned, but it was more of a footnote at the end of the main piece despite attempts by both Sheriff Evans and Officer McCullough to give the deaths of Kira Grace and Andrew Green equal weight.

Tammy, who'd also decided to stay an extra night after Constance had insisted on paying not only for her room, but also for dinner and drinks, was incensed over how the media marginalized Kira's murder.

"Don't stand for it, then," Jane heard Constance tell Tammy as she approached the two women while they sat in the Ian Fleming Lounge.

"What do you suggest I do? Wait until one of the reporters is doing a live shot and then lunge for their microphone?" Tammy asked. "It would take something totally over the top to get them to want to tape me. I'm an aging hippie. A Bohemian soap maker. They won't pay attention to a word I say."

"I'll make them listen," Constance said. "I'll hook them with the poison angle, and when they're on the line, that's when you'll inform their viewers that *the druid's* most recent victim was one of the most talented photographers of our time. You'll tell them how Kira Grace might have talked too loudly and worn crazy clothes, but that she made the world a better place because she was full of life and laughter. Tell them that she was our friend and that we're going to miss her." To Jane's surprise, Constance hid her face in her hands.

"Oh, Connie." Tammy put an arm around Constance's shoulder and squeezed. "Why don't you ever show your softer side to other people? Beneath all that talk of paralysis and necrotic tissue is a woman with a tender heart."

Constance cursed under her breath, and suddenly both women were giggling uncontrollably.

After she'd witnessed so much grief, the sound of their girlish merriment was a balm to Jane's spirit. Glancing away from the two herbalists, Jane gazed around the room. The lounge was crowded. Many of the new guests had checked in that afternoon and still wore looks of wide-eyed wonder. They didn't seem the slightest bit nervous about staying at Storyton Hall, and Jane guessed this was due to the fact that the media had downplayed the resort's connection to the murders. The Internet and television reports focused on images of Andrew Green's homestead, along with photographs of Mr. and Mrs. Earle and select Earle Pharmaceutical's board members in what was now being called the Benetyne Scandal. Storyton Hall was mentioned, but never in a negative light. Because of this, Jane began to believe that their future bookings would remain intact.

Someone barked out a hearty laugh from the far corner of the lounge, causing Tammy to turn and spot Jane.

"Hi, there!" She raised her glass. "Me and the Poison Princess are blowing off a little steam. Would you like to pull up a stool?"

Jane smiled to show that she appreciated the invitation. "Thanks, but I need to get home. However, I didn't want to head out without speaking to you first. Ms. Meredith, do you mind if I borrow Tammy for a few minutes?"

Constance slid off her stool and gave the seat a firm pat. "Keep it warm for me. I'm going to see if I can get us an earlier dinner reservation. I'm famished. I missed all the teatime treats because I was too busy talking to people after my lecture, but that's the price one has to pay for being as inherently fascinating as I am."

Tammy tossed a maraschino cherry stem at her. "They just want to know more about your inherently fascinating friends."

"Actually, that's true," Constance said. "The Medieval Herbalists will be a top Google search for weeks to come." She frowned. "And with Hannah's attention fixed on her sister's defense, who's going to manage our group now?"

"Don't write Hannah off yet," Tammy said. "I have a feeling she can handle both challenges just beautifully."

Constance scowled. "You're such a flake. Always seeing the best in people."

"You know it. Go get us a table, would you? You can bully a waiter or two if that'll make you feel better."

Unable to maintain her frown, Constance's mouth curved upward. She even managed to wish Jane a pleasant evening before leaving the lounge.

Taking Constance's vacant stool, Jane asked the bartender for a glass of water. She then took out her phone and, covertly hiding the screen from the other guests, showed Tammy the image being displayed.

"I wanted you to see this," Jane began. "This is a bulletin board I keep in my office. I call it my Hopes and Dreams board. It's a childish name, I know, but it makes its point. After I write a hope or a dream that I have for this place on a piece of paper, I pin it to the board. Every hope or dream is represented by a different color."

Tammy took the proffered phone. Her lips moved as she read, "'Restore Chekov's Orchard.' You have an orchard?"

"We have fruit trees," Jane said. "Mostly apple varieties. But I have no idea what shape they're in. The whole area is a mass of vines and underbrush."

Looking back at the phone, Tammy continued reading.

"A folly? Cool. I can't imagine how much it would cost to— Wait! A spa? You want to open a spa?"

Jane smiled. "I do. It's the biggest piece of paper on that board. The hot pink one. The falconry program kind of leapfrogged this dream, which is okay because the raptors have been beneficial for the guests, our bank account, and Mr. Lachlan. But the reason I'm talking to you about this now is that I'd like you to be involved in this dream. I can't imagine opening a spa without you. You're the only person I can picture running it."

Tammy stared at her, openmouthed in shock. "Me?"

"Yes. Your products are perfect for facials and massages. All natural, herbal, and environmentally conscious. And far beyond your products, there's your gift for reading people. For sensing their needs and wishes. There's no one more capable and caring. Are you interested?"

"Are you kidding?" Tammy's eyes glittered like a child's at a birthday party. But as she looked at the image on Jane's phone again, the light in her eyes faded.

Jane touched her arm. "I'm springing this on you very abruptly. Take a night to think about it, okay? Many things can happen between now and tomorrow morning. For instance, the door to the Henry James Library, which is normally locked at ten o'clock, will remain unlocked tonight." She felt Tammy stiffen beside her. "A single lamp will illuminate the display case where the antique herbal was displayed. No one will be watching the library or the corresponding hallways. Upon its return, the herbal will be put away in protective storage. Because even though I hate to admit it, some books can be hurtful."

"You knew?" Tammy asked very quietly.

When Jane nodded, Tammy shook her head in disbelief. "And you're still offering me a job?"

"What was your motivation in taking the book?" Jane asked.

"To spare Constance pain," Tammy said. "But that's not

the only reason. I would never have done it if I hadn't just lost Kira. I was also lashing out. You need to know that. It wasn't purely altruistic. I'm no saint."

Jane laughed. "I don't know many saints who can pick locks. How'd you learn to do that?"

Sinclair had already presented Jane with a thick file on Tammy. It was filled with the details a Guardian of Storyton Hall needed to possess before hiring a new staff member. And even though Jane knew all she needed to know about Tammy Kota, she still wanted to hear the answer in person. It would be the first step toward becoming closer to the woman she hoped would run Storyton Hall's spa.

"My dad taught me," Tammy said. "He was a security guard and one of those survivalist types. He wanted me to have certain skills 'just in case.' When I was a teenager, I thought he was nuts, but now, I'm glad I learned so many random things from him." She gave a self-effacing shrug. "I'm pretty rusty, though."

"You got the job done." Jane flashed Tammy a grin and then tapped the clock on her phone screen. "Time for me to go home. Think about joining us, would you? I'll catch up with you before checkout tomorrow."

Optimism flowed through Jane's veins like sunshine. Stepping out on the back terrace, she inhaled deeply. The summer evening air was perfumed by confederate jasmine and honeysuckle, but there was also a faint signature of fresh herbs.

Though she couldn't say why, Jane felt suddenly compelled to spend a few minutes sitting on the low wall of Mrs. Hubbard's kitchen garden, so she changed course, veering away from the paths frequented by Storyton Hall guests to a side path used primarily by staff members.

After she'd ascended several wide steps and entered the

rectangular space located behind the kitchen, the strong aroma of rosemary met her. There, in the corner of the southeast wall, was a bush so large that Jane knew Mrs. Hubbard must have planted it several seasons ago.

Jane moved toward it and reached out to caress a quill-like branch. Thinking of how the herb symbolized remembrance, she bent down and closed her eyes. In the peaceful twilight, she vowed to remember Kira Grace. And if Tammy agreed to become a Storyton Hall employee in the not-so-distant future, she and Jane could decide what would be a proper memorial for her.

Whatever we come up with, we should put it in Milton's Gardens, Jane thought. *As close to the flowers as possible.*

For the first time in days, a sense of serenity enveloped Jane. It was as though the garden sensed all she'd recently been through and was responding by cocooning her in its sweet fragrance and muted, twilight hues.

As she strolled among the herbs, touching velvety leaves, prickly stalks, and silky petals, she realized that she'd never been so aware of the power of each plant until this moment. Like books, plants had the power to heal or to hurt. To woo or to wound.

Jane spotted a small glove at the base of an oregano plant and leaned over to collect it. She smiled when she saw Hem's name written in permanent marker on the cuff. The boys had been working hard in this garden and she loved that they'd taken pride in their work. How she felt about this garden was how she felt about all of Storyton Hall. Every stone. Every book. Every blade of grass on its vast estate.

Jumping up on the wall, she looked out over those grounds now. She imagined all the transformations she wanted to make in the days and years to come and hoped they would prove possible. She wanted to leave a great legacy to her sons, not a dilapidated hotel with untended land.

"You look like a queen surveying her kingdom."

Jane turned to find Edwin standing at the entrance to the herb garden, a bouquet of wildflowers in one hand and a slim, gift-wrapped package in the other.

"There's a line from *The Secret Garden* that reads, 'If you look the right way, you can see the whole world is a garden.'" Jane made a sweeping gesture with her arm. "I'm trying to see things through Frances Hodgson Burnett's eyes."

"Maybe I can help," Edwin said. Shifting the flowers to the crook of his arm, he offered Jane a hand.

She barely had both feet on the grass when Edwin pointed at the wall. "Would you sit down? I want to say something to you, Jane. I promise not to take long, but it's important."

"All right," Jane said, feeling a flutter of anxiety. Was Edwin about to confess another dark secret?

Edwin laid the flowers in her lap. They were a lovely combination of buttercups, Queen Anne's lace, chicory, pink butterfly weed, and purple loosestrife. "I don't know what each flower means," he began. "I don't have Tom's knowledge. I just think they're beautiful. And tough. Like you."

Sitting next to Jane, Edwin held her hand very lightly. However, he looked at her with such intensity that Jane was tempted to squirm.

"Why do I get the sense that you're about to say something that can't be unsaid?" she asked, half in jest and half in dread.

"Because I am." Edwin gave her hand a comforting squeeze. "I know you're concerned about getting involved with me, Jane. You're a mother. I'm a book thief. You're the Guardian of Storyton Hall. I'm The Templar. My life is full of secrets. I understand your reason for hesitating. But I promise you this: I will never put you or the boys at risk. On the contrary, I will do everything in my power to keep the three of you safe." He placed the gift-wrapped package on the wall. "I know you haven't had a chance to finish Lionel Alcott's journal, so I'm going to give away the ending."

Jane shook her head in alarm. It was an automatic reaction. She never wanted to hear how a story ended. She always wanted to find out herself. "No, don't!"

Edwin touched the gift. "This is what he was seeking. It's my greatest treasure, and I want you to have it. Before you make a decision about us, would you open this first?"

The intensity in Edwin's dark eyes softened. Jane saw his desire to win her over. She saw a little fear there too. He always seemed so implacable that it was this glimmer of vulnerability that prompted her to say, "I will."

As she slipped her finger under a fold in the gift wrap, she gave him a coy smile. "You need to stop giving me all these presents."

"And why would I do that?" Edwin asked, tracing the line of her cheek. "I've been searching for you my entire life. I want to devote my days to bringing you flowers, surprising you with gifts, and telling you how smart, capable, and beautiful you are."

"Wow. That'll take the wind out of the sails of my argument." Jane laughed and then sobered. "I do feel a bit guilty because I've never given you a thing in return."

Edwin slid his hand along Jane's throat before burying his fingertips in the loose bun of strawberry blond hair gathered at the nape of her neck. "Give me a chance," he whispered.

"Kiss me," she whispered back.

She thought Edwin might refuse, insisting she open the gift first, but he didn't. His other hand clamped around her waist, pushing her body into his. Their lips met, and Jane gave in to the hunger she'd been trying to ignore since Edwin's return.

When they finally pulled apart, it seemed to Jane that the

garden had become even more resplendent. The flowers looked like pale suns and moons, and a host of fireflies had been drawn by the lengthening shadows. They hovered among the plants like diminutive constellations.

"I really need to go," Jane whispered. "So I'd better open this."

Carefully, she tore the wrapping paper to reveal a letter-sized cardboard box. Inside, she found what appeared to be a sheet of old parchment paper enveloped in Plexiglas.

Jane couldn't read the writing on the paper. To her, the exotic letters looked like a form of Arabic.

"That's Persian," Edwin said, pointing at the graceful calligraphy. "It's a Rumi poem. An original called 'Buoyancy.' There are lines in this poem that kept replaying in my mind when I was a 'guest' of the sheik's. Lines that kept me connected to you even though we were world's apart."

Jane looked down at the elegant lines of script. "Which ones?"

Picking up her hand, Edwin uncurled her index finger. He moved it down the glass and then paused. With his mouth hovering near her ear, he whispered, "It says, 'A mountain keeps an echo deep inside itself. That's how I hold your voice.'" He waited a heartbeat and then spoke again. "I hold you like an echo inside myself, Jane."

Edwin's words moved through Jane like a warm wind. She felt the truth in them. No matter what difficulties they might face as they moved forward, this man loved her. And she loved him. Perhaps that was enough.

"In that case," she whispered in reply, "I'm yours."

After a long moment of contented silence, Jane stood and smiled. "Come on. It's time for supper. And we really need to get these flowers in water."

Edwin gathered up the Rumi poem and the scraps of wrapping paper while Jane collected the wildflower bouquet.

Hand in hand, the couple left the herb garden and crossed the wide stretch of lawn toward Jane's house, walking below a large swarm of fireflies. The insects seemed to be lighting the way, beckoning the man and the woman to continue moving forward. Because even though darkness was falling, the vast expanse of sky over their heads was aglow with undiminished stars.

Keep reading for a special preview of
Ellery Adams's next Books by the Bay Mystery . . .

KILLER CHARACTERS

Coming soon from Berkley Prime Crime!

The flesh would shrink and go, the blood would dry, but no one believes in his mind of minds or heart of hearts that the pictures do stop.

—SAUL BELLOW

"All I think about is death," said Laurel Hobbs. She pushed her empty mug closer to the edge of the table and glanced around Grumpy's Diner in search of Dixie. "I know I sound selfish and whiny, but death has become the theme of my life. Death and dying. It hangs in each room of our house like a light fixture or a pair of curtains. Steve and I whisper about the inevitable moment before we go to sleep at night. When will it happen? Will we be forewarned? Or will it be sudden? Will there be a phone call in those dead hours between midnight and dawn?" She reached behind her head and tightened her ponytail of honey-blond hair. "Even the twins are depressed. They can see their grandmother withering day by day."

Olivia Limoges nodded in sympathy. "It sounds really hard. How's Steve doing?"

"He puts on a brave face," Laurel said. "But I worry about him burying his feelings. This is his mother, and she's dying. Yet, he barely talks about it." Seeing Dixie emerge from the kitchen carrying a glass coffee carafe, Laurel raised her arm and waved.

Dixie responded by holding up an index finger. She then skated over to the *Evita* booth to drop off a check. As she worked her way toward the front of the Andrew Lloyd Weber–themed diner, she paused at the *Cats* and the *Starlight Express* booth to top off her customers' mugs with fresh coffee.

"There won't be anything left by the time she gets here," Laurel complained. "And I don't have time to sit around while she brews another pot."

This grumbling wasn't like Laurel. Olivia studied her friend in concern. Laurel's face was puffy from lack of sleep and she hadn't bothered to put on makeup or earrings. Olivia couldn't remember seeing Laurel without either. Her friend also couldn't keep still. Her fingers moved from her empty coffee cup to her napkin to her wedding band, conveying a sense of anxiety that worried Olivia. Laurel was always full of energy, but it had been a controlled and positive energy—not this neurotic restlessness.

Seeing Dixie stop again to refill a mug at the *Tell Me on a Sunday* booth, Olivia tried to distract Laurel before she leapt up and grabbed the carafe right out of Dixie's hands. "You said that you and Steve talked about things before you went to sleep. Doesn't that count as him discussing his feelings?"

Laurel shrugged. "It's all details. Wills, funeral arrangements, what will happen to his dad—Steve hasn't once said that he's sad or scared. I feel like he's a million miles away these days. I'm trying to be patient and understanding, but I'm also taking care of the boys, my work, the house, the yard, the bills. I also visit his mom when I can and that's not much fun. You know she doesn't like me."

Olivia covered Laurel's hand with her own. "Men don't communicate the way women do. I'm sure Steve is grateful for your support, but you need to take care of yourself too, Laurel. You're running yourself ragged."

Laurel barked out a humorless laugh. "I don't have any other choice. A woman comes in once a week to help with the cleaning, and a landscape service is handling the lawn, but I have to keep up with everything else. Between Steve's work and his parents, he doesn't seem to have anything left to give to me or the boys."

"Here I am!" Dixie exclaimed. She skidded to a halt in front of their table and performed an elaborate series of one-hundred-and-eighty-degree turns by balancing on the toe of her left skate. "Service with flair! You can't get *that* at The Boot Top Bistro, eh?" she teased, referring to Olivia's five-star restaurant.

"It really is shameful that we don't have a single tutu-wearing dwarf in our employ," Olivia admitted with exaggerated embarrassment as Dixie refilled their mugs. "Do you know one who'd be interested in working for a demanding female owner and a moody French chef? My wait staff says the tips are great, but they have to deal with lots of persnickety customers. Being adept at smoothing ruffled feathers is a necessity."

Dixie snorted. "Grumpy's feathers have been ruffled for the last three days over this fishin' trip he wanted to go on and couldn't because of family stuff. Instead of smoothing his feathers, I told him *exactly* where he could shove them! Sometimes that man takes me, and his whole beautiful life, for granted. When that happens, I need to remind him how much the two of us need each other for things to work. Not just around here, but at home too." She stopped and drew her brows together in concern. "Laurel, honey, what's wrong?"

Laurel was silently weeping. "Sorry, Dixie. I'm just tired and stressed. We have a meeting with Rachel's palliative care team today and I'm dreading it."

"Rachel? Is that Steve's mama?" Dixie asked, resting the coffee carafe on the edge of the table.

"Yes. Milton is his dad," Laurel said. She wiped off her tears with her napkin. "Milton and Steve argue about Rachel's care at every meeting. It's just awful. The meetings are scheduled every two weeks, and the closer we get to . . . the end, the more Steve and his dad argue about her care. They've always gotten along so well, but lately, the friction between them comes out during these meetings."

Dixie made a sympathetic noise. "It's hard to let go of the folks we love. But what about Rachel? Doesn't she get a vote on how she lives out the rest of her life?"

"Of course," Laurel said, bristling. "She's stated more than once that her main objective is to avoid pain. She isn't interested in adding weeks or days to her life if it means suffering, but neither Milton nor Steve seem to be listening to her. I've never gotten along with Rachel, but I've been trying to make sure her wishes are being heard. Luckily, the palliative care doc and both of the hospice nurses are very focused on her goals."

Dixie put a hand on Laurel's shoulder. "I can almost feel the weight on you, sweetie. How much time do they think she has?"

"Six weeks." Laurel took a sip of her coffee and then glanced out the window. She watched the passersby for a moment before adding, "I think she'll go sooner. She's been trying to hang on until Christmas for Steve's sake, but whenever I visit, she talks about how tired she is." Laurel sighed. "If Steve and his dad don't make peace with one another *before* she passes, things are going to be even worse once she's gone."

Dixie gave Laurel's shoulder another squeeze and then swept her gaze around the diner. A customer was signaling her for the check, so she turned back to Laurel and said, "I'm gonna pack up some treats for you to take home. I know how much those darlin' boys like Grumpy's apple pie. You hang in there, honey. We're here if you need us."

When Laurel nodded absently, Olivia felt a pang of guilt. Other than taking Laurel out for the occasional lunch or coffee, she hadn't been a very supportive friend. She knew that Laurel was stressed, and even though she and the other Bayside Book Writers had bemoaned her absence during their last two meetings, they'd all assumed that she'd bounce back and make it to the next meeting. Laurel always bounced back. That's the kind of woman she was.

"Have you been able to write at all?" Olivia asked softly. "Outside of pieces for the newspaper, I mean."

Laurel was still staring out the window, but her eyes had a glassy, unfocused look. "No," she whispered.

"That settles it. I'm coming with you to this meeting," Olivia said. "Even if I sit outside in the hall, you'll know I'm close by. You need a friend, whether you realize it or not. And while I'm terrible at all the touchy-feely stuff, I *can* be present." Olivia pulled some bills from her wallet and placed them on the table. "Haviland will be at the groomer's for another hour. He's getting the works today— shampoo, trim, massage—so I'm all yours."

"Maybe I should trade places with Haviland," Laurel said as she shouldered her purse. "I'd love a day of pampering."

Dixie reemerged from the kitchen and skated to the front of the diner, blatantly ignoring the customer in the *Phantom of the* Opera booth who was waving what Olivia assumed was an empty syrup jug in the air in an attempt to flag down his diminutive waitress. However, Dixie wasn't going to miss her chance to show Laurel some love by thrusting a loaded take-out bag into her arms.

"I don't want to hear any thanks from you either," Dixie warned when Laurel opened her mouth. "You've always been there for me and mine. It's our turn to repay the favor. Kiss those boys for me, ya hear?"

And then she skated off, her pink taffeta tutu billowing like an umbrella or the bell of a gelatinous sea creature.

Olivia held open the diner door and gestured for Laurel to precede her outside. "That poodle is shamefully spoiled. It's better not to compare our existence to his. It'll only make you feel glum. Besides, why shouldn't you have a spa day? If you need a fresh crop of helpers, I could ask Kim for the names of reliable babysitters and you, me, and Millay could spend a few hours in New Bern being treated like royalty."

Laurel turned toward her minivan, which looked like it hadn't been washed in months, and sighed. "What if something happened while I was gone? I couldn't live with the guilt."

Would you feel guilty or would your husband make *you feel guilty?* Olivia wondered and then tried to erase the uncharitable thought. She wasn't a fan of Laurel's husband. None of the Bayside Book Writers were. They were friendly to him for Laurel's sake, but Steve never seemed to put as much effort into the marriage as Laurel did. Even after the couple had undergone over a year's worth of marital counseling, Olivia continued to doubt Steve's sincerity. It wasn't fair, she knew, to judge a man she didn't really know, but her gut told her not to trust him. And with her history, Olivia knew it could be foolish to ignore her baser instincts.

He's Laurel's husband. Not yours, Olivia reminded herself.

Laurel, who'd been rooting around in her purse, proffered a business card. "Here's the address. The meeting starts in thirty minutes. I doubt Steve and Milton will be thrilled to see you, but if you're sure . . . well, I'd love to have you there."

"I'm sure." Olivia smiled. "See you in a few."

The offices for KinderCare Hospice were located halfway between Oyster Bay and New Bern, and looked relatively new. Laurel was greeted warmly by a receptionist and told to proceed to the conference room.

"Everyone's in house. We're just waiting on your husband," the woman called after them. "He said he was running late, but that he'd get here as soon as he could."

Though Laurel's shoulders tensed, she smiled and thanked the woman as though Steve's tardiness was no big deal.

Steve's father was far more overt in expressing his annoyance.

"He's *late*?" Milton demanded angrily after Laurel repeated the receptionist's message to the group of people gathered in the small conference room. Laurel's father-in-law was bent over the water cooler in the corner. Now, he stood erect and glared at Laurel. "Are his patients more important than his dying mother? And who's this?" He gestured at Olivia with his paper cup, causing water to slosh over the rim and onto his shirt. "Goddamn it. Now, look at me."

A woman in her late twenties with large breasts, wide hips, and dark brown hair pulled into a loose bun eased the cup from Milton's hand. "Why don't you sit down while I refill that for you?" She spoke in a soothing, almost maternal voice and gave Milton a winsome smile. "I'm sure your son will be here real soon. Dr. Mark had to grab some paperwork from his office, so the timing might work out just fine. Come on, sit down by me."

Judging by the woman's purple scrubs, Olivia guessed that she was one of Rachel's nurses. The second nurse was taller, thinner, and older. She was in her mid-thirties and had luminescent, mocha-colored skin and hazel eyes. Beside her sat a clergyman, and next to him was a dour-faced matron in a wool cardigan. The chair at the head of the table remained empty, but a young woman with an athletic build occupied the chair directly next to it. She wore a white scrub top with pink piping and pink pants and was drawing leaping dolphins and bubbly hearts on a legal pad.

Is she a college student? Olivia wondered. *High school? Maybe she's an intern or a volunteer.*

"Dad, this is Olivia Limoges," Laurel said. "She's just here for me. She won't say a word. I just needed a friend today. I hope that's okay."

Milton was clearly taken aback. "*You* needed a friend? What does *any* of this have to do with you?"

Laurel's face reddened. "You and Rachel are my husband's parents, and I care about you both, so this does concern me. Rachel's illness also affects my family. My sons. My husband. And me. I want to do everything I can to help, and I don't appreciate being made to feel as if I don't matter."

"Well, I don't see how . . ."

Milton's rudeness was interrupted by the arrival of the palliative care doctor.

"Good morning, everyone," the doctor said in a tone of affable authority. He breezed into the room with an air of urgency common to most physicians. However, once he'd settled into his chair, he took a long moment to simply sit and be quiet. A calm came over him and the room. He glanced at each person at the table, greeting him or her with his eyes. Olivia liked him for taking the time to do this.

When his gaze fell on Olivia, Laurel spoke up. "This is a good friend of mine, Olivia Limoges. I invited her to be here today," she added, and again, Olivia heard a note of defiance in her friend's voice.

"Jonathan Mark," he said, extending his hand. "It's a pleasure to have you with us, Olivia." He then quickly introduced the rest of the team members. The busty, dark-haired nurse who'd successfully soothed Milton was Tracy Genvita, and the older nurse with the beautiful skin and eyes was Wanda Watts.

Dr. Mark went on to explain that Haley Hill, the baby-faced woman in pink-and-white scrubs was a nurse's aide, before moving on to the clergyman. His name was Bob Rhodes, and he served as the associate pastor of the church Rachel and Milton attended. Dr. Mark finished up with Lynne Stuart, the dour-faced matron who served as a volunteer for both the hospice and the church. The introductions completed, Dr. Mark shifted his attention back to Laurel. "Will Steve be joining us?"

"He's late!" Milton snapped before Laurel could answer. "Apparently, his practice is more important than his mother."

"Having gotten to know your son a little, I doubt that's the case," Dr. Mark said kindly. "Let's review how things are going. Hopefully, Steve will slip in while we're talking. Okay?"

"Okay." Laurel flashed the doctor a grateful smile.

Olivia listened as the hospice team discussed Rachel's condition. She was impressed by how they presented the facts without sounding remotely distant or cold. If anything, they all seemed to know Rachel and to genuinely care about her welfare. The team didn't focus on just the medical details either. Once those had been reviewed, Dr. Mark asked for feedback from everyone present, and by the time each person had spoken, an entire range of subjects had been covered. They discussed changes in Rachel's diet, her current emotional state, her spiritual needs, her favorite sources of entertainment, and anything else that might have come up since their last meeting.

The team had been sharing for twenty minutes when Steve arrived, out of breath and murmuring apologies about a tricky case.

Milton rolled his eyes and shook his head in unconcealed disgust. Steve ignored these gestures as he pulled out a vacant chair on the opposite side of the table from his father. Spotting Olivia, he paused to glare accusingly at Laurel before asking, "So where are we?"

"The team just finished updating us on your mother's condition," Milton said tersely. "I'm sure they don't have time to repeat everything, so I'd like to talk about our next step." He quickly swiveled his chair in order to address Dr. Mark. "Rachel is eating less and less. When will you consider putting in a feeding tube?"

"I don't think Mom needs one yet. Does she, Doctor?" Steve spread his arms wide, placing his hands flat on the table. He inhaled deeply, filling his chest with air. Olivia wondered if Laurel's husband was trying to appear physically domineering or if it was a subconscious movement.

Jonathan Mark weighed the pros and cons of inserting a feeding tube and patiently and attentively listened to the concerns Milton and Steve had on the subject. Olivia had never encountered a physician with such an unhurried manner. He listened with every fiber of his being—maintaining eye contact, nodding, and repeating each person's concerns to make sure he correctly understood them. By doing so, he managed to defuse the tension between father and son.

Olivia was most impressed by Dr. Mark.

The meeting was eventually called to an end when Tracy's pager went off.

"Excuse me," she said, moving to a far corner of the room. Pulling a cell phone from the pocket of her scrubs, she dialed a number and listened. She then assured the caller that she was on her way.

"Is it Rachel?" Milton asked, his eyes fearful. "Is she okay?"

It was at that moment that Olivia saw him for what he truly was: a man who would give anything to have more time with his wife. And what of Steve? He undoubtedly wanted his mother to live as long as possible too, but he didn't want her to suffer. He was ready to let her go if letting her go meant that she'd have a peaceful death.

Does such a thing actually exist? Olivia thought dubiously.

She wanted to believe in the possibility of people slipping

away in their sleep, caught up in the arms of a sweet dream. She wanted to believe in such a serene passing, but she'd seen too many violent deaths—too many murders—to invest much faith in the other kind. The kind where a person dies in their own bed, surrounded by loved ones. It seemed like a foreign concept to her and yet, that was precisely what Milton, Steve, Laurel, and the people of KindredCare were trying to give Rachel. A graceful exit. A departure on one's own terms.

"She's asking for me," Tracy said, looking at Milton. "I'm late for my shift and you know how changes in her routine can upset her. I'm going to head out."

"Thanks, Tracy." Dr. Mark rose to his feet. "Okay, folks. Let's see how Rachel does over the weekend. I'll check in with the dietician on Monday and we can revisit the topic of the feeding tube then. Feel free to call if other concerns arise. We'll keep working together to provide Rachel with the best possible care."

With the meeting adjourned, the hospice employees left. Steve informed Laurel that he wouldn't be home for supper because he wanted to spend the evening with his mother, and then he and his father also departed, arguing all the way down the hall.

Pastor Rhodes made to leave as well, but Lynne asked him to wait. "I want to tell Laurel about Rachel's request. I'm sure she'll want to do something to help."

Olivia didn't care for the woman's tone. The implication was that Laurel's efforts had been found wanting but that she was now being offered the chance to remedy her lack of daughterly devotion.

"Of course," Laurel said, playing right into Lynne's hands. "What is it?"

Lynne smoothed the material of her cardigan with a self-satisfied air. "You know Rachel's collection of Hummel figurines? One's broken and she'd really like to see it repaired as soon as possible. It's her favorite piece. She's asked both Milton and Steve to take care of it *several* times, but I guess they're both just too overwrought to get it done."

Laurel looked nonplussed. "I don't know how to fix—"

"Fred Yoder would," Olivia cut in brightly. "Give me directions to your in-law's condo, Laurel. I'll get the Hummel and take it directly to Fred."

Laurel's relief was nearly palpable. "Really? Because that way, I could still make it to the grocery store and meet the twins' when they get off the school bus."

Olivia directed her reply at Lynne. Beaming at the pug-nosed woman, she said, "Problem solved. Thank you *so much* for bringing this to Laurel's attention."

Lynne gave her cardigan another tug, muttered something about her Christian duty, and marched out of the room. A baffled Pastor Rhodes followed in her wake.

"I don't envy you," Olivia told Laurel. "You're in the middle of a very trying ordeal. I can see why you can't work on your novel, but do some journaling so you can vent. Don't hold everything inside. Okay?"

Laurel promised to do her best. After giving Olivia directions to the condo, the two friends parted ways.

Olivia wasn't about to face a dying woman alone. She wasn't good with strangers under normal circumstances, and she had no experience with the terminally ill. Also, everything she knew of Rachel Hobbs came from what Laurel had told her over the years, and these anecdotes had not left a favorable impression. Rachel was a doting, overly involved mother. Steve was her only child, and she'd never forgiven him for getting married. She was fond of her grandsons, Dallas and Dermot, but had never shown an ounce of warmth toward Laurel. In fact, she seemed to look for excuses to criticize her son's wife. Nothing Laurel did was ever good enough, even though everyone who knew the Hobbs Family believed that Laurel did a great job balancing a successful career with her home life.

Maybe Rachel has become kindhearted now that her days are numbered, Olivia thought hopefully. She doubted this was true, however. She found that people rarely had major personality reversals. Even when death was a certainty, and in Rachel's case it was close at hand, Olivia didn't think people suddenly just stopped being who'd they'd always been and started being someone else. She knew fear had the power to change people. As did love. She had been molded by both emotions, but she was still Olivia Limoges.

"The Captain now looks more like an Admiral," the owner of A Pampered Pooch told Olivia as she led Captain Haviland into the front room.

"He *is* a handsome fellow," Olivia agreed and leaned down to kiss her poodle on his black nose. He rewarded her with a lick on the cheek and then pranced over to the door, his caramel-colored eyes lit with an anticipatory gleam. He was ready for a ride in the car.

"You wouldn't be wagging your tail so vigorously if you knew where we were headed," Olivia said once she had Haviland safely fastened in his dog harness in the backseat of her new Range Rover Evoque. This was a novel arrangement for them both. Previously, Haviland had enjoyed sole proprietorship of the passenger seat. Now that Olivia was married, however, Police Chief Sawyer Rawlings claimed ownership of that seat, leaving Haviland the bench seat.

As Olivia drove through downtown Oyster Bay, her spirits were lifted by the sight of the tinsel candy canes fastened to the top of each street lamp and the wreaths of fresh greens festooned with red velvet bows hanging from every shop door. Christmas hadn't meant much to her until her half brother and his children had come into her life, but now, she enjoyed the holiday, reveling in her role as the doting aunt.

"We have arrived, Captain. Sandcrest Condominiums," Olivia said, reading the gilt sign attached to the wall of a small gatehouse. Unlike most of the newer planned communities in Oyster Bay, this one actually boasted a working electronic gate and a uniformed security guard. Olivia put down her window as the guard approached.

"Who are you here to see?" he asked with complete disinterest.

"Rachel Hobbs."

"One moment."

The guard returned to his miniature cottage and made a quick call. Olivia clearly passed muster for the gate slid open and the guard gestured for Olivia to drive forward. She did, wondering for the first time how the Hobbs had acquired their wealth. She'd never thought to ask Laurel what line of work they'd been in, but she knew that their Oyster Bay condo was one of several residences Milton and Rachel owned. Because of Rachel's illness, it had become their primary residence.

The condo, which was originally a place for them to stay when they were visiting Steve and his family, was an end unit with a large patio, a lovely garden, and a two-car garage. The interior was also impressive, and when Tracy, the hospice nurse, invited Olivia to wait in the living room while she fetched the broken Hummel, Olivia took note of the expensive furnishings as well as the top-of-the-line appliances in the kitchen.

It wasn't until she moved closer to the locked bookcases that the extent of the Hobb's wealth became more apparent. Each shelf was crammed with costly, leather-bound first editions, delicate Staffordshire and Meissen figurines, and Chinese porcelain that looked, even to Olivia's inexpert eye, like very early pieces. Now thoroughly intrigued, Olivia tiptoed into the hallway and was rewarded by the sight of a row of framed Picasso drawings.

Olivia was drawn deeper into the condo by Picasso's bold, fluid lines. As she marveled over a series of female nudes and then ogled a splendid study of a horse, she couldn't help but overhear voices at the end of the corridor.

"Laurel sent a stranger to pick up my Hummel?" Rachel Hobbs sounded tired and weak, but still managed to convey disgust. "It's too bad Steve didn't marry someone like you, my dear. You're so good to me and I bet you'd know how to take care of him too."

"I like to think so," the second woman replied with a confidence that bordered on arrogance.

Standing in the dim hallway, Olivia balled her fists. She didn't care for the possessive note in the nurse's voice. And why did she say "I like" instead of "I'd like," as though it wasn't just wishful thinking.

Olivia retreated to the living room and tried to calm down. She'd come to Rachel's place to relieve Laurel of one of her burdens, but what if she'd just stumbled on a truth that could tear her friend's world apart?

Is Steve having an affair?

This question was foremost in Olivia's mind as she accepted a small box from Tracy, who flashed her a guileless smile as she showed her out. It was the question that ran on an endless loop as Olivia drove back through town.

This time, she didn't notice the Christmas decorations. She didn't see the tinsel candy canes wink in the December sun or draw a comparison between the red cheeks on the plastic Santa outside the hardware store to a pair of crabapples.

Olivia was far too focused on getting to Rawlings for any of these things to register. She needed to talk what she'd heard—and what she'd felt—over with him. She needed his good sense and his reason. She needed him to make her believe that she was blowing this way out of proportion.

Because if Rawlings didn't convince her not to, Olivia would ferret out the truth concerning Steve Hobbs. And if it turned out that he was cheating on Laurel, Olivia would hurt the man. She didn't have a plan yet, but she would do something. If Laurel suffered, then Steve would suffer.

Olivia would see to that.